THE LONG AFTERNOON

Dusk had begun to fall when the train arrived at Altondale. David, still a little drunk with reading, nearly walked by Mr Dobbs, the idol of his childhood, without giving up his ticket. Mr Dobbs had been called back from retirement when younger men had deserted the station for the army.

He took David's ticket and said, "It's good to see you, Mr David. Captain Harvey, I suppose I should say. Your mother said you'd be coming home on leave, but she didn't know when."

"It's good to see you too, Dobbs. Do you remember the red, white and blue flower bed you planted for Old Teddy's coronation? And how Toby, Felix, and I all wanted to become stationmasters?"

"And now you're all in France shooting at each other. It doesn't make sense."

"No," said David, "it doesn't."

THE LONG AFTERNOON

Ursula Zilinsky

A STAR BOOK
published by
the Paperback Division of
W.H. Allen & Co. PLC

A Star Book
Published in 1985
by the Paperback Division of
W.H. Allen & Co. Plc
44 Hill Street, London W1X 8LB

First published in the USA by Doubleday & Co. Inc.1984
First published in Britain by W.H. Allen & Co. PLC 1984

Copyright © Ursula Zilinsky 1984
Phototypeset by Input Typesetting Ltd, London
Printed in Great Britain by Anchor Brendon Ltd, Tiptree,
Essex

ISBN 0 352 317191

Part 1

SO SWEET A PLACE

Chapter 1

In honour of the coronation of King Edward VII, the stationmaster of Altondale had planted the small railway garden plot with geraniums, lobelias, and daisies in the shape of a Union Jack. The boys thought it ripping. They thought everything about the station ripping. Mr Dobbs, the stationmaster, was their god. All three of them planned to become stationmasters when they grew up.

Nannie, who had come to the station ostensibly to view the patriotic flower bed, but really to keep an eye on things, this being her last summer of power, with Toby off to prep school in the autumn, much approved the flowers but felt, as always, constrained to point out that Master Toby would in due time grow up to be the future Lord Altondale, not a stationmaster. As for Master Felix, who stood to inherit the second-largest munitions works in Germany, why, the notion of his running a railway was enough to make a cat laugh.

No one but Nannie ever called Felix by his full name. To his friends and family he was Flix, and the implications of speed and slyness in the nickname suited his spare, nimble body very well. Felix looked like his mother, the Baronin Sophie von Landeck, who would have been accounted a beauty had her eyes not been too close together. In Felix this flaw had taken on a purely humorous cast. One of his older sisters had once described him as looking like a nutcracker, but a very handsome one.

As to the third member of the trio, Nannie made no comment, for Master David's father was the local vicar and High, while Nannie was a Noncomformist.

It seemed a pity, Nannie often thought, that Mr Harvey, seeing that he wore a cassock and used incense, had not elected to be celibate as well. Instead he had chosen to follow that other tradition of the English clergy, marrying for love instead of money, and having far too many chil-

6

dren, each more handsome than the last. Indeed, Master David was so beautiful as to be, to Nannie's mind, almost improper. She did not consider him a suitable companion for Master Toby, and would not have cared if he had grown up to be a stationmaster.

"Here are the mummys," she said. "Good afternoon, my lady. We were just looking at Mr Dobb's flower bed."

Lady Millicent Strafford, who had been out for an airing in the carriage with her husband's German cousin, the Baronin Sophie von Landeck, smiled at everyone. She always smiled, having been taught as a girl that it was the duty of people in her station in life to present a pleasant face to their inferiors. When she was annoyed, angry, or hurt, the smile grew smaller. It never entirely went away.

"Mummy," said Toby, "wasn't it clever of Mr Dobbs? A Union Jack, you see, because of coronation year. Wouldn't Old Teddy be tremendously bucked if he could see it?"

"Darling, you're not to speak of His Majesty as Old Teddy. It's not respectful. Good afternoon, Dobbs. The garden is indeed lovely. Most suitable."

"We thought it might cheer Old Teddy up if he could see it. His Majesty, I meant to say, begging your pardon, Your Ladyship."

Lady Millicent's smile had grown much smaller. She sometimes wondered whether Dobbs might not be a secret anarchist, but in this she was far afield. As king of his railway station Dobbs merely had a fellow feeling for the king of England, and would have been glad to stand him a pint at the Strafford Arms any day Old Teddy cared to stop by.

"It's nearly teatime," Lady Millicent said to Nannie. "Do let the boys have it downstairs today; it's such lovely weather."

The carriage turned left onto the Dewsbury Road, down the great colonnade of lime trees which formed the entrance to Altondale Park. This was the grand way of going home. The boys preferred the humbler and more interesting approach along the High Street, where they could admire the village idiot drooling and talking gibberish outside the greengrocer's, a large glass jar of peppermint bull's-eyes in the post-office window, and a leech in a bottle inside the chemist's shop.

Past the cricket pitch, where a pony, wearing felt boots, was drowsily dragging a lawn mower back and forth, the village ended abruptly and the country began. Farms, built of tawny stone and thatch, the smells of midden and byre, replaced the gentle curve of the High Street.

Just past the home farm a small green door, almost hidden by a creeper, was set into the rosy brick wall which circled Altondale Park. The gate opened into a part of the park not usually seen by visitors. Hidden among the shrubbery were potting sheds, greenhouses, and the gardener's cottage.

Masses of roses cascaded down the descending terraces; Italian copies of Greek statues stood among the topiary. One, said on no particular authority to be the Emperor Hadrian in person, pointed a monitory forefinger at the stable clock, as if to warn of the lateness of the hour. As they clattered down the flagged walk, the boys heard it strike the quarter, and saw the carriage pull away from the Palladian wing. At a very fast trot indeed they ran past the stable block with its covered exercise yard, the Old House, and Elizabethan sundial announcing: *Horas non numero nisi serenas*, down the steps to the kitchen and up the back stairs with their mysterious smell of wax and housemaid's mops, to the nursery rooms high under the roof, where Nannie was grimly awaiting them, an ominous array of soap and towels at the ready.

Though nursery tea consisted of a ferocious wash, supervised by Nannie, milk, and stodgy strips of brown bread and butter, while drawing-room tea came with a cake stand loaded with cherry cake and meringues, Toby was never entirely sure that it was worth it. For one thing the wash was even more ferocious, and for another cakes and meringues were considered "bad" for children and seldom offered. Children had to sit without fidgeting, and if visitors were present, had to answer such silly questions as my, one

8

had grown, hadn't one, or worse yet, was one a good little boy.

The weather that summer was worthy of a coronation year. Day followed glorious day in an unbroken sequence that seemed positively un-English. It was white flannel weather, boating and cricketing weather. Books were left lying about the lawn, and tea was served, day after day, under the great cedar said to have been planted in the days of Queen Elizabeth by the builder of the Old House.

In its cool shade China tea, pale as straw, fell from a silver spout, while bumblebees nosed into the lavender hedge with the noise of tiny dynamos. The silver muffineer glinted in the sun; the gas flame under the hot water paled to transparency in the brilliant light.

Lady Millicent and the Baronin Sophie were nibbling cucumber sandwiches and discussing the burning question of the moment. Should Toby and Felix be taken to London to see the coronation? Nannie was against it. She considered London unhealthy in the summer, and was sure the boys would make themselves ill with excitement.

"Really, Milly," said the Baronin, "they aren't babies. Toby is ten, and Flix is nearly eleven. And a coronation, that is after all something to see and remember."

"I'm sure you're right, Sophie. Still, one doesn't like to go against Nannie. She takes such umbrage. Sometimes it goes on for weeks. And it's silent umbrage, which makes it worse."

"I cannot understand why you English are so terrorized by your nannies. They are only servants, after all. If Flix's nurse had ever been sulky or impertinent, I would simply have got rid of her and found another."

"Yes, but Sophie," said Lord Altondale, reaching for a piece of anchovy toast, "it's not the same for us. They acquire power over us when we're infants, so that we can never after assert ourselves against them. I think I could dismiss my butler, even my gamekeeper, but Nannie? Never. One's knees knock together at the very thought. All the same, Milly, I think the boys should come to London. They needn't mix with the crowds. They can stand in the window and watch the procession go by. Sophie is right; it will be something for them to remember."

"Of course, Augustus," said Lady Millicent. "Will you tell Nannie what we have decided?"

"Oh . . . ah . . . hadn't you better see to all that, Milly? Children and nannies—it's a woman's department, what?"

Lady Millicent said, "Very well, Augustus." For once her smile was one of genuine amusement.

The boys said how do you do and sat silently in a row while Lady Millicent broke it to Nannie that they were to go up to town for the coronation. She managed to make it sound like their patriotic duty, and mentioned in passing that Nannie would undoubtedly find time to look up some of her old babies, such as General Labouchere at the War Office and Lord Spyke at the Department of Indian Affairs.

With this as a sop Nannie took it pretty well, merely muttering that if the poor little mites got sick, not to say they hadn't been warned.

Toby, while resenting being called a poor little mite, was intensely looking forward to going up to London to see the king. He wished there were some way he and Flix could tell Old Teddy about Mr Dobbs's Union Jack flower bed. At the same time he was exercised about David, who had not been included in the invitation. David was Toby's best friend, and it seemed wrong to Toby's loyal little heart to have a treat not shared by him. But it was one of the cardinal rules of Lady Millicent's and Nannie's, that children must never ask for anything, neither treats for best friends, nor meringues. His eyes slid to the cake tray. There were heaps left. Really, grown-ups were extraordinary. They had eaten nearly all the boring sandwiches, and had ignored the cakes.

Lady Millicent, catching sight of Toby's longing glance, said, "Will you have a meringue, darling? And Flix and David?" She gave one to each of them, on a flowered plate with a silver fork.

And why, thought Toby, rendered philosophical by frustration, must there be a flaw in every pleasure? Why did he have to eat meringues with a fork, when everyone knew

10

they crumbled at a touch. Why couldn't he plop the whole airy thing into his mouth, to let it deliciously crumble and melt, or at least pick up the crumbs with his fingertip. But this was of course unthinkable, as unthinkable as asking whether your best friend might come to London.

Toby ate as much of his meringue as could be eaten with a fork, swallowed, and said, "Oh, Mummy?"

"Yes, darling." Lady Millicent looked a little pained. Children at drawing-room tea were to be seen, not heard.

"Mummy, couldn't David come up to London with us? To see the king," Toby added, invoking higher authority.

David, finding himself the centre of attention, blushed. Lady Millicent's smile grew very small indeed, but her voice was as pleasant as ever. "We shall have to see, darling."

Toby knew that one. It meant no. He looked at Felix. Felix understood and winked. It meant yes. If David could not go to the coronation, his friends would not. They were the three musketeers. One for all, all for one.

Deliberately, Toby picked up his plate again. Slowly he moistened his forefinger with spit. He gathered up the crumbs on his plate, while Lady Millicent's smile did not so much shrink as congeal. "Toby!"

Toby licked his finger clean and said, "Yes, Mummy."

"I do not think the king will want to be cheered on his way to Westminster Abbey by a naughty and disobedient boy. You may get down. Tell Nannie I will speak to her later."

After the boys had gone inside, there was a silence. Augustus, who did not think Toby's crime a major one (he quite often licked up crumbs himself if no one was looking), did not want to become embroiled in a nursery crisis. He abstracted his mind and took refuge in his view.

Capability Brown had landscaped Altondale Park more than a hundred years earlier, but Augustus thought of it as very much his own. And indeed it was far more beautiful now than when Brown had created the series of terraces and streams which led the eye downhill to the artificial lake with its Palladian replica of a Greek temple at the far end.

The copper beeches, oaks, and elms he had grouped amid the rolling hills, saplings then, had grown in magnificence until they stood like thunderheads against the blue summer sky.

"Capital feller, Brown," said Augustus not for the first time. "Care for a walk around the park, Hesso? Get up an appetite for dinner, what?"

At the sound of the word "walk," Culpepper, Augustus's Gordon setter, stood up, panting. Culpepper had a coat of shining black silk and for tail a plume Cyrano would not have disdained. But though he had beauty, he had no dignity. Culpepper's was a slave nature. Augustus was his god. Had Augustus died, Culpepper would without doubt have sat on his tomb until he died too, of starvation, loyalty, and want of intelligence.

"All right then, Culpepper," said Augustus, "come along, come along."

Left alone with Sophie, Millicent sighed, a sigh so small that only an old friend could perceive it. Sophie understood. She knew Milly cared nothing for the rolling Yorkshire hills so deeply loved by her husband. Lady Millicent wanted to have the season in London, go to dinner parties every night, look in at the opera for a scene or two, ride in Rotten Row, gossip with friends, have at-homes.

Of course she had had at-homes at Altondale, but what pleasure was there in giving tea to Lady Lappiter, who was deaf and carried an ear trumpet, or Colonel Molyneux, whose daughters wore ribbons and giggled like schoolgirls, though well on the wrong side of thirty.

Lady Millicent wanted to live in the Strafford's town house on Chesterfield Hill, she wanted to receive elegant young men in top hats, she wanted to be glamorous among glamorous women. Yet very few things could lure Augustus from his beloved Altondale. He might go to London for a few days to sit in the House of Lords, but generally one might as well try to remove Antaeus from his piece of earth. Now if she had had daughters, thought Lady Millicent, she would simply have had to have seasons in London to bring them out.

"Sophie," she said, struck by an idea, "why don't you

give your girls a season in London? We could all stay on Chesterfield Hill and I could present them. Then they could still have the winter season in Berlin. After all, one or the other might quite easily marry an Englishman."

The Baronin, who was religious and therefore considered all things under the aspect of eternity, thought her cousin's craving for town and society trivial. But she was a woman of the world, and had to admit that there was much to be said for Milly's idea. A London season, under the new king, might be fun for the girls, not like those horrible parties she had attended in Berlin before she married, in those overstuffed, stifling rooms, where no window was ever opened.

Of course the girls would still have to come out in Berlin. Perhaps it wouldn't be so bad now, with a new, young kaiser. And then a season in London, presentation at court; yes, it was an idea to be considered.

"I think it's an excellent plan, Milly," she said. "I shall certainly mention it to Hesso. Marit talks about becoming a nun . . ."

"Oh, my dear," said Milly with genuine sympathy, forgetting for the moment that Sophie was a Catholic and a pious one at that.

"I don't think there is much to it. She hasn't the temperament, any more than I had. I went through the same thing as a girl, so I understand her. Perhaps a London season will *changer les idées*. But Milly, she is only fifteen, and Angelika is twelve. Still, we can plan for a few years from now."

Lady Millicent sighed. It was something to look forward to. And meanwhile they were going up to town for the coronation, which reminded her that she must talk to Nannie.

Before going to sleep that night. Toby spent a long time on his knees, asking God to forgive him for his wickedness. He had not at once realized just how bad he had been, or rather, he had been proud of the magnitude of his crime. In one small act of disobedience he had managed to offend God by being greedy, Nannie's Miss Manners, a poor lady

13

who appeared to make her meals off the scraps on other people's plates, and worst of all Mummy, whose kindness in asking him to tea was rewarded by his show of bad manners.

Nannie's scolding had left him unrepentant; he had heard so often that he was the wickedest boy in all the world and was turning her hair grey with the trouble and shame he caused her. Nannie's hair, he reflected with the cynicism of his years, might at her age (which he guessed to be around a hundred) have turned grey quite easily without his help.

So it was not Nannie's scolding which had roused him to repentance, but the gentle words his mother had spoken to him before sending him to bed without supper. Lady Millicent had said nothing about the shame he had caused her in front of guests who would, as Nannie had already pointed out, now be able to tell all their friends in Germany that English children were little Hottentots. With the tact for which she was famous, Lady Millicent had gone directly to the one aspect of Toby's crime which would make him feel terrible for weeks. By asking whether David might come to London, she pointed out, Toby had publicly caused embarrassment to his friend.

God, explained Lady Millicent, had placed each of us in his proper station. Peer's son or vicar's, or peasant's for that matter, each condition had its virtues, its duties, and its rewards. Mr Harvey was a scholar and a gentleman, and David was a gentleman's son. His poverty, unlike the poverty of the poor, was no disgrace. How did Toby imagine he must have felt to hear his friend asking for what virtually amounted to charity?

So Toby prayed most heartily to be made into a better, more tactful friend, and under Nannie's unforgiving eye got into bed and composed himself to sleep—properly, with his hands outside the covers. This, winter and summer, was one of Nannie's inflexible rules. Terrible things, she hinted, happened to boys who touched themselves "down there." The village idiot, who grinned and mumbled outside his parents' greengrocery in the High Street, had probably done that very thing.

14

Toby said, "Goodnight, Nannie; I'm sorry I've been bad," and shut his eyes. He heard her walk out of the room and close the door. She would, he knew, be back. In an hour or two she would enter silently, carrying a lamp, to make sure the hands were still outside, the covers undisturbed. No matter how tired he was, Toby tried to stay awake for this second visit, for Nannie, thinking him asleep, sometimes bent down and kissed his cheek, and then he knew that even though he was the wickedest boy in all the world, she loved him.

In the end Lady Millicent had to wait to go to London longer than she had expected. The king fell ill with appendicitis. The coronation was postponed to August 3. By that time a good many of the more glamorous European visitors had gone home, while the more impressionable members of the English nobility were in bed, recovering from the latest ailment made fashionable by royalty.

Nothing was said about the boys as the family got ready to move to London. They would have come only with the greatest reluctance if they had been asked. August 3 might be Teddy's coronation day, but August 4 was the christening day of the Vicar's newest baby. Felix and Toby had been asked to tea afterward. They would not have missed it for all the coronations in Christendom.

"Any amount of meringues," Toby confided to his cousin. "And no one minds if you lick up the crumbs."

Unlike his predecessor, who had once told Augustus's father that being a parson wouldn't be a bad job except for having to go to church on Sunday, Mr Harvey loved his church, and its annual progression of feast days; its liturgy and sacraments. Though his kind heart misgave him, he could not help enjoying the morose dignity of a High Anglican funeral; being most happily married himself he delighted in performing weddings, and, as the father of a large family, he loved christenings. Best of all he loved christening his own.

This was the sixth time that he had enjoyed this privilege. Lord Altondale, sending for the sixth time a silver porringer, had suggested the name Sexta. Mrs Harvey, weary after a difficult confinement, had pleaded for Ultima, but the Vicar had long since determined that the child would be Julian, after Dame Julian of Norwich, whose peculiarly English mystical writings he cherished above all others.

Never a very firm believer in the doctrine of infant damnation, the Vicar found it particularly difficult to pray sincerely that little Julian might be delivered of her sins. All his babies had been beautiful, but none so beautiful as Julian, who even at birth had not looked red and wrinkled, as a baby should, but pink and smooth and though very small, so perfectly proportioned that she was like an exquisite doll. Her eyes were not dark blue like the rest of the Harveys, but smoky grey. While he renounced the devil and all his works on her behalf, those strange eyes looked past the Vicar, almost, it seemed to him, past the ceiling of the church, and though his wife had told him dozens of times that it was only wind, he could have sworn that she smiled.

Nannie sat between Toby and Felix, bolt upright in the Strafford pew. In spite of being chapel, Nannie invariably insisted on coming to church, partly to keep an eye on Master Toby, but mainly to show by way of pinched nostril and beady eye how deeply she disapproved of candles and incense.

She had been invited to tea with Felix and Toby, but had refused, for there was nowhere in the vicarage where, in her opinion, she could suitably drink this tea.

Mr and Mrs Harvey would willingly have had her at their dining-room table, but their sense of what was proper was not so highly developed as Nannie's, who knew that it would never do. In a properly conducted household she would, of course, have had tea with the Vicar's nanny in the nursery, but the Harveys only had a nursery maid, a mere village girl, and that was no more to be considered than the kitchen. So Nannie thanked the Vicar kindly for the invitation, complimented Mrs Harvey graciously on the new baby, instructed the boys to their mortification to be

16

sure to behave like little gentlemen, and went back to the hall.

"Oh dear," said the Vicar, laughing, "what will she do when she gets to heaven and finds out we are all equal in the sight of the Lord?"

"She'll probably ask him whether he's washed his hands," said Toby.

"Will we be, though?" asked David. "Equal, I mean. Aren't there hierarchies, cherubim and seraphim, and then all the people who were Jesus' friends and relations on earth, His mother, and Joseph, and the Beloved Disciple?"

The Vicar, considering this, led the way through his untidy garden into the dining room, where the large round table was set for the christening tea. This was more like it, Toby thought with satisfaction. Scones, honey in the comb, chocolate cake, and mountains of meringues. There was boring old bread and butter as well, but Mrs Harvey never seemed to mind if one passed it up in favour of better things.

"We were wondering," said the Vicar, when the guests and his own large family had been distributed around the table, "*benedictus, benedicat*, whether we will all be equal in heaven. David thinks not."

"I'm inclined to agree with David," said Mrs Harvey. "There'll have to be a special section for nannies, where they can sit with their bonnets and prams, being superior."

"David," said Mr Harvey, "thought there would have to be favourites. Jesus' mother and the apostles and friends He had on earth."

"I think that would be rather horrid," said Agnes, the oldest of the Harvey children. "His friends weren't a bit nice. Publicans and sinners."

"When I was a girl," said Mrs Harvey, "I thought publicans were people who kept pubs. I could never understand why Mr Riley, who kept the Pig and Whistle at home, and was very nice, should be so singled out."

"I've often thought of making a collection of all the misunderstandings children have of things in the Bible," said the Vicar. "I thought for years they were called the Gathering Swine."

17

Toby sputtered into laughter, choked on a crumb, and had to be hit on the back.

"Sorry, sir, but I think that's rather good."

"Do you really think so?" said the Vicar, flattered.

"I used to think it was 'the stars in their corsets fought against Sisera,' " said Mrs Harvey, at which Toby choked again. When they had all stopped laughing, Felix said, "But aren't publicans pubkeepers, Mr Harvey? I always thought that too. What are they, really?"

"Tax collectors," said the Vicar. "From the Latin *publicamus*, the public revenue." The presence of guests rather than the age of several of his own children kept him from enlarging on the natural confusion with public house, which went back to the French *maison publique*, a brothel, not to mention the Latin *publicus locus*, a latrine.

Toby, chomping on his fourth meringue, wondered why he always had so much more fun at the vicarage than at home. He supposed it was because no child had to wait to be spoken to, everyone was heard as well as seen. Even Julian, in her basket next to Mrs Harvey, now joined the conversation with gurgles and little squeals. Though he was an only child, Toby had spent enough time at the vicarage to have learned not to be afraid of babies. He knew how to hold out his finger to be gripped, and the kind of voice babies liked. He held out his finger to Julian. At first she seemed not to be interested, but when he touched her tiny fist, her fingers closed on his with surprising firmness.

"She has a splendid grip, Mrs Harvey," said Toby.

"She loves holding on. She seems very fond of people. Some babies don't care much, you know. David was always very independent. It's funny how different they all are from each other. Babies look so much alike at first, one tends to think they are all the same."

"Julian isn't the same. Even her eyes are different. All the rest of you have blue eyes."

"Perhaps I should have called her Athena," said the Vicar.

"Why Athena, please, Mr Harvey?"

"After the Greek goddess of wisdom. That was her epithet, grey-eyed Athena."

18

Grey-eyed Julian let go of Toby's finger. She seemed to be looking at the ceiling, yet so strange were those smoky eyes they almost gave the impression of looking beyond it.

"I know what, Mr Harvey," said Toby. "I know what she looks like. She looks as if she were thinking of something else."

Chapter 2

Every summer morning Toby awoke with the first lark song, and patted, barefoot and unwashed, past Nannie's door, down the back stairs to the kitchen, where he poured himself a glass of milk, cool from the pantry. Not even the housemaids were ever down as early as he.

He ran out into the morning mist, breaking through wheels of cobwebs newly spun in the night, past the lake with its ducks and swans still sleeping, their heads tucked under a wing. Rabbits spurted with a flit of white scut into the tall grass at the sound of his step. Geese, with the look of offended dowagers, waddled down the bank and plopped heavily into the water. Coots called their shrill warning down the lake and the moorhens said, Get back, get back.

Toby, who had a tender regard for the sensibilities of animals, wanted to tell them, "Please don't bother to run and hide; I won't hurt you." He tried to walk as silently as Hasselt, his father's gamekeeper, not bending the grass, scarcely casting a shadow. But still the rabbits started away and the moorhens said, Get back. Only the tame deer had learned not to be afraid and looked at him with wide, quiet eyes.

By the sundial, which, speaking Latin, smugly announced that it counted only happy hours, he might find David waiting for him, and if they were in luck they might run across Hasselt and be allowed to go with him to the shed where he was rearing baby pheasants for the big shoots in November.

"How can you bear to let them get shot?" Toby asked

once, holding a warm ball of feathers in his hand, feeling its heart racing against his palm. "How can you, Hasselt?"

"It's what they're for, e'ent it?" Hasselt said stolidly. He ruled over a world that was to Toby full of wonder and terror, beauty and pain, all of it so mixed that he could not separate it out in his mind. The baby grouse and pheasant, reared with such tender care for the guns, the shy small rabbits, with their eager, quivering faces, screaming in Hasselt's traps. "Rabbits is vermin," the gamekeeper said, and broke their necks deftly and without pain. Toby, if he came upon an animal in a trap, would always set it free, to die, he knew, far more slowly and agonizingly than under Hasselt's skilful fingers.

Most terrifying of all was the ferret, stirring in his bag until Hasselt untied the string and let him down a rabbit warren. Toby always had to close his eyes in order not to see that evil face. It gave him nightmares. He knew the sick feeling in his stomach was excitement, and he was ashamed of it; he thought that people who attended public executions had probably felt just like this, but he could not keep away.

"When I try to imagine God," David once said to Toby, "it's Hasselt's face I see."

After he got over the shock of what sounded like blasphemy, Toby began to see what David meant; the stolid, persistent keeping order over so much beauty and pain. A rabbit screaming in a trap or at play in a glade of primroses, foxes bounding in the moonlight or torn by the hounds, a linnet snared as bait for a hawk, and the hawk itself, balanced on his tightrope of air, falling from sight like a stone, to dig beak and claw into the linnet's flesh, wings mantling its victim, thinking itself predator, but in reality Hasselt's prey.

When Toby was away from home, at Eton and Sandhurst, and later in the trenches of Flanders, the beauty and cruelty of Hasselt's woods were what he thought of when he thought of Altondale.

Straffords followed, as gentlemen should, the unlucrative professions; the army, the church, the diplomatic service, and politics. Since they were seldom clever enough to be diplomats, and disliked living in town too much to devote themselves seriously to politics, they usually went into the army, with an occasional younger brother going into the church. Toby's father had served his country in India, where he had remained heroically immune to a foreign culture, and would indeed have considered such a concept a contradiction in terms. Like many of his brother officers, he developed a great liking for the native troops under his command, while ignoring or ridiculing those Indians who, had they had the good fortune to be English, would have been his social equals.

Though he enjoyed his soldiering years, Augustus went to sleep every night thinking of Altondale, hoping that its green woods, soft fogs, and feathery rains would enter his brown and arid Indian dreams.

When word reached him that his father had died, and that his younger brother Algernon was spending the family fortune with terrific speed, he resigned his commission and, with his Indian body servant, returned to England to assume his position as Lord Altondale, sit in the House of Lords, find an heiress to restore the family fortunes, and—it was all he had ever wanted—live quietly on his estates.

The Indian servant died almost at once of English weather and English food. Augustus mourned him sincerely, and would willingly have buried him with the Strafford family, but that he was unfortunately not a member of the Church of England.

In due course Augustus wooed and married Lady Millicent Langland, the plain but rich daughter of an earl. Young Algernon, known to his friends as Algy the Cad, both for his phenomenal luck with women and his disastrous lack of it at cards, was packed off to visit his German relations and find himself a rich bride.

Though Sophie did what she could, trotting out heiresses to steel mills and coal mines for his inspection, Algy, who was not interested in settling down, decamped to Monte Carlo, where he lost at cards a sum which earned him the profound respect of every member of his club. Hauled back to England by his outraged brother, and told to get a job,

21

Algy said he could rather fancy himself in the diplomatic service, and also wished to announce to his family that he had fallen in love with and proposed to marry Miss Rachel Montefiore, only daughter of Sir Abraham Montefiore, the well-known financier and philanthropist.

"Diplomatic service," snorted Augustus. "What does he think, that old Montefiore will buy him the Paris embassy so he can lose money at Longchamp?"

"Rachel Montefiore!" breathed Lady Millicent, having recovered her voice after the first shock.

"I know, Milly. I told him it wouldn't do. But his mind's made up and we can't stop him. He's over twenty-one. Anyway, they're having her baptised."

Sir Abraham raised no objection to the marriage. He was immensely rich and could see no reason why only American fathers should buy impoverished English peers for their daughters. He gave Rachel a slap-up wedding at St Margaret's, Westminster, a flat in Montefiore House, and a large estate in Surrey. For several years after his marriage Algy, looking very nice in striped trousers and a silk hat, footled about the Foreign Office, doing no one quite knew what. Then he was posted to the Berlin embassy in charge of protocol. Everyone at the club had a good laugh about it.

"Old Algy in Berlin. What a thing!"

"Very straitlaced lot; he won't like it much."

"No more wine, women, and song. Poor Algy."

"He will do very well," said Sir Abraham to Augustus. "He is very knowledgeable about protocol and precedence and all those things. I do believe the *Almanach de Gotha* is the only book he's ever read all the way through."

"Oh, he'll play the fool as well in Berlin as elsewhere."

But old General Lappiter, who prided himself on being able to see deeper into a well than most, had his own theory. "Playing at Intelligence is my guess, Strafford. Mark my word."

"Well, heaven help British Intelligence," said Augustus when telling Sir Abraham about it, "if that's the kind of idea they come up with."

Sir Abraham and Augustus had grown quite friendly, often dining together when the House of Lords was sitting.

Sir Abraham gave Augustus some good investment tips, and Augustus felt for him much what he had felt for his Indian servant—dashed good feller for a wog, what?—an attitude he did not trouble to conceal since he saw nothing wrong with it.

Sir Abraham treated him with amused toleration. With the perspective of thousands of years of civilization stretching behind him, he was able to regard the English as blond barbarians, overgrown, unmannerly children, who must be given an occasional treat to keep them from being a nuisance.

With Algy settled in such a satisfactory manner, Augustus was able to devote his life to being a country squire. The House of Lords was a nuisance, since it involved going up to town, but on the whole his life was without complaint. If he had one small grief, it was the knowledge that Toby was to be an only child. His birth had nearly killed Lady Millicent, and the doctor had been very firm when he had told Augustus there must be no more children.

Augustus vacated his wife's bedroom without regret, his own tastes being for young coachmen with high boots and whips. But he would have liked to have seen the Altondale nurseries filled with a dozen little Straffords, for the thought of the estate going to one of Algy's half-Montefiore offspring made him feel hot and cold.

However, Toby was such a dear little boy, so much what one wanted one's son to be, sturdy and manly and straightforward, that Augustus soon forgot to worry, and took him with him as he rode on his daily rounds of the estate; first held in front of him in the saddle, later on his own pony, until Nannie complained the poor little mite would grow up as bowlegged as a cavalry officer.

From the top of Hangman's Knoll (there had never been a local gallows or hangman, but the village liked to think so), Augustus and Toby could see the gashes of black in the green hills, and the pall of smoke which hung over the industrial towns from which they derived much of their wealth. They knew that men spent their days doubled over in a fetid mine, hacking at the coalface, that children pulled

23

carts along underground passages, that men and women spent their lives as servants of the mills and lived in warrens of soot-black houses with one water tap perhaps for twenty-five families and no sanitary facilities to speak of, but the comforting creed of the day was that such people had been created by an all-knowing Providence like oxen, lacking the capacity for suffering fatigue or the sensibility to feel boredom and pain. When Augustus stood on Hangman's Knoll and looked at the smoky cloud on the horizon, he simply felt grateful that he was who he was, and not a miner or a millworker, or worst of all, a foreigner.

One was a dashed lucky feller, he often told Toby. In return for this luck it was one's duty to treat decently those dependent upon one, and to do one's duty to one's country. It was, he told Toby over and over, a very jolly thing to be Lord Altondale.

Chapter 3

At the gracious suggestion of the All-Highest Kaiser Wilhelm, arrangements were made for the heir of Landeck Steel to be educated in Prussia. Lehzen, a military school near Königsberg, was considered the most exclusive and the best. It was here that Hesso delivered Felix after they returned from the coronation of the kaiser's English uncle.

"Good God, but it's a gloomy place," said Hesso as they stepped out of the railway station.

The town was small. Its narrow streets were filled with the sound of gulls. Fog pressed on the roofs. As with all towns near schools, its shops catered to the hungry young; cakes, sausages, and rather splendid toys filled the windows. The school was a half hour's walk from the town. It looked, appropriately enough, like a mixture of medieval fortress and army barracks.

Hesso and Felix were shown into the headmaster's study by a soldier in uniform—everyone at Lehzen wore a uniform—and were received with abrupt Prussian courtesy by Colonel von Hunger. He told Hesso how very honoured he was to have the privilege of meeting him, but ignored Felix as if he were not there. After several more remarks highly complimentary to the Landeck Stahl Fabrik and its products, he rang a bell. A boy of about sixteen, also in uniform, appeared with great promptness, saluted, and stood at attention.

"Ah, Krampitz," said the headmaster. "This is Felix von Landeck, one of our new pupils. Show him to his dormitory. Krampitz," he added to Felix, "will be your prefect."

Heels clicked, another salute was exchanged, Krampitz and Felix left the headmaster's study, and after wandering through several corridors and climbing a number of flights of stairs, arrived at the dormitory where Felix was to spend his nights.

It was a long room with a row of beds lined up on each side. A washstand with a tin bowl on it stood at the foot of each bed. Krampitz, who had until now not spoken, walked down the row of beds, stopped, and said, "You sleep here. Your clothes here, shoes on the left, like this." He pointed to another bed, whose occupant had already unpacked. Felix wondered where everyone was. They had not met a single boy in the hallways.

"Tomorrow you will be measured for a uniform. Until it is ready you will continue to wear your clothes."

The school uniform, grey, scratchy, and ill-fitting, was not, Felix thought, something he would be in a hurry to exchange for his own grey flannels. Colonel von Hunger knew this, of course. Lehzen was the only school at which new boys did not arrive already fitted out with the school uniform. After a week of being that most despised of minorities—a new boy, made conspicuous by his civilian clothes—the vainest or most individualistic was thankful to become one with the mass of ill-fitting grey and clumsy boots. Colonel von Hunger understood the myth of uniforms. With each year at school he permitted them to become smarter, better tailored. The boys in the upper school added red tabs to their collars like staff officers, and were allowed glossy, expensive riding boots. In their senior year they were allowed gold braid and spurs.

"You can go back and say good-bye to your father. Dinner is in half an hour."

This was a shock to Felix, who had assumed that he would be allowed to stay with Hesso until his departure. But he merely said, "Thank you, Krampitz."

"You don't call me Krampitz; you call me I.C. because I'm In Charge. New boys are called warts their first year. If you hear anyone calling wart, you drop whatever you are doing and run there as fast as you can. All right, dismissed."

Felix did not know whether he was supposed to salute or click his heels. He never did this at home, and the idea embarrassed him. He said, "Thank you," again, and turned to leave. He had no idea which of the hallways would lead him back to the headmaster's study. Krampitz stood in the doorway, watching him coolly, offering no advice.

He found his way in the end and learned that his father had obtained permission for him to see him off on the train. They decided to walk back to the station. There was no hurry; Hesso's train would not leave for two hours.

In the station restaurant Hesso ordered a large dinner, though neither had much appetite. Hesso had not liked the looks of the school and was depressed at the thought of leaving Felix there. Still, what could he do? When the kaiser himself makes a suggestion, what does one say? "No thanks, Your Majesty, I think I'll send him to Eton with his Cousin Toby?" Besides, Eton probably wouldn't be all that much different. Schools were wretched places. If only Felix didn't look so very young, sitting there, poking at his sausage with his fork. Hesso wanted nothing so much as to wrap him in his greatcoat and take him back to Landeck.

"Do eat up, Flix," he said irritably. "If I know anything about schools, you won't have another thing fit to eat till you come home for Christmas."

The mention of Christmas cheered them both up sufficiently that they could get through their leave-taking without tears.

His father had given him money for a cab back to school, but Felix decided to walk. He was not frightened at going back, but neither did he want to hurry. He sauntered through the town, looking into the shop windows, particularly the splendid toy shop. Then he took the beach path back to the school, which stood darkly on its hill against the grey evening sky.

In the dormitory all the boys' trunks had arrived, and Krampitz was supervising their unpacking, showing them where to put their things. "You are to keep everything in its proper place at all times. Any food you have brought from home goes into a common pool in the dining room. There is room inspection by the housemaster every morning, and I for one would not want to be the boy through whose untidiness this dorm gets a demerit. Any personal articles must be kept in the trunk. You there, what's your name?"

"Tussow, please, I.C."

"What have you got there?"

Tussow was a very small boy, whose hair grew in a cowlick over his left temple. He tried to hide a plush toy.

"An elephant, please, I.C."

"A toy?" Krampitz managed to put enormous scorn into this question. "Now look, this isn't a nursery, it's a military school. We don't play with toys here. Throw it away."

Made desperate at the thought of losing his most prized possession, little Tussow shouted, "It's not a toy, it's a mascot."

"You're going to need more than a mascot if you ever again speak to a prefect without being spoken to. Now put away that disgusting creature, and all other personal articles. Warts are not allowed books or photographs." He went on telling them the regulations of the school; that they must learn the name of every master and every upperclass cadet their first week or be punished, that they must instantly obey any order given by an older boy or be punished, that they must not talk with each other or be punished.

They were sufficiently terrorised to finish their unpacking in silence. They would remain silent and isolated through a large part of their first year at school. This too was part of Colonel von Hunger's policy.

While they were silently putting away their things, there

was a shout of WARTS in the hall. For a moment they were paralysed, not sure if it meant them. WARTS! The second call galvanised them; they elbowed each other through the narrow door. Krampitz and another boy stood at the end of the hall. They lined up, breathless.

"Don't ever make me call twice again. Tussow, you were last. Why?"

"Please, I.C. somebody's got to be."

"Are you trying to be funny?"

"No, I.C."

"Clean these." He pointed to a bench on which there was a row of muddy football boots. Since this was the first day of the new term, the mud must have dated back to the end of the spring term. It was well dried in. Tussow was still scraping away at it when the bell rang for supper.

"You're horribly slow, Tussow," said Krampitz. "You'll miss supper, I'm afraid. Still, perhaps you'll remember it next time you're feeling funny."

Supper was a poor meal; acorn coffee, coarse bread, and beetroot jam. The coffee could be made drinkable by adding sugar, but the sugar bowl stood in front of Krampitz at the head of the table, and since no one was allowed to speak to him unless spoken to, it was impossible to ask for it. He waited till everyone had choked down his coffee—no one was allowed to leave food on his plate or drink in his cup—then handed the sugar bowl to the boy next to him. "Pass it around; don't keep it all to yourself, greedy pig."

After supper Colonel von Hunger gave a short talk. He welcomed the new boys, said he hoped they would be happy at Lehzen, even felt inclined to promise they would be, if they observed the rules, for happiness grew out of obedience and doing one's duty. But, he added, their happiness was not his primary concern. Lehzen's aim was to turn out, happy or not, at the end of eight years, the disciplined men the fatherland needed to lead its army.

Every eye at this was drawn to the table where the seniors sat, eight-year men, gods in spurs and gold braid, who did not condescend to stare back at the mortals at the other tables.

After the headmaster had dismissed them, one of the seniors said, "Krampitz, come to my study after you've put your warts to bed." He wore an eyeglass and had pale lashes, like a guinea pig. His name was Count Hagen von Hagenbeck. His coat of arms had more quarterings than anyone else's at Lehzen; his family tree went back directly to the Teutonic Knights. Hagenbecks seldom married outside their own family, preferring their own second cousins for breeding purposes. This accounted for their guinea-pig looks and guinea-pig-sized brains. Anywhere but at a Prussian school Count Hagen would have been assessed a capital ass. Here he was a power.

Five other seniors were in his study when Krampitz knocked on his door and was told to enter.

"'Lo Krampitz. Had nice hols?"

"Passable. Papa was kept busy with the Russian situation, but Erich and I got some good shooting at the lodge."

"Lucky devil," said Count Hagen. "I was made to spend the summer with a crammer, working, merely because I failed six subjects last term. Poisonous fellow, that schoolmaster, though he had a daughter who was really hot stuff."

No one believed him, but they licked lips suddenly grown dry. "Lucky dog, Haggy. But then you always are."

"How's your new lot, Krampitz?"

"Scruffy. You know how they always are. I've got your little brother cleaning our football boots, Tussow. He was going to sleep with his toy elephant."

"Oh, is that why he wasn't at supper? Silly little squit."

"I'm told," said Count Hagen, yawning and letting his eyeglass drop, "that the heir of Landeck Steel is a new cadet here. It won't do. This isn't a school for tradesmen's sons."

"Landeck, though, Hagenbeck."

"Steel peddlers."

"Steel puddlers."

"Oh, ow, Tussow. No more of that, or we'll have to fine you again."

"Seriously, I don't like it. I think we ought to get rid of him before pork butchers start to send their sons here."

"Tonight?"

"The sooner the better."

They stood at the foot of his bed like the grey bulk of a nightmare. Dragged from his first sleep, Felix was not sure whether he was awake, or where. When they whispered, "Come with us," he threw back the covers and got up. The touch of ice under his feet helped to orient him; those stone flags belonged to school. He followed obediently, remembering school stories he had read; rags in the dorms, cocoa parties at midnight. But he knew, really, that it was nothing like that. The atmosphere was threatening, the silence not that of suppressed laughter.

Someone opened a door, someone else pushed him inside. It was some kind of broom closet; there were buckets and scrub brushes on the floor, and mops hanging from nails on the wall. Everything smelled damp. It was very cold. Felix hoped they would not think he was shivering because he was frightened.

"What do you want?" He had forgotten that he must never speak first. Yet no immediate punishment followed. One of the grey shapes said, quite politely, "We'll tell you what we want. We want you out of here."

"But why? I haven't done anything."

"This isn't a school for the sons of tradesmen."

"Tradesmen!" Not noticing in his indignation that he differed with them only in degree, he said, "My father is Landeck Steel, not a greengrocer."

This time a hand hit him across the mouth. "You don't talk to us, we talk to you." He felt a trickle of blood on his chin, and cautiously moved his tongue around his teeth. They still seemed to be all there, which was one good thing anyway.

Hagenbeck said, "We're not here to debate with you. We are telling you, go home."

Felix was so angry he was no longer frightened. He said, "I was sent here at the suggestion of my father's friend, the kaiser. If you don't like it, you will have to lump it."

It was probably the bit about "my father's friend" that annoyed them into beating him as badly as they did. Except for Hagenbeck they weren't vicious, and normally they might have remembered that there were five of them and he was very small.

"Have a look at the school chapel," one of them said as they left. "There've been others who didn't belong here. You'll find their memorial plaques on the wall."

He waited till he was sure they had all gone, then picked himself up from the damp floor. He ached all over, but nothing seemed to be broken. He made his way back to the dormitory and crawled into bed. After a little while he noticed the silence and it struck him as odd. It was not the silence of sleepers, but of held breath. Shortly after he'd got into bed, he saw Krampitz get up and walk down the length of the dorm as if he were checking on the sleepers. He did not slow down as he passed Felix's bed, but Felix understood that had he been seriously hurt or uncontrollably frightened, Krampitz would have been ready to help. He fell asleep with confused dreams of toy shops and ordnance.

The bell rang at six. It sounded like a demented fire alarm, like the clatter of thousands of tin pails; it threw them from their beds in a state of shock, to stand at attention even before Krampitz's call of reveille rang down the room.

"You're last out of bed, Tussow," Krampitz began to say, then saw that Felix was moving even more slowly and said nothing.

They washed in the tin bowls at the foot of their beds. It was hard for Felix to move. He was bruised all over, and one eye was swollen shut. No one said anything to him. They let him go first out of the door, though it meant someone else would be last and be given a nuisance job to do. They behaved as if they had learned overnight that he had a fatal disease.

The day opened with gymnastics on the muddy playing field. A sergeant shouted insults at them, made them touch their toes, leap over each others' backs, lie on their stomachs in the mud and do one hundred pushups. Felix could barely move, though after the ghastly hour was over he was warmed, his muscles had loosened, and he felt altogether better.

He was ravenous at breakfast, and bolted his coarse bread and beetroot jam with pleasure. None of the masters commented on his black eye and swollen lip. It was Colonel von Hunger's policy that the cadets took care of their own discipline problems, even if this occasionally led to memorial plaques in the school chapel.

After breakfast they went to class. Each master in turn made an identical speech, assuring them that he was a martinet, was proud of it, insisted on absolute discipline and hard work, and would show no leniency to those who did not meet his standards. They were given uniformly bound notebooks and texts, and informed that these must be returned in the same condition as they were received. They were greasy and spongy, marked by the grubby hands of a generation of schoolboys, and Felix thought that this injunction at least would not be difficult to obey.

For lunch they ate boiled potatoes and a sausage that seemed to be largely stuffed with sawdust. The dessert was tapioca pudding. Felix and his sisters always referred to this as fisheyes-and-glue, but he was still hungry, and had no trouble cleaning his plate.

Lunch was followed by two hours of games. This was not intended as recreation. Everyone, no matter how unsuited, had to join team sports. The coaches looked over the new boys and shook their heads mournfully, saying, as they did every year, that this new lot was the worst they had ever seen.

Pregnitz Minor, a third-year boy who coached junior cross-country running, ignored Felix's black eye and split lip, but approved the spare, small body. He said, "You look like a runner. Ever try?"

Felix, who had been watching with horrified wonder what looked to be a many-legged animal writhing in the mud of the rugby field, decided that running would be far preferable. He said, "I'd like to try. I'm a bit stiff today, though."

Pregnitz, who seemed to be quite human, grinned sympathetically. "We'll leave it for a day or two. If anyone wants you for rugby, tell them you're taken."

"Oh, thank you," Felix began to say, but Pregnitz Minor

had moved off. Felix looked around. No one was paying attention to him. Everyone was cheering the writhing beast on the rugby field. He slipped through a gap in the hedge and felt instantly, magically, at liberty. In spite of his bruises he began to run. He had to get to town and back before games was finished, and he also wanted to begin to train for Pregnitz Minor, who was the first person he had found to like at school. He was still wearing his civilian clothes; the few people he passed on the beach path took little notice of him. Outside town he slowed to a walk, so he would not look hot and dishevelled. His heart beat fast, not only from running.

The toy shop was around the corner, its window gleaming. And yes, it was still there. No one else had bought it.

He wandered around the aisles, looking at anything but what he had come for. The shop owner bowed himself in half and said, "How may I help you, young sir?" No one had ever called Felix "sir" before. He could feel himself blushing.

"I'm looking for a birthday present for a friend," he said, turning his face to the shop owner for the first time.

"Well, goodness me. And what does the other chappie look like?"

Felix relaxed. This was a language he spoke fluently. He had learned it at home, from the grown-ups who worked for Landeck and walked a careful line of jocularity between disrespect for a child and respect for the heir of Landeck Steel.

"You'll have to ask at the hospital," he said, smiling.

The shop owner, who had assessed the value of an expensive English flannel jacket on a boy who would obviously outgrow it before the year was out, to its very last penny, laughed obsequiously.

"What kind of toys does your friend like, young sir? Clockwork railways, meccanos, guns?"

Felix knew enough not to head straight for what he wanted. "Well, railways. He's got quite a collection, though. I might just be buying him something he already has. He collects guns too. Not toy guns, but those replicas of famous ones, you know. Do you have anything like that?"

"Oh, young sir, if you had taken a look in the window," said the owner, just as if he hadn't seen Felix's nose pressed flat against the glass two days running, "you wouldn't have to ask. The only thing is, it's usually fathers or rich bachelor uncles what buys them. I mean to say, young sir, with all respect, they are almost as expensive as the real thing."

Felix, lordly, said, "Let's have a look." He could feel his two short hours trickling away, but he was fighting for his life and could not afford to be discovered as a runaway from school.

The proprietor brought the gun from the display window, laying it down reverently in front of Felix. "Colt .45," he said. "The gun what won the Wild West."

Felix, who had read all the *Leatherstocking* books, and every penny western he could get hold of, went over the gun with an expert hand. "The balance isn't bad," he said with the nonchalance of Natty Bumppo in person. He put the gun back on the counter. This was the worst moment of all. "How much?"

Herr Kasewitz, Prop., bowed himself in half once more, and managing to call him sir twice in one sentence, told him. Including the money his father had given him for cab fare the day before, Felix found he had, give or take a penny, exactly enough.

The local tuck shop would see no coins of his this term. The cakes would sit in the window unbought by Landeck money. He remembered how hungry he had been after he had finished his lunch, but also remembered the memorial plaques in the school chapel.

"Very good," he said. "Will you wrap it up."

Time ticked away while Herr Kasewitz turned the parcel into a birthday present complete with bow, exchanged it for all of Felix's money, and informed him, on being asked, that, young sir, it was exactly half past three.

Felix arrived back at the gap in the hedge with five minutes to spare. He had discarded the ribbon and gift box along the way. While the rugby players washed off the mud, he managed to take the gun from his pocket and slide it under his mattress.

Tea was a repetition of breakfast. He ate it, as well as the lumpy gruel they had for supper, with excellent appetite. Between tea and supper they had more classes. After supper there was a study hall. Since the new boys had no home-work as yet, they were told to write a letter home. "It is quite jolly here," Felix wrote. "I think I am going to like it very much." He had, until then, always been known as an unusually truthful little boy.

When the five nightmare figures met at his bed he was awake and ready for them. He followed them down the hall to the broom closet without demur. At each step the gun in his bathrobe pocket bumped against his thigh. Anyone with more brains than Hagenbeck might have become suspicious of quite so jaunty a step.

"It won't do, you know," said Hagenbeck as soon as he had shut them all in the broom closet.

" 'It is quite jolly here,' " said another. " 'I think I am going to like it very much.' It really won't do, little Landeck."

He had been prepared to face physical violence, but not violence to his privacy. "You read my letter!"

"Prefects censor all letters home."

"Swine," shouted Felix, losing his temper. "Bloody swine."

"Now, now," said a reasonable voice, "let's not start name-calling, or we might have to call you a bloody liar, little Landeck. 'It is quite jolly here. I think I am going to like it very much.' That is not what a truthful person would have written. It is not what *we* expected you to write. 'Dear Daddy, take me away from here before I turn into a memorial plaque in the school chapel,' was more what we had in mind."

Felix put his hands in his pockets, touching the gun. He was sorry it was not a real one. He would have liked to see them dead. "You can whistle for it then," he said. "I'm not going to write it."

"Yes you will," said Hagenbeck, who was so eager to get down to the beating part that he could not trouble himself to reprimand Felix for impertinence. "Last night was just a sample. Tonight is going to be the real thing. Tomorrow you'll write home, if you can still hold a pen."

"I won't, you know," said Felix, his hand firmly on the gun.

"He's insane," said Hagenbeck. "We're wasting time. Let's get started." They had been standing in half circle around him, seeming in the dim light that came from outside the grimy window, figures without dimension or individuality, a solid block of grey; and it was as a solid block that they moved at Hagenbeck's command and stopped at Felix's.

Respect for guns had been bred into all of them. At home, as small boys, and later through eight years of school, they obeyed one rule without question; you do not point a gun at anyone, ever, unless you are prepared to kill.

The dim light from outside glinted along the barrel. "It's not real," said Hagenbeck. "It's a toy." But he did not sound entirely convinced.

Felix, feeling the tremendous physical superiority that comes with holding a gun, and mistaking it for moral superiority, felt he could afford to say nothing.

"I am going to report you to Colonel von Hunger," said Hagenbeck, changing tactics.

"For having a toy gun? You'd look a fine fool."

"It is a toy, I knew it," said Hagenbeck. Most annoyingly his voice cracked, which it hadn't done for almost a year.

"Come close and find out."

The boy with the reasonable voice said, "All right, what kind of a gun is it?" He took a step back and leaned against the wall, hands in pocket, one connoisseur to another.

Felix said, "It's a Colt .45." He had thought this out, running back to the school. "It belonged to an ancestor of mine. He was a bad hat and had to emigrate to America. He was hanged in Tombstone, Arizona."

"Tosh," said Hagenbeck. "There's one in the toy shop in town. I'll bet that's it."

"Possibly," said Felix. He had never felt so well in his life. "You can't afford to find out, though, can you? Look, all of you, I don't know what you're so fond of in this

36

broom closet. It smells of damp mops. Shall we call it a standoff and go to bed?"

"I think he's got us, Haggy," said the boy with the reasonable voice. "We'll have to think again."

Felix felt for the door handle behind his back, swung the door open, and bowed them out. "Goodnight," he said with the utmost politeness.

After they had gone, he ran down the hall, exultant and shaky, wanting to shout, laugh, tell somebody, but ending in bed, the covers pulled over his head, crying.

When he had finished and blown his nose as quietly as he could, he felt relaxed and sleepy, but knew he must stay awake, for he had no doubt Hagenbeck would try to come after the gun. If only it suddenly weren't so difficult to keep one's eyes open. He pretended he was a sentry on guard duty, with Indians moving surefooted and silent through the warm Western night. He pretended he was an Indian, standing so immobile in the dark he was mistaken for a stone. He pinched himself, he propped his eyes open with his fingers, he pretended a firing squad was taking him out to shoot him for sleeping on guard duty. He had just waved away the blindfold with a nonchalant smile and steady hand, when the door handle turned and the dormitory door opened a crack. Hagenbeck moved down the rows of beds till he came to Felix's. Felix kept his eyes closed. There was no danger of his going to sleep now.

Hagenbeck picked up the bathrobe and felt in the pockets. The gun was not there. His hand crept cautiously, a millimetre at a time, under Felix's pillow. Nothing on the left side. He walked quietly around to the right and put his hand out again. The gun was there. Felix brought it smashing down on the groping hand, and hoped the cracking noise he heard was human bone.

Hagenbeck yelped, and clutching his hand, ran out the door. Krampitz, wakened by the noise, said, "What the devil is going on? Is that you again, Landeck? Why can't you keep quiet?"

"Please, I.C. I think it was Hagenbeck. He was looking for something in my bathrobe pockets. Do you think he was trying to steal my money?"

"Don't be impertinent, Landeck. Shut up and go to sleep."

Felix did, sweetly, without bad dreams.

The next morning Hagenbeck appeared with two fingers splinted and bandaged. He said he had caught his hand in a door. Felix noted the bandage and ate his breakfast, thinking that few things tasted as good as acorn coffee and beetroot jam.

The senior with the reasonable voice, observing him, said, "He seems a plucky kid. The kind we need. It seems a pity to waste him."

"He's a tradesman's son."

"Landeck Steel, though."

"That makes no difference."

"It does, you know. I propose we let him be."

"I veto it," said Hagenbeck.

But the others went with the voice of reason, and even in a Prussian military school the majority ruled.

It was decreed that Felix should be sent to Coventry, but during their first year the new cadets were so isolated in any case by the rule which did not permit them to speak to each other, that Felix hardly noticed. Indeed not everyone abided by it. Pregnitz Minor for one remained friendly, and the hours Felix spent running cross-country with him and the rest of the junior team were the happiest of his first year of school.

His classmates treated him with silent respect. No one knew exactly what had happened, but everyone knew that one of them, a mere wart, had somehow managed to hold his own against five seniors.

His schoolwork gave him little trouble, and if the masters were, as David was to write about his at St Dunstan's, poor, nasty, brutish, and short, this was in the nature of things, for who but such a one would choose a life sentence spent in a school?

He brought home good reports at Christmas, but Hesso was not pleased. "He's become secretive," he said to his wife. "He doesn't speak unless he's spoken to! I don't like it."

"He is learning discipline," said Sophie. "It is necessary."

"I haven't any discipline, and I get on all right."

"It is not the same."

"Perhaps not. But they're turning him into a Prussian, Sophie. We should never have sent him to Lehzen."

"You could hardly have refused."

"No, damn it. Sorry, Sophie."

"You know, my dear, things are very different these days from when you were a boy. The whole spirit of the times has changed. All of Germany is becoming more Prussian. I know you don't like it, but it's a good thing for the country and for Landeck Steel. You've only to look at what Germany was like before; all those petty duchies and counties muddling along as if they were still in the Middle Ages. The entire industrial revolution, which made England into the most powerful country in the world, passed us right by. If it hadn't been for a few great men like your grandfather and Alfred Krupp, and Bismarck's vision of Germany's future, we would still be no better off than Italy or Spain. Look how you've forged ahead over these last years. You've said yourself it won't be long till Germany leads the world in industrial production. Do you think that would have been possible under the old system? Felix is going to inherit one of the largest industrial empires in this new Prussian Germany. He's got to be educated in Prussia."

Hesso sighed. "I know, Sophie. I just don't see why it has to be all shorn heads and heel clicking. The blasted school sounds no better than a jail."

"Felix has accepted it."

"I know," said Hesso. "That's what I don't like."

Chapter 4

The housemaids, sleeping two to a bed in attic rooms which broiled in the summer and froze in winter, began their day at six, plunging from their warm beds into the chilly air as into a freezing lake. In haste they broke the crust of ice in

the water jug and splashed their faces, fumbled with numb
fingers at hooks and buttons, and hurried downstairs to
take up their housemaid's boxes, which contained black
lead, soft brushes, leather, emery paper, a cinder pail, and
broom; weapons in the daily battle against soot, tarnish,
and rust. Grates were cleaned and new fires laid, brass was
polished and rugs swept. Occasional tables and overmantels, every inch of their surfaces covered with mementos,
bibelots, boxes of silver filigree, fans, photographs, ormolu
clocks, and vases of pampas grass, were cautiously dusted.
Draperies and portieres and clutter made unending work,
especially when combined with sooty coal fires, but housemaids cost less to keep than a hunting dog, and the
rumblings of William Morris, who preached natural wood,
light-coloured walls, and simplicity, would not reach Yorkshire for some years to come, and when they did, would
be ignored.

At a quarter past eight the staff met for protracted prayers
and a hastily eaten breakfast, and by nine stood ready
at the housemaid's cupboard to collect jugs of water for
baths.

At nine Calais, Lady Millicent's maid, drew the curtains,
said, "*Bonjour, miladi; il fait beau,*" or "*il pleut encore,*" as
the case might be, plumped up the pillows, put a bedjacket
on Lady Millicent's shoulders, and handed her a tray with
tea and two arrowroot biscuits.

Calais had been Lady Langland's maid and had been
passed along as a wedding gift to her daughter. In all she
had lived in England for nearly thirty years. Nevertheless
she claimed to speak no English, much to the annoyance
of Nannie and the other servants, who got even by calling
her Miss Kelly.

While Lady Millicent drank her tea, a footman carried
up cans of hot water and filled the hip bath which stood in
front of the fire in Lady Millicent's dressing room.

Augustus had a bathroom of his own, with a rather
splendid tub mounted on a dais, and a heated towel rail,
but Lady Millicent would have considered it indelicate to
use this.

After her bath, Calais helped her into her dressing gown

40

and slippers. She breakfasted in her sitting room on tea, baked eggs, galantine of chicken, and crumpets, while she read the *Morning Post*.

Augustus always ate a dining-room breakfast. Although he never deviated from his daily kidney and eggs, Cook sent up porridge and cream, bacon, ham, potted meat, and kippers even when there were no guests. With breakfast Augustus read *The Times*. This, like the *Morning Post*, arrived, of course, a day late which irritated Lady Millicent and soothed Augustus.

When he had finished with the paper, the linenmaid ironed it and took it up to Nannie, who daily read the "Court Circular" and the "Births," brooding darkly on Lady Agatha Somebody, delivered of the Hon. Agravaine Somebody, brother to the Hon. Etcetera and Etcetera Somebody, while her own nursery was empty, with no prospect of new babies until Master Toby, aged eleven and away at his prep school, should be ready to take a wife.

While Lady Millicent ate her breakfast, Calais aired her underclothes, heated the curling irons, and brushed the yards of braid sewn inside her skirts to catch the dust and mud. After breakfast she laced Lady Millicent into her corsets and spent an hour doing her hair. With the help of pins, and an Alexandra fringe, she managed to make Lady Millicent's fine, fair hair appear as fashion required, as if her swanlike neck could scarcely support its great mass. Lady Millicent's neck was not really all that swanlike, but the high whalebone collar, made fashionable by Queen Alexandra to hide an operation scar, helped to make it appear so.

After breakfast Lady Millicent went to the morning room, while the housemaids cleaned the bedroom and emptied the slops. The morning room, so called because it faced east, was pleasant in the summer, but on a chill February morning it was, despite a blazing fire, decidedly bleak.

Here Lady Milly read and answered her mail, went over the menus with Cook, and saw Nannie about anything that needed doing in the village. After this her day was essentially finished. In the summer she might walk round the garden, slowly filling a basket with flowers for the house; on her at-homes she gave tea to deaf Lady Lappiter and Colonel Molyneux and his daughters, and during the hunting season she rode to hounds, passionately, absorbedly, sometimes as much as five days a week. But the hard weather after Christmas had put an end to the hunting, and her days were again idle and endless. She might have filled them, as did Sophie von Landeck, with good works among the local poor, but she was never at ease with people not of her class, and besides, Nannie and Mrs Harvey saw to all that.

But there came a day, late in February, which brought an end to her idleness and boredom. When Nannie came to see her after breakfast, she had a handkerchief in her hand and was in tears.

Much alarmed, Lady Milly said, "What is it, Nannie? Is something wrong?"

"Oh, my lady, such dreadful news from the vicarage."

With a sigh of relief that the dreadful news had nothing to do with Toby, Lady Milly said, "Sit down, Nannie. What's happened? Is anyone ill?"

Nannie blew her nose into a very large handkerchief. "Oh no, my lady, not to say ill. At least, I suppose you might call it that."

"I can't call it anything until you tell me," said Lady Millicent, growing impatient. "Come, Nannie, what is it?"

"It's Miss Julian, my lady. Poor little mite. They say the doctor's been and she's blind."

"Blind! Oh, Nannie, no. Are you quite sure?"

"Yes, my lady. I had it from Alice."

Alice was the young village girl who was the vicarage nursery maid. Only catastrophe would cause Nannie to break down the social barriers sufficiently to gossip with her.

"Oh, Nannie, how very dreadful. I must go at once to see if we can help. Do ring and tell them I shall want my carriage and coat."

"Begging your pardon, my lady, but they do say there's

nothing to be done. She was born blind, it seems, poor little dear, only no one knew it."

"One can always help," said Lady Millicent briskly. "You know, Nannie, when I was a little girl I had scarletina and was made to spend four weeks in a dark room. I remember it so very well."

Behind this colourless statement lay the most terrifying experience of Lady Millicent's life. She had never forgotten her sense of isolation; panic at first, loss of reference later, knowing the times of day only by the meals her nurse brought her; and finally, as she was recovering, her lethargy and sense of acquiescence in the darkness surrounding her, so that in the end, when her mother had joyfully pulled open the curtains to release her, she had screamed, not only with the pain the light caused her eyes, but with sheer rage at having to return to a world of people and objects.

Calais brought her coat, hat, and gloves, and told her the carriage was waiting.

"Oh good." So determined was she upon her errand, she did not even pause to ask herself whether her visit would be welcome. Until now, relations between her and the vicarage had been cool. Mrs Harvey, in what little time her large family and her village activities left her, would have been prepared to be friendly, and indeed had seldom time to notice the chill that emanated from Lady Millicent. It was partly a question of social standing. About this Lady Millicent was as unrelenting as Augustus was easygoing. Had Mrs Harvey treated her with less of an all-equal-in-the-sight-of-the-Lord attitude, had she been permitted to patronize and be Lady Bountiful, relations might have been warmer. But that was only a surface reason. There was another cause for her coldness toward the Harveys, one never admitted, or even put into words in her mind, for it dealt with what were to her unspeakable things; the suspicion that the Harveys' large brood of children had been lovingly begotten and joyfully conceived. Under the cover of outward religion and decent family life, Lady Millicent suspected the Harveys of being lovers. That in public they always behaved with propriety did not deceive her. She had sometimes seen their eyes meet—almost involuntarily, it seemed—and Mrs Harvey's plump cheek turn pink. Yes, even in church.

Lady Millicent had been quite properly warned by her mother on the eve of her marriage that certain things must be endured for the sake of an independent establishment and the subsequent blessing of children. Augustus's lack-luster performance had done nothing to change her mind, and she had been quite as relieved as he when Toby's birth had put an end to these unseemly and painful obligations. That Mrs Harvey, the wife of a vicar of the Church of England, could be suspected of deriving pleasure from such distasteful things was, even if only dimly perceived and never acknowledged, quite sufficient to put a chill into their relationship.

If the Harveys looked upon her visit as an intrusion, they gave no sign of it. They showed her into the drawing room and sat down as if they had all day to devote to social calls. Mrs Harvey looked much as usual; a little untidy, as if caught on the run, but by no means devastated. It was the Vicar who showed the effects of the terrible news. Yet no one could know from his composed welcome and offer of sherry, that this morning he had said to his wife: "I wish I did not think that Julian's blindness has been sent to teach me a lesson. I have read enough of the lives of the saints and their own writings to know that no one's relations with God run as smoothly and cheerfully as mine have always done. It would surely have been easy to remember that He is a terrible God. One cannot separate even Christmas from the Massacre of the Innocents. How could I have had the impertinence to think that I was an exception? By what special merit?"

His wife could only say that he was the best of men and must not even think such dreadful things. She reminded him that God had always been hard on his favourites. Look at Job.

' "Yea, though he slay me, yet will I love Him.' I think I could manage that. But when my reproof comes by way of injury to my child, I feel almost that I might take the advice of one of Job's comforters and curse God."

"My dearest, you mustn't think like that. In a little while

you shall go to church and thrash it all out with Him if it takes the rest of the day. But just now I fear I see Lady Millicent's carriage. Another Job's Comforter, I expect."

Lady Millicent proved to be nothing of the kind. She said all the right things—it was part of her upbringing to have the right words for sticky situations—but she quickly moved to practical matters.

She said, "I hope you won't think my visit intrusive. I should not have ventured to interfere in so sad a family matter, but I think I might be of some help. You see, in a small way I have some experience with . . ."—she could not bring herself to use the word "blindness"—"with living in the dark. When I was quite small I had scarlet fever and had to spend four weeks in a dark room. Light was considered dangerous for the eyes. I don't know if doctors still think this, I hope not. But when I heard about your dear Julian, it brought it all back so vividly, as if it had happened yesterday. Of course you will think that it was different. I had my sight and knew the objects around me, and at first this was perfectly true. There was merely panic at being in the dark, and the awful boredom. But after a time this changed. I don't know how long it took, because time was the first thing I lost touch with. My brothers and sisters had been moved out of the nursery for fear of infection, so it was very quiet. There was a hired nurse—Nanny couldn't come near me, of course—and the maid who brought my meals. The nurse didn't stay and talk much. I imagine the dark room upset or bored her. I grew to be quite out of touch with the outside world. And after I got over the panic and the boredom, I began to acquiesce in the darkness and timelessness around me. I stopped wanting things. It was almost like being dead."

She stopped, appalled at herself. All her training had taught her that it was the height of indelicacy to speak about one's private feelings, and here she had gone on at length about the most secret and terrifying time of her life. "Do forgive me for talking so much about myself when you can think of nothing but dear Julian. But you see, in a way this is about Julian." She could not stop talking. The deep waters of memory had caught her in a tide she could not hold back. "I remember so well how, the moment the nurse stopped talking to me, I stopped being aware of her presence. It must be much worse for Julian, because she has no way of knowing that there is a world in all that darkness. We must make sure she is always made aware of people and things. Until she gets old enough to crawl about and touch things, we must bring them to her. That is really what I've come for. I know how busy you are, Mrs Harvey. You have your other children to look after, and all your kind work in the parish, so I do hope you'll allow Nannie and me to help. It would give us both such pleasure."

"It's most kind of you, Lady Millicent," said the Vicar. "Not at all."

"I hope I don't neglect her," said Mrs Harvey. "She has such an angelic temper, hardly ever cries or wants things; perhaps I've taken it too much for granted that she was just being good."

"We shall work with her," said the Vicar, "and turn her into demons, like the others. Would you like to see her, Lady Millicent?"

They went to the nursery, where Alice sat crying and mending some linen, and Julian lay in her crib, fists curled at her shoulders, like a newborn's. She did not react to the noise of their entrance, but when Lady Millicent went up to the crib and put a finger in her fist, she grasped it firmly.

"You little poppet," said Lady Millicent. Julian's beautiful grey eyes appeared to be fixed on a point somewhere beyond the ceiling and did not turn to the voice.

"When she was christened," said the Vicar, "Toby said that she looked as if she were thinking of something else. Of course we had no idea then . . ."

"I blame myself," said Mrs Harvey. "I should have noticed so much sooner."

"You couldn't have known," said Lady Millicent.

"Her eyes never followed movements. She never spent hours watching her own hands the way babies do. I think I did know, in a way, but I was too frightened to find out."

"My dear," said the Vicar, "even if we had known, we could have prevented nothing. You heard the doctor say so."

"Yes, I know. We mustn't give way."

Lady Millicent unpinned her gold watch and held it to Julian's ear, thinking how differently a sighted child would have reacted to the glittering bauble, probably trying to put it in her mouth, certainly wanting to throw it on the floor. Julian listened placidly and made no protest when it was withdrawn. Lady Millicent put an index finger in each fist, and Julian pulled herself up into a sitting position.

"What a clever girl. Can she sit up by herself then?"

Julian appeared to like the sound of this new voice and responded with a pleased gurgle, but when Lady Millicent let go she fell back and lost interest, resuming her pensive look past the ceiling.

"Little darling," said Lady Millicent. "Mrs Harvey, I mustn't keep you from lunch. But I do hope you will allow me to visit often and perhaps let Julian come to the hall when the weather is better. Nannie is quite bereft, now that Toby is at school."

The Harveys thanked her and showed her to the door. After she had left, the Vicar said, "Well, well, Lady Milly. Who would have thought it?"

"Lady Bountiful with baskets for the deserving poor. Am I to produce babies to keep Her Highness's Nannie in a good mood?"

"My dear, she wants to help and she is being kind. For Julian's sake we must accept any help that is offered."

"Yes, of course you are right. It's very good of her. I shall keep reminding myself of that. But Simon, just once I should dearly love to say a very rude word."

"Come into my study where the housemaid can't hear you, and you shall say as many rude words as you like. And then we will have lunch."

Lady Millicent and Lord Altondale sat at each end of the long dining-room table. Even when it had none of its extra leaves in, there was a good deal of distance between them. They ate veal cutlets, fillet of beef and baked potato, apple tart and custard, biscuits, cheese, and fruit.

"Seems to me Cook is taking it very easy these days," Augustus grumbled.

"I'm afraid she always does when we don't have guests. I'll speak to her."

"She might at least let us have a savoury."

"I quite agree. I'll mention it to her. Augustus, have you heard the news from the vicarage?"

"Yes, it's rotten luck. We must do all we can to help. You know, Milly, I never had much confidence in the local sawbones. Perhaps we ought to have a specialist down from London, if the Harveys wouldn't think it interfering. I'd see to the fee and all that, of course."

"That is a very kind thought, Augustus. We must give them time to get over the shock, then I'll suggest it to the Vicar. I'm sure he won't be unreasonable."

"Meaning she might put her ears back? Well, you handle it, old girl. Tact and all that, not my strong suit, what?"

After lunch Nannie and Lady Millicent turned out Toby's toy cupboard and selected a soft, furry dog with a windup clockwork in his stomach which played Brahms's *Lullaby*, a brass wind chime to hang in the window, and a rubber duck that squeaked when squeezed for Julian's bath.

That night Lady Millicent wrote her twice-weekly letter to Toby at his school. She told him about Julian and added: "Nannie and I raided your toy cupboard—we know you won't mind. We gave Julian the squeaky duck and the furry clockwork dog. She seems to enjoy listening to the tune, but she doesn't appear to associate it with the toy itself. She never reaches for anything. I suppose if one is born blind, the outside world literally doesn't exist. Once a thing is no longer in one's hand, it is no longer there. It seems to me a truly terrifying thought to know that everything outside one's own body is only a black void, and we must do everything to teach dear little Julian through touch and hearing that there is a secure, bright, and stable world out there."

This was in February. Julian was six months old. From then on Lady Millicent's letters to Toby constituted a kind of diary of Julian's progress.

"She can sit up by herself quite well," Lady Millicent wrote in March. "Of course she doesn't look about as a sighted child would, but we are trying to get her to turn

48

toward sound—so far without success. The horrid brass fire-engine bell with which, Nannie claims, you used to drive her quite demented, is a great favourite of Julian's. She clangs it with a will, but if she drops it she does not try to find it again. It is as if it had dropped off the edge of the world, as of course for her it has. Nannie and I take it away from her and ring it within reach. She may protest against this briefly, but she does not reach for the sound."

By the end of March Lady Millicent wrote: "The weather has turned charming, so instead of visiting Julian, we bring her up to visit the Hall. She enjoys the airing in the carriage—I imagine it's the rocking motion, for one must remember that the sight of crocuses and snowdrops emerging from the frozen ground means nothing to her. It's too cruel.

"We have fixed up your crib so that, if the weather should turn nasty, Julian can spend the night. She is such an amiable child, and does not appear to mind strangers, though I do sometimes feel that she doesn't quite take to Nannie, and that, I think, is because Nannie can't really take to her. 'It's not natural, my lady,' she says, 'for a child not to smile and hold out its arms when Nannie comes into the room. All my babies loved their Nannie.' Of course I have tried to explain to her that this isn't fair. It isn't natural to be blind. Babies smile and reach out to people they can *see*. When one talks to Julian she smiles quite enchantingly, though it is true that she doesn't hold out her arms to be picked up. She's got three and one half teeth, and her hair is so fair as to be almost white. But I do not think this will last. She looks so much like dear David, that I think her hair will probably turn the same glossy leaf brown. Well, you shall see her at Easter. We're all tremendously looking forward to having you home."

By Easter Toby found Julian established in his crib in his nursery, playing with his toys. "The kidnapping," he said to David, "seems to be complete." They had always, when writing to each other, referred to it that way, at first as a joke, then, on Toby's side, with some trepidation. "What will your people say to it all?" he had written to David after Lady Millicent had told him about getting the crib ready so Julian could stay the night. "Once my Mama makes up her mind to anything, one can't stop her, and your Mama may not be in the mood to lose a daughter . . ."

But it seemed that the vicarage had accepted Lady Millicent's predation calmly. It had all happened so gradually. First an afternoon's ride and tea at the hall, later a boy sent with a message that since the weather had suddenly turned so very damp, might dear Julian spend the night, then an unseasonable snowstorm which rendered the roads hazardous, and by the time good weather and Easter arrived together, Julian appeared to have gone from being at home at the vicarage and a guest at the hall, to being an occasional guest at the vicarage and at home at Altondale Hall.

Mrs Harvey did not seem to mind. For one thing she was once again in a state which Lady Millicent described with distaste as "enceinte," and had arrived at the placid, bovine stage that comes after morning sickness has stopped and before the restless nest-building instinct of the eighth and ninth month takes over. Also, though she blamed herself bitterly for the feeling, she had never been able to love Julian as much as she did her other children. Perhaps, as the mother of so very handsome a brood, she felt Julian's blindness to be a flaw which reflected on her. Had she been an animal (and there was a good deal of that in Mrs Harvey's personality), she might have regarded Julian as a runt and have left her to starve. As a Christian wife and mother she felt guilty and uncomfortable, and was not sorry when the creature who caused these feelings was out of her sight. Particularly as one knew she was splendidly looked after.

The Vicar minded very much indeed. He knew a good parent should have no favourites, but how to rule the unruly heart? From the day Julian was born he had been her slave. He was also the slave of an overscrupulous conscience, which told him that the Straffords could do a great deal more for Julian than he could. An expensive specialist had been brought down from London, unfortunately only to confirm what the local doctor had already told them; that there was no cure for Julian's type of blindness. He could not say what had caused it; possibly Julian's somewhat premature birth, though she seemed strong and healthy in

50

every other respect. He very much approved of what Lady Millicent and Nannie were doing, and promised to send her ladyship a monograph he had written about working with blind children, which tended essentially along the same lines.

Could the Vicar procure so highly prized a medical opinion? Could his wife, with a parish to run and large family to contrive for on practically no money, spend the day playing with Julian, talking and singing to her, trying to teach her, as Lady Millicent and Nannie undeniably did?

Surely only a fiend could object. The Vicar acknowledged that he was such a fiend. He prayed earnestly for forgiveness, and imposed upon himself the penance of silence.

David and Toby kept to themselves during Easter vacation. They were of an age to be more interested in toy railways than in babies. As for the machinations of the grown-ups, they watched those with the detached cynicism suitable to their years.

"I've never seen my Mama so fascinated by anything," said Toby, trying to prop a railway trestle he was building with some mildewed volumes of Chambers's *Encyclopaedia*. "Of course it's very jolly for me. Nannie hasn't once had time to check whether I've washed behind my ears. Oh bloody hell!" he added as the trestle, so carefully constructed, collapsed under the onslaught of a Basset-Lowke goods engine. Toby had learned to swear quite wonderfully from one of the older boys at his prep school.

"Bloody hell, bloody hell," repeated David, laughing at the sheer enormity of it. "Do they really let you say things like that at your place?" David had lessons at home with his father to save money. Next year he would go to St Dunstan's, a minor public school. Toby was of course going to Eton.

"Ho, never," said Toby. "They swish you like anything. Six of the best for a really good curse, but it's worth it."

Even as a little boy Toby had been beaten often and hard by his father, mostly for setting free animals caught in traps. He had once confided to David that at Eton there was a sinister group of upperclass-men known as The Library (somehow this harmless name made them sound even more ominous), who administered savage beatings to the younger boys. He seemed not only to accept this as one of the unavoidable facts of public-school life, but almost, it seemed to David, to relish the prospect. No one had ever beaten David at all, and he could not help wondering what it would be like. He suspected that unlike Toby he would dislike it very much indeed.

Toby said, "Is your Mama having another baby?"

"Yes. In September."

"Oh good. She'd better hang on to this one, or my Mama will come foraging again."

"It's supposed to be twins this time. Perhaps they could have one each."

A month after Toby was back at school, his mother wrote: "You'll never guess who's taken a fancy to Julian. Culpepper. There was a dreadful outcry one morning when Nannie found him, breathing heavily, tail thumping, in Julian's crib. Julian was pulling his fur quite happily. I imagine she thought he was another furry, noisy toy. Nannie was fearfully upset, you know how she thinks dogs are germy, and then poor Culpepper does shed rather a lot. But I think it's important for Julian to have a live toy, so I spoke firmly to Nannie and Culpepper is now allowed to sleep at the foot of Julian's crib. Isn't it extraordinary, though. We always thought he was so completely Daddy's dog. Luckily Daddy's been very busy with the beagles and hasn't really noticed.

"Darling Julian regards Culpepper as an object, I'm sure. She uses him to pull herself upright. You remember how she would never crawl. I suppose babies learn to crawl because they *see* something out of reach they want, and poor Julian has nothing to entice her from where she is. Well, now she clings to Culpepper and lets herself be dragged about. It's not crawling, certainly, and nobody could call it walking. An odd mixture of both. Nannie is afraid she'll get bowlegged from walking so young, but I feel anything, anything at all that gets her away from her immediate orbit is good. Daddy's asked Jimson to make a special kind of harness for Culpepper so Julian can hold on properly.

"We still cannot get her to reach for sound, and I fear I may have become too obsessed by the need to teach her. What sight is to us sound will be to her; it will guide her and teach her the existence of things away from her. If only I could teach her to make the connection."

A week later Lady Millicent wrote again.

"Oh, my dear Toby, she's done it. Our darling Julian has done it at last. And only fancy, it's all Culpepper's doing. I brought him to the nursery with his new harness on, and instead of letting him run to her (she was lying on the floor, just turning on her own axis the way she does), I held him by the door. He resented this and gave that polite little bark of his, and for the first time Julian actually turned *to* a sound. Then, with quite extraordinary speed she crawled *in a straight line* directly to Culpepper and grasped his fur. I didn't know what to do, I was so happy. I rang for Nannie and told her and we both stood there almost crying with excitement. In fact I suspect Nannie did cry; I heard her trumpet quite loudly into her handkerchief.

"We repeated the experiment, putting Julian at one end of the room and Culpepper at the other. Each time he barked she came at him like an arrow. Bless him; I've told the kitchen to give him an enormous steak for his dinner. Though it is humbling to think that a dog could accomplish what all Nannie's and my work could not do."

The letters stopped there; probably Toby at Eton was too happy and absorbed in his new life to bother about saving letters from his mother. But Lady Millicent's interest in Julian did not cease. In her own odd way she had fallen in love at last. It put a shine on her days and lasted her all her life.

Chapter 5

It always surprised David, wretchedly unhappy at his own school, that Toby had settled into Eton so quickly and easily, for of the two of them it had been Toby who had looked forward to public school with the greater trepidation. David, who had been taught at home by his father, had little idea of what to expect, while Toby knew, having been told by an older cousin, that at Eton the boys' names were affixed to the doors of their rooms. Toby had spent the entire summer of his twelfth year in despair that thus his most shameful secret would be given over to the world to sneer at.

Until then it had been known only to his family, the Vicar, and David, whom Toby would have trusted with his life, that Toby was not Toby's real name.

"What is it then?" Felix had asked.

Toby had blushed. He could not bring himself to pronounce it. "You tell him," he said to David.

"Theobald," mumbled David, blushing in sympathy.

"Theobald Peregrine," said Toby, displaying its full enormity. "Theobald Peregrine Strafford."

Felix had lived up to the occasion. "Good God, how bloody. They're going to put that on your door?"

"Yes," said Toby miserably. Confession had not eased his mind. "I don't know how I can stop them."

"Not go to Eton," suggested David.

"But we always do."

"Shoot yourself," said Felix, who at Lehzen had acquired rigorous notions on the correct way to deal with public shame.

"Perhaps nobody will notice," said David.

"They'll notice Theobald Peregrine all right," said Toby, but when he had arrived at Eton he had found on the door of his room only the chaste announcement: The HON. T. P. STRAFFORD. Nothing that happened thereafter could cloud Toby's equanimity. All the stories he had heard were true. The Library did beat people savagely for almost any reason; small boys who had a stammer or red hair, or in any other way made themselves noticed, were forced to drink ink, had their rooms torn apart, and glue spilled over their books. But T. P. Strafford could take it. Besides, he was so obviously the right sort, with his cheerful, sturdy good looks and dogmatic sense of the proprieties, was so plainly destined to grow into a prefect and first-eleven cricketer, that even as a fag Toby's life was never made entirely miserable.

David was not the right sort at all. At least he wasn't at St Dunstan's. Very likely he would not have been the right sort at Eton either.

St Dunstan's was a minor but perfectly respectable public school which catered mostly to the sons of the clergy. In Mr Harvey's day the headmaster had been a considerable scholar, who had surrounded himself with a staff very like himself. When he retired it was taken over by a muscular Christian, who promptly got rid of the mild scholars who had for so long shambled through its halls, and had brought in his own sort; men of muscle and firm opinions, with a great belief in science, the efficacy of group sports, and discipline administered by one's peers.

Undoubtedly this new regime turned out men far more fitted to rule an empire than the old one had done. But there was no doubt that David would have been happier under the old headmaster.

He arrived at school speaking Greek like a sophist and Latin like a papal nuncio, inclined to be dreamy and fall in love with various poets, incompetent at mathematics, suspicious of the physical sciences, and arrogantly convinced that games were for people who hadn't any brains. Unfortunately he had never been taught to keep his opinions to himself. When he rashly quoted Mr Kipling's celebrated line about the flannelled fool at the wicket, the muddied oaf at the gate, it was clear to one and all that he had started off on quite the wrong foot and needed licking into shape.

He discovered that he was physically braver than he had expected, and could bear with the pain of constant beatings, but that he was endlessly depressed by the ill will which expressed itself in tearing his room apart and spilling ink on his books. For consolation he would lock himself and a volume of poetry in the lavatory, where he wept pleasurably for Adonais, Lycidas, and Lesbia's sparrow, and emerged, red-eyed, bowels empty but mind teeming with a kaleidoscope of glorious words, to be waylaid by muddied oafs, among whose few and simple ambitions it was to rescue

David Harvey from the perils of romantic poetry, long hair, and aestheticism. The thought that this might all go on for six years often made David wish that he were, like Lesbia's sparrow, safely deadand buried.

Of course it did not go on for six years. David was after all an irresistibly handsome boy, and by the end of his first year a prefect had begun to take a personal interest in him, and the bullying stopped.

As one member of a large and exceptionally good-looking family, David had never until then regarded himself as in any way unusual. At St Dunstan's he learned that looks such as his were quite as useful as money in the bank or a coronet on one's writing paper. It was a lesson he would have learned sooner or later in any case, but it would have come better to a more mature, less unhappy boy.

Despite the attentions of the prefect, and later of a rather nice housemaster, David never came to like school. He lived from summer to summer, dreaming away termtime with thoughts of the long, happy reprieve of Altondale with Toby and Felix.

Some of these summers Toby and his parents spent at Landeck. David did not really mind this very much; he was perfectly content to sit in his father's study, talking or reading, but Toby and Felix did not find the arrangement satisfactory. They had always been a threesome, and they missed David.

"I do wish he could have come," Felix said once.

"He can't afford the trip," said Toby, who knew all about the vicarage finances.

"Could we give him the money?"

"No."

"Wouldn't he take it?"

"I don't know," said Toby. "I just know you can't offer it."

Even as a boy Felix never rushed at things, having great confidence that, even if it took years, he would eventually have his way. The summer he was sixteen he was sent to the Touraine to polish up his French accent, but when Hesso asked him what he wanted for his seventeenth birthday, he remembered a four-year-old wish and said he would like Toby and David to spend the summer with him at Landeck. Put like this, he felt, in terms of a birthday present, with Hesso paying for both boys, David could accept without losing face.

Hesso, remembering a summer he and Augustus had spent together at the same age, during which they had discovered the pleasures and awful consequences of drink, cigars, and women, said it was an excellent idea. The Straffords were in any case coming over later for Angelika's wedding. Why shouldn't David and Toby come in June, and they could all travel back together.

He bought the tickets and sent them to England with a bundle of French banknotes tactfully addressed to both Toby and David, saying they must have their first French meal as his guests at Mère Catherine's in Calais and to be sure to order the snails, a suggestion both boys were silently determined to ignore.

They had never travelled by themselves anywhere more exciting than their schools, so that going abroad by themselves, just like grown-ups, was a thrilling idea. Nannie was certain they would miss the ferry, be seasick, lose their luggage, and be kidnapped by white slavers.

In spite of these warnings, David and Toby set out on a rainy June day, spent the night with Toby's Uncle Peregrine on Chesterfield Hill, missed neither train nor ferry, and, since the weather had cleared and the Channel was as smooth as glass, were not even sick on the way over. Mère Catherine's proved to be a very small, rather grubby restaurant. Secretly they would have preferred to lunch at one of the posh hotels along the Promenade, but this seemed ungrateful when Hesso had been so kind.

A very old waiter, with a grandfatherly air and a soup-strainer moustache, seated them by an open window, where they had a view of the grape arbour and three dustbins. Mère Catherine's was not one of those restaurants which allowed the view of the sea to distract its guests from the serious purpose of eating.

Toby and David were determined to have nothing to do

with Hesso's revolting suggestion of snails, and ordered steak and *pommes frites*.

The waiter, who miraculously appeared to understand their French, though they had great trouble understanding his, suggested a steak *marchand de vin*. And what kind of soup?

It was really too hot for soup, but before they had got their French adjectives and nouns in the right order, the waiter said leave it to him and disappeared. Neither the forks nor the glasses were very clean, but they were in France and counted it as part of their adventure.

The waiter brought a crisp baguette of bread and a crock of butter, then returned with a soup which was pale green. "*Bon appétit*," he said so firmly they did not dare send it back.

Very cautiously they dipped their spoons. The soup was cold. It tasted creamy and pleasantly bitter, and added to their sense of foreignness and adventure.

The steak was bloody and tender, flavoured with a strong wine sauce. Seeing that he was in France, Toby ordered a carafe of wine. The waiter brought it, saying it was *du pays*, but did not specify which country. David thought it very puckery. Having been warned by Nannie never to drink foreign tap water, he shyly asked whether he could have some *low gazoose*. The waiter, a tolerant soul, quite accustomed to the outrages tourists committed upon his mother tongue, kindly suggested cider, which arrived in a stone jug, cold and sweating from the cellar. It was delicious.

For their dessert they had raspberries with an odd kind of cream. They thought it might have gone off in the heat, but the waiter said it was *fraîche* so firmly they decided they had better eat it. Fresh or not, it tasted wonderful with raspberries.

"Well," said Toby, paying the bill with a large bundle of Hesso's French money, "if that is wnat Nannie calls the nasty way foreigners muck their food about, all I can say is that that is where Nannie's toes turn in."

No one had warned David that French cider has a much higher alcoholic content than English, and by the time he had finished the jug, he was feeling quite as hilarious as Toby on his carafe of *vin rouge*.

They caught their train, still feeling very cheerful, but the heat and the lunch told on them, and both fell into a refreshing sleep, from which the conductor awakened them at Düsseldorf, where they had to change into the local train which took them to Eschenbach. Felix was at the platform, waiting for them. They stepped down from the train into a sound like a monstrous heartbeat. "It's the mills," said Felix. "You'll scarcely hear them at Landeck."

They gave up their tickets and went outside, where a trap was waiting for them. It took them out of town, along a river path lined with moon-struck willows. The drumming of the mills grew less. They turned back to see the night sky over Eschenbach lit by flames shooting from tall towers, and clouds of yellow, rose, and black drift in the night sky.

Ever since the Thirty Years' War, the Landeck family had lived in a former Cistercian abbey, a house which combined dignity and damp to a very striking degree. Felix led them into a high, vaulted room, known as the Abbot's Study, where sandwiches and hot soup awaited them. "We usually eat in here," Felix said to David. "The refectory's really too big for anything but balls and very large dinner parties. I'll show you round tomorrow. There's a vault full of bones, and of course a ghost—not a Landeck; one of the priors, who was supposed to have been excessively wicked."

David, looking about himself with proper English suspicion of things popish, decided that the priors had done themselves rather well. He and Toby fell upon the sandwiches as if Mère Catherine had never existed.

"It's awfully nice you're here," said Felix, helping them to demolish the mountain of sandwiches. "There's been such a to-do over my sister's wedding, I was getting awfully bored."

"Who's she marrying?"

"A man called Kuno von Steenhagen," said Felix, his voice edged with dislike.

Toby yawned and said, "Jolly good," and before Felix

59

could explain why it was not, his parents came back from a dinner party and sent the boys off to bed.

They met Angelika and the fiancé at lunch, to which they arrived late, full of insincere apologies. Angelika introduced Kuno von Steenhagen in an offhand way and sat down by Toby.

"What are you up to? The fish? Thank goodness. I was so afraid you might say the pudding, and I'm starving."

The fiancé, who had found an empty chair at David's end of the table, said, "She's always starving. She even pinches food from the soup kitchen," for which Angelika threw a bun at him. She turned to Toby and said, "I hope you haven't come to see me marry Lieutenant von Steenhagen, because, you know, I'm not going to." Toby liked Angelika because he felt comfortable with her. Usually he was shy with girls; they filled his mind with terrible and forbidden imaginings, but Angelika was just Felix's sister, and he was quite used to sisters; David had such a lot of them.

Marit, Felix's other sister, who had been working at the cottage hospital, arrived so late they had already started dessert. She greeted David without interest, and took the empty chair by his side. She wore a very plain grey dress with a white collar and cuffs, which made her look like a postulant. David recalled that there had been talk about her going into a convent, and this suddenly made him unable to think of anything to talk to her about.

Angelika and Kuno were throwing cherrystones at each other. Toby and Felix were making plans to go down to the stables and take out the horses after lunch, and still David sat, wracking his brain for something suitable to mention to a future nun.

Marit said she would just have a bit of fish, she wasn't hungry, and then turned to David and said in English, "I would like to ask a favour of you, please, Mr Harvey. It is that I would like you to speak to me in English. You see, my sister and I had a year in France being finished, but we only had one season in London, and I would like to perfect myself in your language before I enter the convent. It is not a beautiful language, but it has some nobility, I think."

David, rather resenting this dispassionate slur on his mother tongue, said politely, "You speak English very well, Baroness."

Marit waved this aside impatiently. "Please do not pay me compliments, Mr Harvey. They benefit no one and rouse only the sin of vanity."

David, who had never in his entire life had such a lunch partner, caught from the corner of his eye the amused grin of Angelika's fiancé.

"You must also never speak about the weather, Herr Harvey," said Kuno, "which being English you might be inclined to do. Fräulein Marit converses only on improving subjects."

Marit, who blushed often and painfully, felt the blood mount hotly under her collar. It was surely true that one should not waste God's precious time in silly chatter and idle games, but how awfully priggish it sounded when Kuno put it that way. And now Herr Harvey, with that horrible English levity she had learned to dread during her London season, said, "I'm afraid I don't know any improving subjects, Baroness. Perhaps *you* could improve me."

She knew that in his beastly English way he was making fun of her, that what he said required a flippant answer or none at all, yet, was it not her duty to try and seize the occasion, for one never knew when and how one might indeed improve a fellow creature.

She said, "What is your worst subject in school?"

"Mathematics," said David promptly. "But since I'm on the classical side, that doesn't matter. Where mathematics are concerned, I'd really rather not be improved if you don't mind."

"I'm afraid I would be quite useless," said Marit, acknowledging her shortcomings, as a Christian should. "It was my worst subject too."

For a moment they felt a sense of mutual sympathy, even a kind of ease. David said, "William James calls mathematics a form of low cunning."

"Mr James?" questioned Marit. "Yes, I have heard of him. But I never read novels. They only waste time."

After lunch Marit chose a book of devotional literature

from her mother's shelf and went to her room to rest for an hour before returning to the hospital. In the room she shared with her sister, she found Angelika kneeling in front of a lit candle, deep in prayer.

"What saint are you trying to bribe now?" she asked when Angelika at last got to her feet.

"Winifred. I'm afraid I'm awfully far down the alphabet."

"Winifred? Which one was she?"

"She was Welsh, and a man called Caradoc importuned her. When she refused him, he cut her head off. But the earth opened up and swallowed him, and someone glued her head back on and she became a nun."

"Well, she sounds as if she might sympathize. But Angie, you'll have to marry some day. It is your duty. Why not Lieutenant von Steenhagen?"

"I'm not in love with him."

"That doesn't matter. Mama says it comes afterwards, after you're married."

"And if it doesn't come, you're stuck. Do you think they're in love, our parents?"

"Oh, Angie," said Marit, much shocked, "it isn't proper to speculate about such things."

"I don't think they're in love and I don't think they ever have been either. Did you have a good look at Herr Harvey, Marit? Isn't he heavenly? Just fancy being able to look at someone so good-looking every morning of your life across the breakfast table."

"Good looks don't last. And even if they did, you would soon be bored with them."

"I would never get bored going to parties and the theatre with him and having all the other women turn green with envy."

"You're talking terrible nonsense, Angie. Herr Harvey is much too young and quite unsuitable. He hasn't any money."

"He'll get older, and we have lots, don't we? I think we ought to spread it around." She unpinned her hair and shook it down over her shoulders. A childhood fever had turned it snow-white. She was the only one of Hesso's

62

children to have inherited his wide-set blue eyes. It made for a striking combination, as she very well knew.

"Do you think I could make Herr Harvey pay attention to me, Marit?"

"It would be very wicked to do that while you're engaged to someone else."

"But I'm not engaged. I never wanted to be engaged. *They* told us we were engaged. That can't really count, can it?"

Marit put her arms around her sister. "We had a very big engagement party, and there was a very public announcement. The crown prince was there and we all drank champagne. In fact you drank more than was good for you. You are engaged."

Angelika's eyes filled with tears. "Oh, Marit," she said, "how did it happen? I never meant it to."

When she was seventeen, Angelika had a winter season in Berlin. Marit, who was determined to be a nun, had not come with the family, but had stayed at home, working in the soup kitchen, visiting the sick, and discussing endlessly with Mother Hedwig the reality or lack of her vocation. The next summer Lady Millicent had opened up the house on Chesterfield Hill, both girls were presented at court, Lady Milly had at-homes, there were parties and dances and plays, and rows of quite heavenly young men came to call. Angelika was nearly as happy as Lady Millicent; Marit, who had only come on the advice of Mother Hedwig, pined for the soup kitchen and the deserving poor.

When they got back to Eschenbach, she resumed her endless debates. Mother Hedwig, sworn to patience, nevertheless grew rather weary and said to Sophie, who was an old friend, "I know people in the world think your Marit is exactly the right kind of person to become a nun. And of course she may have a vocation; I cannot know that. Not all vocations come like a Pentecostal flame. But if I had a choice between your two girls, Sophie, I would take Angelika. She would make a wonderful nun."

"Angelika! Oh no, Reverend Mother, you can't know

her well if you think that. Angelika is the most worldly of girls. It has often caused me great worry."

"I know all that, and I do pray for her happiness and yours. And Marit's, of course. But I have seen so many young girls enter the convent, and popular opinion completely to the contrary, I have found that it is not the melancholy, pious ones that make the best nuns, but the merry of heart. The Marys, not the Marthas."

"Well," said Sophie tartly, "you can't have Angelika. She has absolutely no vocation for anything but going to dances, flirting with young men, and drinking champagne."

Mother Hedwig smiled. "So did we at one time, don't you remember?"

"You did, not I. But then you were the pretty one. We shall have to set about finding a good *parti* for Angelika. A husband and babies will settle her."

Lieutenant Kuno von Steenhagen was from every point of view a *parti*. It was true that he had the reputation of being a rather wild young man, but Hesso did not mind high spirits; he had had plenty of those himself.

The Steenhagens were an old Prussian military family; Kuno's father, General von Steenhagen, held an important position in the Ministry of Ordnance and Supply, far too many of whose orders, Hesso felt, went to Krupp instead of Landeck Steel. With a Landeck daughter-in-law, surely the General would look upon Landeck Steel as the family firm. Perhaps he could be offered a directorship to encourage him.

Angelika had to admit that she had danced a great deal with young Steenhagen; he was personable and fun and a sublime dancer, and when Sophie asked her whether she liked him, she said, "He's very nice. I don't really know him."

"You seem to get on so well at parties," said Sophie. "I wondered whether you liked him particularly."

"I never thought about it."

"Perhaps you might."

Hesso and the General lunched at their club. After some general conversation about the deplorable state of the world, what with socialists, anarchists, and the lack of respect for their elders among the young, they came to specifics.

"I do envy you having girls, Baron," said the General. "If you knew the trouble my sons have given me . . . Your Felix seems a nice chap."

"So far," said Hesso cautiously. "He's only seventeen. Plenty of time to be troublesome yet."

"It must be delightful to have girls around the house, I've often thought."

"I don't know. There's all the bother of finding them husbands. Of course Marit plans to become a nun, but that's not really a help. They expect a dowry, just as a husband would." Between a sip of brandy and a puff of Havana, Hesso mentioned what that dowry would be.

The General, far too well bred to show that he had taken note, said, "You surprise me. Aren't they supposed to be very poor?"

"Yes, the sisters live poorly enough. It all goes to the church. Nothing poor about them, you know."

"Please give my respectful regards to the *gnädige Frau* Baronin," said the General when they parted, while Hesso sent his to the *gnädige Frau* General. And so things got under way.

"I think we ought to invite the Steenhagens for dinner," said Sophie the next day.

Angelika said, "Let's ask their Aunt Ida. Perhaps she'll come dressed in her crinoline."

"You're very unkind, my dear child. The Steenhagens are a very old family; naturally there are some eccentrics among them. The poor woman can't help thinking she's Marie Antoinette, and it must be quite dreadful to have to keep waiting for one's head to be cut off."

"Does she know about that?"

"Oh yes. You see, she looked herself up in the historical encyclopaedia."

Kuno said, "I think something is going on. The families are plotting."

"Are they?"

The Steenhagens had dined with the Landecks, and after dinner Angelika had been encouraged to show the young lieutenant the conservatory. It was the very first time in her life that she had been left alone with a young man, and thinking this over, she said, "Oh dear."

"I take it the idea does not charm you, Fräulein Angelika."

"Well no. That sounds rude, and I'm sorry, but it's got nothing to do with you personally. I'm sure you're very nice. I just don't want to get married yet."

"Then we are completely agreed. Neither do I."

"I'm so glad. Could we be friends, do you think?"

"That would be delightful."

Kuno kissed her hand just as the Baronin Sophie and Frau General came into the conservatory. Angelika was not sent to her room to repent, in fact the incident was not mentioned at all, which made her certain Kuno's suspicions had been correct.

"You must believe me, Angelika, we only want what is best for you. A young woman needs her own establishment, a husband, and babies to be happy. Your father and I want nothing but your happiness."

"Well, I wouldn't be happy married to Lieutenant von Steenhagen. He doesn't want to get married either."

"How do you know?"

"We talked it over last night when you sent us to the conservatory."

"But Angelika," said Sophie much dismayed, "that was a most unsuitable subject to discuss with a young man."

"Even one you're trying to foist on me?"

"No one is stopping you from going to your room."

"She's such a pretty little thing," said General von Steenhagen to his son. "I can't think why you object to her."

"I don't object to her; I simply don't want to get married."

"There's a nice dowry comes with Fräulein Angelika. You might think it over. From various things I hear at the Jockey Club, your debts aren't getting any less."

Kuno thought it over.

"Fräulein von Landeck, would you reconsider? I've been thinking ever since our talk in the conservatory, and I've come to the conclusion that the feeling I mistook for friendship is really love."

"Nonsense. You've been got at."

"Truly, I haven't been able to stop thinking about your beauty since I saw you last."

"You haven't been able to stop thinking about my dowry, is what you mean. I've been asking questions about you. You lose too much at cards."

"My dearest Baroness, I know nothing about a dowry. You wrong me very deeply if you think of me as a fortune hunter. Believe me, I would feel exactly the same about you if you hadn't a penny."

"Of that I have no doubt," said Angelika, laughing. "Please, let's not start lying to each other. Our only protection is in being honest and standing up to them."

"You're right, of course. It's the only way."

"But I'm not in love with him!"

"Love. That's what comes of letting her read all those French novels. You talk to her, Sophie."

"My darling child, your father is right. Except in novels, people who marry for love always come to a sad end. The happiest marriages are between people of the same background and class. Parents have far more experience of the world than a silly little girl just out of finishing school. We want only your happiness; you must believe that."

Resistance stiffened on both sides. Additional forces were deployed.

"My dear child, as your confessor I must speak to you very seriously about your behaviour to your parents. Marriage is a holy sacrament; your parents have chosen for you a young man who will make you love and respect him in the course of time. You are very ungrateful if you reject their kindness and care for you."

"I'm sorry, Father, but you're not talking about the sacrament of marriage, you're talking about a merger between Landeck Steel and the Ministry of Ordnance and Supply."

By now everyone had lost sight of the original purpose, which had been to arrange a suitable marriage for Angelika, an alliance from which both families would benefit. Kuno was by no means the only young man Angelika might marry, nor was she the only rich girl Kuno could find for himself. What had seemed a mildly good idea, had grown, fed by resistance, into a power play in which children defied their parents, thus causing great rifts in the fabric of society, rifts which in the end would let in anarchy, socialism, and social disorder.

In the process of doing battle with the adult world, Angelika had grown very fond of Kuno. She knew very little about him, of course; however, there were times when she thought it might be rather fun to be married to him, but that her parents' intransigent attitude had made all thoughts of surrender impossible.

Kuno, with the amount of Angelika's dowry mentioned at least once a day by each of his parents, was willing to reconsider.

"I wouldn't bother you, you know, if that's what you're worried about," he said to her one afternoon when his parents had sent him calling.

"How do you mean, bother me?"

"If you don't know, never mind. It's for your mother to tell you."

"I'm not talking to my mother."

"Angelika . . ." They were calling each other by their first names now, without a Herr or Fräulein, though they still used the formal "Sie".

"What?"

"Never mind. Just remember what I told you."

When both families arranged a surprise engagement party, Kuno and Angelika began to feel that they were caught up in a wave from which they might not be able to escape. Presents began to arrive, the wedding gown was ordered, and ridesmaids recruited. Marit decided to put off her entry into the convent to be her sister's maid of honour. The Steenhagens rented a house near Eschenbach so the young people could see much of each other. Congratulations and gifts began to arrive from the ruling houses with which Landeck Steel did business. Guests were accepting invitations. The kaiser regretted, but the crown prince, who liked parties, said he'd love to come.

"I feel as if I were being bartered for a goat and two cows," said Angelika, showing the presents to her unwilling fiancé. "Your Aunt Ida sent me a sheep from her farm—does she really call it Le Petit Trianon? A live sheep, not a lamb chop."

"Well, your English uncle sent me a dozen of very good port."

"I'm not going to marry you so you can drink port. You must send it back."

"I don't see how we can stop them."

"I don't either, yet. But I will. I am getting help."

"Help? From whom?"

"Saints."

"Saints, Angelika?" Kuno was taking instruction in the Catholic faith, but evidently not making much progress.

"You are a heathen, Kuno, you wouldn't understand."

She had started alphabetically, lighting a candle to St Adelaide, who had, however, had two husbands and was not helpful. Nor, for reasons she could not understand, were various saints who in their own lives had gone to quite drastic lengths to avoid marriage and preserve their virginity. Perhaps they felt obedience to parents was more important than the virgin state, perhaps they were busy elsewhere; at any rate poor Angelika was all the way down to Winifred in the calendar by the time David and Toby arrived.

They were told most of the story by Felix and Kuno that afternoon, as they stood by the railings of the Eschenbach racetrack and watched General von Steenhagen's chestnut two-year-old pour herself over the hurdles as smoothly as water flung from a pitcher.

"I've got a thousand on her for the steeplechase," Kuno said to David.

It seemed to David an appalling sum. "I do hope you're lucky."

"I hardly ever am," said Kuno, smiling into his eyes. "You see, I'm frightfully lucky in love."

At dinner that night Angelika found herself next to David, and remembering that he was a clergyman's son (though unfortunately of a heretical sect), told him about being let down by her saints. "I've only got Zita left," she said, "and though she was unmarried herself, she's the patron saint of household servants, so she mightn't really be interested in helping someone not get married."

"What about Uncumber?" said David.

"Uncumber? What a funny name. Are you sure it's not Cucumber?"

"You couldn't have a saint called Cucumber. Her other name is Wilgefortis. *Her* father insisted on her marrying when she didn't want to, so she prayed for a miracle, and the next morning she awoke to find she had grown a long black beard."

Angelika started to laugh. "Oh, I do know her. She is called Kümmernis in German. But Herr Harvey, I'm not sure I want to grow a long black beard."

David agreed that this might be a nuisance, though his own was as yet scarcely enough to trouble him. "Besides, her father got so angry with her he had her crucified. Not exactly a happy ending."

"All the same, I think I'll keep her as a last resort. Thank you very much."

Because so many guests were expected for the wedding, Sophie had asked the boys whether they would mind crowding into Felix's room, which had an adjoining dressing room with a bed in it. They not only did not mind, they were delighted with the hugger-mugger arrangement, which was as good as Toby's nursery high under the roof of Altondale Hall, with the added benefit that Nannie wasn't there to keep an eye on them.

After one look at the pictures on Felix's wall, Toby elected to sleep in the dressing room, saying with the frankness of an old friend that he had seldom seen anything so hideous.

During his summer in France, Felix had discovered that art need not—indeed, should not—be pretty. In consequence he had grown very sneery about the Lenbachs and Winterhalters which decorated his parents' walls, and had hung on his own an abstract which Toby said reminded him of the kitchen linoleum at home, two Paris street scenes apparently painted in a thick fog, and, worst of all, a sketch of a fat naked woman bending over a washtub, wringing out her long red hair. The flesh tones were purple, the hair carroty, and both David and Toby, accustomed to the Gainsboroughs, Lawrences, Reynoldses, and Stubbses who had painted the Straffords, their houses and horses, thought her an ugly, awkward daub.

"My father says it looks as if it had been painted by a backward child," said Felix, quite accustomed to such criticism. "My mother and Marit think she isn't decent."

"She could hardly constitute a temptation," said David, while Toby went off to have his bath.

Felix said, "It's lucky she is so plain or they'd never have allowed me to hang her. David, have you ever seen a girl without . . . you know, with nothing on?"

"No," said David, wondering what might be coming. It had been Felix, two summers ago, who, having been informed by Pregnitz Minor, baldly, but quite correctly, how babies were made, had imparted this astonishing information to his two friends. David, knowing Felix as a great joker, had indignantly accused him of having invented it, while Toby was rocking back and forth on the floor, helpless with laughter.

"Oh Lord," he finally gasped, quite breathless, "Fancy one's parents!" At this Felix too had begun to laugh, while David, the blood hot in his cheeks, had buried his face in his arms. It was all very well for Toby to think such things funny. His parents had had the good taste to stop with him, and even Felix's had only run to three. But what, David had thought miserably, of Mr and Mrs Harvey and their large brood at the vicarage? He could hardly bear to look at them that night at dinner, and for once was relieved that summer was nearly over and he could return to St Dunstan's. Since then wider reading in the classics had given him a more relaxed view of these matters, while Toby had fallen under the influence of the chaplain who had prepared him for confirmation, and tried hard never to think of such things at all.

David, rather hoping that Felix had not returned from Lehzen with any more arcane and startling information, said, "Only Greek ladies in the museum."

"I have."

"Have you? If you want to talk filth, you'd better do it before Toby comes back from his bath. He's awfully pi these days."

"What?"

"Pi. Pious, you know. He got an attack of religion the year he was preparing for confirmation. It does take some of them that way."

"Oh, I know. Cold baths and long walks. There are some like that in my school too. Anyhow, there's this girl in the village next to the school; she's the baker's daughter and I think she's half-witted, and she lets you for fifty pfennig."

"What, look at her without clothes on?"

"No, stupid."

"Oh," said David blushing. "Flixy, you sod, did you?"

"Well, no. I almost did, once. A whole lot of us went one evening, and I thought I was going to, but it was all rather depressing, standing in a queue, waiting, and the place smelled awful, of flour and sweat, so in the end Pregnitz and I said we were in training, and went back to school. But anyhow that's how I saw."

"How sordid."

Felix said, "It really was, you know, that silly half-witted creature and the smell and everything, but the awful part was that after we got back to the school, I was sorry we hadn't stayed. I half wanted to, you know. I still do."

"Do you?" said David. "Why?"

"I don't know. It's funny, isn't it?"

"Oh, Flixy, it's disgusting. Why don't you just do it with Pregnitz? It would be a lot cleaner anyhow."

"Pregnitz," said Felix shocked. "I couldn't do that. He's my friend."

"Well, some other boy at school then. Or don't you do those things in Prussian schools?"

"Well, people do, quite a lot, really. But you have to make yourself want to first, that's the problem. Is that what you do?"

David nodded.

"Do you like it?"

"I didn't at first. I quite do, now."

"Do you never want to do it with girls?"

"Well, your description certainly didn't do much for me that way."

"You know, I don't think Angelika has any idea. It's going to be a complete surprise."

"All kinds of things are going to be a surprise for her. Where on earth did your family find this Kuno creature?"

"Dunno. I was away at school. Under a rock somewhere, I think. Poor Angie."

"I don't suppose he'll bother her much," said David.

"D'you mean . . ."

"Here comes Toby. Talk about something decent."

While the wedding was to be the high point of the summer, Hesso saw to it that there was plenty of excitement in the meantime for his guests. With Felix as guide they were permitted to tour the steel mills, and one day Hesso took them himself in his new motorcar (the back seat filled with spare tyres) to the small aerodrome the works had recently acquired. This was known to the other steel barons as Landeck's Folly; by no means the first and only one. Some years before, Hesso had bought the very first motorcar even seen in Eschenbach, and lately he had introduced a young lunatic who had built a flying machine in his parents' woodshed, into the design department of the firm; a piece of madness, said the competition with some satisfaction, which could drive a solid concern such as Landeck Steel straight into bankruptcy.

When they arrived, three changed tyres later, at the aerodrome, Toby and Felix found themselves in a new world. There was a smell of petrol, the grass was black and oily

73

underfoot, a canvas shed flapped in the backwash of a plane zooming two feet over its roof.

Toby inhaled this strange new air with exhilaration. "I'd love to go up, Uncle Hesso," he said, forgetting that well-brought-up boys never ask for anything but wait until it is offered.

"Well, let's see what the pilot says."

David very much hoped the pilot would say no. The plane which had zoomed so narrowly over the top of the canvas hangar now hung above them like a tiny black cross. On the ground, another plane, from which a mechanic was slowly detaching himself to come forward and greet them, looked incredibly frail; nothing but strips of very thin wood, canvas, and wire. Not at all, thought David, the kind of thing to which one would wish to entrust one's seventeen-year-old person, with most of life still to be lived.

"Watch," said the mechanic after greeting them. "He's going to dive her to test the wing struts."

Even as he spoke the black cross above them began to drop, growing larger, till they could distinguish its nose pointing straight at the ground, and could hear the wind whistling in the wires. It seemed to be aiming directly at them, but since neither Hesso nor the mechanic made a move, David shut his eyes until he heard Toby give a small gasp of excitement and became aware from a change in the noise that the plane had levelled off. The dive was over. He opened his eyes and watched it coming down in long S-curves, touch ground, hop, and suddenly graceless, waddle toward them across the oily grass. The pilot clambered out, all nonchalance and goggles, a small jockeylike man with a black smear of oil on his face.

He inspected the struts, said casually to Hesso that they would do, and nodded as casually at Hesso's request that his young nephew might go up for a spin. Toby was given a pair of goggles and tucked like a baby into the passenger seat behind the pilot. It was made of wicker, looked like a hip bath, and was surprisingly uncomfortable. But Toby at this point would not have cared if they had strapped him to the wing; he was going to fly.

They bucked across the landing field, lifting suddenly,

the earth leaping back, people, trees, and motorcar falling from them and growing as small as toys. Toby felt as if he were standing on a church steeple, or high in the rigging of a ship, but at the same time borne up by air itself, like a great bird, or a god ascending.

Later they picnicked on the oily grass with the pilot and mechanic. Toby could not stop talking; he was drunk with air and exaltation. Felix, who had flown once or twice and had been sick, said, "Wait till Nannie finds out what you've been doing."

"You wouldn't tell."

"I may not be able to resist the temptation."

"Flying in the face of Providence, that's what I call it," said Toby, who was very good at mimicking Nannie. "God never meant for you to fly, Master Toby, or He would have seen to it that you were born a pigeon. His eye is on the sparrow, and don't you forget it. He that is down needs fear no fall."

"Then there was Master Icarus," said David, taking it up. "Lord Daedalus's son that was. Time after time I said to His Lordship, 'He'll singe his wings,' I said; 'you mark my words.' But would he listen? No. Up he'd go with those silly waxen wings—well, I never, I said to His Lordship, but I might as well have been talking to the clock. And you know what the end of all that was, poor little mite. It all comes of not listening to Nannie."

As a last resort Angelika took a chance on growing a long black beard and lit a candle to St Uncumber, and that very afternoon, while Toby, David, and Felix were picnicking, she was led to a solution.

Like Marit she was something of a bluestocking and very keen on self-improvement. That morning she had asked David to recommend a really interesting English novel which would help her perfect herself in that language. David had looked over the Landeck shelves, and having himself a secret weakness for Mr Rochester, had suggested *Jane Eyre*.

After saying her prayers to St Uncumber, Angelika had put on a large shady hat (it would hardly do to get freckles as well as a black beard), and with the copy of *Jane Eyre* in her hand, had gone into the rose garden. She read, enthralled, till teatime, and could scarcely wait to get back to Jane's adventures. It was rather late at night, for she read English slowly and with some difficulty, that she arrived at the wedding scene, where the brother of the first Mrs Rochester interrupts the ceremony with the unwelcome news of that lady's existence. It was of course too much to hope that Kuno was already married, but it did give her an idea.

The next morning a heavy silver soup tureen arrived from the All-Highest Kaiser Wilhelm himself. Kuno, who being lucky in love, had lost the thousand he had bet on his father's horse, and had found in the morning's mail a very stiff letter from the secretary of the Jockey Club, looked at the soup tureen, remembered Angelika's dowry, and said, "Well, that does it. We'll have to go through with it now."

"No," said Angelika. "Kuno, I've had a marvellous idea. I think it was sent to me directly by St Uncumber, it had to be a miracle, though such a simple one I can't think why it didn't occur to me before. Listen, when they say, 'Do you, Kuno Sigismund von Steenhagen, take this woman etc.,' you simply say no."

Kuno was dumbfounded. The plan had such simplicity and breadth, it truly did seem an inspiration. But at the same time he was horrified. "Angelika. There'll be all those guests, and archbishops, and the soup tureen."

"Well, he's not coming. I don't know if I'd have the nerve to do it with the kaiser right there, but since he won't be . . ."

"My Papa is very cross about it."

"Well, he can't go everywhere. He came to Bertha Krupp's wedding last year and it was ghastly. He stood up and talked for two hours and of course no one could sit down. My feet ached for a week."

Kuno started to laugh. He desperately needed the money, he really had no objection to Angelika, he might never find so good a match again, and heaven alone knew what his father and his creditors would do to him, but the idea of standing at the altar saying no was irresistible. He said, "It's a splendid idea, Angelika. Oh, I can picture it. 'Do you take Angelika Maria Domenica von Landeck to be your lawfully wedded wife?' 'Like hell I do.' "

"You mustn't swear so much, Kuno."

"Well, you can't have it both ways. If you marry me, you can't reform me. Oh, but Angelika, when the time comes, will we have the courage? With all those candles and incense and monsignors."

"There are two of us. If you don't do it, I will. But first we must give our parents one more chance. We must sit down quietly with them and tell them we are determined not to marry each other and beg them most humbly to call the whole thing off."

"Let's not," said Kuno, who was afraid of his father. "Let's surprise everybody."

"No. We must give them a chance to do things properly. It's only fair."

"Oh, all right, Angelika. But my father will be awfully cross. You don't know how shirty he can be."

"They were extraordinary," Kuno later said to David. They had gone swimming in the river, and were lying in the sun. "All they could talk about was the soup tureen. Would English families go on like that?"

"If the king had sent a present? Oh, I should think so."

"Really extraordinary," said Kuno.

The wedding morning could not have been more perfect if it had been ordered, like the wedding dress and the champagne, with no expense spared, directly from Paris. The sun shone from a cloudless sky, a gentle breeze billowed out the bride's heirloom veil as she drove at her father's side through the streets of Eschenbach, cheered by the workers of Landeck Steel, who were having the day off and would in the afternoon have their celebrations with beer and sausages provided by Hesso.

The cathedral, a squat, liver-coloured building of great antiquity and hideousness, was covered with flowers. The groom's side of the church was agleam with cuirasses, silver helmets, and gold braid. The bride's side, while not lacking in uniforms, tended more toward nobility, money, and social rank. In addition to three crown princes—two, alas, from mere Balkan countries—there were so many dukes and duchesses that even Augustus and Lady Millicent were seated halfway toward the back of the church. Behind them were the local steel barons and their families, the directors of the firm, the higher staff, and a rabble of townspeople, old servants, and poor relations.

The groom and his best man took their places, the organ let go with a burst of Lohengrin, and the bride came up the aisle on her father's arm.

She was like a cat stroked during a thunderstorm; her eyes and hair seemed to give out sparks. Tales which later appeared in the press of her being dragged up the aisle, weeping and pale, the helpless victim of a barbaric sacrifice, were journalistic invention.

They stood, bride and groom, with bridesmaids and attendants, and a very little cousin carrying the ring on a red velvet cushion, while the archbishop and monsignors and altar boys moved slowly about their business amid candles and incense.

The ceremony, which included a high mass, seemed to its Protestant visitors rather long, but to Angelika the minutes clicked by like seconds. The Archbishop, who liked to hear his voice echo through the cathedral, went on at some length about so happy a marriage, determined neither by politics nor convenience, nor an overpowering passion which had recklessly broken through the limits of order; the joys of motherhood, and the simulacrum of God's love for his creatures which is represented by the Christian marriage. Angelika would not have minded if he had gone on all day, but at last he wound himself down and came to the point. "Do you, Kuno Sigismund, take this woman . . ." Angelika stole a sideways look and decided that she had never seen such a weak chin in her entire life. Odd how she had not noticed it before. No one with a chin like that would come up to scratch. And as she had expected, Kuno cleared his throat and meekly said, "I do."

"Do you, Angelika Maria Domenica . . ."—heart-pounding and breath choked off—". . . take this man . . ." What, live with someone with such a weak chin and no backbone? Angelika drew a deep breath and in a small but clear voice said, "No."

"With this ring . . . ," the Archbishop galloped on, not having bothered to listen. It was not until he became aware of a faint, questioning rustle in the congregation that Angelika's answer reached his consciousness. Even then he did not entirely believe it. There was nothing for it but to make certain. "Do you, Angelika Maria Domenica," he began again, giving her a chance to correct her error. Poor Angelika had not anticipated having to go through it all twice, but it got easier with practice, and much more firmly than the first time she said, "No."

For the longest ten seconds any of them had ever experienced, the entire cathedral appeared to hold its breath. For Angelika there was only the drumbeat of her heart, for Kuno there was a wild desire to giggle, for Sophie vapours and smelling salts, for Hesso anger, and at the same time a sense of pride in his daughter's pluck. The Archbishop seemed to have totally lost his bearings; he stood with jaw dropped, immobile. Then one of the monsignori whispered something into his ear; he pulled himself together and requested the bride and groom, the bride's parents and the groom's, to step into the vestry.

The wedding guests were left to stare at each other in horrified conjecture. No one knew what to do. Were they expected to leave or stay? Only the press, following deeply ingrained instinct, reacted promptly and stampeded for the nearest telegraph office.

What was happening in the vestry? Would the bride and groom reappear and repeat the ceremony, a repentant bride this time saying yes? And would this not make plain to all, that the holy sacrament of marriage was in reality a business arrangement?

Not that among the grown-up guests there were any who disapproved of this. When you endowed with all your earthly goods, it was best to endow someone who already had plenty of earthly goods of his own.

In the vestry both Sophie and Angelika had fainted;

Sophie in earnest, Angelika because she didn't know what else to do. Kuno confessed that they had never wanted to get married, that he too had been supposed to say no, but had at the last moment reconsidered. Hesso, for all his anger, was getting happier and happier that Angelika was not marrying such a piece of wet flannel. Finally the monsignor who had so admirably kept his head at the altar suggested a compromise. The Archbishop went back into the church and announced that the bride had been taken ill and the wedding would have to be postponed. *Nunc dimittis.*

The excuse of sudden illness was so good the family rallied to it as if it had been a battle cry. By the time Angelika considered it safe to come out of her faint, the family doctor, who had been in the cathedral, was bending over her, fingering her pulse (which was rapid indeed) and advising a long rest. With never an unkind word spoken she was taken home and put to bed, where she was kept through the beautiful summer weeks, a virtual prisoner. She was restive at first, wanting to get up and eat a decent meal, but someone was always with her, saying, "You mustn't overdo; you'll make yourself ill again," until the fiction grew on her too and she began to feel truly weak and ill.

The one thing which kept her going were the left-wing papers her maid managed to smuggle into the sickroom. The more conservative papers had accepted, or pretended to have, the fiction of the bride's illness, with touching headlines of BRIDE SWOONS AT ALTAR, FAMILY JOY TURNS TO SADNESS, and affecting descriptions of a radiant bride whose delicate constitution could not sustain the happiness of her wedding day. The left-wing papers, on the other hand, leaped upon the story as an absolute godsend. Nothing had been so good for circulation since Fritz Krupp's suicide. They dragged it out for weeks, from the first headline: BRIDE SAYS NO, to an exact-to-the-penny accounting in the socialist *Vorwärts* of what the wedding had cost while German workers were earning starvation wages, to deeply affecting tales in the *Zukunft* of an innocent daughter sold to a dissolute young man whose idle, parasitical life had consisted of one scandal after another. One of the lowest rags went so far as to insinuate that several of those scandals were of a sodomitical nature, and while this was true, it was nevertheless libellous and the paper could be closed down by the government. Nothing, of course, could be done about the foreign press, which was, if anything, even redder and more malicious, the French papers in especial spreading themselves in detailed descriptions of Aunt Ida and her sheep, not to mention Uncle Hubert, who had been put away for having successfully conducted a passionate love affair with one of them.

Angelika went from being a daughter of a merchant of death to a Joan of Arc, a martyr to her viciously greedy family, whose courage had triumphed—or had it? Where was *la petite Baroness?* Had anyone seen her? OÙ EST ANGELIQUE? the headlines began to ask. Had her irate family consigned her to a dungeon in the medieval abbey, shadily acquired from the expelled monks during the Counter-Reformation? Had she been locked away, like her sister, behind the walls of a penitential order?

The German papers, which had under strict censorship laws not been able to spread themselves on the subject of Kuno's scandals and Uncle Hubert's predilections, took up this new topic with alacrity. WO IST ANGELIKA? they too demanded, in the largest type, with illustrations of the abbey crypt and the forbidding high wall of the Carmelite convent of Eschenbach.

"*Wo ist Angelika*, indeed," said Hesso to General von Steenhagen. Their friendship had survived the scene at the altar and they continued to lunch together. "She's in her room, reading all those papers her French maid smuggles in to her and laughing her head off. Where is Kuno, come to that?"

"With his regiment in East Prussia. It is a small, dreary garrison town and offers hardly any opportunity for creating a scandal, though if there is one Kuno will find it."

"Is it true, what they said in the papers?"

"I'm sorry to say it is."

"It wouldn't have been very nice for Angelika."

81

"I thought marriage might change his mind. She's such a pretty little thing."

"I don't suppose it would have," said Hesso.

"No, probably not. It was worth a try. As for Angelika, might it not be a good idea for her to be seen in public? Put an end to all the nonsense in the papers."

"Yes. A spa, perhaps, for her health."

"A very good idea. Let's have another brandy."

Angelika and her mother set out a week later for Karlsbad. The press, though particularly asked to consider the young baroness's frail state of health, turned out in force and roared questions at her as she entered, pale but smiling, Hesso's private railway car. That evening the papers were able to describe to their readers Angelika's autumn *tailleur*, as well as her sable toque with nose-length veil and bunch of Parma violets, her pale face and courageous smile, and congratulate themselves at considerable length on having brought about by their relentless and courageous questions the release of the lovely young baroness from the abbey dungeons.

The journey became a triumph of publicity. At every major halt the press converged on the private railway car. Angelika, much to her mother's annoyance, would appear at the window and wave to one and all, and even, unless pulled back, answer questions. Sophie took to sal volatile and her rosary. Never a rapid thinker, it did not dawn on her for some time that travelling in a private railway carriage with the Landeck coat of arms painted on the outside was not the best way of insuring privacy.

Marienbad, Bad Ischl, Gastein, Spa—steamer trunks, lady's maids, couriers, and the press; it was a procession a diva might have envied. At last, at Hesso's suggestion, they relinquished the private car, eluded the press, and went to ground on the gloomy family estate in Silesia now owned by Sophie's widowed sister Paulina.

Paulina lived with a dyspeptic companion and a pug dog in an aura of churchgoing and relentless good works. The day began with morning mass, protracted by the great age of the officiating priest, who moved with tortoiselike deliberation from one side of the altar to the other, and had to be hoisted to his feet after each genuflection by two sturdy altar boys.

Mass was followed by a breakfast of penitential gruel and bad coffee, after which the ladies personally superintended the making of bread-and-water soup from a recipe by Mrs Beeton designed to discourage people from wanting to be poor, which they then served with their own hands to those among the town's indigent they considered deserving. After a midday meal, more drawn out but scarcely more appetizing than breakfast, the ladies retired, presumably to their private devotions, but more likely to have a nap. Angelika was left with the biographies of the less riotous saints and the books of her mother's girlhood—devotional poetry and tales of poor but pious and merry families.

Afternoon coffee was taken in the company of like-minded local matrons, who then joined Paulina and Sophie in the house chapel for the Angelus and rosary. During the evening they knitted grey and scratchy comforters for the poor, while the dyspeptic companion smothered her belches and read out loud from an improving book. How dull it all was, thought Angelika, secretly dropping a yawn into the skein of grey wool.

Angelika's maid thought it dull too. She was not accustomed to households where the only visible male was the ancient Catholic priest, so she tipped off a friendly journalist who had given her his card, and after that even the quiet Silesian backwater became impossible and they resumed their travels.

This time they accepted the invitation of the von Au family—distant relations of Hesso's—who lived on thousands of acres of Hungary and raised horses. Sophie did not care for them, for they were worldly, immensely rich, cared nothing for good works, but lived to breed horses, race horses, go to hunt balls, eat large meals, drink a lot, flirt and laugh through day after day. Of the state of their souls Sophie had little doubt, but the situation of their estate, surrounded by thousands of acres of *puszta*, guarded by herdsmen with long whips, seemed to her the last remaining refuge from Germany's intrepid journalists.

As Sophie had feared, Angelika had a wonderful time in Hungary. The von Aus were a large family of the kind that is never happier than when in each others' pockets. Their house was always filled to the last attic bedroom with relations and friends. Angelika adored them all. Her pale cheeks rounded and grew pink, and she willingly joined in charades, picnics, dances, and pranks.

There was no question here of church twice a day and three times on Sunday. The local priest, a young man who needed no help in getting about, had evolved a kind of huntsman's mass that combined reverence with top speed. He could get through a solemn high mass in thirty-five minutes, and low mass never took more than twenty. Sophie, who tried to slow things down by making the responses and saying the creed in her usual reverent and dignified manner, was simply left behind. The von Aus wore riding breeches to church so that they might be off promptly at the last amen.

There were lots of young men, von Au sons and cousins, and Angelika, with her snow-white hair and violet eyes, not to speak of her recent romantic history, was a tremendous success. If no one asked her hand in marriage, it was only because they feared her drastic measures at the altar.

Fridolin von Au, a captain in the Austro-Hungarian cavalry, who, in the tradition of such officers, seemed to be almost permanently on leave, and in the tradition of his regiment, knew no fear, proposed to Angelika in spite of all he knew about her previous behaviour.

Angelika said very properly that he must ask her parents, but indicated in every way but words that her answer at the altar would be very different this time.

Frido therefore approached Sophie, who, made cautious by recent events, inquired searchingly into his character and past, and found nothing much amiss. Admittedly he had fought a few duels, but that was such a commonplace of his time and background that even Sophie could not make it a cause for objections. More gravely, there had been a number of liaisons in Vienna and Budapest, but, thought Sophie with recently acquired wisdom, at least those liaisons had been with women. She wrote to Hesso, putting these matters before him, and Hesso wrote back that the von Au holdings were considerable and he had always liked young Frido. But, he warned, the one person whose consent must be asked first and foremost was Angelika herself. The family could hardly survive another *blamage* like the wedding to Kuno.

Frido once again approached Angelika, who promised this time to say yes, and on St Stephen's day they became engaged. It was decided to have a very quiet wedding at the village church, more to keep the press away than for fear that Angelika might make it a habit to say no. Nevertheless the journalists of three nations braved the long whips of the herdsmen and were able to report to their readers: ANGELIQUE DIT OUI—ANGELIKA SAGT JA.

Marit was safe in her convent; Angelika had said yes. The Landecks breathed a sigh of relief. With any luck, they thought, they could now put their feet up and relax. They failed to reckon with Felix.

Chapter 6

David went up to Oxford at the beginning of the summer term with a very good scholarship to Oriel, which had been his father's college. He took possession of two rooms under the roof, with linenfold panelling, uncomfortable wicker furniture, a lumpy straw mattress, and a scout called Paston whose duty it was to bring him tea and crumpets, carry up hot bathwater, empty slops, and generally look after the comfort of the undergraduates on his staircase. He appeared to think but poorly of most of David's possessions, and sniffed audibly as he hung away a marvellous jacket of brown velvet on which David had spent an outrageous sum; nearly all that was left of his scholarship money after his fees and battels were paid. Toby too had sniffed at the brown velvet, thinking it both wasteful and extravagant, but David had thought it all out and looked upon it as an investment.

His headmaster at St Dunstan's had said to him when he took his leave: "In the long run it may be true that it's what you know that counts. But in the short run, it is always *whom* you know. And most of life's chances come in the short run."

David had no great opinion of his headmaster, but knew that in worldly matters he was usually right. That was why he had bought the brown velvet jacket. "If one can't afford a lot of good clothes," he had said to Toby, "one has very few choices. One can be shabby-genteel, but that would be fatal, because one would end up meeting other shabby-genteel people. One could be spartan, and indeed I shall have to be in many private ways, seeing that this damned coat has left me with scarcely two and six a day for bread and cheese, but I don't want to be spartan where it shows. The obvious solution is to be a dandy. A dandy with only one coat, admittedly, but that a glorious one."

During his first day at Oxford, however, the brown velvet coat remained in the cupboard, and David, properly dressed in white tie and black gown, went to be welcomed in elegant Latin by the vice-chancellor and handed a blue book: *Statuta et Decreta Universitatis Oxoniensis*, which he studied over tea and toast in his rooms.

Written in a seventeenth-century Latin far less elegant than that of the vice-chancellor, it enjoined him among other things from hunting wild beasts with dogs, traps, or guns, forbade him to carry a bombard or crossbow, or even a falcon on his wrist, though he might, if he intended it for honest recreation, carry a bow and arrow.

Drinking his tea, David thought about the elegant and rowdy undergraduates who had given rise to such injuctions. His mind was still on them as he went out for a walk, encountering no one carrying either crossbow or bombard, only a procession of choirboys, their surplices flapping in the breeze, and undergraduates making a row.

He had been at Oxford once before, when he had sat for his scholarship. Then it had been empty of undergraduates. Now they were everywhere, shouting at each other, making plans for drinks and dinner, being noisily chummy.

As on his first visit, so now Oxford failed to charm. He

was happy to be here because he was done with St Dunstan's and was free to begin his real life, but the feeling other people, his father among them, had for Oxford, eluded him.

"You expected the wrong things," his father had said when David had told him of his disappointment with the place after his first visit there. "Nobody falls in love with Oxford at first sight except American tourists. It grows on you slowly, like a snail's shell."

Just now, looking pensively at the tame deer in Magdalen Park, David did not regard Oxford as a snail shell in whose convolutions he would one day make his home, but as a stepping-stone towards London.

He loved his family and was fond enough of Altondale, but he had no intention of spending his life in a small town. Just how he would spend it he did not quite know. The expression "having to make one's way in the world" was clear enough in its meaning but horribly vague in application. His choices were limited by a lack of money; one needed a private income for all the more interesting professions. The diplomatic service, which he vaguely thought he would have enjoyed (seeing himself pin-striped and silk-hatted, speaking admirable French) was unthinkable without money of one's own. Even the least distinguished regiments, he knew from Toby, expected their officers to have a hundred and fifty pounds a year, while in the more fashionable cavalry regiments three thousand was barely considered enough. Joining the family firm did not appeal to him; he had no call for the clerical life. Besides, his brother Freddy, who even now spent his vacations in Birmingham missions, taking what Lady Millicent called an unseemly interest in the lower classes, had determined from a very early age to become a missionary with a tribe of particularly voracious cannibals or, failing that, unusually contagious lepers, and one clergyman per family, David and his father were agreed, was quite enough.

He supposed he would end by doing something literary, but he was vague even about that. His very facility for writing pleasant verse made him doubtful of its quality. His gift for languages, background in the classics, and want of money pointed him with hideous inevitability to one career and one only: that of schoolmaster. Well, they could hang him by his thumbs and drive red-hot slivers under his nails, they would not get him to set foot inside a school again. Somewhere among this great crowd of noisy undergraduates someone would surely be found who would take him into the world of money and frivolity. There was no hurry. He had three years, his wits, and his face.

Quickly weary of rowdy schoolboys, David turned to go back to his college. As he moved across Carfax he became aware of a sudden silence. Everyone had turned to look at a group of four undergraduates moving down the street. They were still dressed in the white tie and black gown of the vice-chancellor's reception, and so had the air of a small processional, but what arrested everyone's attention was the fact that the tallest of the four carried a hooded sparrow hawk on his gauntleted wrist.

In their black gowns, with the rufous, black-bordered bird digging his talons into the leather gauntlet, they seemed to provide for David's private pleasure an illustration of one of the forbidden things in the *Statuta et Decreta* he had been reading over his tea.

He wondered whether the small processional had something to do with OUDS—were they recruiting actors or audience—but it was surely too early in the term for that, and besides there was nothing theatrical in their progress; they gave nothing out. For all the attention they paid their watchers, they could have been walking a dog. The youth with the hawk, tall and very fair, might have been as hooded as his bird, he was so inward and absorbed.

David's own interest in falconry had not outlived the brief enthusiasm of one summer, when he, Toby, and Felix had watched Hasselt train a peregrine—the hunting bird of an earl, Hasselt had explained—for, like people, falcons and hawks had their assigned social stations, from the eagle for an emperor, the merlin for a lady, down to the goshawk for a yeoman.

Refusing to be seen gaping like a country cousin, David turned his back on the procession as they approached him, though he continued to watch their progress in the glass of a shop against a background of mugs and tobacco jars with the college arms imprinted on them.

"That's the Duke of Frome's youngest son," said a spotty youth standing beside him. "He had that falcon at Eton."

David had no intention of being drawn into conversation with so unprepossessing a creature. "It's not a falcon," he said, moving away, "it's a hawk."

He was to hear a good deal more about the four young men in the course of the winter. There is always one set at the university which is talked about more than any other, and these occasioned a great deal of gossip.

Even at Eton, it was said, they had aroused attention by their extravagance and wickedness. They had attended the first night of the Diaghilev Ballet at the Châtelet, where they had been seen conversing during the intervals in easy French with Fauré, Forain, Bakst, and Debussy. They were said to be great frequenters of the Grafton Galleries, to know all about modern painting, to understand the music of Stravinsky, and the verse of Laforgue and Apollinaire. Their books, like their champagne, were imported from Paris.

They were forever in trouble with the authorities for their absences at London parties and opening nights, or, if present at Oxford, for their predilection for pubs frequented by Jericho bargemen. But it was only the hawk who was sent down. Someone beside David had apparently read the *Statuta et Decreta*. David remembered him, however, and when, nearly a year later, he found himself during Eights Week, standing next to the tall fair youth, he said, "Shouldn't it have been a peregrine? Sparrow hawks are for priests."

The Landecks usually sent their sons to various foreign universities for their education, so that they could emerge, at the end of four years, both cosmopolitan and polyglot. Felix did his year's military service, and was then sent to the Sorbonne, where he devoted his time to buying Post-impressionists, and to a lady of easy virtue called Nellie de Lafayette. Nellie was, as Felix wrote David, an education in herself, but she was not exactly what the family had in mind, and when various spies in the pay of the family reported that Felix had not once been seen attending a lecture at the university, he was sent, instead of his next quarter's allowance, a railway ticket back to Eschenbach.

"I did think they might have waited till the end of term," Felix wrote David. "Well, she came rather expensive, and this will save a Christmas present. Apparently Cousin Algy told my father that a monastic and womanless atmosphere prevails at Oxford, so I'm being sent off there, at once, right in the middle of term—it seems Algy was able to fix this up; what a bore influential relatives are—so you may expect to find me on your doorstep any day now, ready to acquire the English virtues of sobriety, thrift and chastity."

"Are they English virtues?" David asked his friend Anthony Fielding.

Anthony laughed. "Foreigners have very odd ideas about us I've often noticed it."

Felix arrived exactly one week after his letter. Looking pale from an agitated Channel crossing, he went without stopping at his own rooms in Christ Church, directly to Oriel, where the porter informed him that Mr Harvey was out. Hunting.

"Foxhunting?" asked Felix, thinking this an expensive sport for the son of a poor Yorkshire vicar.

"Riding to 'ounds with the 'Eythrop," said the porter severely.

When did the porter think Mr Harvey would be back, Felix asked. Mostly not till the gates closed, said the porter, seeing that Mr Harvey generally took his tea and often his dinner with Lord Anthony Fielding at Magdalen. The son of the Duke of Frome that would be, the porter explained, relishing every syllable.

Felix thought this over. He knew about Magdalen, which had been Algy Strafford's college. It was considered the most elegant and snobbish of all the Oxford colleges. Royalty from all over the world sent its sons to Magdalen. Once, Algy had told Felix, when the Japanese crown prince, Prince Chichibu, had been an undergraduate there, the president, inquiring whether the name meant anything, and being told that it meant Son of God, had serenely assured the young prince that he would find the sons of many other distinguished parents at Magdalen. How on earth, Felix wondered, had David, that penniless scholar, got himself mixed up in such a crowd? And who was Lord Anthony?

Felix was rescued by Paston, who enquired whether he was the German gentleman Mr Harvey had said might be arriving any day, because if so he was to come up to Mr Harvey's rooms and be given whatever meal was appropriate to the hour of the day. Tea, said Paston firmly, in case the German gentleman should not know this.

Felix, who had lost breakfast and lunch on the cross-Channel steamer, accepted the offer gratefully. He was taken up a narrow stair and ushered into a room with admirable linenfold panelling and rickety wicker furniture. David appeared to have added to this nothing except hundreds of books, which was in character, of course. What was not at all in character was the large bowl of hothouse hyacinths, which filled the room with their expensive springtime scent.

Paston put a match to the fire and said, "I'll have your tea in a jiffy, sir."

"Will Mr Harvey really not be back until the gates close?"

Normally, said Paston, he wouldn't. But His Lordship, Lord Anthony Fielding as you might say, and Mr Harvey, had promised to look in when they got back from hunting in case the German gentleman had arrived.

"Very good of them," said Felix, who was cold, hungry, and entirely at fault, not having written David the exact time or even day of his arrival.

Paston went to get tea. Felix picked up a book left lying on the table, Corbière's *Les Amours Yaunes*, bound in morocco with the ducal crest of Frome on the cover. Its motto: *Bonus-Melior-Optimus*, made him smile at its simple ambition, yet this expensive volume increased his sense of unease, just as the hyacinths had.

The tea and crumpets were consoling. Felix had finished his third cup and fourth crumpet when he heard voices and

91

laughter on the stair. The door opened and David, looking incredibly handsome in his scarlet coat, blinked in the unexpected light, looked at the glowing fire, and said in the mildest of Oxford tones, "Flixy, how nice." Behind him a shadowy form, also in hunting pinks, moved into the room; an exquisite creature, taller than David, with thistledown hair and sapphire eyes, and the languid, attenuated air of an overbred whippet. David introduced him as Lord Anthony Fielding. Felix, remembering a long list given him by Algy Strafford of things one might not do at Oxford, refrained from clicking heels or shaking hands.

"Did you have a good crossing?"

"I really prefer not to be reminded."

Lord Anthony laughed. David, pulling off his gloves, said, "I'm going to change. I'm one mass of mud."

"You must learn to stay on your horse on wet days, my dear," said Lord Anthony. Noting the intimate tone of voice, and David's cool withdrawal from it, Felix thought, Oh Lord, he's a case, and began to feel more kindly toward Lord Anthony, as one does toward those one can pity.

David returned, wearing a beautifully cut coat of brown velvet, which Felix admired in a puzzled way. Algy had told him that the only possible thing at Oxford was three-piece broadcloth.

David said, "Shall we have tea here?"

"No," said Lord Anthony. "You never give one anything fit to eat. Let's go to Clem's." He turned to Felix and said, "Do come too," and Felix, not knowing what else to do with himself, came.

"Clem is Clemence Barton, a great friend of ours," said David. "His rooms are on the same staircase as Fielding's."

Clemence Barton's rooms contained neither college furniture nor college tea. The predominant colour was peacock blue, to match the Bakst costume sketches tacked on the wall. Through a haze of Sobranie smoke Felix discerned a number of undergraduates sitting languidly on peacock cushions on the floor, drinking Dom Perignon, and eating caviar from a skull with a hinged lid. One of these, a youth with a round choirboy face disfigured by a black eye, smiled at Felix and said, "What heaven, you've arrived." Lord

Anthony introduced him as Ned Mandeville, then presented their host.

There was nothing three-piece broadcloth about Clemence Barton; he matched the decor of his room in peacock velvet. To Lord Anthony and David he said, "The unspeakable and the uneatable have returned. It only wants our rowing blue and we'll be a party." He turned to Felix and said, "Have some champagne."

David said, "Have a heart, Clem. Anthony and I are starving. We want tea with muffins and real eggs, not those foul black things."

While Clem Barton shouted down the stairs for tea, eggs, and muffins, David lowered himself cautiously on a.peacock cushion. Lord Anthony said, "Tucker's fence strikes again."

"Be fair," said David; "it struck Colonel Pierpont too."

Ned turned his battered choirboy face to Felix and said, "Colonel Pierpont is the MFH and has a wonderful line in curses. What did he say when he got thrown, David?"

"It wasn't goodness gracious me, that much I do remember."

A scout brought tea, someone held out a box of cigarettes, someone else pushed the caviar in Felix's direction. No one asked after his journey or his opinion, as a newcomer, of Oxford. They treated him as if he had just strolled over from another quad.

Felix was not deceived by the mildness of their manners. He knew he was there on approval, but he was on foreign territory and did not know what would be approved. It was like the first day at military school, except that Lehzen had never left its cadets in the least doubt as to what was or was not approved behaviour.

For David's sake, a David so at ease among them that he was not even troubling himself to talk, but sat, turning the pages of a book, he guessed that they would give him every benefit of the doubt. He also knew from Algy Strafford that he would need it. Germans were these days highly unpopular at Oxford, thanks to the Rhodes scholars who were personally chosen by the kaiser and therefore shared to a considerable degree their sovereign's boorishness, boastfulness, and suspicion of all things foreign.

"Where is Andrew?" asked Lord Anthony. "Still on the river? It's nearly dark."

"Well, you know Andrew."

"My brother rows for the college," said Lord Anthony to Felix, making it sound like an amiable failing. Even as he spoke the door opened, and a young man in shorts, showing very blue knees, came into the room. He wore a long wool scarf wound around his neck, but seemed otherwise unconscious of the cold.

"I never really grasped the full meaning of 'rowing blue'," said Clemence Barton, "until I saw Andrew's knees. This is David's friend, Felix von Landeck."

Lord Andrew acknowledged this introduction with the absent courtesy of someone who has been training hard all afternoon and has just caught sight of a tray laden with muffins and tea. The others, digging occasionally into the pot of caviar, sipped champagne while the haze of Sobranie smoke grew thicker. David seemed absorbed in his book. Clemence Barton said, "Do have some more champagne," and settled down beside Felix, taking up a piece of needle-point. "I'm copying one of the Bakst designs for *Scheherazade*," he said cosily. "Isn't it pretty?" Felix, with a sudden spurt of fatigue and irritability, caught himself thinking, Bloody poof, and decided that early as it was he would find his rooms and crawl into bed. He would have liked to take David away with him, to rescue him, was what he really meant, from all these foul people, except that David did not think they were foul people, was indeed very much at home among them.

He was on the point of making his excuses, when Lord Anthony said, "Don't read in the dark, my dear; it rots your eyes," and turned up a lamp behind David.

David said, "This poetry rots my brains," and threw the book aside. As Anthony bent to pick it up, his shadow moved, light filled a dark corner, and Felix's eye was caught by a small painting on the wall, a tiny stretch of beach, a few inches of ocean, ladies in bustles and parasols, gentlemen in dark suits and top hats. Suddenly he felt comforted and even happy.

"Is it a Boudin?" he said to Clemence, who looked up from his embroidery and said, "Yes. Do you like it?"

"May I?" said Felix and got up to have a closer look at it. Clemence took it down from the wall and carried it to the table, where there was a better light. "I bought it in Paris last year," he said, "and paid a shocking amount for it. 'It's such a little painting, Monsieur Liebestraum,' I told him, but he wouldn't have it. He always knows when I've fallen in love with something and charges accordingly."

"Yes, I know Liebestraum," said Felix, no longer offended by needle-point and peacock-blue velvet. "Definitely a first cousin to St Peter. I'd hate to tell you how much he got out of me for a Picasso gouache just before I left Paris. I tried to convince him that it had an air of fatigue—he doesn't like cubism, you know, and isn't at all happy about the direction Picasso's taking—but he merely said, 'I, Liebestraum, personally promise you that Picasso's best work is still ahead of him.'"

Clemence choked into his champagne. "What heaven, did he really say that? Come and see my other things. I keep them in the bedroom, because one's guests get a trifle clumsy sometimes after they've had champagne."

They dined at the George on rather poor food, and Felix generously forgave Clem, since he owned a Boudin, the very obvious passes he was making at the waiters. David and Felix got back to Oriel as Big Tom began to strike nine. Felix yawned and said, "I feel as if I'd been put through a mangle. It's being so sick on the boat, I suppose, and then all that champagne afterward."

"Don't bother to move into the House tonight," said David. "You can stay with me."

While David lit the lamp, Felix took off his jacket and put on a rather glorious silk paisley dressing gown he had found hanging behind the bedroom door. He accepted a glass of very good whisky, looked at the hyacinths, and said severely, "David, what have you been up to?"

"How do you mean?"

Felix took a sip of his drink and said, "I expected to find you, poor and studious, sitting by a very small fire, eating bread and cheese, deep in your books. Instead I arrive to be told that you are riding to hounds with the Heythrop, and find you intimate with a very odd circle of people. Not at all your sort, I would have said."

David said, "I *am* poor and studious. I'm reading Greats, I mean to get a first to please my Papa, and I mean to do it in three years so he won't have the expense of two of us at Oxford at the same time, Freddy not being the kind to get scholarships. I mostly do live on bread and cheese and stewed tea. But you're wrong about one thing; they are very much my sort."

"It seems very odd."

"Flixy," said David, amused and touched, "you're not seriously proposing to lecture me, are you?"

But Felix was proposing to do just that. Full of champagne and whisky he went on and on like a Dutch uncle about hunting pinks, hothouse hyacinths, and twelve-year-old Scotch whisky.

"But it's none of it mine," said David. "It all belongs to Anthony. I'm not running up debts, if that's what you mean."

Felix thought that there were debts and debts, and that all these lovely things belonging to Lord Anthony made things worse. For reasons not entirely clear, the hunting pinks bothered him most. In a way this was a relief to David, who thought Felix might take it into his head to go on about the silk dressing gown.

"They're borrowed," said David, "that's all. You borrow Toby's waders when you go salmon fishing."

"It's not the same," said Felix.

Knowing it wasn't, David said, "It's exactly the same."

Felix said, "I do understand that one of the main reasons one goes to the university is to meet the right people, to make connections for one's future career. But those people, David!"

"Yes, I could have done better at your college if I were a serious person. Everyone there is working at becoming prime minister. It's very dull."

"One could never say that of your crowd."

"No, one couldn't. Which is why I like them. And they have taught me things."

"I can imagine."

"Try not to be stuffy, Flixy. I meant things like French poetry and Russian ballet, learning to like music that isn't by Handel, and the right kinds of paintings, the kind you like." Mimicking the emphatic tones of Clem Barton, David said, " 'Monet and Manet, my dear, not Tuke and Tonks.' "

Felix could not help laughing. "I can hear him."

"There, you see. You know, Flixy, I don't really want a career in the sense that you think of it. I don't want to do frightfully real and earnest things. The trouble with not having money is that one must do something to earn it."

"What do you have in mind?" asked Felix.

"I'm not quite sure. Something literary, I expect. I quite often earn a guinea even now winning the poetry competitions in the *Westminster Gazette*."

"I shouldn't call that much of a living."

"No, I know, of course."

"How's Toby?" asked Felix.

"As always. He got into Sandhurst, as I suppose you know."

"Yes. Does he like it?"

"I can't see why not. As far as I can tell all they do is get drunk, rag people who aren't in their set, and play polo. I expect you'll see him soon; he comes here quite often, between chukkas, so to speak."

Felix wondered what Toby, who was something of a prig, made of David's Oxford friends. He said, "Who gave Mandeville the black eye? Barton?"

"Oh no. Some bargeman in a Jericho pub, most likely. It's not the first time. Ned has a liking for low company. Barton looks after him, as much as anyone can look after someone so bent on self-destruction."

"Why is he bent on self-destruction?"

"I don't know. Why is anyone anything?"

"And the exquisite Lord Anthony? What is he bent on?"

97

"On being exquisite, I should think. Why should he trouble himself to be anything else?"

"He's in love with you."

"I know. There is nothing I can do about it. I wish he weren't." David and Felix had few secrets from each other. There were taboo topics with Toby, things he simply would not talk about or listen to, but none between Felix and David, with the result that Toby thought far better of his friends than they did of each other. David said, "Anthony's mother used to collect writers; mostly not very first-rate ones, William de Morgan rather than Morgan Forster. But all the same, a literary salon. I thought I might get to meet some of them, become a private secretary or something to a Man of Letters. I'd quite like that, I think. But just around the time I first met the duchess she'd decided to take up religion and ill health and had moved to the country, so now it's all doctors and monsignors."

Felix began to laugh. He said, "David, my dear, you are a bloody tart. The only thing that makes you tolerable is that you're such an unsuccessful one."

Love, thought Anthony Fielding, was very much like toothache. Not the excruciating kind, the nagging sort that never lets up and never lets you forget it's there. Of course the pain wasn't in one's mouth but in the pit of the stomach—a romantic would have called it the heart, but it was quite definitely the stomach—and one couldn't go to the dentist to have it out.

He was lying curled in a patch of sunlight on David's bed. David had dressed and was sitting by the fire. Anthony had seen his eyes glance sideways to the book he had put down and now wanted to take up again except that he was too polite to do so.

"Felix and Clem have gone up to town to the Grafton Galleries," he said. "They've hit it off tremendously."

"Felix," said David, "would hit it off with Jack the Ripper, if Jack the Ripper collected Impressionists."

"I'm very glad," said Anthony. "It would have been so uncomfortable if they hadn't taken to each other. I do like Felix so much." How have I come to this, he wondered, to this constant ache, this idiotic wish to say what will please, even to lie. He had always been run after, sought out and courted. At Eton he had led a queen-bee life, making lingering choices between equally spotty boys, devastating clean-living captains of cricket, playing idle and vicious schoolboy games, beloved, never lover; cat, not mouse. It did not occur to him even now that David too had played these games, but having learned in a harsher school, played more ruthlessly and not for amusement.

Anthony had been aware of David since his first day at Oxford. Despite his seeming self-absorption he had noted that haughty back turned on his piece of showing off with the hawk, had noticed too those extraordinary looks, and over the months to come had been struck by a solitude that was plainly a matter of choice.

David had come up to Oxford with something of a reputation. He had had poems published in *Public School Verse*, and soon followed this up with others in the *Isis* and the *Cherwell*. Anthony's set were a literary lot; a published poem counted with them as much as a rowing blue did in more hearty circles.

Amid the frantic freshman rush to join everything from OUDS to the Fabian Society, not to miss out on new people to be met, friends to be made, David's solitude had seemed to Lord Anthony, who could not bear his own society for more than five minutes at a time, to have something arrogant and unattainable about it, so that, run after as he and his set were, when David said, "It ought to have been a peregrine," he felt the address as an accolade.

For all his aloofness David had proved to be easily acquired and should have been as easy to discard. How then, Anthony often wondered, had this obsession started? When had the pain lodged itself, seemingly permanently, in the pit of his stomach? Was it the first time he had noticed David's eyes move to a book put down half an hour before, and had realized that he was longing to get back to it? Or the first time David had got up and got dressed and sat by the fire, leaving Anthony alone in the bed? Or was it when he had finally admitted to himself that David was being polite; that having no love to give he was generous instead with his time and his body.

Though he thought about these things almost as obsessively as he thought about David himself, Anthony had no answers. All he knew was that he had fallen in love like falling down a well. He could see the stars at noon, but he could see nothing else.

David said, "Do you want some tea, Anthony?"

"I'd really like champagne."

"You know I haven't got any."

"Let me send you some."

"Not for the first time, no thank you." Since Felix's arrival he had grown as touchy on the subject as he had been at the beginning of their friendship.

"Why can't you ever take a present?"

"Because it's not my birthday. Stop being tiresome, Anthony. You knew when this started that my end of it was bread and mousetrap cheese and Lipton tea. If you don't like it you can always go back to Magdalen."

"Will you come too?"

"Yes, of course, if you want me to."

"And you don't forget."

"I didn't forget, Anthony. Felix and I sat up talking till all hours, and I was reading a very dull book for my essay and fell asleep. I said I was sorry."

The kettle began to make spitting noises. David filled the pot, and in a few minutes poured out two cups and handed one to Anthony.

"Is it really Lipton's?"

"It's Earl Grey."

"You shouldn't have bothered."

David drank his tea, poured the dregs of his cup into his saucer, and said, "My tea leaves tell me we are going to have a quarrel if you don't stop it, Anthony."

"Let's not. I'm sorry I annoy you. It's really only that I've never known a poor person before."

David laughed. "That is what Oxford is for, to broaden your social horizon and teach you new things."

Anthony did not join in the laughter. "I ache so," he said like a child.

"I know," David said gently. "I'm sorry. I would do anything to make it stop."

"It won't make it stop," said Anthony, grasping his chance, "but it might help if you would come home with me for Christmas."

Their friendship had begun during Eights Week, with the Long Vacation looming ahead. It was perhaps the threat of such a long separation so soon (and David's lack of panic at it) which had laid whip and spur to what might otherwise on Anthony's part have been just another pleasant affair. He never asked people to his home, for his father was of an eccentric and irascible temperament and invariably took against guests he had not himself invited. But at the thought of an entire summer without David, Anthony found that he no longer cared whether his father took after his guest with a horsewhip, so long as he, Anthony, might be allowed to bind up the wounds. David, duly warned, had accepted the invitation, adding that if Anthony did not mind a lot of Harveys crowded together like a Calcutta slum, he might like to spend part of the summer at the vicarage.

Anthony's fears had proved groundless; David had charmed the duchess and had circumspectly managed not to give offence to the duke.

"You were very good with Papa," Anthony had said after they were settled at the vicarage. "He's so difficult as a rule. I do wish he were more like yours."

Anthony loved being at the vicarage; he loved David's family noisily crowding around the large dinner table, with every kind of guest, a renowned Oxford scholar visiting the Vicar, or a layabout trading a day's yardwork for a meal or two (for the Vicar's Christian principles would not allow such a one to be fed at the back door), and David's cheerful, disputatious brothers and sisters. There was no port to separate the ladies from the gentlemen and the grown-ups from the children. Everyone sat for hours, elbows on the table, engaged in endless and learned talk, with even Adam and Eve, the nine-year-old twins darting like minnows between the Latin quotations and Greek syllogisms. Here Anthony felt himself free of the label he carried with him everywhere—the Duke of Frome's son—and became for the first time in his life simply Anthony Fielding, David's Oxford friend, and a temporary member of this large and peculiar family.

It was very naive of Anthony to think that no one in the vicarage thought of him as a duke's son. The Vicar might, under the aspect of eternity, regard him as not much different from himself or a visiting layabout; the twins, after half an hour's shy silence and an uproarious game of racing demon, might take to calling him, despite David's reproving "Lord Anthony to you, please," simply by his first name; but there was one member of the household who never for a moment forgot his prospects. Mrs Harvey, with five poor but beautiful daughters to marry off, thought of very little else. She studied his family tree in *Debrett's* and entertained happy daydreams of Lord Anthony falling victim to a hopeless passion for Jenny, who was the prettiest, or Fanny, who was the brightest. She was far too innocent to guess that her David had already gone as far down that road as it might be travelled.

After their successful summer vacation, Anthony had not worried about Christmas until the arrival of David's German friend, who was, he understood, invited to spend the holidays at Altondale Hall, which was also the home of David's oldest friend, Toby Strafford. Were the three of them planning a reunion which held no place for him?

"Not that I can really recommend Frome at Christmas," he said a little desperately. "Papa is always at his worst on holidays, but I expect it will be a fairly good party if there is hunting."

"I'm sorry," said David, "but I've got to spend Christmas with my people. Why don't you come too and then we can go on to Frome for the new year."

Suddenly much happier, Anthony said, "Thanks, I'd love to come to the vicarage. It will be heaven to miss the Frome Christmas treat for the grateful tenantry."

"You forget the Altondale Christmas treat. We too have a grateful tenantry, and if they aren't grateful enough, Toby's Nannie will let them know in no uncertain terms."

Felix, David, and Anthony travelled from Oxford to Altondale together. Toby, who had promised to meet them at the station, was not there. Bolt, the Strafford's coachman, said he had not come back in time from his day's hunting. He saw to their luggage and they set off along the gentle curve of the High Street. The greengrocer's window was bright with tinsel and cotton wool. The village idiot peered out at them, his breath frosting the panes. At the vicarage Anthony and David got down. In the bright rectangle of the door Felix saw the silhouette of a girl in a coat and hat accepting David's hug. They walked up to the carriage together, David's arm around her shoulder. A black dog followed at their heels. Culpepper, Felix remembered, and the girl must of course be David's blind sister.

David said, "You remember Julian, Flixy? She's going back to the hall, so you can drive up together. We'll see you tomorrow. If there isn't a frost we might have some good hunting."

Felix greeted Julian and handed her into the carriage. The coachman turned the horses back into the High Street. In the early dusk, front gardens Felix was accustomed to seeing abloom with roses looked bare and melancholy. Gaslight shone lambent from windows; behind drawn curtains shapes moved as in a shadow play, setting a table, getting tea. Someone opened a window and sprinkled breadcrumbs on the sill. Sparrows whirled like pieces of brown paper, settling to feed. Julian said she had been giving a hand at the Altondale Christmas treat, which was held annually at the parish hall. Lady Millicent was nominally in charge, but it was Nannie and Mrs Harvey who saw to the decorations and found a suitable gift for everyone; flannels, wool socks, knitted caps, comforts of a practical rather than festive nature. The festivity came later, when everyone had tea and Christmas cakes, and Lady Millicent put in an appearance, graciously accepting a cup of tea and moving among the tenantry, saying a suitable word to everyone.

Julian described it composedly, in a grown-up manner which reminded Felix of Lady Millicent, whose social conscience would never allow a silence to fall. A last edge of sunset bordered the distant hills, which were darker

103

shadows in the dusk. Culpepper, a shadow amongst shadows, loped along at their side with lolling tongue. Downhill past the home farm, the horse trotting briskly, knowing its stable near, they entered the path to the park. The lodge windows were alight; a curl of smoke stood on the windless air. A woman's face appeared at the window and a hand waved a greeting into the dusk. Julian waved back.

"How did you know she waved at you?" Felix asked.

"She always does. And even if she didn't, it wouldn't matter, wasting a wave."

As they pulled up at the stable block, the clock chimed the half hour over their heads. Toby, his gloves spattered with mud, was just handing over his horse to one of the grooms. He looked reproachfully at Felix and said, "I was coming to meet you. You must have been early."

"Or you late."

Toby helped Julian down from the carriage and stood with his arm around her, smiling at Felix. Culpepper put a muddy paw on his knee, and Julian said, "Get down, Culpepper." How did she notice everything, Felix wondered.

At the door to the Palladian wing they met a young woman who was scraping great clods of mud from her shoes.

"Kitty, what a day to go walking," said Toby. "Oh, this is my German cousin, Felix von Landeck. Mrs Snow, my American cousin, or aunt—we haven't quite worked it out yet."

They shook hands. In the dim light of the entrance Felix could only tell that she was small and slender and wore black. Then Mortman opened the door, and as the light poured out he saw that she had red hair; a tangle of curly filaments, each of which seemed to catch and give back the lamplight shining through the door.

She said, "How was the Christmas treat, Julian?"

Julian, who was scraping her boots on the scraper looked up and said, "Feudal."

Kitty Snow laughed. "Is that a new word of yours?"

"Oh no," said Julian. "I've always known it."

The quiet mockery with which she said this seemed to Felix far too adult for so young a girl. She was, if he remembered correctly, only ten. Had he and Toby and David judged the grown-ups as coolly when they were children? Yes, he supposed, if they had troubled to notice them, they had. He remembered the various speculations they had entertained about their sex lives, found himself looking at Mrs Snow, and felt the blood warm in his cheeks.

"I'm going to change my shoes," said Kitty. "Don't be a pig and eat all the cakes, Toby."

Mortman asked whether she would like him to send a maid to help her. She went off with an amused, "Gosh no, I can take off my own shoes; I've done it for years."

"She can too," said Toby. "It's because she's American. Mortman and Calais don't know what to make of her. She does her own hair and dresses herself—if she weren't our cousin, they'd suspect she isn't a lady."

"I never knew you had American cousins," said Felix.

"We're ashamed of them. One of them was a bad lot and fought with General Washington, instead of against him. Kitty's his great-great-something-or-other-granddaughter. Her husband is dead. He was a clergyman and left her very badly off. Algy and Rachel found her giving music lessons and living in lodgings, so they brought her back with them. Then Algy got recalled to Berlin, so Papa invited her for a long visit. She has a little boy who was going to one of those public schools they have over there; you know, the kind anyone can go to, but Papa is going to send him to my old prep school and to Eton, if they'll have him. Poor kid, he's having a thin time of it up in the nursery with Nannie. Americans aren't used to it the way we are. Come and have some tea; you must be starved."

They found Lady Milly and Augustus in the small drawing room. Lady Milly, rather tired after the afternoon's charitable activities, sipped china tea. Augustus, very muddy and red in the face after a brisk day after the fox, was gobbling crumpets.

"Dear boy," said Lady Millicent, giving Felix her hand, "how nice to have you here again. Sit by me and tell me about your dear parents. How is your mother?"

Felix greeted Augustus, accepted a cup of tea, and settled down to the inevitable family talk. Toby and his father went over the day's hunting. Julian came in with Culpepper. She kissed Lady Millicent's cheek, and settled down by Toby, who put his arm round her shoulders and drew her close.

While Felix was giving an account of his family, he watched her with some curiosity. At first glance she seemed as plainly dressed as any village girl, and he wondered whether Lady Millicent were mean. But he quickly realized that everything she wore was of the best quality and beautifully made. The plainness, he guessed, was due to her blindness, which would make ribbons and frills a nuisance for her. She looked, thought Felix, like a very expensive young Quaker. Except for the colour of her blind eyes, she also looked so much like David as to be almost laughable; she had the same straight nose and marvellous modelling of cheek and jawbone, the same exquisite line of mouth with its slight upward tilt at the corners, the same silky brown hair, glowing with light, as if it had only yesterday shed the gold of childhood. Only her eyes were not like his. Julian alone among the vicarage children had inherited her father's grey eyes, while David's were his mother's, a clear, dark blue.

Julian had slid to the floor by Toby's feet, and was feeding bits of cherry cake to Culpepper. Her perfect little nose twitched happily at Toby's strong smell of horse, leather, and sweat. It was one of her secrets that she preferred such smells to the soft violet scent of Lady Millicent's cheek.

Her life was full of secrets, her own and those of the people around her, of the woods and the house. She heard what no one else did: the rustle of mice in the wainscot, the nearly silent scuttle of blackbeetles in the kitchen. Long before anyone else, she was aware of the sweet smell of dry rot gnawing into the beams behind the stairs. She gathered people's secrets as well, knew what the housemaid whispered to the shy, young undergardener at the kitchen door, and what Augustus and his coachman did in the small flat above the stables. She never spoke of any of these things, neither at the hall nor at the vicarage, where she went every morning to do lessons with her father and then sat, remote and silent, at the noisy, crowded lunch table.

She had little interest in her older brothers and sisters, but would have liked to be friends with the twins, who were nearest to her in age. But Adam and Eve were shy with her (who were shy with no one else, not the Provost of Oriel or even Nannie), and Julian had too little experience of people her own age to know how to put them at ease. The formal manners Lady Millicent had taught her were a glass cage from which she could not escape.

There was never enough help at the vicarage, and it was the twins' job to help with the washing-up after lunch. Julian would have liked to help too, but she was never asked. While she put on her coat and hat to go back to the hall, she could hear their cheerful voices raised in argument (those endless vicarage arguments; when Noah was told to put two of every animal into the ark, did that include fish?) or songs, rude parodies of the soppier *Songs of Praise*, most of them written by their father, who had an unchristian dislike of sentimental Christianity. Sometimes, if they were in a gentle mood, they would sing a lovely Latin lyric David had taught them on his last visit home: "*Vidi, viridi, Phyllidem sub tilia . . .*"

Adam had at that time a very pure, fragile soprano voice, and listening to the pretty tune, Julian, who even as a baby had never found the relief of tears, felt a small pain, like a bruise inside her throat, which she did not recognize as a wish to cry.

Back at the hall she would go to Lady Millicent's sitting room, put her blind muzzle against the soft cheek smelling of violets, and tell about her morning, what she had learned, said, and eaten, for no detail of her life bored Lady Millicent. Julian talked, guarded her secrets, told her what she wanted to hear.

Felix, watching her, drank tea and answered Lady Millicent's questions about his sisters. "Angelika is well, and very happy," he said. "The babies are rather nice, if you happen to like babies. You know that Marit has left the convent."

"Your dear mother must be relieved."

107

"I'm not sure. Marit's behaving rather oddly—well, she always did, of course. She's . . ." He stopped as the door opened and the fire flared up in the sudden draught. Julian, who had heard Kitty's step in the hall before anyone else, turned her face toward the door and smiled.

Nothing had eased her loneliness like the arrival of this strange American lady. Nannie wasn't sure she was a lady at all, she had such odd ways. And it wasn't suitable, Nannie said, for Miss Julian to spend hours talking and giggling in her room with her. What on earth could they find to talk about?

Perhaps it wasn't suitable, Julian agreed. There were twenty years between them, yet she felt that Kitty was the nearest thing to a girlfriend she had ever had. She seemed to be unaware of the twenty years' difference between them, and treated Julian as if she were the same age as herself, and neither of them was sure whether that age was thirty or ten.

"Oh, Cousin Augustus, you've eaten all the crumpets," Kitty said.

Augustus, who derived a lot of simpleminded pleasure from being teased by such a charming American voice, said, "Well, m'dear, I've been out hunting all day and it's given me rather an appetite. Have some cherry cake."

"I hope you didn't kill any foxes," said Kitty.

"Foxes are vermin, m'dear, and have to be kept down."

"But they're so beautiful and hunting's so cruel. How would you like being torn into little pieces by a lot of yapping dogs. Why can't you just shoot them?"

In the light of the drawing room, Felix realized that she was both older and plainer than he had thought her in the entranceway. Her black dress was shiny at the seams with wear. Except for the oriflamme of her hair there was nothing to arrest the eye. Her voice was delightful and her laughter festive, but her face was marred by freckles and she completely lacked the two attributes most prized by women of fashion, a complexion and a figure. Nevertheless Felix found himself putting down his teacup and joining her talk with Augustus, who, after a quick look round to make sure that her horrible solecism about shooting foxes

108

had not been overheard, had quickly changed the subject. They were talking about her son Oliver, who was not enjoying life in the nursery with Nannie.

"I think Nannie will do Oliver a world of good," said Kitty, when Augustus had kindly sympathized with the little boy's misery. "I've noticed ever since I came here how beauty-fully English children are brought up. Look what an angel Julian is. Mothers really aren't very good at bringing up their own children. At least I wasn't."

"Yes, but all the same," said Augustus, "think of it from his point of view. It's different for us. We're brought up to it. But to be suddenly stuck in the attic with Nannie after spending all his time with you does seem hard."

"It doesn't matter if it is hard, it will benefit him in the long run," said Kitty. "You know, Cousin Augustus, I have a theory. I think some people are natural-born children, and some are natural-born grown-ups. Natural-born children usually have blissful childhoods, and get more and more miserable the older they get. Natural-born grown-ups are miserable, mopey kids. They're sure nobody loves them, they hate school, and feel chronically misunderstood. Then when they're grown up everything suddenly falls into place, and the older they get the happier they get. I know that was true in my case; I've never been happier than since I turned thirty."

Felix looked at her, shocked. For one thing he had not thought her quite so old. (He had just turned twenty, and anyone aged thirty seemed to him almost to belong to his parents' generation.) For another thing he had never before heard a lady so casually admit to her age. In his circle women pretended to be younger, until they turned seventy or so, at which time they usually began to add another ten years so that everyone could say they would never have thought it.

Lady Millicent said, "I wonder if Kitty isn't right," and Felix knew she was thinking of her sunny childhood at Langland.

Augustus said, "I'm sure she is. I had an absolutely rotten time at my prep school, but things are very jolly now."

"Really, you know," Kitty said to Augustus, "turning thirty was like being newly born for me. I remember waking up on the morning of my thirtieth birthday and realizing that my life was probably half over, and that for thirty years I'd been somebody's daughter, somebody's wife, somebody's mother. And I said to myself, from now on I'm going to be Kitty Snow, and if you don't like it you can lump it. Of course they didn't like it—my husband, my mother-in-law, the congregation—nobody liked it. But *I* felt a lot better."

Augustus said, "But what exactly did you do?" He hadn't had such an amusing tea in years.

"You'll laugh at me, but the first thing I did, I stopped putting rice powder on my nose to hide my freckles. You see, I was always ashamed of having them, and then I was ashamed all over again for powdering my nose, because in Boston nice women—especially ministers' wives—don't. Then I joined the Bloomer Society and stopped wearing corsets. My mother-in-law said that's what killed my husband, but the doctor said it was pneumonia. Then I became a suffragette."

Augustus, who had been delighting in a tale that in an Englishwoman would have profoundly shocked him—not that an English lady would have mentioned corsets in mixed company—now felt compelled to make a protest. "Oh really, my dear . . ."

Lady Millicent hastened to her husband's support. "My dear Kitty, you must not say such things. Perhaps it is different in America, but in England they are quite dreadful women."

Kitty said, "Dreadful how?"

"They are not ladies," said Lady Millicent. "Women who voluntarily put themselves in a position"—she leaned closer and lowered her voice—"being pawed and handled by men . . . policemen, of course, but still men. No lady would dream of doing such a thing."

"Frustrated old maids," said Augustus, whose carriage had been hit by a suffragette cabbage during last year's coronation procession. "Only way they can get a man to come near them, I expect."

Felix had never paid attention to the subject of women's votes, and would not have done so now had it not been brought up by this amusing American visitor. At home in Germany he had never heard of a suffragist movement. Things were done gradually and decorously. His own mother had installed the first woman doctor ever seen in Eschenbach as head of the cottage hospital against much masculine opposition, and he himself had bought a painting by Mary Cassat. Let women earn their place of equality as men have done, by merit, and the vote would be granted them.

Luckily he did not voice these sentiments, but merely asked, "Why do you want to vote, Mrs Snow? Do you really think it will improve politics?"

"No," said Kitty with great frankness. "I know that's the official line, but most women I know are idiots and are just as likely to vote for the handsomest man as the most competent one. But most men are pretty idiotic too, so I don't think that ought to disqualify us. It simply isn't fair that men can vote and we can't."

"I must say I agree about voters being idiots," said Toby. "Some Strafford or other has almost always represented Altondale in the House of Commons. Just now it's Colonel Lapitter, but before him it was my great-uncle Peregrine, who was completely gaga and spent most of his life in a bin. Yet he was voted in election after election."

"Toby," said Lady Millicent, "Uncle Peregrine was eccentric, not mad."

"Mad as a hatter," said Augustus. "Shot foxes and thought he was the Antichrist."

Lady Millicent turned to Kitty. "My dear," she said, firmly changing the subject, "won't you play for us?"

There had always been a piano in the small drawing room at Altondale, though no one at the hall played. Twice a year a piano tuner looked after it; for the rest of the time it served to display a cloisonné vase filled with pampas grass, an Indian silk shawl, a collection of silhouettes cut out by Augustus's aunt, several china plates painted by the same lady, a small easel displaying photographs of Lady

111

Milly's parents, and a stereopticon with scenes of India from Augustus's army days.

Felix went to open the piano for Kitty and said, "I'm a very good page turner. May I?"

"Can you lift the pampas grass down is more to the point. And can you sing?"

"Yes to the pampas grass and a qualified yes to the singing. I can carry a tune and have an untrained, slight but not unpleasing voice. Will that do?"

"Good enough for here," said Kitty. "Is there anything in particular you'd like, Cousin Augustus?"

"Well, my dear, I'm not very musical. What about that thing you played on Friday—no, Thursday it must have been because that was the day we dragged Le Bredon's spinney and Lapitter's mare caught her hock on a bit of barbed wire. I've never heard a man curse like that. Da dum dum, da dum dum, d'you know the one I mean?"

Kitty played the Schubert impromptu thus described, then a Boccherini minuet for Julian, and for Lady Millicent, who felt it her duty to keep abreast of the latest in culture despite her exile in Yorkshire, Sinding's *Rustle of Spring*.

Felix was impressed by Kitty's musicianship, and the uncondescending seriousness with which she performed for people whose general idea of music was the annual performance of the *Messiah* by the Dewsbury Choral Society. "You're awfully good," he said, and realized when she laughed at him that he had not kept his astonishment sufficiently disguised.

"It's what I was doing in Boston when Cousin Algy found me," she said. "Giving music lessons. I used to think I'd like to play professionally, but my family behaved as if I were going to run off with the circus, and then I got married and had Oliver, so I never got around to it."

She and Felix sang "Sheep May Safely Graze" for Augustus, whose favourite tune this was, possibly because it reminded him of his own Yorkshire fields, dotted with brown-faced lambs, and "Where'er You Walk" for Lady Millicent, who liked the notion of nature at the service of the English upper classes.

When Lady Millicent at last glanced at the clock, she

was astonished to see that it was time to change for dinner, and smiled gratefully at Kitty.

She had not been pleased when Augustus's spontaneous act of generosity had landed her with an American widow of uncertain background. Making every allowance for her being transatlantic, Lady Milly could not possibly approve of someone who not only wore no corsets and discussed this fact in the drawing room, who made no secret of her age and poverty and showed little respect for social rank. But there was no denying that Kitty made the time pass. The long winter afternoons had not gone by so quickly since the happy days when she and Nannie had, like children absorbed in a new toy, taught Julian to reach for objects she could not see.

Dinner passed like tea, with verve and no longueurs. This was not because it was a brief meal, as always when it was "only family" it consisted of five courses: hare soup, lark pie, veal à la jardinière, vol-au-vent, and plum pudding.

As a special treat the children were allowed to eat downstairs, so Felix got to meet Oliver Snow, an unprepossessing child with carroty hair and a peevish expression. His eyes, much his best feature, were his mother's; tawny, with green flecks—lion's eyes, Felix thought—but his nose appeared to belong to someone else, his father probably, though he might of course grow into it. He acknowledged Felix's presence with the air of one who knows that life holds only unpleasant surprises, then turned his gaze upon the hare soup with a look of profound disapproval. He spent the first half of the meal picking things up on his fork and putting them back on the plate, but by the time the veal was served this occupation lost interest, and forgetting, or never having learned that children were there to be seen, not heard, he turned to Julian and said, "Can you taste your food?"

Surprised but always polite, Julian said, "Yes, of course."

"Because I read somewhere," Oliver went on, "that if you eat in the dark you can't taste what you're eating."

His unfamiliar accent drew attention. There was a

shocked silence, then Kitty said cheerfully, "Try not to be an idiot, Oliver. You can find out for yourself, you know, instead of asking stupid questions. Here, open your mouth and close your eyes." She picked up a strip of vegetable on her fork and put it in his mouth. "What are you eating?"

"Turnip," said Oliver, "and I hate it."

"That's very interesting," said Toby. "Is it just Oliver, or is there something to it?"

"Shut your eyes," said Felix. Toby obeyed and Felix fed him a bean.

"Bean," said Toby.

"Veal."

"You liar. Here, you try it."

Soon they were all laughing and accusing each other of cheating. Lady Millicent watched with incredulous horror her dinner guests spearing food from each others' plates and feeding it to their partners or, worse, to people across the table, making a good deal of mess and mostly failing to identify what it was they were eating. The vol-au-vent was unrewarding, and she thought she might resume possession of her dinner party, but when dessert came Julian drew her into the game. As always, Lady Millicent was unable to resist Julian's coaxing, and accurately identified a piece of suet from her plum pudding.

"Fluke," said Augustus.

"Oh no, my dear," Lady Millicent told him, "experience."

When Julian had first come into her life, Lady Millicent had bandaged her own eyes and, battling her terror of the dark, had taught herself to find her way about her own room, and presently through the house. The experiment, at first so frightening, bringing back memories of being shut in a dark room as in a coffin, had rewarded her with an extraordinary sensitivity of touch, smell, and hearing. Though it would never have occurred to her to do something so unladylike as playing games with food, it now appeared that her sense of taste too had refined itself, to the point where, challenged by Augustus, she easily distinguished currants from raisins, and lemon peel from orange. No one except Julian came anywhere near to equalling her performance, and though she could not really approve of such informality and hilarity at her dinner table, she was warmed by everyone's admiration, especially Julian's, who said, "You were wonderful. I had no idea you could do that."

After the ladies withdrew, the gentlemen continued the game. Augustus wondered whether they would be able to tell the difference between whisky, gin, and brandy blindfolded, and Toby and Felix assured him that they certainly could. This was a game after Toby's heart. He fetched bottles and glasses, and they tasted far more than was necessary to answer Augustus's question. When they finally went to the drawing room to join the ladies, they found it empty. Everyone had gone to bed.

Felix, who had made sure the day before that Kitty did not ride to hounds, sent word the next morning that he would not hunt.

"Hung over, I expect," said Toby to David and Lord Anthony when they met outside the Strafford Arms.

At Altondale David hunted, as he always had, in tweeds. Lady Millicent deplored this. It would have been unthinkable at Langland. But here, in what after twenty-five years of marriage she still thought of as the back of beyond, a small Yorkshire village where every farmer rode to hounds, foxhunting still held to its original purpose, which was not, whatever Lady Millicent might think, to separate those who could afford a scarlet coat from those who couldn't, but to have rip-roaring fun while keeping the foxes out of the hen runs. She therefore had to content herself by letting the perfection of her own turnout be a silent reproach to those less correctly appointed.

"Flixy doesn't get hung over," said David. "I expect he's up to something. You know how devious he is."

"I can't imagine what," said Toby, tipping back a whisky, while the hounds roiled at their feet and a huntsman's horn sounded thin and high across the park. Augustus's hunter pricked up his ears; the dogs whimpered with excitement. They handed their empty glasses to a waiter and galloped off, starting a fox who led them six miles over a country of hedgerows and fences before going to earth in a sett under an old coal mine where it was no earthly use trying to dig him out. But another fox broke cover almost at once, and they were off again. It was a perfect day, with long runs and hardly a check. Nothing could convince Toby that this wasn't as much fun for the fox as it was for him, except right at the last, of course, but he had the professional soldier's attitude toward violent death, and did not trouble his head about it.

In the early dusk of a December afternoon they trotted their blown, lathered horses back to the stable block and went in, very ready to wolf down scones and Christmas cakes.

Felix, it turned out, had spent his day in ways which were not only blameless but seemed, compared to the excitement of a day's hunting, unbelievably dull. He and Kitty had taken young Oliver for a long walk, so that Felix could show him the artificial waterfall, the gamekeeper's cottage with its awful reek of dead weasels and squirrels nailed up on a gallows as a warning to other predators, and the railway trestle, where they stood while the London express roared under their feet, covering them in black smoke; in short all the delights of his childhood summers at Altondale. Oliver had proved morose and uninterested. Nevertheless Felix had accepted Nannie's invitation to tea in the nursery with Oliver and Kitty.

"Nursery tea?" said Toby, not quite believing this, gulping a boiling cup of his own.

David laughed. "You must be full up with Christmas spirit."

On Christmas morning Julian and Oliver dived into the Christmas stockings which had appeared overnight tied to their bedposts. This was a new experience for Oliver, whose father had not approved of the heathen trappings surrounding the birth of Our Lord. He grew less and less peevish as he dug out tin soldiers, coloured pencils, a clockwork engine, and, in the toe, an orange and a shining new sixpence.

No one, not even Toby and Augustus, came down for breakfast on Christmas morning. Everyone felt torpid and liverish from the Christmas dinner—nine courses, twelve guests—which was an annual Strafford tradition, and one of the high points of Altondale's social year. In anticipation General Molyneux polished up his medals, Lady Lapitter rubbed her ear trumpet with a shammy till it shone, the two Molyneux girls got into a frightful quarrel about which of them was to wear their late mother's hair ornament of cairngorms and egret feathers, Mrs Harvey was laced by her daughters until she could, breathlessly, fit into her last year's best dress. Kitty had a little tussle with Calais, who had done something clever and Parisian with her "other" black dress.

"Oh, Calais," she wailed, "it's much too low."

"*Non*," said Calais. "At dinner, *il faut montrer ce qu'on a.*"

"But I don't have it," said poor Kitty.

"Neither does *miladi. Le bon dieu* 'elp those who 'elp themselves."

"Ruffles? Oh, Calais, I can't."

"You must," said Calais with such decision that Kitty gave in and even allowed Calais to do her hair, and touch her cheeks with rouge and her freckled nose with powder.

Lady Milly and Augustus's Christmas present to her had been a ruby which had belonged to the mother of a scapegrace revolutionary who was Kitty's ancestor. Calais fastened this to the black velvet ribbon Kitty wore around her neck, clipped, despite Kitty's protests, one of Lady Millicent's hair ornaments of diamonds and feathers in the glowing copper hair, and stood back, saying, "*Voilà*," like someone who has produced a rabbit out of a hat.

Kitty's transformation had its effect on Felix, who spilled a good deal of sherry at the sight of her. When she laughed at him, the ruby trembled like a drop of blood in the soft hollow of her throat. All through dinner his eyes returned to it, irresistibly. He could hardly attend to anything else, not to Lady Milly, in her new gown by Worth, nor the brave sparkle of Lady Lapitter's ear trumpet in the candle-light, nor the splendour of the hunting men in their scarlet coats. Throughout the evening he was scarcely aware of the festive company which sat around the Strafford table with smilax and holly winding down the centre, and ate its way steadily and without flagging through two kinds of soup (hare and clear), fish, fillet of beef, oyster patties, turkey, curried rabbit, partridges, a savoury and plum pudding, with the result that on Christmas morning no one except the children could face anything but a cup of tea and a Seidlitz powder.

At St Michael and All Angels holly and pine was wound around the font and choir stalls. The blanched light of the wintry sun poured in through the windows, turning the candleflames transparent. Grubby little boys with runny noses were transformed by cassock and surplice into angelic beings, who stood in the choir stalls and sang the anthem in high, perishable voices. Kitty, moved by a pure descant, put her arm around Oliver's shoulder, having a sudden, strong, if unlikely vision of him as one of these angelic creatures. Felix smiled at her. It was the first Christmas away from home for both of them. Both were happy to be here.

Christmas lunch at the vicarage, to which Toby and Felix were invited, was soothing in its nursery plainness of cutlets and Christmas pudding. Afterward Toby suggested a long walk up to High Fenton and across the ridge to the ruins of Fenton Abbey. It was a brilliant, cold day. From the crest of High Fenton they looked at the fields spread below them in their different shades of winter brown, with the stone walls winding along the folds of the hills. In the distance one could catch, now the leaves were down, a glimpse of the stable clock and the crisp shimmer of sun on the lake.

Toby, who would one day inherit most of the land at their feet, stood modestly by while the others admired, and settled themselves on broken bits of abbey wall to have a cigarette and grow philosophical about life and love in the pale winter sun.

It was Felix, of course, who introduced the topic of love. It was much on his mind, and he was never good at keeping things to himself. The others smoked and said, "Well, yes of course," "Oh, but Flixy . . ." "Yes, of course she . . . ," but mostly they let him ramble on while the sun finished its low circle of the hills and shadows fell upon them, so that they felt the cold and resumed their walk, still talking.

"Is that why you were looking out the forbidden degrees in the prayer books this morning?" asked Toby. "I wondered."

"They are very odd. 'A man may not marry his grandmother.' Who would want to?"

When their silence had lasted a moment too long, Anthony said politely, "She is only thirty. That isn't so very old."

"Flix is twenty."

"I'll get older."

"So will she."

David said, "Flixy, what exactly do you propose to do? She isn't a person you can set up in an apartment like Nellie de Lafayette. And you can't marry her. You'll have to marry tin mines and iron ore and a lady who comes with them."

"A papist lady," said Toby.

"My mother did not marry a Catholic."

"Nor did any of our mothers. That's neither here or there. You can't marry an American widow with a child and no money, whatever her age. None of us can."

"David can."

"The only one of us who's poor enough to marry for love."

"Rather a waste," said Anthony sadly. "David doesn't fall in love."

"Neither do I," said Toby, who had been in love only once, with the captain of his cricket eleven at Eton. It was then that he had taken to prayers and cold baths, had duly recovered, and had by now very nearly forgotten that such things were.

"I do," said Anthony. "I am."

"You're a younger son," said Felix. "Can't you please yourself?"

"Younger sons are dreadfully poor and I have expensive tastes. I shall have to marry ten thousand a year at least."

The road narrowed and they split up, first in Indian

119

file, and later, when it widened again, by twos, Felix and Anthony ahead, Toby and David trailing behind.

"But what am I going to do?" they heard Felix wail. "I can't just worship from afar like that silly knight in the poem."

"Sometimes afar is better," said Anthony.

"Fellow sufferers," said Toby, amused. "Is Fielding's passion as hopeless and unsuitable as Flixy's?"

"Even more so," said David.

"No ten thousand a year?"

"Not a bean."

Felix had not planned to spend the entire winter vacation at Altondale, had in fact made arragements to see people in London, to visit galleries and dealers, go to the opera and the theatre. Yet he stayed on, hunting when there was no frost, refusing an invitation to Frome when David and Anthony went there for the new year. Daily proximity failed to bring boredom and to put an end to so unsuitable an infatuation.

"Which proves it isn't infatuation," he said to David when he came back from Frome.

"Perhaps it will happen when we are back in Oxford," said David. "Distance may do what propinquity didn't."

"It would be rather nice in one way," said Felix. "Yet in another I wouldn't like it at all."

He asked Kitty whether he might write to her when he was back at Oxford. She was rather surprised at his formal German manners, but said yes, of course. "Only I won't be here any longer. I'm going to London."

"London?"

"Yes. I have to earn a living, you see. It's very kind of Cousin Augustus to have me here, and to offer to pay for Oliver's education. I can't refuse charity for Oliver, but I won't accept it for myself."

"But what will you do?"

"Give music lessons, like I did in Boston."

"Does that pay?"

"Not very much. But I don't need much, especially now that I don't have to think about Oliver. You know, I'm

120

looking forward to London. I'm not a country mouse by nature."

"Where will you live?"

"I don't know yet. Somewhere cheap. Cousin Augustus says Chesterfield Hill—that's his townhouse, you know—but that's ridiculous."

"Why is it ridiculous?"

"It's in Mayfair, Baron," she said, as if she were naming some forbidden quarter of town. "I'd have to buy proper clothes and behave like Lady Milly."

"Don't you want to behave like a lady?"

"Not her kind of lady."

"What kind of lady?" he asked and felt his heart giving a hard bump against his ribs.

"A lady who has some fun," said Kitty.

From someone like Nellie de Lafayette a statement like that could have been taken as an invitation to provide that fun. But Felix was never sure with Kitty. She reminded him of a story he had read one day while waiting for David in his rooms. It too had dealt with an American abroad—a girl, not a widow—whose behaviour, natural to her American upbringing, had been regarded by Europeans as great impropriety. She had finally been carried off by a fever, as a punishment, one was left to suppose, for having gone to the Colosseum in the dark with a young man.

He could never tell with Kitty what she would laugh at or where she would draw the line, quite suddenly and firmly, often about things he considered perfectly proper. He sometimes asked himself whether he had been tapping timidly at the door when he might have knocked down a wall. They did not even address each other by their first names yet.

This much at least he might remedy; gain a piece of ground before he went away. He said, "There is something I would like to ask you; not to call me Baron. After all, if I am a cousin of the Straffords, and you are a cousin of the Straffords, it must follow that we are cousins of each other."

She laughed, the festive laugh he liked so much, and said, "Does everyone at Oxford talk like that? Of course

121

I'll call you Cousin Felix if you like, and you can call me Cousin Kitty."

It was not what he had had in mind, adding as it did, a touch of incest to an already complicated state of affairs.

Augustus was very much exercised by Kitty's decision to go to London. He was fond of her and enjoyed having her about; he hated to think of her having to cope with straitened means, and above all he did not like to think of anyone he liked having to live in London.

Kitty was very fond of Augustus too, fond enough not to be able to tell him how dull she found living in the country; how desperately she longed for galleries and concerts, walking along lit streets, looking into the windows of fashionable shops. She could have told this to Lady Millicent and found ready sympathy, but she and Milly had somehow never quite hit it off. Her smile, when Kitty's move was under discussion, grew very pained and small indeed.

What, Lady Milly asked herself, would one's friends say? A poor relation in America was all very well; many of the best families had those, but a poor relation in London, where one knew people, was an embarrassment. Besides, what would Kitty do? She was not at all suited to being a governess or a lady's companion, and what other possibilities were there for a gentlewoman?

"I'll give music lessons, of course," Kitty said when Lady Millicent delicately brought up this distressing subject.

It was, Lady Milly supposed, respectable enough, though not what one had ever expected of a relation of one's husband, however distant and transatlantic.

"And where will you live?" asked Lady Millicent.

Kitty said, "Somewhere cheap," as she had said it to Felix.

In this matter Sir Abraham Montefiore was able to help. He had, he told Augustus over lunch at his club, recently bought a block of houses in Tite Street, and would be delighted to let Augustus's American cousin rent one. Augustus asked where Tite Street was exactly, and on being told Chelsea, put his ears back and said, "Oh, ah, is that quite . . . ?" for to Augustus Chelsea meant artists, loose living, that awful bounder Oscar Wilde, orgies, and opium. He was reassured, however, when they went to look at the houses of solid, hideous brick, which Sir Abraham had bought as a speculation. One couldn't, he thought, visualize much *vie de bohème* going on behind such a dull, liver-coloured facade.

Sir Abraham named a very reasonable rental, of which Augustus, unknown to Kitty, proposed to pay half. Subject to Kitty's approval, everything was settled that afternoon.

Kitty, while freely admitting that it was a very ugly house, was delighted with it all the same. Its walls were thick, it was on the river end of the road, and Chelsea, still almost a village, with the King's Road not yet paved, delighted her.

Lady Millicent had insisted on sending her a housemaid from Altondale for the sake of respectability, Sir Abraham found her pupils among his numerous musical friends, Felix often came to take her to the opera or for long walks along the towpath, while Augustus, who had taken to attending the House of Lords more frequently than had been his habit, was given his own armchair by the fire, from where he could bemusedly listen to Kitty's new Chelsea friends, who always seemed to be sitting all over the floor, arguing noisily about modern art, modern music, free love, Fabianism, socialism, and someone called Dr Froyd, who, if he had indeed written the kind of things Kitty's friends said he had, ought to have been horsewhipped.

Women who had cut their hair short, and men who had grown theirs long, demonstrated their accomplishments by showing pictures which looked to Augustus like cubes done in brown gravy, and banging out on Kitty's piano (a gift from Augustus) compositions which sounded like the cat being sick. Poets, who under no circumstances could stand comparison with Mr Kipling, declaimed verses of impenetrable opacity, while everyone talked about plays by people called Ibsen, Strindberg, and Wedekind, all of which seemed to deal with people of doubtful morals and unstable home lives, and had to be performed in out-of-the-way theatres in Hammersmith and Shepherd's Bush. And who, said Augustus, giving Lady Millicent a censored account of these doings, was taking Kitty to see these unsuitable performances? Cousin Felix was who.

"Felix," said Lady Millicent, more upset by this last piece of information than by all the rest.

"I think they go about together quite a bit."

"But Augustus!"

"They're cousins, m'dear."

"Not really."

"No," said Augustus thoughtfully. "Not within the forbidden degrees at any rate."

Within a week after this conversation Felix had a letter from his father, suggesting that he might consider spending the spring term at Harvard rather than Oxford. Spring, Hesso had been given to understand, was the only really good time to be in New England, the summers being too hot and the winters too cold.

Felix knew of course that the family was moving into action. No doubt Lady Milly (or even Augustus) had dropped a hint in a letter that he was seeing a great deal of a poor American widow, and it was proposed to move him away from danger. He obeyed with sadness but without reluctance. His pursuit of Kitty Snow was the peculiarly painful kind that can have no end. Even were he to win her love, what could he do with it? It was as clear to him as it was to everyone else that he could not marry a widow ten years older than himself and quite penniless, and it had not really needed David to point out that Kitty was not the kind of woman one establishes in an apartment and keeps on the side. To Felix the world of women was very clearly divided into those who did, and those who did not. He was in a dilemma that had no solution and escape was almost welcome.

His farewells from Kitty were unsatisfactory. She said she would miss him, it is true, but it was a promise most casually made in the same breath as the assurance that he would love Harvard and the request that he would write Oliver, who collected stamps. He did not know that both

124

Kitty and her maid, Annie, stood at the window after he had left and watched his slight figure move down the street with a deep sigh of regret.

"Oh dear, Annie," said Kitty.

"Yes, miss."

Felix had turned the corner and they could no longer see him. Kitty sighed once more. "Tell you what, Annie, make us a cup of tea."

"Yes, miss. Shall I put in a drop of brandy?"

"Yes, Annie. The situation does seem to call for it."

The friends were dispersed once again. Toby was in Ireland. After Sandhurst he had joined Princess Victoria's Own Yorkshire Rifles, recently returned from India and now stationed in Ulster, where trouble was expected to erupt at any moment. Toby liked Ireland. It was splendid hunting country, the local gentry was hospitable and fond of drink, and if the peasantry was poorer and more exploited than the poorest Yorkshire farm labourer, that was not the kind of thing to trouble Toby's mind.

The Vickies were nowhere near Larne on the night when twenty thousand rifles manufactured at Landeck Stahl Fabrik and sold illegally through a good many middlemen, were unloaded in the dark and rushed to Belfast on motorcycles, but, Toby wrote David, they were all hoping for a good scrap on July 12, a hope which David received with very little sympathy.

This being their third year in Oxford, Anthony and David had moved out of their colleges into shared lodgings, a pretty Queen Anne house which Ned and Clem Barton had rented the year before. The peregrine had been brought back from exile at Frome and stood on a curved wooden perch over a circle of sand in the garden.

Sadness tainted all Anthony's days. The Trinity term had begun, and no one knows more keenly than a lover how terribly quickly eight weeks can draw to an end. Though he knew it bored David, he could not keep off the subject of their coming separation; what will we do, how will I bear it?

"You will become a cavalry subaltern in India," David

said, "pig-sticking and clapping your hands for chota pegs, whatever they may be, going to tea with Mrs Hauksbee and falling in love with her nubile daughter. As for me . . ."

"Why not stay on another year and work for a fellowship. You know your tutor says you're sure to get one. I expect I could talk my people into letting me stay in England another year."

"I have to have something to live on, Anthony. I'm skint, literally."

"Why not talk to your father? He wants you to get a fellowship, you know he does."

"I can't ask him for money. Freddy's coming up to Oxford, my sister Agnes is marrying a curate—he'd support me for another year while the family lives on bread and mousetrap cheese."

"I wish I could help."

"I wish you could. Now if you were your MP brother, you might need a secretary. I think I could do that quite nicely."

David had not mentioned the idea of being a secretary idly. It was a step he had been considering for some time. Apart from being decorative and possessed of good manners, he had few qualifications for such a job, but he did not see why that should hinder him. He could hand teacups with the best of them, and wrote a neat and legible hand.

The notion had first struck him when Lucas Ryder had come to Oxford to give the Mesurier Lectures on English Prosody. David had fallen in love with the poetry of Lucas Ryder while still a schoolboy at St Dunstan's, and had carried his books like a talisman in his pocket long after he had the poems by heart. When he had tried to picture the poet, it had usually been in exalted terms, someone like Shelley, splendour moving among shadows, a schoolboy notion which died painlessly at first sight of the poet. Lucas Ryder, who at the time of the Mesurier Lectures was in his mid-fifties, was a formidable man with the look of a personage rather than a person. Andrew said he looked like a hanging judge who enjoys his work; Clemence thought he was more like one of those Roman emperors who are described in the Latin bits of the *Decline and Fall*. "You know, the kind who held the corrupt empire together by day and feasted all night on peacock breasts and lark's tongues and beautiful boys."

There had been in fact a rather beautiful young man in Lucas Ryder's entourage who appeared to be a kind of private secretary, and it had occurred to David that this must be an interesting and pleasant way to earn one's living. He did not know how one went about getting such a job—did one write a letter to a man as famous as Lucas Ryder saying that he was one's favourite English poet? The idea seemed gauche and even ludicrous. David had never met anyone's private secretary and could not ask advice, but suspected, correctly, that, as with most other things in life, it was a matter of introductions and knowing the right people.

The Duchess of Frome had, in her London days, been a keen, if undiscriminating, literary hostess. Henry James had sipped china tea in her salon, but so had Anthony Hope and Ernest Bramah, and no one knew which she preferred. When David, spending the Easter holidays at Frome with Anthony, mentioned the Mesurier Lectures, the Duchess said, "Dear Lucas, he used to come to all my parties. His plays are delightful, I think, but I must confess I can never understand the poems. I'm always sure I shall—they look so simple on the page—but when I begin to read them, I seem to slide off their smooth surface. What about you, Anthony?"

"I think I have much the same problem. On the whole I prefer my poems in French. You must ask David; he's our great Ryder admirer. He sat through all the lectures."

"I can *always* understand dear David's poems," said the Duchess. "They are quite delightful. You ought to send some to Mr Ryder, David. He is sure to adore them."

David rewarded this happy suggestion with one of his best smiles, but said, "I couldn't do that, Duchess, I'd never dare. And I don't know Mr Ryder."

"But I know him very well. If you will let me, it would give me great pleasure to send him your poems."

David demurred as long as a charmingly modest young man should, but in the end the Duchess had her way, as he had always meant her to.

All his adult life Lucas Ryder was introduced as someone who needs no introduction. Success had come to him with his first book, and finding him a pleasant host had not deserted him since. He wrote for the better part of his life in a peculiar vacuum; there were no other major poets writing in England. Tennyson and Browning were dead; Hardy was still largely considered a novelist. As a playwright he was up against the formidable competition of George Bernard Shaw, and the great popularity of Barrie and Pinero, but his fellow poets scribbled verses of sheep and sheep meadows, pleasant enough, no doubt, but aptly described by Lucas Ryder himself in a review of *Georgian Poetry*, as pastoral piffle.

Even at Oxford, where it is not done to go to lectures, Lucas Ryder's had been packed to the last seat.

David had made no effort at the time to meet the poet. He never did anything as part of a crowd. But while he sat talking with Anthony about his future, he had a letter in his pocket from Lucas Ryder's secretary, inviting him to tea at the Dower House, Rye.

"What can you be doing?" said Anthony the next morning, finding David surrounded by *Bradshaw* and several pages of paper with numbers scribbled on them.

"I'm trying to work out a timetable for getting to Rye at teatime with a stopover in London to visit the Elgin Marbles."

"I shouldn't bother," said Anthony, quoting an earnest tourist Felix had once claimed to have overheard in the British Museum; "they're all broken." He picked up the timetables and said, "It seems a fearful lot of trouble for a cup of tea."

"Don't be such a Philistine. It's Lucas Ryder's tea. Look at it in the nature of a pilgrimage. Pilgrims expect to go through a lot of trouble."

"Be sure to tell him that. He'll lap it up, I expect."

"I'll try and weave it unobtrusively into the conversation. Why are you angry, Anthony?"

"I'm not angry. Well, yes, I am. David, must you be quite such a tart about this?"

David looked at him in silence, and for one moment Anthony had a glimpse of someone he scarcely knew behind the beautiful face and charming manners. Then David smiled and said, "I know. Society has some rather nasty words for what I am about to do, but society troubles itself very little about the sons of poor parsons, so they must take trouble for themselves. Probably nothing at all will come of it, and school-mastering will engulf me in the end."

"Yes. Don't expect *me* to wish you luck."

On a bright day at high tide the shimmer of the sun on the water of the estuary trembled in the air and almost hurt the eyes. Watery reflections danced on the ceiling of Lucas Ryder's study. All the windows stood open to the sun and the shrill warning cries of nesting marsh birds.

Lucas Ryder balled up a piece of paper and threw it at the wastebasket, but missed. "It's definitely stopped," he said to his secretary, "right in the middle of a poem too, blast it. Still, it's nice to have it over with for a time. Like getting over flu."

"I have a feeling you are getting into one of your irresponsible moods," said the secretary, picking up the crumpled paper and putting it tidily into the wastebasket. Lucas Ryder agreed that he probably was.

Irresponsible moods regularly followed one of his bouts of poetry. All his other work, essays, criticism, even the plays, were written with disciplined, daily application, but his poetry came upon him like a Pentecostal curse, which for weeks and sometimes months allowed him neither rest, sleep, urbanity, nor mental balance. It was like an illness—flu was putting it very mildly—and his recoveries, coming as suddenly, left him lighthearted and light-headed. At such times, as a young man, he had set out on long tiresome journeys, up the Amazon or across the Sahara. At the exact midpoint, when it would have been as much trouble to turn back as to go on, he usually repented of the whole enterprise, began to long for hot baths and dry sherry, and out of sheer frustration and bad temper settled down to writing a book about it. As he grew older and less inclined to physical exertion, he committed follies more easily remedied; bought a new motorcar or took a new lover.

His present secretary, familiar with such moods, wondered whether his own tenure with Lucas Ryder was drawing to an end. In part this would depend on the guest they were expecting for tea. He had read the poems (undergraduate stuff, Lucas Ryder had said of all but two), but he had also read the Duchess's letter. "He is a delightful young man," the Duchess had written, with the word "delightful" underlined twice, "so beautiful to look at, and quite unspoiled where almost anyone would have grown vain." "Quite" and "vain" were underlined as well.

The secretary mentally absolved the Duchess of any wish to pander. He was certain that she had no suspicions of Lucas's private life; to her he was a charming bachelor, and during her social days in London she had done her ingenious best to find him a suitable wife. Yet, had she got a fee for bringing them together, she could hardly have written a more cleverly phrased letter. Of all social vices, Lucas Ryder held, vanity was the most destructive to relationships, because it was so boring. The secretary, who was very vain himself, and not much good at hiding it, was curious to meet this latest paragon of the Duchess's. As for himself, he was not greatly concerned. In such matters Lucas Ryder had a reputation for behaving honourably. Among his large circle of distinguished acquaintances there would undoubtedly materialize a post rather better than the present one. It was only the humiliation of the thing, and people in such positions soon grow accustomed to being humiliated.

David arrived in Rye in time to have a look around and let himself be beguiled by the pretty town built on the slope of a steep hill. If he had wanted to live in another small town, which he didn't—he wanted London and city life and liveliness—there would have been no place more easy to fall in love with than this town of narrow cobbled streets, its cottages leaning their roofs together like gossiping crones, its larger houses impeccably Queen Anne or George I at the very latest. From the church tower one could see for miles over the reclaimed marsh dotted with sheep, to the estuary gleaming in the spring sun, and ship masts rocking tranquilly in Rye Harbour.

He stood for a few moments outside Lamb House, wondering respectfully whether Mr Henry James was even now at work on one of his convoluted, beautifully balanced sentences, had a quick look at the thirteenth-century Ypres Tower (pronounced Wipers by the locals), and then set out along the coast road toward the clump of willows which hid the Dower House from view.

He pulled the bell punctually at four, and was admitted by a young man who introduced himself as Mr Trevelyan, and was not, David noted, the same young man Mr Ryder had had with him at Oxford. He reflected that Lucas Ryder appeared to change secretaries rather frequently, and followed Mr Trevelyan into a house which was like only one other he had ever seen.

It was very light, for the walls were not papered, but painted a creamy white which gave back the sunlight streaming through the windows. The floors were bare, the furniture appeared to be for use rather than show, no swags of drapery kept out the leaping reflections of water. Not only were there no dead birds and dried flowers under glass, no pampas grass and overmantels, the house looked as if there never could have been any such clutter within its walls. Nothing had been taken away. The rooms were as the owner had meant them to be, spacious, light, and orderly.

For sole ornament there was a blue vase filled with cut flowers, and over the chimneypiece a portrait of a man who looked like a hanging judge and a woman with a profile like a Roman coin. When the secretary said, "Mr Ryder's parents," David was not in the least surprised.

Then Lucas Ryder came in, introductions were made, and David, who would in any case have said something agreeable, was able to say, "What a beautiful house," and mean it.

"Oh, do you like it? Most of my friends think it looks like a barracks, or, as one put it, as if the bailiffs had just been through it."

"They left all the best pieces of furniture," said David, "very unlike bailiffs, I imagine. I've only ever seen one other house like this; the one George III built at Kew. I've read somewhere that he preferred it to all his palaces."

"Yes," said Lucas Ryder, "I know the house in Kew. This one's of the same period. It was built by the Lord Longacre of the day for his mother-in-law; his very own contribution, it was said, to her rheumatism."

"I suppose it's silly to judge people by their houses," said David, "but I must admit that when I saw the one in Kew I instantly revised my opinion of George III, and decided that he must have been not only a charming person but one of our better kings."

Lucas Ryder noted to himself that his guest had a nice way with a compliment; he didn't come straight out with it, leaving you shuffling your feet and saying, "Oh, that old thing," but tucked it neatly inside the conversation, so one could put it aside and enjoy it later. He turned to his secretary and said, "Will you tell Mrs Placid there will be three for tea, Bunny. If Mr Harvey has walked all the way from Rye, he must be very ready for it."

David caught himself thinking, Bunny forsooth, and as the secretary went out noted a look of amused speculation in Lucas Ryder's eye which made him wonder uneasily whether Mr Ryder read minds.

"Is your cook really called Mrs Placid?" he asked. "It sounds almost too good to be true."

"Yes. She isn't a very good cook, but I engaged her on the strength of her name, hoping that it would have influenced her personality."

Tea was carried in by a housemaid. Bunny Forsooth handed cups very nicely. Lucas Ryder, going back to what they had been talking about, said, "It's odd when you come to think of it how kings are taught to us by categories. Good Queen Bess, Monstrous Richard III, Merry Charles,

132

Mad George. As if they'd ever only done the one thing. Have you ever in all your life been taught one good thing about James I? Yet he was responsible for the King James Version of the Bible—the only work of art ever produced by a committee—and Shakespeare did most of his mature work under him rather than Elizabeth. And what do we learn in school? That he hated tobacco and drooled."

"Perhaps the English don't like their royalty imported from Scotland," said David. "Or from Germany, for that matter."

"Or kings who have favourites," said Bunny meaningfully.

David did not object to this rather heavy-handed introduction of the subject. In a country where such tastes can get you two years in Pentonville, it was as well to play with all the cards on the table. Lucas Ryder, however, perhaps feeling that the foray was a trifle premature, said, "That would hardly apply to George III, who was very happily married. And look how sentimental we English are about Richard Lionheart."

"We were very unkind to Charles I and Edward II," said Bunny with the tenaciousness of the stupid. Lucas gave it up.

"How is the Duchess?" he asked. "I haven't sen her for ages."

"She is very well," said David, "but please don't tell her I said so. She would never forgive me."

"No, she wouldn't like that at all," said Lucas Ryder, laughing, and since Bunny had brought up the subject, decided it might as well be settled once and for all. "She says you're great friends with one of her boys; I forget, was it Andrew or Anthony?"

"It's Lord Anthony," said David. He often wondered afterward what would have happened if he had said that it was Lord Andrew. Would he have been given a cup of tea and a watercress sandwich and been sent on his way?

"Ah yes, Anthony," said Lucas, not displeased. "Tell me about yourself. What will you do after Oxford?"

Through the open windows came the smell of new-cut grass. A breeze from the estuary stirred the curtains and

133

fingered the pages of an open book like an inquisitive guest. With a sigh David said, "I don't quite know. Schoolmastering, I expect."

Lucas held out his cup for more tea. "You don't sound as if you'll like that very much."

"I won't like it at all. But I must earn my living, you see. My father is a clergyman, quite a poor one, with two more sons to educate and five daughters to marry off." David had long since discovered that far from despising him for his poverty, people tended to like these frank admissions, and he made them, these days, more often than not.

"What would you have liked to do if money were no object?" Mr Trevelyan asked.

"I think I should have liked to be a gilded young ass about town," said David.

Lucas laughed. "Not a poet?" he asked.

"I should hardly dare to mention such an ambition in this house."

"Why not? I thought your sonnet about Thucydides very good indeed. How did you come to write it?"

"A German friend, who's a reserve officer, was reading Thucydides one night at Oxford. He says he reads it as a corrective for too much military enthusiasm. When he came to the part where the Athenian army embarks for Syracuse, pouring libations from gold and silver cups, all those glorious ships racing each other as far as Aegina, hurrying off to defeat and slavery in the quarries, he read it out loud to me. And the next morning I woke with the sonnet more or less ready in my head."

"Just like that? You write easily then?"

"I think one ought to, don't you?" said David, it being one of the most cherished tenets of the Fielding set that art ought to be achieved without huffing and puffing.

"I'm the wrong person to ask. When I'm writing I go about like Sir Philip Sidney, biting my truant pen and beating myself for spite," said Lucas Ryder, and David realized that he was being politely reproved for talking rubbish.

"I find that difficult to believe," he said to retrieve the

situation. "Reading your poems I always have the impression that they arrive as easily and perfectly shaped as a new-laid egg."

Lucas Ryder laughed at this, but Bunny Trevelyan, watching David's easy progress, said acidly, "You are from the country, I take it."

David, thinking, Careful, Bunny, people like us mustn't show temper, said cheerfully, "Darkest Yorkshire."

Lucas Ryder said, "Come and see my bit of beach. It belongs to the Longacres, the big house on the hill, but I have the use of it." They went out through the French windows. Bunny Trevelyan stayed behind, which David considered an encouraging sign. "The last dowager who lived here," Lucas Ryder went on, "was quite dotty by all accounts. She was the widow of an admiral who went down with his ship, and from the day she got the news of his death she stopped all the clocks and would have stopped time itself if she could have. She survived him by thirty years, but she insisted on having her clothes and her servants' uniforms made in the fashion of the year when her husband died. I saw her once when I was here on a visit. She looked exactly like Queen Victoria, short and dumpy, with a big black hoopskirt and a lace bonnet. One day she told her maid that the admiral was coming home and she was going out to meet him. Apparently she walked into the sea under the impression that he was expecting her. The house got a reputation for being haunted after that, quite undeservedly, I'm sorry to say. Or perhaps I'm just not the kind of person ghosts show themselves to."

"What kind of person do you think ghosts prefer?"

"In my experience, housemaids who shriek and drop a tray loaded with your best Lowestoft."

Their talk ranged easily, neither being the kind of conversationalist who bones up on one subject and keeps at it till it and his hearers are exhausted. From ghosts they got on to romantic poetry (David preferred Shelley, Lucas Keats), the advantages for a poet of dying young ("It's good for one's reputation," said Lucas; "otherwise I consider it a mistake"), and Greek versus Roman civilization. David opted for the Greeks. "It isn't their vices that get me down about the Romans but their food," he said. "I can't feel for a people who put fish entrails in a jar, let them rot, and use the resulting mess as if it were Worcestershire sauce."

Lucas mentioned the black broth of the Spartans.

"Yes, there is that. Actually the later Greeks got fairly decadent too. There is a recipe in Athenaeus for a dish made of birds' brains, eggs, wine, and roses."

Lucas Ryder, who as a rule chose his secretaries for their looks rather than their brains, was immensely enjoying his walk with someone who was decorative, intelligent, and well-read into the bargain. "How disgusting one's ancestors are," he said.

"Ours were probably very earnest, dull Britons who painted themselves blue and ate bread and cheese."

Their walk had taken them past the water meadows of the estuary down to the beach. The water, scarcely moving with the outgoing tide, reflected the rays of the evening sun. Above the level marsh the town on its hill seemed suspended in the transparent gold of the air.

"It's the way I would imagine a mirage to be," said David.

"Or one of those towns sailors claim to see submerged in the water, with all the church bells chiming."

From the marsh came a moorhen's warning call; a flight of swallows fled toward the tall grass. A sense of unease stilled the lively bird-chatter in the water meadow. Lucas looked up and pointed. Like a tiny cross a kestrel hung in the sky, riding the wind. Lucas quoted a line of poetry David did not recognize ("I caught this morning morning's minion") and noted the quick leap of pleasure in his companion's eyes.

"It's beautiful," said David after a moment's silence. "Is it yours?"

"How I wish it were. It's by a Father Hopkins, a friend of my Oxford days."

The clock on the tower of St Mary's struck three quarters, its sound carrying clearly across the marsh. David said, "If that is a quarter of six, I have to catch my train."

"I'm sorry you have to leave so soon," said Lucas, meaning it. He was dining out, otherwise he would have invited him to stay. Instead he found himself saying, "My secretary is leaving me soon. I don't know if such a post would interest you."

David, who had not expected success to arrive quite so promptly, allowed Lucas one of his rare smiles.

"Think it over," said Lucas. "It might not suit you. I live very quietly here and see few people."

The sparrow hawk had fallen from the sky, but they had not noticed him stoop. The swallows darted across the grass again, showing their creamy bellies. David said, "I don't have to think it over. I should consider it a very great honour."

Bunny Trevelyan saw David to the door. David wondered whether he suspected that he was about to leave his present employment. He was being just a touch too charming. David respected him for this. Had the situation been reversed, he would have done the same.

Chapter 7

The flower beds at the Buckingham Palace end of St James's Park were planted with red geraniums, and Kitty, who was shaking with nerves, said morbidly to her companion that they made her think of lakes of blood.

"Rubbish," said Mrs Castlemain, weaving a stout chain through the palace railings. When she had finished, she handcuffed herself to Kitty and pushed home the lock. "There," she said, "if they want to arrest us they will have to take us both." She dropped the key down her firmly corseted front with a flourish.

"Oh, Cass," said Kitty, remembering Lady Millicent's warnings, "do you think you should? Suppose they try to look for it."

"Let them try," said Mrs Castlemain, a note of challenge ringing in her voice. "Let them if they dare."

Kitty looked admiringly at her friend, cheered by being chained to someone so intrepid. Mrs Castlemain had a deserved reputation for belligerence; no one had been more delighted than she when the Women's Social and Political Union had turned from polite and legal protest to militancy. Policemen dreaded having to arrest her, presiding magistrates muttered oaths when she appeared in their court, even prison wardens groaned when she was delivered to their door. Kitty found her a great comfort.

Mrs Castlemain had been her very first friend at the WSPU. A woman of vision and imagination, she had taken one look at the slender American widow and had seen her possibilities.

"How absolutely splendid," she had said. "You are exactly the kind of person we are looking for."

"Really?" Kitty had asked. "In what way?"

"It's your figure, my dear. The very thing."

No one had ever told Kitty that her figure was the very thing before. Both her Bostonian mother-in-law and Lady Millicent's Calais had been frank to the point of brutality about her lack of it. She gazed in some bewilderment at Mrs Castlemain, and said, "My figure?"

"Well, your not having one," said Mrs Castlemain, equally frank. "We can dress you up as a young man, you see."

"I'm not sure . . ."

"Of course you'll have to cut your hair."

Kitty had not been offered a chair by her redoubtable new acquaintance. She sank into the nearest one without being invited to do so.

"Mr Asquith is going to speak against the Conciliation Bill next week. We'll dress you up as a young man-about-town. You shall sit in the Visitors' Gallery and at the appropriate time you will break out the WSPU banner and shout VOTES FOR WOMEN."

"I see," Kitty said weakly.

"You won't be doing it alone," said Mrs Castlemain reassuringly. "There will be others. None of you young gels have figures nowadays. It's not attractive, but it is very much to our purpose."

"I'm not a 'young gel'," said Kitty, this being so far the only arguable point Mrs Castlemain had made. "I'm a middle-aged widow from America, and I really don't think I can cut my hair and dress up in trousers to shout VOTES FOR WOMEN at Mr Asquith. Couldn't I go as myself?"

"They would never let you in. You see, we've all heckled them so much and made such nuisances of ourselves, that they won't let anyone in skirts come near them nowadays. And surely your hair is a trifling thing to sacrifice for The Cause." Mrs Castlemain always spoke of it like that, in capital letters.

So Kitty had cut her hair for The Cause, had put on trousers, had shouted VOTES FOR WOMEN in the House of Commons, had unfurled WSPU banners at public meetings, and heckled speakers, and as a final argument permitted herself to be chained to the palace railing to direct the attention of His Majesty to the plight of voteless women.

Mrs Castlemain raked the windows of Buckingham Palace and said, "If he is looking, it must be from behind a curtain. I cannot see anyone at the windows."

"Do you suppose he'll look at all? He wasn't a bit interested when Miss Bloomfield knelt down in front of him and begged him to stop forced feeding."

"Well," said Mrs Castlemain, "he is a man, after all. One can't expect too much." Her own husband, a suffragan bishop, had imbibed. Kitty supposed one couldn't call it drink when it was a bishop. But no matter how politely his failing was spoken of, Bishop Castlemain had indulged it until he died of it, and his behaviour had given his relict an uncompromising view of men in general.

"The queen's not much better, though she is a woman," said Kitty. "When Emily Davison threw herself in front of the king's horse, he asked after the horse and she asked after the jockey, but it was Emily who was dead."

"A very unbalanced gel," said Mrs Castlemain, who had marched, dressed in purple, at the head of the funeral procession.

Her eye went up and down the palace railings, checking that all was in order. While she and Kitty had been talking, women had arrived by singles and twos, and were now standing against the railings like so many country cousins gawking at the palace. Like country cousins they wore large shawls and carried unfashionably capacious handbags.

"I think everything is ready," said Mrs Castlemain to Kitty. "We can begin."

At her signal, WSPU banners and placards suddenly appeared from the depths of the unfashionable handbags. Shouts of VOTES FOR WOMEN rang out. A crowd collected almost instantly and began to catcall and boo. Kitty was happy to see a policeman approaching. She was far more frightened of the hostile crowd than she was of the police, though the London constabulary had amazed her by its ferocity. They were not at all the courteous English bobbies of whom visitors said, "English police are wonderful."

She had undoubtedly been the more shocked because she had come upon it newly and had not, like Mrs Castlemain, lived through the years when suffragettes, marching earnestly behind their placards and banners, had been considered a great joke, and had been treated with condescending kindness. Gradually feelings had grown exacerbated, culminating in a six-hour battle in Parliament Square on a day always referred to by the WSPU as Black Friday. Since then those large, slow, pink-faced men, feeling themselves made fools of by minds more subtle than theirs, defeated constantly in the exercise of their duty by the guerilla tactics not of male bandits—this could have been endured if not tolerated—but by females, ladies by and large (not counting Sylvia Pankhurst's frightful shock troops of East End working women), who had not long ago been content to sit in their cluttered parlours, sewing a fine seam and caring tenderly for the fragile egos of their menfolk. Something had turned them into creatures bewitched, monsters against whom it was entirely permissible to use the only kind of force in which men were superior: to trample, kick, lock up, ram metal gags into their mouths and rubber tubing down their throats.

All the same, Kitty, surrounded by a jeering mob, was happy to see a very young, very large policeman approach. He must have been new on the job, or he would not have been deceived by the rotund, motherly air of Mrs Castlemain into addressing her first.

"Now then, now then," he said, "what's all this? You know you're not allowed to demonstrate here, miss."

"Mind whom you call miss, young man," said Mrs Castlemain, drawing herself up to such height as she could command. "I am the mother of six sons, every one of them born in wedlock."

"Now, now," said the young policeman, blushing at the mention of such an intimate subject. "We don't want any trouble. Just you move along quietly, miss."

Mrs Castlemain said politely, "I am sorry, but I can't." She pulled aside her shawl, showing the chain. As if she had given a signal, every woman along the railings began to clank and rattle her chains. "Lumme," said the young policeman, "now what do I do?"

He was hit in the shoulder by a handful of dirt from the geranium beds. It had been meant for the chained women, but well-meant intentions seldom improve these situations.

"You might attempt to keep order among the rabble," said Mrs Castlemain grandly. "*We* shall not escape you."

The young policeman would very much have liked to escape her, and was relieved to see re-inforcements arrive in a phalanx of blue from the other end of the park.

For the next hour London's beleaguered police worked hard at keeping the mob off the women, who rattled their chains and howled like banshees for the vote. Geraniums were torn from the flower beds and flew through the air with a good deal of dirt still clinging to their roots. Saws and burglar tools arrived from Scotland Yard, and the police, much hampered by kicks from dainty black boots, set to work freeing those who had no wish to be freed.

Presently everyone was stuffed into a prison van. Kitty, still chained to Mrs Castlemain, was half laughing, half shaking with reaction, and the anticipation of what was to come.

It was the first time she had been arrested. Mrs Castlemain had been in prison eight times, hunger-striking and being forcibly fed each time. She now put her free hand on Kitty's shoulder and said briskly, "Not to worry, my dear."

"What happens now, Cass?"

"I expect they will book us overnight and have us up

before the magistrate in the morning. We make a big row, shout him down and throw things so that he'll understand that no mere man has the right to decide what is to be done with women. Then, I expect, he'll remand us to Holloway."

"Oh, Cass."

"Ah well," said Mrs Castlemain, "there it is, you know; it's no use fretting."

After a night spent in crowded cells, the women were brought up before the magistrate in Bow Street. In spite of their shouts of protest, and much flinging about of powder and even boots, he managed to sentence old acquaintances like Mrs Castlemain to two weeks in prison. Kitty, as a first offender, was let off with a warning. She felt she ought to beg him to send her to jail with the others, but could not help being relieved when Mrs Castlemain said, "Don't be a fool, child. You can do a lot more damage out here than in jail."

Then the van came to take her friend away to Holloway and the feeding tube. Kitty wept, and feeling bedraggled and let down walked to Chelsea where Annie met her with a nice cup of tea with a drop of rum in it. She spent the rest of the day addressing envelopes filled with red pepper to the members of His Majesty's government, which soothed her jangled nerves.

David arrived at the Dower House at the beginning of July. He was taken by a parlourmaid to the terrace, where Lucas Ryder was drinking tea, a book propped against the pot, its pages kept from blowing in the breeze by a very sticky jar of honey. David, who had been brought up by his father to treat books with respect and consideration, could hardly bear it when Lucas, saying, "How nice to see you," marked his place with the butterknife and told the parlourmaid to bring another cup and a fresh pot of tea. "Did you have a pleasant trip?" He picked up the book to assassinate a wasp, adding the squashed body to the butter and honey stains. Noting a disapproving expression on David's face, he said, "Does that bother you? The book or the wasp?"

"I'm sorry," said David. "Was I looking pained? It's the book."

"Well, thank goodness for that. I once had a secretary who'd grown up in India and wouldn't swat flies or step on beetles. He said they were working out the great chain of being. It was rather a bore, feeling one ought to apologize every time one stepped on an ant."

"I don't at all mind swatting flies."

"Only books?"

David, who had thought he might be shy of Lucas Ryder, of whom he was very much in awe, was relieved to find himself talking so easily. He said. "It's my father's fault, really. I think he secretly believes that books have feeling and scream silently when one dog-ears a page or shuts the paperknife inside to mark one's place."

"That's a very idolatrous notion for an Anglican vicar," said Lucas Ryder. "Some atavism at work, I expect."

"You mean the thought of some monk spending his life illuminating a book of hours?"

"Fortunately the printing press has freed us to treat books with no more respect than newspapers. I'm afraid you'll have to unlearn your upbringing with me. You see, I get sent an enormous amount of books, most of which aren't worth reading, let alone keeping. Come, I'll show you."

They went to Lucas's study, a large, sunny room facing the kitchen garden. "I used to work in a room that looked out over the water meadows," he said, "but I found that I was capable of sitting for hours gazing pensively at the view instead of getting any writing done. So I moved myself in here. Somehow peasticks and rows of cabbages offer far less temptation to daydreaming. Look." He pointed to a large table which stood along one wall. It was covered with proof sheets, manuscripts, letters, and books, sent by publishers, authors, booksellers, all of whom wanted introductions, reviews, or just a kind word. "Trevelyan's only been gone for a week," said Lucas, "and look at it."

It had not occurred to David that others, like himself, might send their poems to Lucas Ryder; undoubtedly having them accompanied by a letter from the Duchess of Frome had done them no harm. He sent a grateful thought to Lord Anthony and said, "How awful. It never occurred to me when the Duchess said she wanted to send you my poems—what a bore for you."

"It had its compensations. Do you think you could cope? Don't bother now, leave it for tomorrow. It's much too pretty a day. Let's go for a walk before dinner."

This, David was to find, more or less set the pattern for his future days. They worked in the morning and David got very good at deciphering the scrawled palimpsests which constituted Lucas Ryder's manuscripts. Like many another writer Lucas tended to go into a panic at the sight of a clean white page, so that he preferred to do his writing on the backs of people's letters, lists of books, or even the margins of pages he had already filled. David answered Lucas's mail, handed teacups when they had guests, exerted himself to be amusing company on their walks, and even tried to master the typewriter, a large, baleful monster which stood on a table of its own in the little room he used for an office. But David and machinery never got on well, and he soon gave it up.

The servants treated him, as they will with people of marginal station, such as governesses and secretaries, with a finely calculated degree of respectful insolence. But even here a handsome face and an occasional smile did wonders. The housemaid was soon mending his shabby linen, and Mrs Placid, who had a weakness for handsome young men, decided that he needed feeding up, as a result of which the cooking improved considerably.

"Mrs Placid's in love with me," David said when Lucas commented on this at lunch one day.

"I thought we were all expected to be that."

"She says, 'If only I were thirty years younger,' in a rather threatening way. I must say I'm very glad she isn't."

"Please do nothing to discourage her," said Lucas. "This soufflé is very good."

His life went on with a swing these days; it was only by that that Lucas realized how bored he had grown. It was his own fault, of course; he was a fool for a handsome face and would forgive its owner even stupidity, for a time. Nor had he ever been the Byronic type of poet who goes on tiger shoots, interferes in foreign revolutions, and conducts public and scandalous love affairs. He had always lived quietly and privately, cultivating a few clever friends, a well-designed garden, and the pleasures of table and cellar. For lovers he chose the Bunnys of this world, who can be put on and cast off with small emotional wear and tear. All his intensity of feeling had been hoarded for his writing, but it was only now, when it had returned, that he knew that for the last few years there had been nothing to hoard.

The move to the Dower House, a change of secretaries (for change's sake, not for the better), had partly hidden the boredom, but now that he looked back he was appalled at the way he had taken the slackness of his days for granted, as he took for granted his increasingly cumbersome body and grey hair. He had allowed time to drift, drinking too much wine at lunch because Bunny's talk bored him, dozing till teatime, thus spoiling the night's sleep, drinking too much at dinner, nodding over a book till he went to bed to find himself restless and very thankful for Bunny's company, because the one place Bunny was never dull was in bed.

Now there was good talk at the table again, with someone whose mind was still tough and supple from its three years' hard training at Oxford. And with it there was the blessing of that face. What have I done to deserve it, said Lucas to himself at least once a day. I must have been someone frightfully good and saintly in a previous incarnation.

He began a play he had carried at the back of his mind for thirty years, about no less audacious a subject than William Shakespeare's years in London, and found in David a companion as easily swept up into literary enthusiasms as he was himself. Together they read everything from Coleridge to Bailey, as well as all the plays and poems. They went for long walks in the afternoon, often talking so hard that they did not notice how far they had gone and to their surprise found themselves in places like Northan and Fairlight, quite ten miles from home.

"What I want to get away from," said Lucas, "is The Bard the way he's taught to schoolchildren. He can't have been anything like that. He was a petty bourgeois, dying for a coat of arms so he could impress the lieges of Stratford, and very ready to put in any amount of crawling to get it. To the Gray's Inn dandies he must have seemed nothing but a bumpkin with the wrong accent."

"The lout from Stratford?"

"Well no, that's too one-sided. There must have been such a lot of Shakespeares; the icon of Trinity Church, the hack who wrote to order, the playactor, and the dandy of the Chandos portrait with the gold hoop in his ear. The trick is to pull them all together into one person."

Once or twice a week David took the train to London to look up background material for Lucas at the British Museum. He loved his quiet days in the reading room, amid the musty smell of books, but for Lucas the hours David was away crumbled in his hands, leaving nothing behind but impatience and waiting. On one of them he went to have tea at Lamb House with his old friend Henry James, who, having been in a very similar predicament in regard to the young novelist-on-the-make, Hugh Walpole, held forth on the delicacy of the affections in sentences so convoluted they made Lucas gasp for a semicolon. When it was time to meet David's train he went down to the station.

"What an impatient creature you are," said David, giving up his ticket. "Worse than a child who can't wait to see what a visitor has brought him."

"I had tea with Henry. Did you know that little Hugh calls him *cher maître?*"

"I did know, as a matter of fact. Walpole once told me that when they first became friends he asked what he ought to call him, and Mr James suggested *cher maître* without so much as a blush. Americans really are extraordinary. Did you get any work done?"

"I never seem to when you're not here."

"I don't think there's much reason for me to go back," said David, "unless you need something specific looked up."

They returned home to find that the afternoon post had brought a letter from Lucas's oldest friend, the actor-manager Jago Portman. David recognized the writing on the envelope, for it had over the weeks of summer kept them apprised of a triumphal American tour, with students in New York, demented with enthusiasm, unhitching his horses and pulling his carriage down Fifth Avenue to the wrong hotel. Rapturous press clippings were enclosed, their margins decorated with many exclamation points.

"A London postmark," said David, handing the letter to Lucas. "The triumphal tour has come to an end."

"One cannot deprive England of its greatest cultural treasure for too long," said Lucas, and smiling, read the letter, which said, "Can I have a cup of tea on Thursday? China, *not* Indian, lemon, no milk, *No Sandwiches*, NO SCONES, and absolutely NO DEVONSHIRE CREAM!!!"

Lucas, laughing, handed the letter to David, who said, "It sounds like a scream of anguish. NO DEVONSHIRE CREAM!!!"

"He's been overeating in America, I expect. Now he's doing penance. What it is to be an actor and have to keep one's figure."

"You look awfully pleased at the prospect of this penitential tea."

"Oh yes. Nicholas is my oldest and dearest friend."

"Nicholas?"

"That's his real name. Nicholas Jago-Portman, with a hyphen, you know. When he first started acting he dropped the Nicholas; he said it would make people think of a paunchy old man in a red suit. Practically everybody now thinks Jago is his first name."

"I see," said David. At the time of the publication of Lucas's first book of poems, a section entitled *To N.* had raised Victorian eyebrows by its erotic warmth. The strictures of the critical Podsnaps had added considerably to the book's sales. David, reading the poems for the first time at St Dunstan's, had wondered a good deal about who "N" might have been. Of late he had come to assume that "N" had simply been the first of the long line of Bunny Trevelyans in Lucas's life, though it was not easy to imagine one of them inspiring such passion and poetry. The brilliant and flamboyant actor-manager Jago Portman was a bit more like it. Tactfully David suggested that perhaps he might go to London on Thursday to do some more work in the reading room.

"Don't be silly," said Lucas. "It's you he's coming to see."

"Me? Why?"

"Insatiable curiosity. Have you ever dangled a gold watch in front of a chimpanzee?"

David, who had no watch, said, "No. But I see what you mean."

On Thursday Lucas sent his motorcar to the station to meet his guest. "He does so love a conspicuous entry," he said to David.

"Perhaps we ought to meet him in the trap, unhitch the horse and drag him in triumph across Romney Marsh. Like those students in New York delirious with admiration for his *Hamlet*."

"Have you ever seen it? The *Hamlet?*"

"Four times. I used to go without dinner so I could afford the tickets. Anthony's set didn't approve; they never believed anything that wasn't French could be really good."

"There is a French *Hamlet*, you know, an opera. I saw it once. Ophelia dies, but Hamlet survives and assumes the crown."

"I shouldn't think Mr Portman would care for that. It used to take him at least half an hour to die."

"Yes. Like most actors he is very fond of dying."

David spent the time between lunch and tea rereading the play. At four he went downstairs. The drawing-room windows stood open, for the day was unseasonably warm, of that intense, glassy clearness which promises rain before nightfall. Lucas was reading through a sheaf of newspaper clippings. David recognized them as the ones which Jago Portman had sent from America. "I was just going over them to make sure I remember them all. He'll expect us to have read them, carefully and piously, like Holy Writ."

"A Hamlet unique in the annals of the English-speaking theatre."

"An Othello to wring a tear from this jaded eye."

"Stupendous."

"The theatrical thrill of the century."

"Yes," said Lucas, "I think we've got them all correct."

Jago Portman announced his arrival with a commanding peal of the bell. When the drawing-room door opened David got to his feet and was surprised to find himself looking almost a foot too high; Jago Portman was much shorter than he appeared on stage. He had an actor's bad skin, and the muted air of one who is too considerate to unleash the full force of his personality on a tea party.

To avenge himself in advance for the frugal tea he had ordered, he said, "Lucas, for shame, you are growing stout," and acknowledged David's introduction with all the interest a duchess might bestow on the children's governess. But David had caught a saurian flick of eye, and knew the mild, uninterested glance had contained an experienced actor's summing-up.

The talk was naturally entirely about the triumphal American tour. David handed teacups and removed himself out of range of the conversation to the window seat. When he wasn't showing off, Jago Portman could tell a good story. David especially liked the one about the theatre manager in Little Rock, who had implored Jago to play Othello in whiteface, since Southern audiences took a dim view of black men marrying, not to mention strangling, white ladies of good family.

Lucas laughed and drawing David back into the talk said, "Harvey is a great admirer of your *Hamlet*. He went without dinner four times so he could afford the tickets."

"Really," said Jago, turning his muted gaze on David. "How very guilt-making. You must let me give you dinner one night when you are in town."

Very much the nice boy from the vicarage, David said, "Thank you, but I'm never in town in the evening, and I've made up long since. Mrs Placid's a very good cook."

"I think she harbours a secret passion for Harvey," said Lucas. "It has improved her cooking immensely."

People rarely turned down invitations from Jago Portman, not, at any rate, when they knew who he was. He murmured, "Well, of course she would," relegating David to the category of flashy young men with whom cooks might be expected to fall in love. He turned back to Lucas and said, "How is my play coming along?"

"I love the way you say 'my play'. It's coming along very well. Harvey's been a tremendous help. He's only just down from Oxford and has kept his scholarly habits. Would you like to see it?"

David said, "Shall I get it?"

"No," said Lucas, knowing that Jago Portman would have to be given his innings with the new secretary sooner or later. "I will."

David understood this too, but would have preferred to be left face to face with a Jago Portman sated with Devonshire cream, rather than the starving hyena he suspected of lurking behind the muted gaze. He said, "Would you care for a cigar?"

Jago Portman shook his head. "Thank you, but I must pamper my voice."

If he had expected a compliment at this point—his voice being in fact an instrument of considerable beauty—he was disappointed. David merely said, "Yes, of course," and went back to his window seat. Jago Portman decided to waste no more time. "Tell me," he said, "how did you come to meet Mr Ryder? Through Bunny Trevelyan?"

"No," said David, "through the Duchess of Frome."

"That sounds most respectable," said Jago as if he were discussing a housemaid's character. "Mr Ryder says you are something of a poet. Are you working on anything interesting?"

David, resenting the belittling "something", said, "Not at the moment. Are you acting something?"

"Not just now. When I am you must let me send you a free ticket."

"It's very kind of you, but I'm never in town."

"I expect Mr Ryder would give you an evening off if you asked him nicely. We might have supper afterward. I still feel guilty when I think of all those missed dinners."

Cruelly, David said, "If you only knew how guilty *we* felt about the China tea, no scones, no Devonshire cream. Aren't you absolutely starving?"

"I seldom think of food," said Jago smoothly, at which

point Lucas opportunely returned, saying, "Sorry I was so long. I had another look at it and almost decided to throw it away and start again. Here, Jago, take it before I change my mind."

Jago Portman looked at the title page. "LORD STRANGE'S MEN. What gall, Lucas Ryder putting Shakespeare on the stage."

"Not really. It's you who'll put it on the stage, and you they'll throw rotten eggs at if it's no good."

Jago touched the top of his head, where the hair was indeed growing thin, and said, "Typecasting. Why couldn't you have written it thirty years ago? I would have loved to do Southampton."

"I wouldn't have had the nerve thirty years ago."

Jago began to riffle through the pages, his attention settling here and there briefly, with an occasional laugh, a "Yes, I like this, it will play beautifully," undoubtedly, thought David, picking out his own lines, like a greedy child snatching the biggest chocolates. Finally he turned back to page one. "*Lord Strange's Men*. I don't think I care for the title."

"It was the name of Shakespeare's acting company," said Lucas. "But you're right, it is dull."

"What about *A Cry of Players*," suggested David.

Jago, scenting an insult, said, "I am very well known for my ability to weep on cue, Mr Harvey, but that seems hardly enough reason to name a play after it."

"It's a term for a collection of things," explained Lucas, "like a pride of lions, or a worship of writers." David, unable to resist it, said, "An ostentation of peacocks."

"Oh, I see," said Jago, ignoring this jibe, "you mean actors in a group are called a cry of players."

"Yes," said David. "It's a very old term. It's in Dame Julian."

"I like it," said Lucas, and Jago agreed. He turned back to Act I Scene I and began to read again.

The play opened with a spirited quarrel and the firing of Kemp, the company buffoon, witnessed by Shakespeare sitting silently downstage. When Jago Portman let out a yell of anguish, David knew that he had discovered that Lucas had denied him an entrance.

Lucas tactfully suggested a drink. Jago said, " '*Et tu*' " his voice plangent with pain.

"Yes, me," said Lucas, who had been prepared for this reaction. "Now listen, Jago, I knew you'd scream, but this will play, you'll see. Frankly, I'm sick of all those grand entrances, and I expect audiences are too."

"You are not," said Jago, with his very best enunciation, "an actor."

"No, I'm not. Jago, it's a barbarism to have a scene come to a dead stop while everyone applauds the entrance of Popinjay Encore, the celebrated tragedian. You are not going to do it to my play."

"No," said Jago bitterly. "I am going to be hidden away in a dark corner like the merest walking gentleman. I have borne with a great deal from you over all these years, Lucas. I have put up with your pathological vanity and your barely adequate plays for the sake of our friendship, but this time you have gone too far. I must have an entrance."

"No. But I'll let you do the Ghost in *Hamlet*. You'll enjoy that."

David could not decide whether it would be more tactful to leave or stay. He decided to stay. They had ceased to notice him, and he was enjoying the performance.

"No entrance, no Jago Portman," said Jago.

Lucas had expected this too. "That's quite all right, Jago," he said. "I understand."

The silence was out of a Greek tragedy, just before the protagonist begins his big speech. But no speech followed. In a voice broken with grief Jago said, "Who . . . ?"

"Pemberly's been after it for months," Lucas said with brutal cheerfulness. "I think he will do well by it."

"Pemberly. Don't make me laugh. Pemberly! You're losing your grip, Lucas."

Lucas went across the room, put his hands on his friend's shoulders, and pushed him into a chair. "Listen," he said, "I don't want Pemberly, I want you. You are my Shakespeare. But you are going to sit upstage, with not so much as a spotlight on you, and you are not going to sneeze, or blow your nose, or scratch your head, or use any of your actor's tricks to draw attention. Remember, you have not yet written *King Lear*, and you are watching the way the world treats old men. When you finally do move downstage, you will do so very quietly. If you do not faithfully promise to do it like that, I will give the play to Pemberly tomorrow."

"Blackmail," said Jago so mildly that they knew he was beginning to see himself upstage, without so much as a spotlight, riveting the attention of the entire house by sheer force of personality.

"You'll be magnificent," said Lucas. "And now do have a drink."

"A whisky, thank you. They say it causes wrinkles, but I need it."

David poured out two drinks, gave one to Jago and the other to Lucas. Their eyes met, but they refrained from smiling. David said he still had to write some letters, and turned to Jago to take his leave. The actor, remembering a time when he had played Pope Hildebrand, held out his hand as he had done for the cardinals to kiss his ring. David, ignoring the gesture, shook it like a hearty St Dunstan's schoolboy. Jago visibly winced.

When they were alone, Lucas sat down in the window where David had earlier sat. The room was full of leaping light from the estuary. Autumn clouds were blowing across the sky, printing shadows on the water meadow. Lucas said, "Well . . ."

"I don't know about well. I preferred Bunny."

"Bunny was nice-looking but stupid. You could discover the law of gravity or come up with the most brilliant epigram since Oscar Wilde, and Bunny would say, 'Fancy.' "

The expressive face creased into a smile. "Don't I know it. It's what made him so safe. I don't think your David is safe at all. I see troubles ahead."

"Yes, so do I. In fact I think they may already have arrived."

"You mean you have fallen in love."

"No fool like an old fool, so they say."

"Have you told him?"

"I'm not so great a fool as that."

"Why? Would he become troublesome?"

"No, I'm sure he wouldn't. He's really a very nice person. We all are."

"I'm not."

"I'm aware of that." They were silent for a moment, old memories reviving briefly, and settling back again into the forgiving past.

"What are his feelings on the subject, if any?" asked Jago. "Do you know?"

Lucas considered this question. "Yes," he said, "as far as one can ever know such things, I think I do know. He's a romantic object, not at all a romantic himself. Well, people as beautiful as that hardly ever are. One must keep that in mind. I think most of his attitudes were formed by reading the Greeks. Like them I suspect he would regard falling in love a madness or a disease sent by an angry god. If it ever happened to him, which given his temperament is very unlikely, he would probably just grit his teeth and wait it out as one does an illness."

"It looks a trifle bleak for you, my dear," said Jago not without satisfaction.

"Well no, because he's also a bit of a hero-worshipper. So long as I can keep my head sufficiently to remember that if David loves at all—and I think in that sense he does—it is not the *who*, but the *what* you are he loves; if I can swallow that, I shall be in clover."

Jago thought this over. "If that is so," he said, "if it isn't a question of who but of what, then it doesn't matter who the what is."

Lucas laughed. "That was very neatly put, Jago." The suggestion left him unperturbed. They had poached each other's territory for a good many years, using their pivileged position as old friends to borrow and purloin each other's lovers. It was hardly more than a game to them, and in this particular case, Lucas was sure, presented no danger.

"But how did it happen?" said Jago. "You've always been so careful. All those moronic handsome secretaries."

"I wasn't very careful about you."

"We were awfully young. Besides, you feel safe with actors. You think we're nothing but a profile and a lot of tricks."

Lucas refilled their glasses and said, "That's not true. The reason I've never fallen in love with an actor is because I am extremely fond of making love, and actors as a general rule are terrible in bed."

Very coldly Jago said, "Are they indeed?"

"Yes, because they're always concerned with how they look, whatever they're doing, eating, walking, talking. You simply can't be good in bed and worry whether your better profile is turned to the audience at the same time."

Jago burst out laughing. "A devastating observation, and probably quite true. Still, it is worrying, Lucas. You know you do your best work in tranquil, even boring circumstances. The very last thing you need right now is a *grand péché radieux*."

"You mean while I'm working on your play."

"You must admit it's very poor timing. How could you let it happen?"

"I don't quite know. The Duchess sent me some of his poems, I invited him to tea, we talked, we went for a walk along the beach, we saw a kestrel, I quoted Hopkins, and I suddenly heard myself saying, 'My secretary is leaving me in June; would you be interested in the post?' "

"It's what he was after, of course."

"I imagine so. He's the son of a country parson with eight children and a small stipend. It was me or schoolmastering."

"If he fancies himself a poet, he will want to go to London and meet publishers and people, you know."

"Yes. He hasn't said anything, but of course he will. We'll be coming up to town for rehearsals in any case, so that's not a problem."

"I still think you might have got yourself a decorative secretary without falling in love."

"Another Bunny Trevelyan, you mean. Do you know, I'd almost forgotten what fun it is just to talk. We sit up half the night sometimes. And of course there is that 'decorative'. I mean the constant pleasure of having him to look at. Heads actually turn when he goes down the street. They really do."

"Yes, that was the first thing I thought when I saw him. 'Lucky, lucky Lucas, to wake up with that head on the pillow beside him every morning.'"

"I expect that would be very nice."

"Good heavens," said Jago shocked, "do you mean to say that sitting up half the night talking is all you do? How very unlike you."

"Yes, isn't it?"

"But why, Lucas. Do you think he's not . . ."

"Well, no. He was Anthony Fielding's great friend at Oxford, and you know our Anthony."

"Do I not. But why, then?"

"I don't quite know. Everything seems different this time."

"Listen, Lucas," said Jago, so exasperated by his friend's folly that he forgot to pretend to be years younger, "at our age all this Sir Galahad nonsense is most unwise. This may very well be your last chance. Don't waste it like a silly mooncalf. Is that clock right? I must go and catch my train."

"Won't you stay for dinner?"

"I dine on a glass of lemonade. To see you and the beautiful Mr Harvey wallowing in cutlets would be more than I could bear without growing vicious."

Lucas, who had seen Jago vicious before, did not repeat his invitation, but rang the bell for the car. "It's been heaven to see you," he said, embracing his old friend.

"And you, my dear. Do take care. Great care."

"I'll write you a comedy about it when it's all over."

"A tragedy, you mean."

"No. The slippered pantaloon in love is always a subject for farce. It's odd, you know, but I'm really very happy."

"That is why you should take care."

Left alone, Lucas went back to sit in the window. He knew Jago's "take care" had been well meant, though it had come too late to be heeded. Even if there had ever been a time when such a warning might have made a difference, he was sure he would have ignored it.

Love that comes late in life has its special perils and pains, but it was a gift it would have seemed to Lucas meanspirited to refuse. It is love graced by patience, perspective, and intelligence, but bereft of hope. If a balance is achieved, one side is unavoidably weighted by the awareness of time passing and past.

The passing of time is a sore subject for poets, particularly for one who has lately and secretly observed his fifty-eighth birthday. Jago had been right about one thing at least; it was folly to waste more time.

Outside the windows the late sunset still held the light; only the room had grown dim. Lucas made no move to light the lamp. He saw David returning from a walk, his hair blowing in the wind. An edge of lemon light lingered over the water meadows.

Then David came in, said, "Are you sitting in the dark?" and lit the lamp.

"Have you been walking?" asked Lucas. "You look rather wind-tossed."

"I think it's blowing up a gale. Is it time to dress for dinner?"

"There is no hurry. Come and sit down a moment. There is something I want to tell you."

David came across the room and sat as he often did, on the floor at Lucas's feet, his elbows on the window seat.

He had wondered at times that this had not come sooner, had even asked himself whether he could have been wrong about Lucas, knowing himself not to be particularly good at these guessing games. But there surely could have been no possible mistake about Bunny Trevelyan.

He had not much minded either way; it was not something which was important to him; if necessary he knew he could manage on relentless charm alone.

In lighting the lamp he had plunged the garden and the estuary into darkness. There was nothing beyond the window now, except the sense of the tide seeping silently and secretively into the sands, and the sound of the wind. When Lucas had finished speaking, David turned from the shadows of the window corner into the light and said, "My dear, did you really think you had to ask?"

In a little while he said, "Do you remember that the Longacres are coming to dinner with Lady Penreath and Miss Bolton?"

"Oh no. Damn, who could have asked them?"

"Who indeed?"

"It's time to dress, I suppose."

"Yes."

"Later then?"

"Yes. Later."

It was a good many hours later, and David was half asleep when Lucas spoke his name.

"*Cher maître.*"

Lucas laughed at this but persisted. "David, you don't by any chance think that this is an unwritten part of the terms of your employment with me, do you?"

Amused, David said, "Oughtn't you to have mentioned that rather sooner?"

"It has only just occurred to me."

"What an innocent you are. It occurred to me when you asked whether I wanted Bunny's job. When I said I would be honoured, of course I meant this too."

When Lucas came down to breakfast the next morning, David, to his annoyance, found himself blushing. To hide it he busied himself with the morning's post.

"Someone called Hermione Goldenrod invites you to a party on the eleventh. In fact she invites me too. She refers to me as your delightful young secretary. Unless of course she means Bunny."

"I've no doubt that Bunny's departure and your arrival are well known to Hermione. She is the wife of one half of my publishers, Asquith and Goldenrod. And she is a great literary lion hunter. You can meet no end of useful people at her parties. Would you like to go?"

"Only if you do."

"Oh, I? Like the ogre in the fairy tale I would like to lock you in a remote castle where no one but me ever gets to see you. But I fancy it was definitely one of the unwritten terms that I should make it possible for you to meet the people who might be helpful to you."

"I wish you wouldn't go on about those unwritten terms," said David. "There weren't any written ones I know of, and you are making all these up." He brought him a cup of coffee and said, "Dear Lucas, I am perfectly content to stay as we are."

Certain that David was lying, and rather touched by it, Lucas turned to look out the window. The long spell of sunny weather had finally broken. The first of the autumn gales was flattening the sodden grass and stripping the golden leaves from the beeches. Rain dashed against the windows like flung pebbles.

"What a day," said Lucas. "One might as well be in town."

Chapter 8

London was still a city of country smells, horses, and horse manure. Motorcars were a fashion but not yet a convenience. Roads were bad, and punctures so frequent it was customary to load the backseat full of spare tyres when going on a journey. There were motor taxis in town, and electric trams, but by and large London still travelled by horse and smelled of it.

Chelsea, where Lucas owned a house in Upper Cheyne Row, had retained a good part of its village atmosphere; it scarcely considered itself a part of London as yet. As in a village, high and low were very much in each other's pockets. Mr Oscar Wilde, in Tite Street, had been obliged to hide his view of the squalors of Paradise Walk with a Persian screen.

Lucas lived in a three-storey house built of that peculiar yellow brick known as Old London Stock, which absorbs soot like a sponge and always looks dirty. The inside was pleasing, with two large rooms to each floor, kitchen and servants' rooms in the cellar, and a large attic with a skylight

Lucas had turned into a study. David fell in love with it on sight.

As a young man Lucas had briefly shared the house with Jago Portman, which, he said to David, proved nothing except the foolishness of first love and the resilience of youth, for no one in his right mind could be expected to live with Jago Portman for any term longer than five minutes. "He should be made to live on a stile, like St Simon," said Lucas with the mildness gained from a perspective of more than thirty years.

This stormy ménage came to an end with a quarrel during which Jago, in a voice trained to carry to the last row of the highest gallery enunciated his grievances from across the street to the intense delight of the neighbourhood.

Chelsea was well accustomed to high drama, having experienced at various times the lovesick screams of Mr Dante Gabriel Rossetti's peacocks, not to mention those of Fanny Cornforth, his model, mistress, and doormat of many years, when she learned that he had transferred his affections to his best friend's wife. And then there was the memorable day when Mr James McNeill Whistler's Jo fought for the possession of his person with Beatrix Godwin in the garden of Number Two, The Vale, Mr Whistler having prudently locked himself inside the house.

Unlike Jago, however, these ladies lacked an actor's training and breath control, and it was generally conceded that Mr Portman's tirade had lasted the longest and was the most clearly enunciated.

Lucas's house had at one time been lived in by Leigh Hunt, and Lucas showed David a letter by Jane Carlyle, describing Mr Carlyle going there to tea and finding Mrs Hunt soundly asleep, dazed with drink or laudanum, the children wearing nothing but shifts, in spite of which they had played host most courteously, and had given Mr Carlyle a very nice tea.

"It's really because of its literary associations that I bought this house," said Lucas, showing David through it.

"Were you hoping to see the ghost of one of the Hunts?"

"Hardly. They didn't live here long enough. They never lived anywhere long, because they always owed the rent.

Tobias Smollett lived here too, you know, right at the corner, in Lawrence Street. He used to invite poor fellow writers every Sunday and feed them beef, pudding, potatoes, port punch, and Calvert's entire butt beer. Understandably he was soon as much in debt as his poor guests. This street must have been beset by duns for two hundred years."

"You must have been a nice exception. Or were you a poor starving poet in an attic when you started?"

"No, I never had occasion to follow that tradition. When I came down from Oxford and told my family that I planned to be a poet, they were dismayed but very nice about it. My father was a doctor and I knew he wanted me to come into the practice with him and was disappointed, but he didn't send me off to the colonies or disinherit me or any of the traditional things Victorian fathers were supposed to do. In fact he very kindly made me an allowance until such time as I would earn some money."

"He must have had great confidence in your talent. So many poets never do earn any."

"I doubt he ever read anything I wrote. He wasn't at all literary; in fact there was nobody literary on either side of the family on whom they could blame such a peculiar outburst. But my mother remembered having gone to a tea party before I was born, where Mr Tennyson read *Maud* out loud, all of it, and when someone incautiously applauded, he read it again. My father said it was a very unscientific theory, but I think my poor mother went to her grave feeling responsible."

"Did your father buy you this house?"

"Oh, no, he'd never have picked Chelsea. Too raffish. No, an aunt who had left me 150 pounds in her will very kindly died just about the time I came down from Oxford. Of course the lawyers wanted me to keep it invested in consols or whatever it was, where it would have brought me an income of something like four pounds ten a year, so I asked my father what he thought I ought to do with it, and he said, 'Buy a house.' He had a great prejudice against flats and lodgings. Of course there weren't many parts of

London, even then, where you could get a house for 150 pounds, but Chelsea was one of them."

"It's a wonderful house," said David, walking through the uncluttered, plain rooms, their walls painted white, their furniture all for use, not decoration.

"Whistler's responsible for the interior," said Lucas, "though I admit I've added a few sticks of furniture since then. When he was in the throes of his Japanese period, he made all his friends throw out their Victorian clutter, whitewash the walls, hang one painting—preferably by Whistler—and have one celadon vase with one spray of white lilac for decoration. Later he got more elaborate and wanted to paint fans on the ceiling, but by that time I'd got used to having it plain and wouldn't let him. I shall never forget my mother coming to see me one day when Jimmy happened to be here. She was horribly shocked by how bare everything was; at that time Jimmy was such a purist he wouldn't even let us have chairs. My mother said I could have the set of Jacobean ones from Wimpole Street, and Jimmy, in that high-pitched American voice of his, shouted, 'No, no, no, Lady Ryder, NOT chairs from Wimpole Street!' My mother asked him where I was going to sit, to which Jimmy said with great dignity, 'On a mat on the floor of course. The Japanese, who are the most civilized people on earth, have done it for thousands of years.' My poor mother had always thought the English were the most civilized people on earth; she and Jimmy never did get along well after that."

"Did he do that drawing?" asked David, looking at a picture over the fireplace in Lucas's study. It portrayed Lucas at his most formidable, looking very like a Roman bust, but one on whose nose naughty schoolboys have perched a pince-nez.

"Yes," said Lucas. "He always saw through me, blast him."

"Felix, you know, my German friend I told you about, is in Japan right now," said David. "I think he and Mr Whistler would have seen eye to eye. Judging by his letters he doesn't ever plan to leave."

"What will Landeck Steel think of that?"

"Very, very little," said David.

"Can they make him come home?"

"Of course, quite easily. They'll stop his allowance and send him a steamer ticket. They've done it before."

Felix had not much cared for Harvard, and had not stayed to take his degree. He had gone on a year's travel to the countries with which Landeck Steel did business. In Russia he paid one courtesy call on Putiloff Steel, and thereafter spent all his time at the house of a tiny man with beetling eyebrows called Sergei Shchukin, who had nothing whatever to do with steel and guns, but owned the best collection of Impressionist painters outside France. Felix sent Kitty a painting of blue horses, which gave Augustus the opportunity to say that Felix must be getting colour-blind, and he didn't see why people couldn't paint like Stubbs nowadays.

From China Felix sent David a large piece of jade, which he used for a paperweight, not realizing how valuable it was. Judging from his letters, Felix did not care very much for China. It was probably too noisy, sprawling, and untidy for his German tastes. He did fall in love, instantly and unconditionally, with Japan. It was not known whether he ever went anywhere near the Mitsui Armament Works. According to his letters to David he settled down in a house with paper windows and a garden which contained neither flowers nor vegetables, only stunted trees, carefully placed rocks, and white sand raked into new patterns every morning by a silent old man. He shared this house with a lady of easy virtue whose name was O-Hisa. She chattered to him in a pleasant voice like a bird—it seemed Felix had learned to speak Japanese in a very short time, though never to read and write it. She played the koto and sang songs which he found unfamiliar but pleasing to the ear, she made a tremendous to-do about pouring out a cup of tea, and presented him with elegantly arranged dinners consisting of two shrimps and a lotus blossom on a lacquer tray. He was hungry all the time he was in Japan, and often had a meal in a restaurant before going home to dinner.

O-Hisa taught him to enjoy communal baths in a large wooden tub, gave wonderful massages, and did things in bed even Nellie de Lafayette had never thought of. As in the days of Nellie, Felix went into considerable detail in his letters to David, perhaps to show him what he was missing and persuade him toward a more natural way of life.

It was astonishing, David thought, that under such circumstances Felix should remember a scrawny American widow with red hair and a freckled nose, no money, and a peevish and spoiled son.

He did not, in fact, remember her all the time. For weeks on end he did not think of her at all, then suddenly she would come into his dreams, usually in some intensely erotic manner, which did not at all reflect the actual state of their relationship, in which he had never kissed any part of her except her hand. Once he dreamt that he and Kitty were making love in a punt on the Isis, while along the shore a fashionably dressed throng of parents and undergraduates applauded as if it were Eights Week.

When he dreamt of Kitty he grew moody and absent for days, while his companion, suspecting another woman in his life, behaved like the heroine in a Puccini opera and threatened to commit hara-kiri to make him lose face.

He sent Kitty a fan with a spray of morning glory and some lines of verse painted on it, and asked David to look her up now they were neighbours, since her letters of late had grown rare and more than usually vague.

David had seen a good deal of Kitty Snow when Felix was still at Oxford, and had found her very pleasant company. He therefore went to the house in Tite Street a few days after he had received Felix's letter, and rang the bell. The door was answered by a red-haired lad with a tweed cap pulled well over his forehead, whom it took him one stunned moment to recognize as Kitty.

"Mrs Snow *en travestie?* Are you doing theatricals or charades?"

She drew him into the hall and shut the door. "I'm so sorry," she wailed. "I know I asked you for tea, and I really am awfully glad to see you, but something's come up and I have to go out. Come to tea tomorrow and say you forgive me."

"If you'll promise to tell me the whole story."

"Oh, all right, I promise." Annie suddenly appeared in the hallway, carrying what looked like a box of workman's tools, which she handed to Kitty. Kitty said, "Look, I've got to go or I'll be late. Swear you won't tell anybody about this, Mr Harvey."

David did not swear and told Lucas that night. Lucas said, "How very odd. Could she be a burglar? Mind you go to tea with her tomorrow; I'm longing to hear the story."

When David went to Tite Street the next day, he found his hostess properly dressed in a skirt, her face disfigured with a black eye and cut lip, awaiting him in the drawing room.

David, shocked, said, "What happened to you, Mrs Snow? Did someone beat you up?" He was beginning to wonder whether Lucas's guess was not a correct one.

"I got thrown out of Number Ten," said Kitty with dignity.

"Downing Street?"

"Well, of course Downing Street. I wouldn't waste my time on Number Ten, Gasworks Road, would I?"

"May I ask what you were doing there?"

"Pretending to be a plumber's assistant," said Kitty, as if this were the most natural thing in the world.

"Was it on a bet?"

"Certainly not," said Kitty. "It was so I could shout VOTES FOR WOMEN at Mr Asquith. I got caught and thrown out before I got to his study, but I did shout it at his butler."

"You wouldn't like to start this story from the beginning, would you?" said David, thinking it was no wonder that her letters to Felix had grown so vague.

Kitty was perfectly willing. While she poured out tea and handed muffins, she told him about Mrs Castlemain, who had seen her potential at a glance, of heckling politicians and unfurling the WSPU flag from the visitors' gallery in the House of Commons, of chaining herself to park railings and being had up before the magistrate at Bow Street.

"How very brave you are," said David, mocking but impressed.

"Oh no," said Kitty, "I'm always terrified. But all the same, you know, it's a lot more fun than Dorcas Guild meetings."

After this David often stopped in to see her between rehearsals and time to dress for dinner. Waiting in the ugly drawing room with its Altondale cast-off pieces of furniture, reading back issues of *The Freewoman* and *Women's Dreadnought* until someone had finished hammering out "Für Elise," seemed to David these days the only time he had to catch his breath.

Life with Lucas in town, he had discovered, was a very different matter from life with Lucas in the country. Lucas in the country had got up early, worked all morning, and cherished his solitude. Lucas in town proved to be both the idlest and most social person David had ever known. He did no work, lay in bed all morning (he had once said to an interviewer that his greatest ambition was to become a chronic invalid so he need never get up at all), made havoc of his breakfast tray, the *Times*, and his letters, and if reminded by David that he had promised to review a friend's new book, said, "You review it for me. And be sure to say something nice about it."

"How can I, it's so awful."

"Yes, but we went to prep school together and he'll do the same for you one day."

They were rarely at home for a meal now, going to lunches, teas, dinner, and suppers after the theatre. It was odd, David thought, how one couldn't stay at home in London. At the Dower House they had spent evening after evening by themselves with none of the sense of urgency that was in the very air of town. David did not really miss those long evenings by the fire, evenings so quiet that one grew conscious of darkness and the tide filling the river and marshes. He was having too much fun in London meeting Lucas's friends, going to parties, and finding that his handsome face and pleasant manners were quite sufficient for social success.

Even when they stayed at home they were seldom alone these days. Friends came to call, and would-be disciples were daily to be found on the doorstep, damp with admiration, clutching flowers and sheaves of their own poems in their tremulous hands, and not above giving Lucas to understand how very willing they would be to take David's place in his life.

David wasted no time worrying about them. Lucas had given no sign of tiring of his company. And if it happened—David never for a moment forgot that it had happened to Bunny and all Bunny's predecessors—he too had by now gathered his share of offers, blatant or oblique, from people who had let him know that they were willing to take Lucas Ryder's place in *his* life.

Watching other young men situated as he was, aware how fatal it would be to be thought available, something to be passed around among friends like a plate of cucumber sandwiches at tea, David had developed for such occasions a nice-boy-from-the-vicarage manner which managed to say no thank you without offence of finality.

He was happy in his new life, but there were times when he felt like a juggler who is keeping one orange too many in the air, and it was at such times that he liked to go and have a cup of tea with Kitty Snow.

The dress rehearsal of *A Cry of Players* went as dress rehearsals are traditionally said to go. By the end of the first act Jago Portman was in hysterics, Queen Elizabeth and the Dark Lady were both in tears, and the Earl of Southampton had threatened to walk out then and there unless a grovelling apology were forthcoming from every member of the cast. When he was reminded that he had a contract, he had clutched his side, miming a sudden and severe attack of appendicitis, but the mention of his talented understudy had given him pause. He called Jago a spavined bitch, the Dark Lady was given sal volatile, Queen Elizabeth had a calming nip from a silver flask, and David, who had been quietly sitting in the stalls, taking notes for Lucas, decided that there was nothing to be gained by staying on.

Jago, as unruffled as a dowager at a charity tea, intercepted him at the stage door and said, "Do give Lucas all my love and tell him it's going splendidly."

167

"Is it?"

"Oh, but yes, my dear. With a dress rehearsal like that it's bound to be a brilliant success tonight."

"I'll tell him."

"You might kiss me for luck."

David, not even troubling to put on his nice-boy-from-the-vicarage manner, said, "You don't need luck, Mr Portman. You can do it on pure genius."

It had begun to snow, big woolly flakes, like a picture of winter in a child's book. The air shimmered white around the streetlamps. Despite a hole in the sole of his shoe, David decided to walk back to Chelsea, partly because he liked snow, partly to save money. He couldn't think why he was always so hard up. He had his lodging and food for free, and Lucas paid him well. But one needed such an awful lot of clothes in London. The brown velvet jacket, its lining patched by an infatuated housemaid, did very well in the country, and even at the Goldenrods, where poetesses arrived dressed in what looked like window curtains, and one young poet, who lived in the Albany, but had read too much Tolstoy, presented himself wearing a blue, belted smock and high leather boots. But it did not do at most of the parties to which they were asked, so David had put his money where it showed and skimped what he thought of as inessentials, such as shoes and overcoats. Lord Baden-Powell had recently publicly declared that a gentleman could always be recognized by his boots, but David doubted very much whether anyone cared that his had a hole or two in the sole. Whenever he did happen to have a little money to spare, it seemed always to be a dry and sunny day, on which the problem of new shoes did not loom very greatly, and knowing what a difference an extra pound or two could make at the university, he often sent what money he could spare to his brother at Oxford, though knowing Freddy he was fairly sure it would end in a mission for relapsed hop pickers, and Freddy, like all the Harveys, would continue to walk about, devastatingly handsome, down at heel, and out at elbow.

He looked for some time at a brightly lit shop window in Bond Street, in which there was a truly glorious winter

coat. Of course the least hint to Lucas would produce it as
a present, but like most people in an ambiguous position,
David had set up a careful dividing line between what one
could, keeping one's self-respect, or could not accept from
an employer who was also one's lover. He turned from the
bright shop window and looked instead at a florist's display
of white lilac. Without having ever bought anything so
luxurious, he had a good guess what they might cost, nor
did he have to count the money in his pocket, for he knew
to a penny how much he had and how long it would have
to last. Nevertheless he opened the door and entered into
warmth, and the scents of summer.

The shop assistant, who also had a hole in her shoe and
knew to a penny how much money was in her purse, found
herself smiling at the sight of him.

David emptied his pockets of all but bus fare—one
couldn't very well walk home in the snow carrying sheaves
of lilacs—and said, "I'll take however much of the white
lilac I can get for this, please."

Oh well, the young shop asistant thought, there it was.
He had a young lady somewhere, and he was squandering
all his money on her. Just as well, really. She couldn't
afford to get sentimental about beautiful young men in
shabby overcoats, not with a hole in her shoe and her way
to make in the world. All the same he had brightened her
afternoon, and she gave him a lot more lilacs than he had
money for.

"Do you want it sent, sir?"

"No thank you, I'll take them with me. Could you wrap
them extra well; I shouldn't want them to catch cold."

"They're lovely, aren't they? Here you are, sir. I do hope
the young lady will like them."

"Who? Oh yes, of course. I'm sure she will."

David let himself out into the moist cold air with a feeling
of relief. There was something cloying about flower shops
after the first moment. He caught a bus and got back to
Chelsea in time for tea.

Lucas was in his third-floor study, looking out the
window at the snow. He hadn't turned the lamps on yet;

169

there was only the glow of the fire, and the milky light coming through the snow-covered skylight.

"You're home nice and early."

"Mr Portman sends his love and says the play is going to be the most tremendous success."

"Was the dress rehearsal as bad as all that?" Lucas asked. He never went to rehearsals. He said they only made him quarrel with Jago, and what was worse, Jago invariably ended by being in the right.

"I've never been to one before," said David, "so I can't really compare, but I'd say it was about the worst possible. Everyone was crying or screaming insults. Nigel called Jago a spavined bitch."

"It sounds about as usual. Can dogs be spavined?"

David gave him the flowers. "These are for you. I think only horses."

"White lilac? You are very extravagant."

"I saw them in a window with the snow coming down and I couldn't resist them."

"Oh my dear, thank you. Nothing could be nicer." Lucas put the flowers into a celadon vase—relic of Whistler's blue and white Japanese decor—and put them on the windowsill. They were like snow drifted against the glass, with snow falling more and more thickly outside. David lit the lamps and rang for tea. Lucas thought, He looks all lit up. Is it just the walk through the snow, or has something happened? Has he met someone and fallen in love at last? No, not someone, something. He's in love with backstage; all the trashy, meretricious world of acting and first names, kisses, quarrels, dressing up. How could he not be? It's the most fatal, longest-lasting infatuation in the world. How well I remember it happening to me, meeting Jago for the first time. I've never recovered from it, not really. And because I've opened that world up for him, he brings me flowers when he needs a pair of shoes and a new overcoat. For Lucas, though David did not know this, was very much aware of his wants and of the dangers of supplying them.

"Did Jago ask you to kiss him for luck?" Lucas said after the parlourmaid had brought the tea.

"He did."

"And?"

"I said, 'You don't need luck, Mr Portman. You can do it on pure genius.'"

"He probably thought you meant it seriously. It's no use ragging Jago."

Though he tried to behave with the senatorial calm of one who has never had a failure in the theatre, Lucas was restless, paced his study floor, and ignored his tea. David watched him in silence for a while, then said, "Don't worry."

"That's easy for you to say. It's not your play. Supposing it's no good?"

"Oh, Lucas, you can't possibly believe that. You must know it's good."

"How? Nobody can ever judge his own work."

"Oh shut up. You know it's good."

"It might still be a fiasco."

"Yes," said David. "It's unlikely, but it might."

"I've never had a fiasco before. I won't know how to behave. What does one do?"

"One retires to one's house in the country to lick one's wounds in dignified silence and reminds oneself at least once a day that the year Aristophanes wrote *The Birds*, the prize for the best play went to a piece of rubbish called *The Drunken Revellers*."

This was sufficiently soothing so Lucas could stop pacing and come to rest at the window, where he watched the snow come down in thick, wet flakes. "If this snow keeps up, no one will come to the theatre," he said gloomily.

"It's very wet snow; it's not sticking to the road. And I rather fancy they'll flock to a Ryder opening night, snow or no snow."

David was right, of course. "Not an empty seat in the house," he said, having scanned the sea of black and white, diamonds and bosoms, below their box. They had taken care to arrive late, but Jago always managed to be later than anyone else, because he hated having his effects spoiled by people looking for their seats. Other actor-managers coped with this by having a one-act comic curtain raiser, or an opening scene in which a pretty maid goes around with a feather duster, discussing with herself the odd behaviour of her employers. Jago Portman simply waited. It took gall and timing, and Jago had plenty of both.

The curtain rose with no preliminaries on the middle of an actor's brawl, which left the audience, still settling into its seats, as disoriented as if, in reading an intricate story, they had accidentally turned two pages at once. There was a faint, questioning rustle as people turned toward each other as if to ask whether there had not been a mistake. Had Act I Scene I been accidentally skipped?

Then Kemp, the old buffoon, got a laugh from the gallery (the one-shilling seats were always the first to see a joke), and the stalls too turned their attention to the stage, where the old lion out of fashion was having his teeth drawn and not suffering it in silence.

In a dim corner upstage, Jago, looking very like the Chandos portrait, with a gold ring in his ear, sat picking his teeth with a quill.

Damn him, thought David, remembering the battle about this scene at the Dower House. Lucas made him promise not to blow his nose or sneeze or scratch his head, but he didn't say anything about not picking his teeth. The trouble was, David realized, watching him, that if you had jugglers, a public execution, and two elephants copulating upstage, and Jago Portman picking his teeth in a dim corner, every eye in the house would be riveted on Jago.

Kemp walked off, roaring and helpless, like a blind bear being whipped for the amusement of the lieges in Paris Gardens, and the young dandies from Gray's Inn invaded the theatre, making sport of sweet Master Shakespeare with compliments, as crude and insolent as bearbaiting mastiffs.

Odd, thought David, how, after having copied and recopied these scenes till he had every word, every comma by heart, after having watched them in rehearsal till all the life had gone out of them for him, they were revived and new now in the actual performance. Was this true for Lucas as well? He could not tell from his face in the gloom of the box. Lucas had on his formidable look, and David suspected that he was amused.

He turned his attention back to the stage. The Earl of

Southampton, with his own, seemingly genuine admiration, turned aside the insolence of his friends, making their compliments sound suddenly real. I can't believe it, thought David. Horrible Nigel's going to be all right. He's even good. He had not been presumptuous enough, knowing his own lack of experience, to criticise anything in the play or Jago's staging of it, but he had argued endlessly with Lucas about the casting of Nigel Davenant as Southampton.

"He's one of the most stupid people I've ever met," he had said. "Stupid and vain. If you take his comb away from him, he won't know what to do with his hands, and he panics if he finds himself in a room without a mirror. Southampton may have been vain, in fact I'm sure he was, but he wasn't stupid."

"He'll be all right on the night," Lucas had said. "Jago and I have known him for some time, and he always is. Besides, he's got the right looks for the part; pretty, with that requisite air of festering lilies. And you needn't look at me like that because I haven't. Jago and Nigel had a brief affair some time ago, but Jago said he couldn't stand all those haircombings in his bed; it was worse than having a dog that sheds a lot."

And here was Nigel, the shedding dog, being much more than merely all right on the night. I'll never understand actors, thought David, watching their first scene alone together, Nigel and Jago acting out the delicate minuet Lucas had spun around the Lord Chamberlain and his blue pencil.

The end of the first act left the audience not knowing quite what to think. The country bumpkin with the wrong accent was not what they had expected the Bard to be like. They had been taken by surprise and suspected a joke against themselves, so the applause was resentful and those who came to call on Lucas in his box were circumspect in their praise.

Act II, with the Dark Lady and Southampton as its polar characters, the plague and worldly success for background, proved the popular one, as Lucas had known it would. It had been easy to write and was easy to like. By the end of the second act the applause was long and enthusiastic.

"So flattering of them to go on and on," said Lucas, "when you know they're really dying to rush off to the bar for a drink."

Their box quickly filled with friends. There was champagne, and the congratulations were wholehearted. Hermione Goldenrod stopped by, clutched Lucas to her bosom and reminded him that he and David were coming to her party and that she would never forgive them if they stopped at Lady Crystal's or the Duchess of Birmingham's along the way. David, hoping to avoid her embraces, said to Lucas, "I'll just go along and say hello to Mrs Snow. She'll be far too shy to come and see us."

"Is Mrs Snow here? We should have remembered to send tickets."

"We did." He pushed his way through the crowd to the stalls, where he found two empty seats. Of course Kitty and Mrs Castlemain (if that redoubtable suffragette had agreed to come to a play written by one member of the male sex about another) might have stepped out for a breath of air, or have gone to talk to friends, yet it seemed odd that nothing had been left behind to show that they had ever been here. The other empty seats all bore some mark that they had been occupied; a programme, a scarf, or a pair of gloves. He waited till the houselights went down, then returned to Lucas's box. There could of course be all kinds of reasons why Kitty wasn't there; he hadn't even troubled to ask her if she were free, but had merely sent the tickets in case she felt like using them. Yet a sense of unease stayed with him through the third act, while Jago worked every trick in his repertory to wind up the play with not a dry eye left in the house. The audience rewarded his efforts with a standing ovation which David timed as lasting a good ten minutes.

On their way to the Goldenrods he tried to remember the mixture of excitement and apprehension with which he had looked forward to his first literary party in London, but there had been so many such evenings since that he'd begun to grow a little bored.

"There's very little cause for excitement," Lucas had told him at the time. "Writers are a dull lot by and large, always saving their best bits for their books, and as for apprehension it is totally out of place. The Goldenrods haven't much in common but they do agree on one thing; she adores beautiful young men and so does he."

All Hermione's parties were large and boisterous, with too many guests and too much to eat. Hermione had never quite got over the notion of children's parties; she always liked to have some special, odd guest to amuse the crowd in her drawing room, as a clown or a magician had amused the guests of her younger years. There had been at various times a rajah encrusted in jewels, the Blackbirds, and while the craze lasted, Madame Zoe, the celebrated medium. This night she presented her latest protégé to Lucas and David, a very large American boxer who had recently flattened the English heavyweight champion. He shyly held out a large black paw to each of them and smiled, showing a gap where his front teeth should have been.

"Isn't he a poppet," Hermione said proudly.

"Are we going to have a prizefight?" asked Lucas. "How exciting."

Hermione, who had felt that her boxer was novelty enough, nevertheless began to look over her guests as if searching for a volunteer. Then she burst into her basso-profundo laugh. "Mr Ryder is making a joke," she explained to her boxer friend, who once more treated them to his gap-toothed smile.

"Go away, Lucas, and find someone to talk to," said Hermione, who never troubled herself to be subtle. "I want to have a tête-à-tête with your divine Mr Harvey."

David, who had not been called divine in public before, hoped he was not blushing, but allowed her to lead him away across the room. Before they could get to whatever dim corner Hermione was aiming for they were stopped by a small man with a leonine head of hair, who put out a commanding hand and said, "Halt."

"Do you mean us?" asked David.

"No, only you, sir. I have already done Hermione; she is of no further use to me."

"Really, John, you are impossible. This is Mr Harvey. Sir John Haidon."

David recognized the name. Sir John was a member of the Royal Academy, well known for his large canvases of historical subjects in modern dress—Julius Caesar being assassinated by conspirators dressed in striped trousers and morning coats, and Boadicea leading the charge in Rotten Row, riding sidesaddle and wearing a black riding habit and a bowler hat. His portrait of Hermione as Salome, dressed in a divided bicycling skirt and looking as if she were about to take a bite out of John the Baptist's nose, hung in the Goldenrod dining room.

"Mr Harvey, you are an answer to prayer," said Sir John. "Exactly what I have been looking for."

"What are you working on now, John?" asked Hermione. "Did you see his painting of the Last Supper with the apostles dressed in football jerseys, Mr Harvey?"

"I can't think how I missed it," said David gravely.

"It's a pity you did," said Sir John. "However, I am at work now on another evening meal of sorts, Plato's *Symposium*, and you, Mr Harvey, are exactly my idea of Alcibiades."

David, looking around for rescue, saw Lucas talking with the boxer and wondered what they could be discussing.

"Everyone will be dressed in cricket flannels," said Sir John.

"How symbolic," said Hermione.

"Why cricket flannels?" David asked respectfully.

"Why not cricket flannels?" said Sir John.

"I only thought," David said diffidently, "since it was an evening party, wouldn't they be wearing white tie and tails?"

Sir John waved this objection aside. He had a vision of a cricket eleven, and to this he determined to remain true. "It doesn't matter in the least what they would have worn," he said. "The ancient Greeks wore either nothing at all or else their blankets. Here is my card, Mr Harvey. Please come to my atelier tomorrow. I start work at the first light."

"I'm afraid I'm leaving for Peru tomorrow," said David with great presence of mind. "I'm so sorry."

"Peru," said Sir John, a faraway look coming into his eyes. "The Incas. Or were they Aztecs? I can never remember. Human sacrifices, Montezuma . . ." David, edging away, was certain that he had been present at the conception of yet another masterpiece. He could picture it in his mind's eye; an Incan priest (unless he was an Aztec), dressed in knickerbockers, holding the knife aloft over his bound victim.

"Do come and sit down a moment," said Philip Goldenrod. "Did Sir John ask you to pose for him?"

"Yes, as Alcibiades in cricket flannels. I'm sure it's a great honour, but . . ."

"The kind of honour one never lives down. You were wise to say you were emigrating. I wanted to talk to you about your poems. Lucas let me read them; I hope you don't mind."

David, who had been hoping that Lucas would do just that, said, "He shouldn't have bothered you."

Philip Goldenrod looked like a snail suffering from excessive sensibility. This stood him in good stead when talking terms, for young authors often got the impression that if they mentioned anything so crude as money he might melt.

He said, "Not at all. I enjoyed it. Very accomplished work, I thought. I told Lucas so."

What he had really said was, "Undergraduate stuff, but not unaccomplished," which was not exactly the same.

"You mean," Lucas had asked, "not publishable?"

"I don't see why not. With his picture on the cover it might sell quite well."

"You're much too kind," said David, remembering that as a schoolboy, he had had fantasies of his name appearing between those of Harte and Hawes in the index of his *Oxford Book of English Verse*.

"Not at all," said Mr Goldenrod. "Come and see me at the office one day next week and we'll have a proper talk."

"Thank you very much indeed, I should like that."

He found Lucas in the dining room listening to a critic from a highbrow quarterly explaining to him what his poems were really about. As David joined them, Jago and his acting company arrived, very late, noisy and drunk. Jago still had a few smudges of makeup left where they would do the most good, but could be construed as accident by those who did not approve of that kind of thing. He posed in the doorway, while a footman waited to take his cloak.

"I'm always thanking you for things," David said to Lucas, in a low voice. Lucas was about to answer him, but Jago's pose demanded silence. He waited for Hermione to come up to him, then foiled her attempt at an embrace with the gesture with which, as Hamlet, he put by Gertrude's advances, and said, in a voice which compelled the attention of even the bridge players in an adjoining room, "My dear Hermione, tell me, was I magnificent or was I not?"

"You were magnificent," said Hermione, who was tolerant of actors, "as of course you should have been, with such a play."

"The play—oh yes," said Jago, remembering that there was such a thing. On stage he often had the delightful feeling that he had written everything himself. "Of course, the play. Where is Lucas? I must kiss him."

Lucas, who was quite used to these performances, said, "I am here, Jago, and you shall kiss me. You did me proud."

Jago proceeded to work the room for compliments like a cutpurse at a county fair. When he came to David, he struck a pose and said, "Well my dear, what have you to say?"

David, who was damned if he was going to have compliments forcibly extracted from him, said, "That was quite an entrance."

"Entrances, my dear Mr Harvey," said Jago in the intimate voice that could be heard in the last row of the gallery, "are the entire secret of acting. You can slink or crawl off, but you must enter well. Now that entrance of yours, my dear, I've often wanted to tell you, but I didn't want to make you shy, the way you hesitate at the door, as if you were too young and modest to march boldly into the room, but in reality simply to give everyone time to say, 'Who is that stunning young man?'—that entrance is sheer and absolute perfection."

David, wishing Jago didn't attract quite so large an audience every time he spoke, joined in the general laughter. Jago took a glass of champagne from a passing footman and said, "I'm afraid I've had an awful lot of this tonight. We had a bit of a celebration backstage before coming here. Hermione's parties are really too large to be amusing. But of course one must just stop in, kiss hands, and be charming to dowagers who arrange charity matinees. It's the least agreeable part of an actor-manager's life. However, now that I've done my duty, would you care to come back to my place? I'm having a small celebration, just a few intimate friends."

"Thank you. Let me just see what Mr Ryder wants to do."

"Mr Ryder is not invited. It would hardly be a celebration if Lucas were there as well."

David looked at Jago in silence, then said, "You are a very odd friend, Mr Portman."

"Odd? How, odd? I am a very good friend."

"You no doubt have your own ideas about that."

"Not at all. It was Plato, wasn't it, who said friends should have all things in common. As well as a good friend, I am also a very old friend, and I do assure you from many years' experience, that should you choose to accept my invitation, Lucas will not mind in the very least." His air was that of a conspirator planning to assassinate Julius Caesar; despite the compelling voice he had somehow managed to rid himself of his audience. No one was listening.

"I can't entirely believe that," said David. "It's been an exciting evening. I expect Mr Ryder will want to talk about it."

"No doubt. I never suggested that Lucas should go home alone, only that he should go without you. Don't pass it up, my dear; I'm really very, very good."

David allowed him one of his best smiles. "I don't doubt it," he said politely. "But it was also Plato, wasn't it, who said that the good is the enemy of the best."

"Did he invite you to a small, intimate celebration?" asked Lucas when David joined him.

"Yes."

"You would have found yourself the only intimate there."

"I suspected as much. Are you tired? Would you like to go home?"

"Not tired. But yes, I would very much like to go home."

Lucas awoke at dawn. The air outside the window, reflecting the night's snow, was like milk. In a moment he realized that it was the silence which had awakened him so early. Chelsea mornings were usually noisy with carriage wheels and the shouts of street hawkers. Now the snow had swallowed all sound.

Inside the ponderous curve of Lucas's body, David lay still asleep. Lucas looked at the beautiful, remote face and smiled. It was undoubtedly a victory of sorts to have him here, in his own bed. Until now it had always been Lucas who had knocked at David's door.

Not, in all fairness, Lucas thought, that David had ever made him beg. Not once had he refused by a pretence of sleep or the excuse of a headache. Always he had moved willingly to make room in the bed, had come without reluctance into his lover's embrace. Yet there was something disconcerting to Lucas in this very willingness; a disturbing sense that such unfailing acquiescence could be based on nothing but a profound indifference, that for David this really did not count, that he was merely a body handed over to someone else's use. Not coldly or grudgingly, it is true, but affectionately, like a coat offered a friend on an unexpectedly chilly night.

But last night it had been David who had knocked on Lucas's bedroom door under the pretext of bringing him a brandy and soda, saying he had sent the servants to bed. There had been very little of a coat lent for a chilly night in their lovemaking when they had gone to bed themselves. David, Lucas thought, smiling to himself, had fallen a little bit in love at last. He might have known earlier. The white lilacs, like a snowdrift in his study window, had been a lover's gift.

Cautiously he moved his numb arm from under David's

head. The movement was enough to break the concentration of his sleep. He opened his eyes, and seeing Lucas, remembered and blushed. Lucas could not help laughing at this.

"Are you laughing at me?"

"I suppose I am. There are so many unexpected sides to your character, you never fail to amuse me."

"In what way?"

"Oh, the nice boy from the vicarage side, that blushes in the morning for what it did at night, the penniless young man so politely and ruthlessly on the make, and now suddenly a wholly new and unexpected side, a side which finds such silly things as success and applause and public admiration sexually stimulating."

"Only your success."

"It's very nice for me, because it's something I can supply. All the same I would prefer to be like the crossing sweeper, loved for myself."

"What makes you think crossing sweepers are loved?"

"Do you think it's a sentimental notion, wanting to be loved for oneself?"

"It's great nonsense. What self? Even the crossing sweeper surely gets loved for something. Do you mean I should only love the physical side of you? I do, you know. You're a wonderful lover, because you have audacity and imagination. But those are the qualities that make you a wonderful poet too. Without them you wouldn't be Lucas Ryder."

"It sounds very flattering, put that way, but all the same there's something lacking. Being loved *for* something is cupboard love. Perhaps everyone's secret ambition is to be loved in spite of."

"What an idea. You know, you're shocking me, Lucas."

"Dear puritan."

In the milky light of dawn the room seemed to have an air of secrecy, almost of strangeness. Even they themselves seemed changed and less familiar. "You are very beautiful," said Lucas.

David half smiled. "Does that still matter?"

"It matters a good deal to me."

"Then think how safe that makes you. Your gifts will be yours till the day you die. We all know how a long a pretty face lasts. What time is it?"

"Nearly seven."

"I'd better go and make my bed look slept-in before the housemaid comes to make up the fire."

"Oh damn the fire and the bloody housemaid and her morning cups of tea. At least the crossing sweeper isn't beset by a gaggle of housemaids in his bedroom."

"You'd soon start complaining if no one made up your fire and brought you tea."

"I expect I would. David, now that the play's out of the way, let's go away for a bit."

"Away? Where?"

"Oh, anywhere. Right away, where there aren't any fogs and slushy roads and housemaids with morning tea. Italy. Anywhere at all. Wouldn't you like that?"

David, who did not mind fogs or slush and was very happy in London, where a handsome face and nice manners went such a long way, turned smiling to Lucas and said, "Thank you. I should love it."

The unease which David had felt at the sight of the empty seats for which he had sent Kitty two tickets, had not left him by morning, and after breakfast he said to Lucas, "Do you mind if I leave you to gloat over your reviews and go round to Tite Street? Call me a fussy old maid if you like, but I can't get rid of the feeling that something is wrong."

"Yes, of course, do go," said Lucas, only half emerging from the review in the *Morning Post* which compared him favourably with the subject of his play.

The snow had already started to melt, and ice-cold water seeped into the hole in David's shoe as he crossed the King's Road. He was beginning to think that there might be something to be said for sunny Italy, when he caught sight of Annie hurrying toward him. The next moment he found himself standing amid a crowd of morning shoppers, holding a hysterical housemaid.

"What's the matter, Annie?" said David. "Do please stop." He tried to disentangle himself, keenly aware of the amused glances of the shoppers. But Annie could neither stop, nor, between sobs and hiccoughs, give a coherent account of herself.

Since he could not calm her, David took her back to Upper Cheyne Row, where Mrs Placid took one look at her and said severely, "There my girl, just you calm down now, or we'll have to give you sal volatile."

This threat silenced Annie. Mrs Placid made her a cup of tea, and after Annie had drunk it, still spluttering a good deal, she said, "There now, that's better. When's the last time you've eaten, you silly girl?"

While she busied herself finding some food for her unexpected guest, David said, "Can you tell me what's happened, Annie?"

"Please sir, it's Mrs Snow," said Annie, beginning to sob again, though more quietly this time. "She never came home last night, so I went round to Mrs Castlemain's, but Mrs Castlemain's Nettie said they hadn't looked in and she thought they must be in quod—prison, sir. Miss Kitty made me promise never to tell His Lordship if she was arrested, but I can't stand the waiting, it's driving me barmy, honest it is, sir. That's why I came to look for you. I never promised not to tell *you*."

"When did all this happen, Annie?"

"They went out night before last and I never saw them again. I've been that upset, sir."

"Of course you have, Annie. Look, you stay here and have something to eat and a nice rest. Mrs Placid will look after you. I'll see if Lord Altondale's at his club. If not I'll send a wire, and then I'll come back here and take you home."

Augustus was not in London, but replied promptly to David's wire that he would have the express stopped and be in London in the morning.

David met him at King's Cross. Augustus hailed a cab, then said, "Nasty business, what?"

"It seems to be unusually so. Mr Ryder kindly offered to stand bail, but they wouldn't hear of it."

"What had she done, do you know?"

"Nothing very much. She and Mrs Castlemain wrote NO VOTES NO GOLF in acid on a golf-course lawn."

"You call that nothing much? My dear David, we English are a patient race, but anyone caught mucking about with our putting greens must expect to be shown the full severity of the law. I expect I'd better go and see the Home Secretary."

David felt comforted by being in the presence of someone who could march in on the Home Secretary without asking for an appointment. He said, "What do you hear from Toby, sir? Felix writes quite often, but Toby's a wretched correspondent."

"He takes after me," said Augustus. "I don't suppose I hear from him any more often than you. If he wants to let you know something he sends a telegram; if he's got a funny story to tell he saves it up till he sees you. He seems to enjoy Ireland. Odd place to enjoy, I should have thought."

The Home Secretary, who had been at Eton with Augustus and often shot grouse with him, said the suffragettes were a confounded nuisance, but obligingly wrote a release order for Kitty and they set out for Holloway Prison.

"I must say Kitty broadens one's horizons," said Augustus, as they were shown into the prison governor's office. "I never expected to see the inside of a jail."

The prison governor read the Home Secretary's release order. David thought he looked uneasy, but he sent for Kitty without making difficulties.

They waited in silence. At last the governor's secretary returned alone, saying that Mrs Snow would not come out of her cell because she refused to owe her freedom to a man.

Augustus, manfully, said, "Rubbish, bring her out," whereupon she was dragged from her cell by two sturdy wardresses and handed over to her rescuers. Her revulsion against Augustus's maleness had been a momentary hysteria; when she saw him she burst into tears and collapsed sobbing into his arms.

"My dear Kitty," said Augustus, deeply shocked by her appearance. Her face was bruised, her lips and gums torn and bloody. She was scarcely able to stand on her feet; her pretty American voice had turned into a raven's croak.

Augustus handed her gently to David and turned to confront the prison governor. "What happens to these women in your jail, sir?" he said. He was icily calm; only David, who knew him so well, realized how angry he was. "Be assured that you have not heard the last of this. Good day to you."

Between them he and David half carried Kitty to their cab and took her home to Tite Street, where Annie put her to bed. A doctor was sent for, and diagnosed pleurisy. It happened sometimes during forced feeding, he told Augustus, that a morsel of food might be inadvertently introduced into the lung, especially if the prisoner engaged in a foolish struggle. Mrs Snow must keep very quiet. He would have a prescription sent round for her.

Kitty remained in bed, very ill and weak. Augustus visited her every day, sent her flowers and baskets of lovely things to eat from Fortnum and Mason's, and felt his heart torn into little shreds whenever she thanked him in the ragged whisper which was all the voice they had left her.

He did not change his opinion of the suffragettes—he considered them more than ever dangerous nuisances—but he found it intolerable (for all the chivalrous reasons they would have resented most) that a gentlewoman should be so treated.

At Kitty's bedside he met Mrs Castlemain, herself again at liberty after four days in Holloway. She explained to him, her voice still hoarse, that she was free under the cat-and-mouse act, a legal device which provided that women be freed, no matter how long their sentence, before their health could be seriously affected, thus avoiding the unfavourable publicity which would undoubtedly have resulted had one of them died of forced feeding. Augustus suspected that Mrs Castlemain, redoubtable creature, regretted the fact that as yet none had.

Under the cat-and-mouse act the women could be rearrested to finish out their sentences when they had recovered their strength. Both Mrs Castlemain and Kitty were thus liable to be returned to jail.

"We must put a stop to this," said Augustus with the calm decision of a man who has only to command for a thing to happen. Mrs Castlemain, who had no opinion of men at all, was nevertheless willing to admit that they had their occasional uses. Augustus, for example, could make a speech in the House of Lords, which she could not.

As soon as she was well enough to travel, Augustus took Kitty to Altondale to be put to bed and cautiously spoon-fed by Nannie (grumbling all the while about such goings-on) back to health.

Augustus himself, despite weather which promised glorious hunting, returned the next day to London, and with Mrs Castlemain's help put together a speech to be delivered in the House of Lords.

Mrs Castlemain was herself in prison once again (and would on no account have been admitted to the visitors' gallery, where she was far too well known) on the day on which Augustus rose and asked their lordships indulgence while he drew their attention to an abuse which, he felt, was a stain on the honour of a country known the world over for its sense of fair play and chivalry. He reviewed the glories of English justice, from the abolition of torture and the star chamber, to the act of habeas corpus and trial by jury.

When he had them purring "hear, hear," thinking them-selves very fine fellows indeed, he took from a pocket a metal gag and asked their lordships whether they knew what it was. No, he had not expected the noble lords to recognize this implement of a horrible practice, borrowed from the brutalities of the lunatic asylum. He begged their pardon in advance for the distressing details he had now to lay before them, and gave what his peers, sleepily trying to digest their lunches, felt was a far too graphic description of the act of forced feeding. Turning their muttered protests to his purpose, he told them they were right to protest, to express their shock at these things which were being done three times daily, perhaps at this very moment, in English prisons, to English women, who might be their lordships' sisters and wives.

Remembering something Sir Abraham Montefiore had recently said at lunch, he flung himself into his peroration.

"It has been put to me," he said, "by a wise and much travelled person, who has had occasion to view us with an outsider's impartial eye"—Sir Abraham had been born in Wapping, but Augustus always tended to view Jews as intrinsically foreign—"that we English are subject to a kind of circular reasoning. We say torture is un-English, therefore what we are doing is not torture. But I put it to you, my lords, that to hold down a desperately struggling woman, to jam a metal gag into her mouth, to force a rubber tube down her throat, to pour hot gruel down that tube—not indeed to sustain life, since feedings administered under such stressful circumstances are inevitably vomited up again—but as a punishment for holding an unpopular opinion, again I put it to you that such treatment is the most barbarous of tortures, and it is being committed in England."

It was not a popular speech, but the House of Lords allows its members great latitude, and Augustus was far too solidly one of themselves to be taken on in open battle. The art of compromise at its finest was brought into play. "Poor Strafford is getting very eccentric," they said at his club. "Augustus is losing his grip. Wonder what Milly makes of it all. She can't like it much, being married to a suffragist."

Lady Millicent did not like it. The women of the WSPU were appalling, but its male adherents were merely ridiculous. There was poor Mr Lansbury with his East End constituency and his cockney accent, Mr Keir Hardie, whose taste in clothes kept *Punch* supplied with never-ending materials for jokes, not to mention Mr Sheehy-Skeffington, with his flaming red beard and piercing Irish voice. Was Lord Altondale to be numbered among this ludicrous lot?

Though Lady Milly made it very plain that she was not happy, it looked as though Augustus meant to be just that. He kept on making speeches, buttonholed the members of his club, badgered the Home Secretary. He wrote letters to the papers, which, to Lady Millicent's mortification, he did not sign *Pro Bono Publico* but with his own full name and title. Old friends began to avoid him.

"They think I'm a suffragist," he said to Sir Abraham, one of the friends who remained loyal to him during those trying days. "I'm not, that's what makes it all so funny."

"There is no reason why women should not have the vote," said Sir Abraham, "but they will not get it like this. Both sides have gone too far for compromise. It will have to come to them sideways, as a result of something else, when no one any longer cares very much."

"How do you mean, sideways."

"I don't quite know. It will happen when our attention is distracted by something more important. War, perhaps."

"War? With Ireland?"

"No," said Sir Abraham, who travelled much in Germany. "Not Ireland."

Felix had been almost a year in Japan and showed no signs of moving on. His letters home had grown rarer; it was reported that he never went to parties at the German colony, that he had been seen wearing a kimono, that he was in danger of going native.

When he went next to the bank to collect his quarterly allowance, he was instead handed an envelope which contained a steamship ticket to Bremen.

Felix said, "Dear Papa, always so direct, so effective. How much money have I got?"

Mr Matsuko, who handled the finances for the small German colony in Tokyo, looked politely inscrutable.

"Yes," said Felix, "I suspected as much."

He was very sorry to have to give up his pretty house with the rice-paper windows, and his pretty O-Hisa, who gave such marvellous massages and did such delightful things in bed, but remembering that boats were notorious for giving their passengers far too much to eat, he cheered up a little. He was getting awfully bored with slices of raw squid beautifully arranged on a black lacquer tray.

And of course, he reminded himself, he would see Kitty again. It was after all less than a day's journey from Eschenbach to London.

In April David and Lucas returned from what Lucas, feeling the need to defend himself against too great a happiness, always mockingly referred to as the Italian Honeymoon. Lucas said it would be unpatriotic not to be in England in April, but the real reason they came back was that David's first book of poems was about to be published.

Like many another minor poet before him, David had found Italy stimulating, and had managed to do a good amount of creditable writing. Major poets of course can write equally well in Clapham Junction or at the North Pole, though not, in Lucas's case, when they are in love. He had simply been too happy to trouble himself about paper and pen, or for that matter, Italian architecture and scenery, except insofar as they made a background for David, who, tanned, his hair streaked blond by Italian sun, had never looked more beautiful or been more—Lucas's mind censored the word "obliging" and tried to substitute "loving," but it resisted him unless he was willing to take it on David's terms, David, who thought him the most amusing and easiest company in the world, and England's greatest poet, and was willing to reward him for this with the delightful present of his person.

Philip Goldenrod, who read David's new peoms over his tea, said, "Good. Now we can get rid of most of the Oxford things. This is quite decent work. What about you, Lucas? Did you really write nothing at all?"

"Very nearly nothing. One poem. I think it's a good one."

"I look forward to reading it."

"You must ask David. I gave it to him."

"How do you mean, you gave it to him?"

Lucas smiled, remembering waking early one morning, with David asleep beside him and the first line of the poem unravelling in his head. The next line and the next had come with a certainty that required no revision. He had written it out and left it on the pillow beside David, who had later come down to breakfast with the piece of paper in his hand, saying, "Is it really for me? Thank you, it's beautiful;" a look on his face Lucas had learned to know well, not a smile, but a glance both happy and grave to tell him how much he loved it.

"Just what I say," Lucas told his publisher. "It's David's to do with as he likes. If he wants to shout it from the rooftops he may; if he wants to keep it for himself—much more likely, incidentally, as I know him—he may do that. It no longer has anything to do with me."

"You *are* in love. Nothing else could turn you into such a fool."

"Yes. Yes, I am. Fancy it happening to me, so late in the day, too."

"Would you rather it had happened sooner?"

"No, I don't think so. I don't think I could have coped with it when I was young. I might have spoiled it. It's a disciplined life, you know, being in love."

Philip Goldenrod did not know. With the envy of those who have never achieved successful love, and therefore think that it must be both easy and pleasurable, he said, "Under the aspect of eternity it is scarcely more important than the mating of mayflies, Lucas."

"Less so, I should imagine. At least mayflies produce other mayflies. But then I make no claims of importance."

"I mean that it is your poems that matter, not the presence of beautiful young men in your life."

"That, my dear," said Lucas, "is where we happen not to agree."

"Well, tell your David I'm pleased with him. As I've said before, with his photograph on the cover we should do well."

Lucas protested against the idea of the photograph, which he privately thought vulgar, but Hermione backed her husband, and David himself seemed somewhat lacking in delicacy on the subject and gave no sign of minding.

The book was reviewed favourably and at considerable length in the more important literary journals by Lucas's literary friends, and with the help of the photograph on the back cover sold very well indeed.

David was pleased to have produced a book, and liked the reviews and compliments, but found that on the whole it made no great difference to him. It was a pleasant thing

190

among the many pleasant things that had been happening to him since he had come to live with Lucas Ryder. He remembered Lucas once saying that he had never felt like a real person until the day he had read his own name on the spine of a book; that in a manner of speaking this had been his birth certificate. Of course Lucas is a real poet, thought David, looking at his own name on the cover of his book. But what am I? Not really a poet, evidently, or I should feel validated by having my name on a book. Not a scholar, or I would have managed somehow to get that fellowship at Oxford. Perhaps I'm nothing but a fairly successful tart. I am twenty-two years old. I wonder if I'll ever find the thing that will validate me.

Chapter 9

During the first week of May, Hesso, who was in Berlin on business, lunched with Algy Strafford, that wizard of precedence and quarterings. In the brilliant summer sun all Berlin seemed to be taking the air; even the hideous marble statues of the kings of Prussia along the Sieges Allee seemed blessed by the sun.

Algy had just returned from a brief holiday in England. It sometimes struck Hesso that for someone who was supposed to be *en poste* in Berlin, Algy travelled a good deal. Still, who could blame him?

"How was everything in England?" Hesso asked.

"Like everything here. So peaceful. Heavenly weather. One thinks it can't last, yet it goes on, day after day."

"The weather?"

"And other things."

Hesso thought of the cannons, rifles, machine guns, and howitzers pouring day after day from the Landeck Stahl Fabrik. He knew that Algy was thinking of that too. He said, "When you were little, did you have serial stories in the boys' magazines? The hero is tied to the powder keg, the fuse is lit, and it says: 'to be continued.' "

"Of course the Irish are rumbling," said Algy. "Perhaps it is only that."

"Everything possible has been done."

"I know. That's what's so frightening. All those alliances and *ententes*. Triple this and triple that. Six powder kegs to go up instead of two."

"Unthinkable."

"That our two countries should be at war? Yes, it is."

"Now France . . ." said Hesso, who felt about his neighbour the way one so often does about neighbours, that they were an unmannerly lot, whose food, wine, and women were much too good for them.

"It does seem odd for England to have them as allies," said Algy. "Still, there it is. How are your young people?"

"All well. The grandchildren are flourishing—two now, did you know? And Felix is on his way home."

"What an interesting year he's had."

"A little too interesting, if you ask me. Why must he always settle down so? We weren't like that when we were his age."

Algy laughed. "Not we. We kept strings of them, like polo ponies."

"We shall have to find a wife for him before he settles down permanently with someone quite unsuitable. There was that American widow too." He poured out a wine which was pale green and tasted faintly of flint.

"Your own?" Algy asked.

"Yes. Austrian. A mountain wine. I bought the vineyards a few years ago—there is a red too. It will be enough to keep the family supplied in case."

"In case you are cut off from France, you mean?" said Algy. They drank and turned to look out the window at the peaceful summer day. A company of cuirassiers paraded down the Sieges Allee, their silver helmets gleaming in the sun. They looked festive, not threatening. "Unthinkable," Algy said again.

Hesso thought about it nevertheless. "What we ought to do," he said, "is get the families together this summer. We haven't done that in years—not since Angelika's wedding."

"That was rather an occasion. What a good idea, though. Where do you think? London?"

"Fallon," said Hesso, as if he were pronouncing a magic formula.

Algy, who had spent some of the happiest summers of his boyhood running wild on the Landeck island in the North Sea, smiled at his German cousin. "Yes," he said, "of course. We'll all meet on Fallon."

The Landeck family did not, strictly speaking, own Fallon Island. It had been leased by Hesso's father to use as a testing range for top secret experiments. He had built a simple cottage where he and his cronies could spend some time undisturbed, salt-water fishing and getting drunk. In time children—well, sons anyhow—were taken along, more rooms were added, but the accommodations remained, until Hesso married, very crude.

Sophie did not approve of men going off by themselves. She suspected rightly that unsupervised they might indulge in behaviour less pleasing to God than if she were there to keep an eye on them. Her religious faith made her impervious to discomfort, but other wives, invited along, shared neither Sophie's strong principles nor her firm Christian purpose. They came once and thereafter refused all invitations to spend a summer holiday at the island with honeyed but unshakable determination.

So plumbing and water were laid on at tremendous expense; in time an electric generator began to whir in its shed. Rooms were added for the ladies and their maids, and Fallon House took on the air of a ramshackle, haphazard, but extremely comfortable summer hotel.

Sophie very much approved her husband's idea of a family get-together. She was tired these days, and as she wrote out invitations she pictured herself in her mind's eye sitting on the shady verandah with Milly and Rachel, in their white summer frocks and shady hats, felt the gentle melancholy which is the gift of long summer afternoons to those past middle age, who know their dreams of adventure or romantic love have not come to pass and now never will.

To be idle for a few weeks, sit with her hands in her lap,

talk with intimates in gentle, polite sentences punctuated by the smallest of sighs, drink pale tea with bullets of sunlight at the bottom of the cup . . .

She drew a piece of writing paper toward her and dipped her pen. "My dear Toby . . ." she wrote, thinking of him, his round cheerful face with the mop of straw hair; he enjoyed soldiering, Cousin Milly had written, loved the hunting and fishing in Ireland, played polo for his regiment. There never seemed to be problems with Toby; no involvements with foreign women, no involvements at all. If there had been, she would soon have known. Theirs was a gossipy family.

"My dear David . . ." How well he too had done for himself, she thought, a First in Greats at Oxford, a book of poems published and well received at age twenty-two, private secretary to no less a personage than Lucas Ryder. Sophie was a great reader, with a tremendous, if ignorant respect for writers. She wondered whether she might invite Lucas Ryder to spend a holiday at Fallon. No doubt he had many more glamorous invitations, but she might mention it to David and see what he thought. David too, as far as she knew, had kept himself free of emotional entanglements. Was it all due to the famous phlegmatic English temperament? Or had she done something wrong, erred in some ways in Felix's upbringing? Well, he was on his way home now. They could begin to look about for a suitable wife; he was quite old enough to get married, and a young woman of sound Catholic background might settle him down, as she had Hesso. On a new sheet of paper she began to make a list of eligible young women, then, remembering Angelika's wedding, tore the list into little pieces. They must proceed with great tact and caution. Thank goodness Angelika was happily married now, and the babies were a delight, so healthy and brown and cheerful, but why, oh why, were her children so headstrong, so very difficult, when other people's were so good? Her thoughts turned to Marit, for it was Marit, of course, not Felix or Angelika, who fretted her until she was worn out with worry and guilt; Marit, who had always been the hardest of her three to love. Had she guessed it, for all the trouble Sophie had taken to hide it? Was it love she had so obsessively sought in the convent, and now among the poor, in a single room in the worst part of town, where soot lay thick and sour in the yard, and the landlord's pig grunted in its pen under her window?

Marit's poor were not the poor whom Sophie herself cherished, the unlucky or thriftless, ill or unemployed who constitute the underside of any industrial city. Sophie's poor were so by accident or ill luck; poverty was not the state they had chosen and God still had them in his keeping.

Marit's poor were drifters and down-and-outs who had long since slipped through God's fingers, who chose their state and asked for neither charity, work, nor prayer. Every industrial community has such people. In Eschenbach they lived under the Schiller Brücke, the first cast-steel railway bridge built in Germany, and named not after the great poet, but after the engineer who designed it and happened to have the same name. The river which ran under the bridge had little in common with the purling stream whose charming curve wound itself along the parkland of the abbey. Here it ran sluggishly, poisoned with waste and sewage. By its shore, sheltered under the arches of the bridge, lived a community which, constantly chased by the police and respectable town dogs, winnowed by malnutrition, alcoholism, syphilis, and knife fights, seemed nevertheless to maintain remarkably stable numbers—Marit's chosen poor.

Not that they welcomed her attention; they cursed her for a rich bitch out slumming, in language so debased and brutal it seemed scarcely like human speech. Marit brought them food, which they might one day snatch at and devour like starved dogs, another throw back into her face; she washed their sores and bandaged them while they kicked at her; she never mentioned God or religion to them, nor did she reprove them for their drunkenness and brutality.

Sophie visited Marit as faithfully as she visited her other poor, carrying a basket filled with warm clothing and a nourishing stew. There was no fire in Marit's room, and when next she came a grey mould had crept over the stew. "Why?" Sophie asked. "Why must you live like this?"

Marit only smiled, her eyes like a gull's, fixed on things far away.

"Dearest Milly . . . ," Sophie wrote, "My own darling Angelika . . . ," sending out letters to Ireland and Hungary and Yorkshire, "Rachel, my dear . . . ," leaving the hardest till last.

It was, she knew, no use inviting Marit to Fallon, where there were no poor, only the Landecks and their kin and friends, and servants as sleek as their masters. Nevertheless she must of course be asked. "My dearest Marit . . ." No, she couldn't do it. One couldn't send a written invitation to a daughter in the same town. She would go and invite her in person, listen to the pig grunting in the greasy yard, look at the milk curdled in its bottle on the windowsill, and ask herself why, what have I done wrong?

She piled the letters into a neat square for the butler to stamp and mail, and rang for her coat and hat. She would go now, right away, while her resolution was firm and she could still call to mind the rectangle of letters, the promised reprieve of a summer of peace and idleness, sitting on the verandah, chatting about nothing, her hands in her lap.

Her Royal Highness Crown Princess Victoria's Own Yorkshire Rifles were a hard-drinking regiment, and kept to a benign tradition of silence at breakfast. Toby opened Sophie's stiff letter with care; on the morning after a guest night the crackle of an envelope could sound like heavy artillery to a throbbing head. Focusing his eyes with some pain, he read his way through Sophie's ornate lines. Felix was on his way home from Japan, they were planning a family get-together on Fallon, she hoped so very much that Toby would be able to get leave and join them.

Leave was not a problem, Toby knew. He was entitled to two months and could have more for the asking. But he was not sure that he wanted to ask.

Never in his life had he been happier than this last year with his regiment. He lifted his eyes from his letter and looked at his fellow officers, seated at the long mess tables, while cat-footed waiters circled silently with porridge and jugs of coffee. From Colonel Molyneux, who was drinking his customary morning glass of claret, down to Second Lieutenant Bill Castries, their latest arrival, who was pulling his sparse moustache in the hope of hurrying its growth, Toby loved them. There could not be a group of better chaps anywhere in the world, and he had waited and worked all his life to become one of them. The Vickies were his father's regiment, his grandfather's and great-grandfather's as well, and ever since he was a very little boy Toby had known their history and had been able to recite the battle honours inscribed on the tattered colours, even the very hard names like Chilianwala and Bloemfontein.

He knew every regimental custom before he went to prep school; that only officers from the rank of major up were allowed to stand on the hearth rug of the officers' mess, that newly arrived subalterns might not speak unless spoken to for three months, that the port must always be circulated to the right, that officers were permitted to smoke cigars and cigarettes (Turkish, never Virginian) but not a pipe, that Vickies always addressed superior officers as "sir" and each other by their last names, like public school boys.

They were a county regiment, originally levied by the Strafford of the day to keep Napoleon's army from camping on Ilkley Moor. His Christian name, like Toby's, was Theobald, and his regiment was inevitably dubbed the Baldies. Hair therefore became an obsession with them. When pigtails were discontinued in 1808, Baldies continued to wear their hair long, and whether or not moustaches were required by army regulations, they adorned their upper lips with soup strainers and their cheeks with dundrearies just to show. When at the battle of Bloemfontein a very thin red line of Baldies had held off a Boer attack, losing every officer and all but a dozen of their men, HRH Crown Princess Victoria had graciously consented to become their honorary colonel, which had given them a new nickname they much preferred to being called Baldies.

Other ranks, of whom the officers saw little except on parade, consisted of Yorkshire ploughboys and whey-faced factory hands who, having incautiously accepted the offer of a drink from a recruiting sergeant, found themselves the next morning with a terrible headache, the Queen's shilling in their pocket (if it hadn't been pinched), and their lives signed away to the army. They were then taken in hand by the NCOs, who drilled, cursed, bullied, brutalized, and flogged them until they became that most reliable of fighting instruments, the English regular soldier.

Though the Vickies' depot was in Dewsbury, which was not fashionable, there was nothing unfashionable about the regiment's officers. It could never be said derisively of them that they could live on their pay. They were expected to keep hunters and polo ponies. Major de Lacy had given a pack of foxhounds to First Battalion. They had high mess bills, owed huge sums to their tailors and bootmakers, and kept a French cook. It was said of them that they scarcely seemed like infantry at all. Colonel Molyneux took this to be a compliment.

Vickies' officers were expected to ride to hounds and play polo at every opportunity, but those few eccentrics who preferred to do needlepoint or liked to read were tolerated. Major de Lacy, who kept a pet wombat and knitted, was loved by everyone.

At the time Toby joined the Vickies they were stationed in Ireland. The first night he had entered the mess, wearing his new bottle-green tunic, taking great care to stand well back from the hearth rug and not to speak unless spoken to, Toby had known that life could hold no happier moment. It had been worth it, all of it, the harsh years of public school, the constant work and discipline which had made of his body an obedient instrument, even the ghastly months at a London crammer's after he had failed his entrance examination into Sandhurst had been worth it; he would have undergone far greater hardships to be allowed to stand under the tattered battle honours, amid the shining mahogany and gleaming silver.

The Vickies had not disappointed him; they were everything he had hoped and wanted. He had only one small regret, that they had never fought together. During the glorious days in India and Africa, where, taking their dominion over palm and pine for granted, they had hacked at brown and black flesh, and were quite often themselves hacked to pieces by irate natives who did not see eye to eye with them, an officer had been able to get his fill of fighting. But though they were ready, even eager, to begin hacking away at the heathen Roman Catholics of Ireland, Gaelic genius for muddles, internecine quarrelling and general fecklessness made it seem unlikely that a proper uprising would ever get off the ground. Still, the regiment had hopes of 12 July, Orangemen's Day, and though Toby very much wanted to see David and Felix again, he did not want to miss any possible fighting.

After breakfast he went to the stables, where he knew he would find his colonel, and put his problem to him. The colonel, feeding lumps of sugar to his black hunter, said, "I should go, you know. If anything interesting looks like happening, I can always send you a wire. Personally I think it's all a lot of talk. No organization, you know, the Irish. None at all."

At the Dower House there was never any need for silence at breakfast. Lucas these days drank judiciously, David hardly at all, and their breakfasts tended to be cheerful affairs during which they read funny bits from their letters out loud to each other, while David tried without much success to keep Lucas from getting marmalade all over *The Times*.

"The twins have discovered Aristophanes," said David, reading a letter from his father, "and are scandalizing the village."

"In the original Greek?"

"No. They think it's much too funny to be kept secret and are busy translating all the most unsuitable bits." David removed the butter knife before Lucas could use it to open a letter with a German stamp on it. "Is it from Professor Pflock about his monograph?"

"No, it's from a Baronin von Landeck. She says she asked you to spend the summer with them at their island in the North Sea, and would be no end honoured if I would join them as well. She has read all my poetry in English and German, and admires it most respectfully, not to mention that the Eschenbach Amateur Dramatic Society's performance of *Pippa Passes* in German translation was a most tremendous success last spring."

Pippa Passes was a one-act farce Lucas had written while an undergraduate at Oxford. It was full of horrible puns, mistaken identities, and farfetched coincidences, and he would willingly have forgotten about it, but that it had become the darling of amateur actors everywhere.

"Oh Lucas," said David delightedly, "think of it. *Pippa Passes* in German performed by the Eschenbach Amateur Dramatic Society! I do wish we'd seen it."

"The things we missed, going to Italy."

David, who had planned to take a short holiday at home while Lucas visited old friends in Scotland ("Very old—my parents' friends really—very sweet, very dull; I won't inflict them on you"), sorted through his letters till he found the one from Landeck.

"Oh good, Flixy's coming home, and everyone's going to have a grand get-together on Fallon Island. Toby's coming too. It will be fun seeing them again. You'll come, Lucas, won't you?"

Lucas, shutting a piece of buttery toast inside a glossy book of poetry sent him by its glossy publisher in hopes of a glossy review, shook his head. "Thank you, my dear, but I think I'd better stay with my original plans."

"Couldn't you go to Scotland later? I think you'd like Felix and Toby and the Landecks."

"I'm sure I would. But all the same, no."

David looked at him suspiciously. "I can always tell when you're keeping something back. You have a reason for not wanting to come."

"Yes, if you must know. The truth is, I don't think I could bear another house party with you. All that pretending you're my secretary . . ."

"Well, so I am."

". . . and sneaking off to your room after everyone's gone to bed, like some beastly French farce."

"You never minded that before."

"Italy must have spoiled me."

"I know. It spoiled me too. But Lucas, what else can

people like us do? We can't very well ask for a nice room with a double bed."

Lucas laughed at this. "No. We can only be very strange and well bred or stay at home."

"Home?" David looked out over the estuary shining in the sun and relinquished his own plans with regret but no resentment. "Is that what you want to do, spend the summer here? Well then, let's."

At such times Lucas had formerly asked himself whether this easy acquiescence to his whims was a measure of David's affection for him, or merely a sign of his indifference. Since Italy this was no longer a question he felt he needed to ask.

"My dear," he said, touched, "how very nice of you. But, you know, I don't think we ought to start making sacrifices and giving things up for each other. It gets to be a habit, and it's so bad for one. No, I'll go visit my bores for the good of my soul, and you go to Fallon, and then, in the autumn I thought we might go to Greece."

David, who had been pouring himself a cup of coffee, spilled some of it into the saucer. "Greece?"

"Would you like that?"

"Oh, Lucas, more than anything in the world."

"I warn you, you'll be disappointed. It's not a bit like those books you're always reading, people in white chitons walking up and down the Acropolis having high-minded conversations. It's smelly and dirty and quarrelsome . . ."

"I'd noticed that, really, reading Aristophanes."

Lucas laughed. "It's a lot more like that than like Plato. Personally I've always enjoyed it very much."

"Oh no," said Lady Millicent. Sophie's letter had arrived with the afternoon post, and she was reading it over her tea.

Lady Millicent disliked everything about Fallon Island. The sheets were always damp, and the sand got into her shoes and stockings, into the hem of her skirts, and no matter how much Calais shook and brushed, it got into her bed. "No," she said again, "most decidedly not."

She and Rachel had planned to open the house on Chesterfield Hill and have a proper London season with theatres, dances, and parties, and she now said so to Augustus.

Augustus, who considered a summer spent in London, season or no season, a wicked waste of good weather, would not hear of it. Both he and Hesso were in a very robust mood that summer; perhaps the prospect of war had inspired it.

"You go to Fallon then," said Milly, "and I shall send my excuses."

Augustus said no. The party was meant to be for the whole family, a grand get-together for everyone. Diplomatically he suggested that a few weeks by the sea would do Julian no end of good. She had been coughing all winter. The bracing sea air might be exactly what she needed.

"Nannie doesn't like the seaside," said Lady Milly.

"Good God—sorry, Milly—we surely don't need Nannie. Julian's twelve; what does she want with a nanny?" He began to tell Julian stories about the island, about childhood summers he and Algy had spent with Hesso on Fallon. "You can lie in bed with the windows wide open and listen to the sea as you go to sleep," he said. "There is no way to get there except by boat; everything is brought in on Uncle Hesso's yacht and once a week a boy rows over from the mainland and brings the mail and newspapers. Some nights the water turns gold, it's algae or something scientific like that, and if you put it in a bottle to save it it's only saltwater the next day, but on a moonlit night it's a sight to see." Augustus often forgot that Julian could not see, and that she was not a member of the family who could claim Hesso von Landeck as uncle, and she never reminded him.

"It sounds lovely," said Julian, and partly because she wanted to go, but mostly because she liked to see how far she could make other people do what she wanted, she rubbed her soft young cheek like a little cat against Lady Milly's, and said, "Dearest Lady Milly, don't you think we could?" and Lady Millicent, on consideration, said, "If you'd like it so much, my darling."

"Do bring everyone," Sophie had written, not knowing that Kitty was staying at the hall and was therefore by every canon of good manners invited to spend the summer on Fallon.

And so Felix, who had sailed across the Pacific to San Francisco, had travelled by train all the way across the United States to New York, and had there embarked for Bremen, and Kitty, who had come by way of the Women's Social and Political Union, and Holloway Prison to Altondale, met once again on a sunny summer day by the North Sea.

"It had to happen," said Felix, kissing Kitty's hand. "I see now that it was meant," while on the other side of the island the gulls whirled screaming into the sky at the whipcrack of a new rifle which Hesso and Toby were trying out on the testing range.

It was a happy holiday; an unbroken chain of sunny days and clear, starry nights. Lady Millicent's unselfishness was rewarded; from her shady seat on the verandah she could watch Julian paddling happily in the shallow water, growing a little fatter and more pink-cheeked every day, and never coughing at all anymore. For such a reward she could bear with damp sheets and sand in her stockings.

With Kitty and Felix, Julian went for long walks along the shore, collecting pebbles smooth to the touch, tiny white shells, and once a hermit crab.

Sophie and Lady Milly worried about those long walks. Surely Felix and Kitty should not spend all that time together. Yet what could they say? Short of offering to share their walks—and neither of them was ready to expose herself to wind, sun, and sand—they could do nothing. And it was true that neither Felix nor Kitty ever gave a sign that they minded if Angelika and her boys offered to come with them, or Julian begged to be taken to the top of the dunes, where the wind blew from the sea, tugging and unbraiding her hair, and turning Angelika's parasol inside out.

Kitty, never as careful of the conventions as she should have been, had put by her blacks, and in a white shirtwaist, with a black ribbon at the neck to show grief, looked frail and somehow much younger than when Felix had first known her.

To mark her disapproval of the prematurely discarded

mourning, Lady Millicent gave Kitty an elegant French evening dress of black georgette for her birthday, which fell in the middle of their holiday. Kitty, accustomed to the blunt speech of her Bostonian mother-in-law, was not subtle enough to appreciate so delicate a reprimand, and merely said, "You *are* kind, Cousin Milly; it's much too good for me," with which Lady Millicent silently concurred.

Hesso, Augustus, Oliver and Toby spent their days on the testing range playing with Landeck Steel's latest in dangerous toys. At the end of June Hesso took Algy, Toby, and Augustus on his yacht to Kiel to take part in the great festivities being held there by the English and German navies. (Felix, claiming that he was a martyr to seasickness, elected to stay on the island with Kitty.)

Steel manufactured by Landeck Stahl Fabrik armoured the dreadnoughts of both nations. The sun shone, boat races were held, the English and German guests feted each other at lunches and dinners. "Friends now, friends forever," was the popular toast that June.

When at the end of the month the heir to the Austrian throne was assassinated by a schoolboy in Sarajevo, no one paid much attention. The kaiser's yacht lay no longer at anchor amid the great gathering of ships, Algy went back to Berlin, but the parties went on, and the toasts to friendship now and forever continued to be drunk. At the beginning of July Hesso and his party returned to Fallon, and David arrived a few days later.

It was the first time the three friends had been together in more than a year. Toby seemed the most changed; his drooping blond moustache made him seem almost a stranger at first. Both he and David had expected Felix to have returned from the Orient, slant-eyed and inscrutable, but Felix, despite his many journeys and adventures, had changed the least of the three; he was as always unsuitably in love and full of talk about it.

Felix and Toby had found a secluded cove where they could bathe with nothing on. Stupefied with sun and the wine they had drunk at lunch, they would doze there and listen to Felix's talk.

"You're brown all over, like Angelika's babies," Felix said to David the first time they went there to bathe.

"Yes, I've been in Italy. We had a house on the top of a cliff, looking out over the sea. Only the birds could spy on us."

"What about servants?"

"Italian servants sleep all afternoon. And even if they'd seen us they'd only think we were some more eccentric English milords. Italy's full of them."

Soberer than his friends, David had brought a book to read, but the sun and the salt air soon caused the letters to blur, and he cast his mind adrift, nodding sleepily, while Felix talked on and on about his great and seemingly insoluble dilemma. He was in love with Kitty, he wanted to marry her, he had asked her every day on those long walks they took, but she would not, saying she was too old, too poor, widowed, foreign.

"Yes, Flixy, of course," they would say. "But Flix, you've got to consider . . ." "Well, no, of course not . . . ," sleepily feeding him crumbs of their attention while they dozed in the sun, until Felix, with a cry composed of rage and anguish would dash into the water and come back, shaking drops all over them like a dog, cursing their tepid English temperament.

"I always expect a cloud of steam to rise up into the air when Flix rushes into the water," said Toby.

"Poor old Flix. Celibacy must be hard on him, after that nice geisha, and the Anglo-Indian widow in need of consolation he met on the boat coming back."

"More Indian than Anglo, I suspect," said Toby, who had heard a good deal about that lady's amatory skills, and could not imagine a decent Englishwoman, even if raised in a hot climate, getting up to such tricks.

Muzzy with sun and wine, Toby seemed these days more willing than he had been since he had got religion at Eton, to take part in this kind of conversation. "It's our English educational system," he explained to Felix, who berated him and David for their want of passion. "We never get the chance to acquire your filthy foreign habits, so of course

205

we don't miss them when we're marooned on an island wooing a respectable widow."

"I went to an all-boys' school," said Felix.

"Yes, but there was that half-witted baker's daughter. Nothing like that at Eton, you know. The only female I ever saw was the housemaid or other chaps' mothers and sisters."

"What about Oxford and Sandhurst?"

"Well, you know Oxford," said David. "It's where they sent you to keep you out of trouble. As Toby says, other chaps' sisters during Eights Week and Commem, and that's about it."

"At Sandhurst they made us go to dances," said Toby. "It was awful, having to talk to girls."

"What a ripping frock," said David, parodying what he knew from Toby to be the standard Sandhurst conversational opener.

"How jolly of you to like it."

"And isn't it a ripping band."

"Yes, ripping."

"Stop," groaned Toby. "I can't stand anymore. Naturally the moment we'd done all our duty dances we went off with the other chaps to get drunk."

"So you see, Flixy, while you were taking lessons from the baker's daughter, Nellie de Lafayette, O-Hisa, and the Anglo-Indian widow—what a thing you seem to have about widows—we haven't even met an available woman yet. And that," said David, "is why Englishmen of a certain age and class are all either buggers or virgins."

"Just about everyone is here," David wrote to Lucas that night, knowing the interest he—an only child of only children—took in large families and their doings. "Lady Millicent, the Baronin Sophie, and Rachel Strafford sit swathed in veils on the verandah and talk obstetrics. Angelika, the one who said no, is here with her two little boys and their Swedish nursemaid, Fröken Ilsa, who feeds them on grated apples, raw carrots, and nuts, and lets them play naked in the sun. She is immensely proud of the result of her advanced methods, and displays her two charges like exhibits at a cattle show—little porkers perhaps. You can imagine how Lady M. feels about this (and we can only thank heaven Toby's Nannie isn't here to see it), but the Baronin says it's the very latest thing in Germany, along with deep breathing by an open window, and walking barefoot in the dew first thing in the morning. Certainly it seems to be good for the Porkers; they are as brown and healthy as Mowgli, and just about as ignorant. Mrs Snow and I tried to sneak them a little civilization by way of the Brothers Grimm, but Fröken told us off very firmly; she wants nothing to do with fairy tales, so full of wicked stepmothers and horrible torments.

"The island itself is very nice, with lots of secluded coves for bathing. Toby, Felix, and I have taken possession of one, and the younger ladies have another. The other day Rachel Strafford got a fish down the front of her bathing dress. We heard awful shrieks and wondered whether someone was drawning, and if so, whether to be rescued by three men wearing nothing but their skin would be considered a fate worse than death. Felix decided on rescue, perhaps thinking it was Kitty in danger, while Toby opted, very typically, for death and decorum. Luckily the shrieks stopped before Felix could take action.

"Felix's romance keeps us entertained, though so far it does not seem to consist of anything but endless argument and long walks on the beach accompanied by Julian. How like Felix to find a blind chaperone! Kitty steadfastly says no. Meanwhile his poor parents are worried to death and completely helpless. Kitty is their guest, and they can't very well present Felix with a railway ticket back to Eschenbach, can they? Perhaps there will be a war to solve their problems; there is some talk it seems of Austria declaring war on Serbia.

"The Baronin asks me to renew her invitation—she would be deeply honoured and greatly pleased. I leave it to you to guess who would be the most pleased. Do reconsider and come."

Sophie and Hesso were indeed concerned over the amount of time Felix was spending with Kitty. Their helplessness took them in different ways. Hesso's mind dwelt as always on railway tickets and such outlying districts as Timbuctoo and Alaska. But what would be the use? You could send Felix off to the iciest waste of the Arctic and bet the entire Landeck fortune that in no time at all he would be cosily settled in an igloo with an Eskimo lady of easy virtue, collecting primitive art.

Sophie, who looked at all things in a wider aspect, wondered whether some divine plot might not be at work on Felix's behalf. The family had removed him from the wiles of a French courtesan and sent him to Oxford, that most masculine and celibate of universities. As a result he had met Kitty Snow and had, it seemed, fallen head-over-heels in love. Removed from this temptation, he had contracted an alliance with a Japanese lady of very doubtful moral background, and rescued from her had found himself, after travelling clear around the world, right back with the American widow. Surely this went past coincidence and pointed to some higher plan.

Sophie put herself to work to learn more about this odd woman of whom Felix seemed to be so unaccountably enamoured. She invited Kitty to sit on the verandah with herself and Lady Millicent and Rachel, and talked in her gentle voice, her sentences punctuated by faint sighs.

Kitty answered her questions with great frankness. She had nothing to hide; her family was respectable, and everyone knew that she had no money except what she earned, and was thirty-two. But she found these talks with Sophie intensely dull; they even panicked her a little. Was this what middle age was like? No more rollicking on the beach with Felix and Julian and the Porkers? (David's name for the two little boys had spread like an epidemic; in spite of Fröken's disapproval, they were the Porkers to everyone on the island.) Was she supposed to sit for the rest of her life with other women, doing embroidery (Kitty hated all forms of needlework) and making polite conversation?

There was one thing which bothered Sophie more than any other about Kitty Snow: her age. Christian charity had embraced her short hair, the fact that Kitty had been a suffragette (Sophie herself believed strongly in equal rights for women, but could not approve the violent methods of the WSPU), even the fact that the person who might possibly become her daughter-in-law had been in prison. She disapproved but forgave the fact that Kitty was careless and hiked up her skirt to play catch with Fröken Ilsa and the Porkers, that the wide-brimmed straw hat which should have shielded her from the rays of the sun, was usually full of pebbles and shells Julian collected on their walks, so that her nose was always peeling and a thousand freckles covered her face, but she could not come to terms with the fact that Kitty was thirty-two.

Felix was after all a crown prince of sorts, and must provide heirs for Landeck Steel. Punctuating her sentences with small sighs, she said to Kitty how nice Angelika's little boys were, and how sad it often made her to have only one son. Did Mrs Snow agree?

"Oh yes," said Kitty. "I always thought it was an absolute disaster, Oliver being an only child. It's what makes him so spoiled and peevish, I'm sure. It would have served him right if I'd had a baby a year—I enjoyed having Oliver—but my husband . . ." Here even the outspoken Kitty came to a stop.

"Yes, my dear," Sophie said kindly.

"He had a bad heart, you see," said Kitty, blushing.

Sophie did see; her sigh this time was one of pure relief. It had been entirely the Reverend Mr Snow's fault that Oliver was an only child. Why, if Kitty and Felix put their minds to it they might have five or six before she turned forty.

"Did you really like having Oliver?" asked Angelika, who was in that delicate state Germans refer to as being in other circumstances, and took a great interest in such matters.

"Yes, I did. I wasn't sick a single day, I got nice and round, and Oliver arrived so fast my mother-in-law scolded me. She said it was indelicate not to suffer more."

This, Sophie thought, was good news indeed. The sight of Kitty's flat chest and narrow hips in her bathing dress had not been reassuring, but in her work among the poor Sophie had often noted that slim girls can be good breeders, and that was what a Landeck was expected to be.

As for money, thought Sophie, or rather the lack of it, did it really matter so much? The Landecks were so rich, surely they could afford one marriage without a dowry. She said as much to Hesso that night as they were preparing for bed.

Hesso was dumbfounded. He knew his wife was a progressive woman with forward-looking ideas (had she not brought a woman doctor to Eschenbach?), but the suggestion that a Landeck might marry a woman without a dowry was positively revolutionary.

"It's never been done," he said.

"Yes, I know. But not doing a thing because it's never been done isn't really a very good reason. We could make two people happy for so very little."

"What do they want to be happy for? That's not why people get married."

"No, I know, Hesso. All the same . . ."

"I thought you didn't approve of marrying for love."

"I didn't. But I'm beginning to wonder whether I wasn't wrong. Perhaps parents don't always choose well. I don't think we did with Kuno, yet when Angelika chose for herself she got a splendid person. And look how happy she is."

When in public, Sophie dressed, as became a woman of her station, with elegance and even high style. But for bed she wore, year in, year out, the same voluminous kind of nightgown—cotton in the summer, flannel in winter—she had worn as a girl in her convent school. Because the sheets were always damp on Fallon Island, she had prudently brought her winter flannels. They made a nice soft cushion under her knees when she got down by her bedside to say her prayers. It was one of her few self-indulgences as she got older and her knees bonier. She said, "Goodnight, dear Hesso, sleep well," as she had said for nearly thirty years, and settled to her prayers.

Hesso, who knew that these would be lengthy, turned his back, pulled up the sheets, and said, "Goodnight, Sophie."

He knew she would not mention the subject of Felix again until he brought it up himself. She had given him something to think about, and his sleepy thoughts dutifully took up their task.

So Felix was determined to marry for love. How very odd. Hesso had thought only people in novels and the lower classes did that. What an extraordinary thing marriage was, come to think of it. You become engaged to two coal mines, some Bolivian tin, an iron foundry, and a chunk of cash, and after some parties and a few words spoken by a priest, you were expected to enter at once and without rehearsal upon life's most intimate relationship with the woman who came with the coal mines, the tin, the iron foundry, and the cash. (Sophie had spent her wedding night reciting the Sorrowful Mysteries of the Rosary out loud, which had very nearly put poor Hesso off his stroke.) With this woman you had children, buried children, worried about children, ate uncounted meals, and at the end of thirty years knew her less intimately than you knew your private secretary. And yet marriage worked. That was the extraordinary thing about it. It worked. With some exceptions, it worked very well.

He thought of the wives of the other steel barons; ladies whose backs never touched the back of a chair, who never raised their voices or laughed out loud, who ruled their large domains with wills of iron and voices as soft as a breeze. And he thought of Felix's American widow. Could Felix's feckless wooing result in as successful an alliance as, say, his and Sophie's?

It was not impossible. There were things in Felix's favour. For one thing he appeared to be naturally monogamous—look at the way he always settled down with one woman. Felix was a nest-builder; must have got it from Sophie's side of the family. It wasn't a Landeck trait.

As for Kitty being so much older, Felix seemed to have a taste for older women. The Japanese lady, according to all reports, had been well past the first blush of youth, and as for Nellie de Lafayette, on whom Hesso had called in person to make sure there were no outstanding debts which could cause trouble later, Hesso had found her a mature, charming, and intelligent woman of the world, really, he had thought indignantly, much too good for that young scamp Felix.

Hesso had nothing against Kitty. Augustus seemed to be very fond of her, and Augustus was no fool. She made him laugh and kept him entertained, and Hesso had to admit that now that Angelika was no longer at the abbey he very much missed her laughter and high spirits. He was sure Sophie would have determined that there was nothing about Kitty that would render her unsuitable as a bride for Felix (apart from her being poor) before she had mentioned the possibility to him. If Sophie thought they would be a successful match, they probably would be. Sophie was seldom wrong about such things.

He heard her rise from her prayers and get into bed. She never liked being talked to after she had been talking to God, so he saved what he had to say for the next day, but he did so with regret. The notion of approving something so extraordinary as Felix's marriage to a middle-aged American widow with no dowry had stimulated him, so that he was wide awake. He listened to the waves retreating with a gentle leaching sound from the pebbles on the beach. If only, he thought, she weren't so very plain. He himself liked opulent women like Rachel Montefiore, and could find nothing to admire in Kitty's walking-stick figure and sunburned, freckled face.

Of course Felix didn't look at things like the rest of them. Look at the paintings he had sent home from his journeys; Japanese faces like devils, enough to give one nightmares, and from France portraits of women, heaven help them, with both eyes on the same side of their faces and their noses all anyhow like a defeated boxer's. Really, compared to the women in some of those pictures, Kitty wasn't bad-looking at all.

Early in July a telegram from Colonel Molyneux was delivered with the rest of the post. Toby, thinking he might get a bash at the Irish—12 July was only a week away—cut short his holiday without regret. David thought he might go back with him, but Felix, with the simple selfishness of a young man in love, said David must stay; he would go mad without someone to talk to. Since Lucas was still in Scotland, David agreed to stay another week or two.

12 July passed, according to a postcard with a picture of the Blarney Stone on it, without incident, much to Toby's regret. The tensions between Serbia and Austria had grown more exacerbated as the month wore on, and Hesso said if all went well, what with the blessings of the *Dreibund* and the Triple Entente, Toby might get a chance to bash Felix instead. No one took him seriously, not even, it seemed, the German army, for Felix, who was a reservist, was not called up.

"I think my parents are coming round," he said to Kitty as they went out after dinner to look for shooting stars. "Mama hinted as much."

"There is nothing for them to come round to," said Kitty.

"You said you would never marry me without their approval," said Felix. "Well, I think they will approve. There has been a distinct air of relaxation all day."

"Has it ever occurred to you," said Kitty, "that I might not want to get married? I've been married, and I can tell you, it's very dull."

"It won't be dull with me."

"Oh yes it will, living in the country and doing nice things for the poor."

"We'll live in Paris, drink champagne for breakfast, and go to the opera every night."

"There's Oliver too," said Kitty. "You surely don't want to be a stepfather to Oliver."

Felix did not. Oliver was not at his best on the island, where he spent all his time watching the cheerful diversions of the others as a missionary might regard the incomprehensible and unappetizing rituals of a particularly benighted tribe. Still, Felix reflected, Oliver would be spending the next ten years or so in boarding schools, Lehzen or Eton, Felix did not much mind which, so long as it was nowhere near Eschenbach. He said very untruthfully that he had grown fond of Oliver, and promised to be a loving stepfather to him.

"Nonsense," said Kitty. "Practically nobody is fond of Oliver. Even I'm not all the time, and I'm his mother."

Felix, not really interested in discussing the peevish child on such a splendid, moonlit night, said, "Look, a shooting star. I can make a wish."

After the first and solitary shooting star, others began to drop from the sky, as if a hand had opened, releasing them. Everyone came out on the verandah to watch. Felix said to Kitty, "Hundreds of wishes, all of them the same."

"It's a meteor shower," said Kitty. "It said so in the papers. Meteors don't count."

July was nearly at an end when Hesso's secretary arrived on the island. He had come over with the boy who brought the mail and the papers, to tell them that Austria, a very good customer, had declared war on Serbia, a very bad one.

"Very silly," said Sophie.

"Most uncivilized," Lady Millicent agreed.

"I do wish Algy would come back," said Rachel; "he always knows what's going on."

"Do they expect the war to bring the crown prince back to life?" asked David.

"I don't think you quite understand how these things work," Hesso told him. "He's an excuse, not a reason."

"The boy who brings the mail said the sea might turn gold tonight," said Felix to Kitty. "If the algae or whatever they are, cooperate, that is." They walked away from the others, and sat down in the shade of a dune.

"Marry me, Kitty."

"I can't, Felix. Please stop."

"Why can't you?"

"Stop!"

"You've run out of reasons. Kitty, do you love me?"

She mumbled something indistinct which he chose to take as affirmative. "Well then?"

Two large tears suddenly detached themselves from Kitty's lashes and rolled down her cheek. "My darling," said Felix, "what's the matter? Have I bored you that much?"

"It's not that," she mumbled, shaking her head. And with a sudden spurt of temper, she added, "It's so hard to keep saying no when you really don't want to."

Felix put his arms around her. "Then why do you keep doing it, you silly creature?"

"Because," she said, sobbing freely now, driven to the truth at last, "because I can't marry somebody that when I'm forty is going to be thirty. It's too humiliating. I have my pride."

He let her go; he was too angry to be tender. "Do you mean," he said, in a voice of pure exasperation, "that you have been driving me insane all these weeks because of a stupid idea like that?"

"It's not stupid. You wouldn't think it stupid if you were me," said Kitty. "You'll be a young man at thirty. I've got crow's-feet, I do, you only have to look."

The corners of her eyes were indeed marked with the faintest of lines. Felix took her face in his hands and kissed it. "You've got crow's-feet, and freckles, and no figure to speak of," he said gently, "and you are the silliest woman I've ever met, and when you're forty and bald and without a tooth in your head I'll love you every bit as much as now. Do you understand? Can you grasp that with your tiny little brain? How salty your tears taste, Kitty. I don't ever want you to cry again."

She sniffed and wiped her arm across her nose. Felix said, "What a pig you are. Here, take my handkerchief. Now blow your nose. Good. Did you know that there is an old Westphalian custom that says that if you use a man's handkerchief it means you are engaged to be married?"

"You made that up," she said indignantly, and began to laugh till the tears started to spill over again.

"WILL YOU MARRY ME?"

It was as if she had been holding her breath for weeks and now could let go. "Yes," she said all in a rush, "of course I will. I don't mean to sound eager, Felix, but yes, yes, yes."

The boy who brought the mail had been right; the sea did turn to gold that night. Even the knowledge that there was some silly scientific explanation, algae or something,

215

could not take away from the enchantment of that trans-formation. Golden waves curled at their feet, the Porkers squealed and screamed, dripping gold like Italian cherubs. Even Sophie and Lady Millicent braved the sands to watch. Kitty suddenly ran into the house to fetch a bowl, then dashed into the water, ruining her beautiful black evening gown. Felix ran in after her, while Fröken dashed sprays of golden drops from her hands into the moonlight.

"It won't last, you know," Augustus said to Kitty when she came out of the sea, carefully balancing her bowl of golden water.

"Of course it will," she told him, and turning to Felix, said, "Do you think it's a good omen?"

He said, "There could be none better."

The next morning a rented yacht steamed at full speed from the mainland, its wake creaming behind it. Algy, impeccable as ever, wearing white flannels and his Eton blazer, stood in the prow. He had come to tell them that Germany had declared war on Russia. It was inevitable that England and France would therefore declare war on Germany. If they could all pack as quickly as possible he would take the English guests to Calais to catch a cross-Channel steamer. Hesso's yacht could take the German contingent back to the mainland.

Felix and David looked at each other. Felix was a reservist and would be joining his regiment. David guessed that he was thinking of Toby, who had been recalled, everyone had thought, to fight in Ireland. Neither could think of anything to say.

"Everyone says it will be over by Christmas," said Algy.

Kitty looked down at her bowl of golden water. Augustus had been right. The gold had vanished. It was just a bowl of water, with a sediment of salt on the bottom.

Part 2

LIFE AT THE MARGIN OF THINGS

Chapter 1

Augustus and his party were stranded in France for nearly a week, camping out in the lobby of a seaside hotel, along with hundreds of English holiday makers the war had taken by surprise. By paying a bribe which in more peaceful times would have bought a nearly honest politician, Augustus was able to secure a tiny bedroom under the roof for his wife, Rachel, Kitty, and Julian. It had formerly been shared by two waiters, was stuffy and hot, and smelled of cooking grease. Kitty said she would rather sleep on the beach with David and Augustus. Lady Millicent, cross with heat and worry, felt it her duty to point out that this was not the preference of a lady, and they nearly quarrelled.

Augustus daily joined the queue at the ticket office, trying vainly to buy passage back to England. No linguist, he simply kept repeating his demand for tickets to Dover, and when the clerk responded with Gallic shrugs of incomprehension said the same thing more loudly and slowly. David, whose French was very good, offered to talk to the clerk, but Augustus said, "Nonsense, my dear boy. It doesn't do to give in to these foreigners, you know. That clerk could understand me perfectly well if he only tried," as indeed, when the bribe Augustus was prepared to offer reached suitably astronomic proportions, he could.

The cross-Channel steamer was packed like a cattle boat, but fortunately the water was smooth and no one was sick.

They passed many steamers going the other way, loaded with their cargo of khaki. Everyone cheered them except Kitty, who surprised her party by bursting into tears. David said, "What is it, Mrs Snow? Are you feeling seasick?"

"No," said Kitty, accepting his offer of a handkerchief. "It's just that it's so awful, those poor boys going off to get killed, and us cheering them on. It's horrible."

"Mustn't talk rubbish, Kitty," said Augustus. "It's high time those Prussians were taught a lesson. Teach them to

218

rape nuns and hang priests in bell towers like clappers. Not cricket, you know."

Calais had been full of rumours of bayoneted Belgian babies, murdered priests, raped nuns, and houses burnt over the heads of the sick and old. It had not occurred to David that anyone could seriously credit this revolting nonsense, and he was surprised to find Augustus doing so so readily.

"Can't expect much of the frogs, you know," said Augustus. "Look at the poor show they put up in '70. No, ours are the lads to do the job. They've the right fighting spirit."

David, with a sudden vivid recollection of Felix sitting by the fire in his rooms at Oxford, reading Thucydides, recalled the Greek saying that war is sweet to the untried. But he said nothing, for he felt in himself a secret envy of those singing young soldiers with flowers in their caps, and wished he were going with them.

London streets were crowded with eager young men queuing in front of the recruiting stations. In their straw boaters in the brilliant August sun, they looked happy and excited, as if they were waiting to buy tickets for a daytrip to Boulogne. But Augustus, who considered it unthinkable that an Altondale boy should volunteer for any but his county regiment, scouted David's intention of joining such a line and gave him a letter of introduction to the colonel of the Dewsbury Depot. The Vickies, by tradition something of a stunt regiment, had managed to get themselves included in the British Expeditionary Force, and were already fighting in France. David had found a letter from Toby awaiting him at Upper Cheyne Row. He was, Toby had written, having a spiffing war.

Colonel Molyneux, who knew David and might have been willing to overlook his amateur status, had been promoted to brigadier, and was with the regiment in France. His replacement at the depot appeared to have been brought back from retirement if not from another century. He sported a marvellous set of Picadilly weepers and flowing white locks in the best Vickies' tradition of the

1890s. He read Augustus's letter, recalled their pleasant times pigsticking and natives-sticking in India, and informed David with courteous regret that, seeing there was a war on, Victoria's Own had unfortunately no time to trouble itself with amateurs. If Mr Harvey were really serious about joining the army, he might try them again when the war was over.

A little dashed but not really surprised, David returned to London and joined a long line of Kitchener volunteers. When by late afternoon this line had moved scarcely three houses down, David concluded that Lord Kitchener did not want him as much as he had pretended, and caught a cab back to Chelsea. In the sunny street newsboys were bellowing headlines about a battle at Mons.

"I think I'll give it a few weeks till things simmer down," said David to Lucas.

"It seems a good idea. Have some sherry."

Lucas had had very little to say about David's call on the white-haired colonel, or his afternoon on the sluggish recruiting line, though David had made an amusing story of it. "You're uncharacteristically silent about all this," said David, shaking his head no to the offer of sherry. "If you disapprove, say so."

"You must do what you feel you ought to," said Lucas. "My disapproval or approval doesn't matter."

"It matters to *me*."

Lucas went and stood by the open window. The sun was low in the sky; the street below him began to fill with tall shadows. From the King's Road they could hear the shouts of the newsboys.

"I don't disapprove of *you*. I do disapprove very much of supposedly civilized people in the twentieth century trying to settle their differences by massacring each other's young men. And I disapprove most passionately of old men and women screaming for blood, when they're not going to be called upon to do the bleeding. But I find it very difficult to get on a moral high horse, because I suspect that very selfishly I simply disapprove of the war because it might put you in a position where people can shoot at you."

They spent the late summer and early autumn at the Dower House. For the moment David made no further attempt to volunteer. Judging by the newspapers the British Expeditionary Force was getting along very well without him. After the first headlong retreat it had stopped the Germans within thirty miles of Paris. The Germans were forced to go back to the river Aisne, where they dug themselves in for the winter. At Le Cateau Toby was awarded the Military Cross. In typical Vickies' fashion he attributed this to a clerical error, and David had to look up the citation in the *Gazette* to learn that under Toby's command A Company of the First Battalion had held an exposed flank until Sordet's cavalry had been brought up. It had been a costly stand; Toby had lost more than half of his men, and nearly all his junior officers, but it was a stand very much in the tradition of First Battalion, who were the Vickies' death-and-glory boys. Since the days of Napoleon First Battalion had had the highest number of battle honours and the highest casualty rates in the regiment, and they were proud of both.

In November, while an autumn gale blew across the estuary, and the battered BEF dug itself in at Ypres, David had a letter from Andrew Fielding. He had been botanizing in the Hymalayas at the outbreak of the war, he wrote, and it had taken him all this time to get back to England. His attempts at volunteering had met with no more success than David's, "but," he wrote, "I'm told that if a whole group volunteers, it's quite easy to get in. I don't understand why this should be so, but we're getting together some of our old friends from Magdalen, Ned and Clemence and some others. Since you were Anthony's closest friend, I thought you might care to come in on this. We're prepared to overlook the fact that you are an Oriel man.

"Poor Anthony, by the way, is still stuck with his regiment in India, and is sick at missing all the fun."

David handed the letter to Lucas, who said crossly, "He sounds like an awful snob. Oriel man indeed."

"That's meant for a joke. Andrew's jokes are all like that. A bit ponderous."

"Is he at all like his brother? I never saw much of him; he always seemed to be away at school or scout camp."

"Yes, Andrew is very hearty," said David, feeling that on this point at least he could set Lucas's mind at rest. "The others were always teasing him about it."

"I take it the others were not hearty at all."

"Well, no. But you know, I think it was more of a fashion than anything else. I expect they're all married with twelve children by now, and think the rest of us ought to be horsewhipped."

"You want to join up, don't you?"

David looked out of the window, where the gale was bending the willows and the rain dashed against the glass like bullets, and tried to picture himself under canvas or in a trench. He said, "It seems very odd, seeing that life with you is so extraordinarily pleasant, Lucas, but yes, I do. It doesn't seem quite fair to let Toby and the others do all the nasty work. So I think I ought to, don't you?"

"You'll never get an unprejudiced opinion from me."

"Be fair. If you were my age, what would you do?"

"I don't know," said Lucas sadly. "Grow a moustache and join the army, I expect."

Lord Andrew lost little time in getting his group of volunteers together, and within two weeks David found himself forming fours in a farmer's muddy field, and sleeping on sacks in the farmer's drafty barn. Lord Kitchener's call for volunteers had been answered in the hundreds of thousands; there was simply nowhere to put them. There were no uniforms; they wore their thickest tweeds and stoutest boots, ate out of tins with their pocket knives, and slept in schools, barns, and warehouses. With the regular army fighting in France there were few officers to train them; veteran NCOs of the Boer War, and retired Indian army colonels were brought back into active service for the purpose. Anyone who had done OTC in school or at the university was instantly promoted to second lieutenant.

"If this keeps up," David wrote to Toby, "I may get to be a major before you. We are quartered at the moment in an infant school, and listen to lectures seated at tiny forms with our knees under our chins. When we're not being lectured we march in massed formation, and slope, order, present, trail, reverse, and pile an assortment of walking sticks and umbrellas instead of rifles. I can't get over a sneaking suspicion that we are preparing for quite the wrong war."

Very gradually uniforms and rifles caught up with Lord Kitchener's New Army, and they began to look like soldiers as they drilled and marched together through the frosty winter days. Despite the cold and discomfort David found he was happy. Those winter weeks had an air of holiday and child's play about them. Many of the volunteers had never been in the country before, and experienced for the first time as reality the Christmas card world of frost and holly berries, and red-breasted robins in the snow.

Then the snows thawed, hedgerows blossomed, spring came a bit drearily, very English, with sudden squalls and a persistent, steady rain. The second battle of Ypres, with its gas attacks, left over a hundred thousand casualties, but the opposing armies still more or less in their old positions. Andrew and David made repeated application to be sent to France, but though they had had nearly a year to think it over, the War Office still could not decide what to do with Lord Kitchener's volunteers. The nearest David and Andrew got to the fighting in France was a camp on the south coast, where they trained new recruits.

Toby came home on leave early in the summer and stopped off to see David on his way back to Folkestone.

"How are they all at home?" asked David, who spent his free time with Lucas and had not been at Altondale since he had unsuccessfully tried to volunteer for the Vickies.

"Oh, fine. Fanny looks as if she were going to boil over, so I expect the baby will arrive any day now. I like her husband; he seems a very good sort."

David's sister had married a gunnery captain who had been wounded at Mons and, only fit for home duty, had become an instructor at the new gunnery camp at High Fenton.

"Yes," said David, "I liked him too, the one time I saw him."

"Everyone's madly busy," said Toby. "The war's like a new toy to them. Father's training the Home Guard, Mummy and Nannie had turned the Palladian wing into a convalescent hospital, the tennis court is a vegetable patch, and there's a bring-and-buy at least once a week, not to mention knitting parties, sewing parties, bandage-rolling parties, and lint-picking parties. Never a dull moment."

"Well, it's bloody dull here," said David. "You know, Toby, it's damnable to sit on one's backside and listen to the guns across the Channel and not be able to get out there. What on earth did they call up a volunteer army for if they're not going to use it?"

Toby, who had very little use for amateur soldiers himself, looked around the tin hut David shared with Lord Andrew. "I can't think why you're so hell-bent on coming out," he said crossly. "It's much nicer here." No one going back to the front was ever in a good mood, and Toby was no exception.

"I'm sure it is," said David, "but I don't think I ought to want a nice war."

"I shouldn't mind, myself," said Toby. "You wouldn't have a drink, would you?"

"Andrew has some whisky. I'm sure he wouldn't mind your having it. Do you want water in it?"

"Not too much. David, if you're really determined to be uncomfortable, why don't you join the Vickies? At least you'd get a regular commission, not one of these jumped up temporary affairs," said Toby with all the regular officer's contempt for the volunteer and makeshift.

"Didn't I write you about that? They told me to run away and play and come back after the war was over."

"Yes, but that was when we were still at full strength. We're four subalterns short this very moment and have been for weeks. I could talk to Uncle Peregrine. He's something rather grand at the War Office these days."

"He can't still be alive."

"Not the dotty one. His son. Though judging by the way this war's being run, he may be fairly dotty too. You know, David, I can't in all honesty recommend Flanders. It is without any doubt whatever the arsehole of the world. But if you're determined to make yourself miserable, I'll have a word with Uncle P."

Uncle Peregrine set to work, and after suitable delays not only David, but Lord Andrew, Clem Barton, and Ned Mandeville found themselves in the officers' mess of the Dewsbury Depot, remembering to stand well back from the hearth rug and to speak only when spoken to.

If it pained their hosts to see Vickies' commissions going to what were, in spite of their spiffing new uniforms and proper public-school accents, young men who had never seen the inside of Sandhurst, the Vickies' code of politeness to newcomers held firm until the port began to circulate. After his third glass, Major Tillyard, who had lost an arm at Mons, which had not sweetened a normally irascible temper, said he never thought he would live to see the day when Kitchener volunteers were going to be given regular commissions, and moreover commissions in the Vickies' First Battalion. Clem Barton, quite as full of sherry, hock, and claret as Major Tillyard, took offence at this and said, "Why? Are you afraid we'll contaminate them?"

The white-haired colonel started the port on another round and said, smiling, "I doubt that you will have the time, Mr Barton. I am told the average life expectancy of a subaltern at the front is exactly six weeks."

Chapter 2

I gotta motta, always merry and bright
Look around and you will find,
Every cloud is silver-lined,
The sun shines bright, although the sky's a dark one.

It was their favourite song; they requested it every week. In their blue uniforms, with their bright red ties, the convalescent soldiers, Kitty thought, looked as merry and bright as the Cuthbert in the song.

225

> *I've always said to myself, I've said,*
> *Cheer up, Cuthbert, you'll soon be dead,*
> *It's a short life, and a gay one.*

She wouldn't have thought they would want that reminder; they surely lived every moment of their days with the knowledge that they were only being patched up to be sent back to the trenches, yet they applauded cheerfully and asked for more. Kitty sang whatever they requested, songs about roses round the door making them love mother more, and bonnie lassies as pure as the lilies in the dell. Mrs Castlemain supported her with a firm, episcopal contralto.

Sister, her veil so stiffly starched that she looked as if she might take wing, sat, arms folded, in the last row, keeping a commanding eye on the revels. When Sister and Mrs Castlemain had met, a throne had spoken to a throne. They had a great respect for each other.

> *Joshua, Joshua,*
> *Sweeter than lemon squash you are . . .*

Kitty sang in answer to another popular request. The awful rhyme bounced back at them from the vaulted ceiling.

> *Yes, by gosh you are,*
> *Josh-u-osh-u-*AH!

When Sister rose it meant there was time for one more song. Sister preferred this to be a hymn. Something quiet, a bit depressing but hopeful, she thought, and communicated with Cass with a nod. Cass said something to Kitty, who once more began to play.

> *Hobgoblins, nor foul fiend*
> *Can daunt his spirit,*
> *He knows that at the end,*
> *Shall life inherit . . .*

Did they find it consoling, she wondered, who would soon be going back where hobgoblins and foul fiends could be little more than comic relief.

> *Then fancies fly away,*
> *He'll fear not what men say,*

He'll labour night and day,
To be a pilgrim.

She smiled as the men crowded around her, shy and inarticulate, to make their thanks, but though these weekly sessions at the hospital were always cheerful ones, and except for Sister's presence might easily have become riotous, they invariably left her deeply depressed.

"Come back to Earl's Court and have some tea," said Cass, after Sister had thanked them most graciously and commanded a probationer to see them to the door. They took a bus through the early dark. There were Christmas decorations in the shop windows. Everything looked bright and happy. Kitty remembered how everyone had said the war would be over by Christmas. But that had been a year ago. One did not hear it so often now.

Outside a brightly lit toy shop they saw a girl hand a white feather to a man in civilian clothes. Cass made a noise which in anyone less dignified than a bishop's relict would have been a snort.

Mrs Castlemain regarded war as typical of the kind of swinishness men got up to when not restrained by the more reasonable hand of their womenfolk. When Kitty had returned from France, she had found her friend at work at the dinner table which was littered with maps, railway timetables, and blueprints.

"I'm very happy to see you," she had said to Kitty. "I have been studying how we can put a stop to all this nonsense. I have a list of army depots here, and my young nephew Alastair, who is at that very tiresome age when boys can think of nothing but railways, has been most helpful in supplying me with the schedule of troop trains going to Folkestone. We can lie down on the tracks, blow up their depots, and set fire to their ammunition dumps. Why, with our experience and organization, I should think the WSPU should be able to put an end to this ridiculous war in a week."

"Cass, you're wonderful," Kitty had said. But Mrs Pankhurst and her daughter Christabel had failed to see their old friend in the same light. The WSPU officially determined to set aside their long struggle for the vote and to join with their masculine oppressors in the fight against Germany. Instead of putting lighted matches into pillar-boxes, smashing the windows of fashionable shops, and unfurling their green, purple, and white banners, they devoted themselves to making recruiting speeches and handing white feathers to men not in uniform. Cass's plans for sabotaging the war lay gathering dust at one end of her dining table. Both she and Kitty had seen nothing for it but to resign their membership in the WSPU.

They admitted to each other that they greatly missed their friends, the days of uncritical comradeship, the unquestioning acceptance, and the certainty that so long as you saw things the same way as everyone else, nothing else mattered. Life without the WSPU seemed dull and empty, so they spent hours each day at each other's houses, drinking sherry to cheer themselves up. Sometimes it worked, and they grew giggly and reminiscent, recalling how one of their members had herself hoisted aloft on a painter's scaffold to appear like a heavenly visitation in the open window of Mr Asquith's dining room to scold the assembled luncheon guests, and how the Pankhursts had given out the information that they planned to hold a gigantic WSPU rally in Parliament Square, to which no one had come except three thousand red-faced members of the London constabulary.

But at other times they simply got lower and lower, and unable to keep from thinking about Felix, Kitty would drop great tears on the khaki socks she was knitting for David and Toby.

Cass, who did not approve of idleness and moping, soon found them another occupation. Passionately as she disapproved of the war and the men who waged it, those men, having been shown the error of their ways by shot and shell, became her new project. With Kitty in tow she visited hospitals, read aloud to the wounded, and wrote letters for those who could not hold a pen. A chance remark led Sister to discover that Kitty gave music lessons, and they had added the weekly sing-alongs to their busy schedule. Kitty had declared herself very willing to play for the soldiers, but had explained to Sister that she could not sing. Her voice had never entirely recovered from the injuries of forced feeding; her pretty, fragile soprano now held a husky note, like a boy's just before it breaks. But Sister had firmly told her that she wasn't asking her to sing opera, just to do her bit to cheer up the convalescents and take them out of themselves, and this had proved so easy to do, her audience being totally uncritical and grateful for everything, that she had long since forgotten her first embarrassment.

It was Mrs Castlemain's maid's day off, so Cass went to the kitchen to prepare tea. Kitty put some coal on the fire, then pulled a khaki sock she was knitting for David from her workbag and began to turn the heel.

Cass was deeply suspicious of those socks. She only tolerated men who were stretched as helplessly as upended turtles on their backs in hospital beds, not those on their feet in the line, requiring woollen socks. But when she taxed Kitty with having a secret lover at the front, Kitty only laughed. "I could never fall in love with David Harvey," she said; "he's much too beautiful." She would have liked to tell Cass about Felix; simply to be able to talk about him would have eased her heart.

Their parting had been so hurried and muddled she had at first hardly found time to be sad. They had made hasty and customary lovers' pledges; to think of each other while gazing at the moon, to write every day, though they knew the letters could not be posted; but there had been no sense of tragedy, for everyone had expected the war to be over in a matter of weeks. "And then," Felix had said, "the very next day I shall be on your doorstep, my darling." He had kissed her hand very formally, for they were surrounded by hurrying servants, luggage, the Porkers, and Fröken Ilsa, and before she knew it, Kitty was standing at the railing of the rented yacht, waving, while Felix's slight figure grew smaller and smaller, and finally disappeared.

Kitty had determined not to wash the hand Felix had kissed; she wrote him first thing every morning, but the purely physical difficulties of leaving the back of one's right hand unwashed defeated her, and after a while the daily letter with no hope of reply became a chore to be put off from day to day. As the war showed no sign of coming to an end, the thought of Felix grew to be nothing but an aching lump in her throat, with no relief or consolation. She did not have the kind of imagination that is much given to thinking of lovers as wounded or dead; the presence in her mind was always Felix as she had seen him last, moving irretrievably out of reach.

But this she could not tell Mrs Castlemain, who would only have said that, heaven having been kind enough to remove the Reverend Mr Snow, it would be flying in the face of Providence for Kitty to saddle herself with another husband. So she went on longing for Felix and knitting socks, and if her tears dropped on her knitting it did not much matter. The lamb's wool was full of lanolin and quite waterproof.

With the Eighth Army in Russia, Felix, wearing his great-coat, a captured Russian fur hat, fur mittens and fur boots, covered by three blankets and a bearskin (belonging to a bear shot by Pregnitz Minor's father in the Masurian Lakes), lay on his bed, thinking of Kitty and waiting to get warm enough to go to sleep.

He was having a splendid war. He was in command of a crack company in a regiment full of old schoolfriends and one very old enemy. Hagen von Hagenbeck was his CO.

From Tannenberg, where German victory had laid to rest after five hundred years the humiliation of the Teutonic Knights' defeat at the hands of the Poles, to the tremendous push that had driven the Russians out of Poland for the first time since Napoleon's day, the Eighth Army had marched from strength to strength. Time and again the Russian divisions, though far outnumbering the Germans, had fled in disorder, leaving behind their guns and horses, their wounded and dead.

Snow now covered the bloated, green corpses, and the only enemy for the moment was the Russian winter, sending its knife-edge of cold under the door.

Over his bed Felix had pinned one of Gustav Klimt's designs for Beethoven's *Ninth Symphony*, a red-haired and androgynous muse who reminded him of Kitty. He would have liked to write to her, but the ink was frozen inside his pen. He often did write to her, feeling a little silly since he knew he could not send the letters, but deriving a good deal of pleasure from it nevertheless. He thought of her in bed in her house in Tite Street, not carnally (he was too cold for that) but comfortingly; a Kitty wearing a flannel nightgown, surrounded by hot-water bottles, under an eiderdown quilt. He pictured himself under the covers with her, thawing slowly, deliciously warming to lust. Or would his touch freeze the hot water? Would his kiss, like the Snow Queen's, turn her heart to ice?

He thought of David and Toby too, wondering what Toby's war could possibly be like. He could not picture it at all. He read of tremendous battles in the papers, first and second Ypres, Neuve-Chapelle, Festubert, yet when the colonel's orderly was told to move the pins on the map into their new positions, there never seemed to be any change.

He pictured David, looking elegant in brown velvet, doing something useless but delightful, writing patriotic poetry, perhaps, or scribbling nonsense for the Ministry of Propaganda, if England had such a thing. What fun it was going to be after the war, should he or Toby manage to survive it, to compare notes.

His sleepy thoughts turned back to Kitty in that soft, warm bed in Tite Street. He was very tired. With a sigh he pulled the fur rug closer and put his arms around the bear's head. He could hardly pretend that the bristly cheek was Kitty's, but as he drifted into sleep he found comfort in its warmth. The glassy eye of the bear stared into space, looking baleful, as well it might.

"Look, sir; it's a flahr."

Dressed, not in brown velvet, but in a sopping wet uniform, David was in charge of no. 3 Platoon revetting the side of a trench that had taken a direct hit earlier in the day, burying three men. He had not been out of his rain-soaked clothes and boots for six days, had not slept more than an hour or two at a stretch for more than a week, and was in no mood to listen to loose talk about flowers.

231

"Don't try that loony bit on me, Hamish," he said. "It's the MO you've got to convince."

"Honest, sir, it's a bleedin' flahr." Hamish's voice took on a note of grievance, as if to say that it wasn't his fault if a flower elected to grow at the edge of the parapet. He had been a butcher's apprentice in civilian life, and was A Company's best middleweight boxer, hardly the kind of person, David thought, to wax sentimental about a flower.

"Oh, all right," he said crossly, and looked where Hamish was pointing. Where the trench mortar had churned up the mud and burst the sandbags, its bulb half torn apart, dropped the elegant white head of a snowdrop. David could not believe it. There was nothing here but frozen mud and ghostly tree stumps. Rats and soldiers were the only things alive. David, who had arrived in early winter and had never known it otherwise, had forgotten that spring was bound to come even to the Ypres Salient. "Good Lord," he said, feeling a little stunned, "you mean to say there's actually going to be spring? Right here in bloody Flanders?"

"'ad one last year," said Hamish. "Didn't we, Nobby?"

Nobby Oakroyd, a slow and deep thinker, gave this question the full weight of his ponderous mind.

"Garn, Nobby, you remember," said his quick-witted friend Josiah Noakes. "They sprung the bleedin' gas attack on us and turned all our buttons green."

Hamish, with fists like hams, gently bandaged the torn bulb with moist earth. Then he looked up with a grin and said, "Honest, sir. Bleedin' nightingales and everything."

David laughed and went to report to Toby. His relations with his platoon were of a cheerful and easygoing nature of which Doolittle, his platoon sergeant, deeply disapproved. From the first David had made it clear that he thought no. 3 the best platoon in the best company in the best battalion in the English army, and that he had every intention of keeping it that way. For several weeks his men had held aloof, not quite knowing what to make of an officer who said please and thank you when he gave an order, and treated other ranks as if they were human. But when discipline proved not to suffer from his peculiar ways, and the platoon continued to carry on in its accustomed death-and-glory manner, they concluded that while amateur officers were in principle to be deplored, their Mr Harvey was a bit of all right. A good many platoons were arriving at the same conclusion at the same time as Kitchener volunteers were beginning to replace the regulars who had been wounded or killed. Only Platoon-Sergeant Doolittle persisted in his belief that an officer who had not been to Sandhurst was against nature. "Mr 'Arvey does things right, but 'e doesn't do them proper," he confided to his friend Sergeant-Major Pickett, and continued to exude a sense of disapproval which was palpable and not always silent.

David found Toby seated at a makeshift table covered with a blanket and the piles of inevitable bumf with which the staff boys well behind the lines proved to themselves that they were fighting the war. He listened to David's report in silence; it was a formality that had to be got through even though he knew it all already, and knew too what David must be feeling. Even in the Salient, where death was constant and cheap and squalid, it never lost its power to shock, and if it was someone in one's own platoon there was added to the sense of loss a deeply personal grief, and an irrational but nevertheless powerful sense of guilt.

When David had finished, he said, "Have a cup of tea. It's quite fresh."

"Thanks, I can do with it." David hooked an empty crate of bully beef toward him with his boot and sat down. The tea tasted of the inside of the petrol tins in which the water was carried up to the line, and of a heavy sprinkling of chloride of lime, but it was hot and David drank it gratefully. He was grateful too for Toby's silence and reassuring presence.

"I'm bloody sorry, David," said Toby when David had finished his tea and might therefore reasonably be considered to be in a better frame of mind. Very small things, Toby knew from experience, could comfort one in the line.

"Thanks. It doesn't get any better with practice, somehow."

"No," said Toby. "It gets worse. Look, go and get some sleep. Not sleeping makes things seem ten times as bad as they really are."

"Yes, I'll do that. I'll just get off the letters to their families first."

Toby, judging that David would sleep better with that chore behind him said, "Do that. And then sleep. That's an order."

"Yes, sir." He pushed aside the gas curtain, then turned back to the dugout, where Toby was already at work again on the papers at his table. "Oh, Toby," said David.

"Yes."

"Hamish's found a snowdrop."

The dugout David shared with Lord Andrew was down a traverse nostalgically called Primrose Lane. A small fire was burning in a petrol tin with holes punched in its sides, and his batman had put a pot of tea beside it to keep warm. Andrew was asleep on his string bed, the dead sleep of a man who has gone without for days.

The same bumf that littered Toby's table covered theirs; along with a book of Andrew's called *Wildflower Rambles in Wiltshire*, and David's *Oxford Book of English Verse*, open to a page of Spenser, whose English flowers, pinks and purple columbine, coronations and sops-in-wine, he liked to marshal in his mind's eye against the frozen Flanders mud. He did not reach for it now, for such small memories can stub and bruise the heart, and he still had work to do.

He reached for the box which held the regimental writing paper with its embossed white Yorkshire rose. Condolence letters were routine, one quickly got used to writing them. There was a formula to it; you said how sorry you were, mentioned some detail of the dead man's life to make it sound personal, said how well liked he'd been and how much he would be missed, lied, nine times out of ten, that he had been killed instantly and had felt no pain, and signed yourself with deep regret D. Harvey, Lieutenant, no. 3 Platoon, A Coy. He'd written dozens of them since coming out, for even on quiet days there were casualties from shelling and snipers. Staff, with its customary regard for the lives of line soldiers, called this wastage.

It had not taken David long to discover that Toby had by no means exaggerated when he had called Flanders the arsehole of the world. It was frozen and bleak and cruelly dangerous, yet he had found himself from the first content to be there. An unexpected Puritan streak in his nature made him welcome hard living; he was as impervious to cold, discomfort, and bad food as only someone who has spent six years at an English public school can be, and he had discovered in himself a flair and liking for soldiering he had never suspected he possessed. If he had once wondered what would validate him, as Lucas Ryder had been validated by his first book, he now had no doubt at all that it was his muddy khaki uniform, with lice nesting in its seams.

"He will be very much missed by his friends in the company," he wrote for the third time. "I hope it may be some consolation to you to know that he died instantly and did not suffer." He remembered the dead boys' faces, mud in their eyes and mouths and ears, tongues purple and swollen like a hanged man's. To put an end to these thoughts he reached for the nearest book, Andrew's *Wildflower Rambles*. The morocco binding, with the ducal crest of Frome, felt very familiar to his hand. He turned the pages till he came to the engraving of a snow-drop—*Galanthus nivalis*. The eighteenth-century parson who had written *Wildflower Rambles* had appended a moral to each engraving. His piety was seemingly greater than his knowledge of Latin, for under the snowdrop he had written a brief homily about the gallantry of the modest little flower venturing through the snow. What would he have said, David wondered, if he could have seen one so gallant it grew on a parapet of a frontline trench.

He signed his name for the third time and put away the writing paper. There was still a small pile of his platoon's letters to be censored. He was very tired suddenly. Remembering the pot of tea stewing by the fire, he got up and poured himself a mug. Yawning, he turned back to the letters.

Of all an officer's duties, censoring his platoon's mail had at first been the one he disliked most. To be forced to intrude into their pitifully small ration of privacy seemed to him so outrageous that he had read with mind averted, looking only for place names and other proscribed information. But gradually, almost against his will, he had found himself drawn into these repetitive, ill-spelled missives, finding that he learned from them more about his men than he could have in any other way. They were so accustomed to having their mail censored that they had put it out of their minds and wrote as naturally as if they could step outside and drop the letter into the nearest pillar-box.

He was always touched and amused by the men's lying efforts to assure those at home that they were warm, dry, safe, and well fed, in short, in the pink. He knew who was cheerful and who was worried, knew that Noakes had a new baby and Dartrey a nagging wife, and that Hall was at the end of his tether and needed a cheerful word to get him through the night's sentry duty.

As usual, Fatty Outhwaite had covered two unorthographic but enthusiastic pages thanking his missus for the pork pie she had sent. As a sign of Fatty's esteem, David had been given a slice of that pie, and had come to the conclusion that Fatty must have the digestion of a hyena. Secretly he had fed most of it to Sergeant Selden's pet rat, which was the size of a tomcat and had fur like a mink in winter.

Nobby Oakroyd, as always, had confined himself to the convenience of the Field Service postcard. Breathing heavily, thinking slowly and deeply, he had ticked off the appropriate statements: "I am quite well," "I have received your parcel," and, though he had never in David's experience been known to write a letter, "Letter follows at the first opportunity."

Josiah Noakes, writing to his uncle who was a successful bookie, had spread himself a good deal on a wiring party of a few nights before, and David feared that by the time he had drawn his pen through everything censurable, Uncle Alf would be getting a very short letter indeed. He had a soft spot for Noakes, who had brightened his first Christmas in the line with a letter addressed to: The Queen, Buckingham Palace, London.

"Dear Queen," it had said. "Taking pen in hand to thank you for your kind Christmas card; please don't think I presume but it was cheery to know you remembered the PBI on Christmas; we all said What price the Queen, please excuse mistakes, wishing you a very happy New Year, respectfully yours, Noakes J. Private." PBI stood for Poor Bloody Infantry, but David had let it pass. Who could regret Christmas at Altondale when one could spend it in a muddy trench with Noakes J. Private.

As he bundled the letters together, something caught at the corner of his eye and he looked up to see a rat by the foot of Andrew's bed, winsomely cleaning his whiskers. David, feeling a cold trickle of disgust down his spine, reached for his revolver, then remembered Andrew asleep, and threw a boot at it instead. The rat, quite undismayed, poured himself into the shadows and vanished. Andrew stirred and grunted, then sat up and rubbed the stubble on his face. David gave him a mug of tea. Andrew looked at it with a puzzled frown. "What is it?"

"Tea, of course."

"Nonsense, it's ink."

"It was tea, earlier on."

"Haven't you slept at all?"

"We had a bit of trouble. A mortar hit Little Venice and the whole wall caved in."

"Oh," said Andrew, not liking to ask for particulars.

"It buried three men. We dug them out, but of course it was too late. I've just been writing to their people."

Andrew did not ask their names. He knew how David must be feeling. "Why don't you get some sleep," he said. "Things seem to have quietened down. I'll look after your lot for you."

"Thanks," said David, "I will. Oh, Hamish has found a snowdrop."

"A what?"

"*Galanthus nivalis*, you bloody botanist."

"Oh, a snowdrop."

"Yes, that's what I said."

237

"Here? I don't believe it."

"Ask him to show it to you. If I know Hamish, he's charging a shilling admission by now."

He took his *Oxford Book of English Verse* and lay down on his cot. It was all right to remember now. *Against their Bridal day, which was not long: sweet Thames, run softly till I end my song.* Softly along the Embankment and under the Albert Bridge, the rats, which at low tide scampered on the muddy edge of the water, scampered into David's dreams.

All that day members of A Company came to see the snowdrop, walking on tiptoe, as if it were a small animal which might take fright. By evening stand-to it was plainly dying.

In May the Vickies were ordered south to the Somme. They marched through the spring landscape, along dead-straight Roman roads, looking dazed upon benign meadows and trees in leaf. As they marched they groused as they had not done on the bitterest winter day in the Salient.

"I think they're happy," said David, as Toby rode up along no. 3 Platoon.

"Yes," agreed Toby, amused. "And they'd rather go back to Wipers than admit it."

Before 1 July 1916, the Somme was known to be a very cushy stretch of trench. The French, who had held it for two years, had shared with the Germans a live-and-let-live attitude which made the life there sound to the bone-weary defenders of the Salient, like life in the royal apartments of Buckingham Palace. The trenches at the Somme, it was rumoured, were cut into chalk, ten feet deep and dry as bone. Flowers grew in no-man's-land, and the sun shone every day.

The Vickies weren't green enough to suppose they were being moved south because they needed a rest. There was much talk of a major offensive—the big push—which would get them out of their soiled trenches into the open, back to a war of movement again, straight on to fuckin' Berlin. Pleased with the prospect they complained bitterly that it was always the poor bleedin' Vickies as got thrown in. Couldn't start a bloody offensive without them, could they.

When they were not grousing they sang, about the mythical Mademoiselle from Armentières, the landlord's golden-haired daughter with the lily-white tits, and the sergeant-major's encounters with the army mule.

The chalk dust of Picardy, stirred by marching feet, lay white as flour on the grass, and powdered their uniforms and hair. A line of another citizen soldier came to David's mind as they marched. "Dust, the dumb messenger of an army." Had the road to Marathon been like this, the hair of the young Athenian knights turned white with dust? Though he knew he was marching into battle, David had never felt more at peace.

Chapter 3

Toward the end of September Felix went home on leave. Between trains in Berlin, feeling that after so many months at the front he was due for a bit of coddling, he decided to lunch at the Esplanade. Oysters, he thought, the first of the season, sparkling on their bed of ice; champagne, of course, and then a steak, seared black on the outside, so tender it yielded to the knife like butter, with a great well of blood gushing from the wound. A bottle of Chambertin (the wine Napoleon had pined for outside the gates of Moscow) if they still had it in stock.

At the Esplanade they greeted him like the prodigal son, but it seemed there was to be no fatted calf. No oysters, at any rate, though there was steak, and yes, they still had a few precious bottles of the Chambertin.

The proprietor himself appeared with the dusty flask in its basket to do the honours and drink a glass to Baron von Landeck's health. With the first sip Felix felt himself returned to civilization; had he not been wearing his uniform he might have fancied himself back at lunches here with his father or Algy Strafford. The steak appeared, and the proprietor, wishing him a good appetite, discreetly vanished.

The steak was appetizingly scorched on the outside, and yielded easily to the knife, but no blood welled from the wound, which was a tender, springtime green. The waiter, summoned to explain this marvel, said that the Herr Hauptmann must not think of it as a steak *an sich*, but a triumph of patriotism and German ingenuity. Since there was no beef to be had in Berlin, all available meat going to the army—here the waiter permitted himself the fleetingest of reproachful glances at Felix's uniform—the chef at the Esplanade had concocted his own version of steak, a victory steak so to speak, consisting of spinach, cornmeal, potatoes, and ground-up nuts bound together with egg-substitute.

Felix consoled himself with another glass of wine. The cake they brought him for dessert was green also, since it was made with mashed beans, and the coffee was the same brown water extracted from roasted acorns they drank in the army. The brandy, however, was sublime.

From Berlin he shared a railway compartment with an infantry officer who had been lightly wounded during the battle of the Somme, and was now returning to his regiment. They exchanged cigarettes and talked about their respective wars. "Perhaps you can explain to me," said Felix, "something which has long puzzled me. Why is it that after every big battle one hears about in France, the pins on the adjutant's map are still in the same place?"

"That," said the infantry captain, "is the nature of this particular war. At least it is on the Western front. While you go sweeping across East Prussia and Poland, we progress vertically, digging ourselves ever more deeply into the ground."

"But if nothing ever moves," said Felix, "how will it end?"

The infantry captain shrugged. "We will all die of boredom or old age. You will be in Moscow long before we are at Amiens or they at St Quentin."

"But seriously," said Felix, who thought this lack of push, this acquiescence in stalemate, very strange. "Do you believe that you will reach Amiens?" He could see that under the circumstances it would not have been polite to ask about Paris.

"Yes, eventually. Trench war is won by attrition, you see. Despite the fact that nothing ever moves, the casualties are very high. The advantage is always with the defending side, and the English, bless their thick skulls, have been slow to realize it. They are very brave, but they have no imagination. Before the big attack on 1 July, they shelled our trenches for one entire week. It was not pleasant; the noise became almost unendurable, but our trenches were dug very deep and though there was always the secret fear of being buried alive, we got through it the way soldiers always get through such things. We played cards, drank beer, told funny stories, and most of us probably prayed. We knew what they were going to do, and therefore we knew what *we* were going to do, and that is always comforting. We knew that the moment the barrage would lift, we could bring our machine guns to the parapet—we had practised this hundreds of times so that we could do it with split-second precision, and of course the Landeck machine gun is so easy to carry and set up—are you familiar with it on the Eastern front?"

"Personally," said Felix, "I know it very well indeed. Allow me to introduce myself." He waited for his new acquaintance to say that it was a small world, then went on. "Unfortunately on the Eastern front it is the Russians who have it. I myself negotiated the sale when I was in Russia in '13. It was one of the few times I ever displayed an ability for business, and my family was delighted with me, but personally I have had many occasions to regret it. But I have interrupted your story. Please go on."

The train rattled through the featureless Brandenburg landscape, laying over it a plume of black smoke. The captain said, "In spite of all those rehearsals and our careful preparations there was one fear which haunted me. Supposing the English lifted the barrage just long enough to let us get to the top and set up our guns, then resumed shelling our trenches; there would have been nothing left of us. Nothing at all. Yet it did not happen."

Smiling, thinking of Toby, Felix said, "It would not have been sporting."

The infantry captain did not smile. "There was nothing

sporting in what followed. They came toward us very slowly in an extended line and we cut them down. It went on all day. They are the enemy, I know, but I have nightmares about it still."

When he was back with his regiment Felix had occasion to remember his talk with the infantry captain. They were stationed near Kovel, having been moved South to stiffen the Austrian lines crumbling under General Brusiloff's attacks. When the Russian advance had exhausted itself, they began to move forward again at such speed that they outstripped their supply lines and artillery and Hagenbeck walked into a trap. It was not the first time that this had happened; his ill-considered displays of keenness and élan had got his battalion into trouble before. It was the early bird, Hagenbeck liked to say, who got the worm. Felix had once rather snappishly pointed out that it was the early worm that got eaten by the bird, but Hagenbeck was not very quick in the uptake, and it was not till the middle of the night that it occurred to him that Captain von Landeck had called his superior officer a worm. He spent the rest of the night wondering whether this was a court-martial offence, and by dawn came to the reluctant conclusion that it probably wasn't.

They had moved through an immense forest all day, following the debris of a retreating army, but never seeing a live Russian. Suddenly they came to the end of the wood and stood, sun-blind, looking out over a parched plain with a dried river course and a range of hills to the east. No sign of life showed anywhere except a solitary bird circling high above them; a scavenger, Felix thought, a kite or a carrion crow. There was something disquieting to a German eye, accustomed to landscapes punctuated by field, house, tree and hedge, in this featureless and empty plain. Hagenbeck kept staring at the ridge of hills. If he took them he could command the entire plain to the east. He could already hear the faint clink of the *pour le mérite* as it joined the other medals on his chest.

To some of his fellow officers it did seem strange that so important a strategic feature as this ridge should be empty and undefended. They suggested waiting till dark and sending out a scouting party, but Major Hagenbeck waved their objections aside. If he waited another German battalion might come up and rob him of the glory of having taken the hills. They lay before him, tempting him like a deadly sin. Not a sound, not the curl of smoke from a cooking fire or the whinny of a horse disturbed the silence. He gave the order to cross the plain and rush the ridge. Too late they discovered that it was held by an enemy whose machine-gun fire cut off their advance as well as their retreat to the woods, leaving those who were still alive only the shallow shelter of the dried-out riverbed. Using their own dead for a parapet, they hacked at the dried dirt with their entrenching tools, trying to dig themselves in. When darkness fell someone suggested they try to make their way back to the wood, but Hagenbeck declared that German soldiers do not retreat. They worked all night, turning the riverbed into a trench and carrying their wounded to its shelter. There was a full moon, they were nearly as visible to the Russians on the hills as they had been in the bright sun, and their snipers did not let up on them all night.

They sweated out the next day behind their inadequate and flyblown parapet. The riverbed was as dry as a bone. They gave the dregs from their water bottles to the wounded, and waited. When the sun was low enough to dazzle the eyes of sentries looking west, Hagenbeck led a raid on the hills from which he and almost no one else came back alive. A night raid led by Felix proved almost as costly but netted a prisoner, a young subaltern with blond chicken fuzz on his chin and cheeks, who spoke about as much French as Felix spoke Russian. He was however very ready to talk, for though he longed to be a hero, he had no wish to have his ears and nose cut off and be impaled on a bayonet and slowly roasted over a cooking fire; things which every Russian child knew were routinely done to their prisoners by the German devils.

In poor French and worse Russian a good amount of information was elicited. The ridge of hills, the young subaltern said, was held by one company of Russian cavalry.

"One?" asked Felix.

"One." The young subaltern held up his index finger so there should be no confusion. But lest this should bring comfort to his captors, he added quickly that the company was commanded by Captain Katiloff, and with Captain Katiloff, Felix gathered, a platoon would have been enough.

This captain—the little subaltern rubbed his chicken fuzz, a gesture which led Felix to conclude that the Russian captain had a splendid beard—there was not another like him. The subaltern tapped his forehead, indicating that Katiloff possessed that rarest of all military commodities: a brain. He had studied abroad, at St Cyr and the Polytechnique, and as a young officer had travelled to South Africa as an observer to the Boer War. The Boers had taught him many good tricks, for time after time they had led the thickheaded English into traps, taking their positions behind rocks or scrub, silently, stealthily, while the redcoated English marched up in square formation, providing an easy target. They had done it over and over, and the English had never learned.

In General Brusiloff, Captain Katiloff had encountered a commander whose ideas were as unorthodox as his own. Brusiloff, disdaining the long artillery barrage, which not only gave ample warning of an attack but churned up the ground so that the attack became bogged down, preferred to use shock-troop tactics of surprise and quick advance. He had readily recognized the value of a small tactical force which could be deployed rapidly, and had got into the habit of using Captain Katiloff and his highly trained company as a kind of commando unit to be placed where surprise or the ability to move quickly would be worth more than ten divisions and a seven-day barrage.

The ridge of hills dominating the plain through which the German army was likely to advance, had struck Katiloff as forcefully as it had Hagenbeck. They had spread out among the rocks, emplacing their light, portable machine guns to command the widest possible angle of fire, and

Captain Katiloff had put his company on total silence, forbidding them to light fires or even a cigarette. He had threatened to hang anyone who so much as breathed noisily, and *pour encourager les autres*, had in fact executed a corporal who had had the misfortune of dropping his mess tin on a rock. The horses and cookers had been moved far back, and during the nights of waiting Captain Katiloff had permitted small detachments of his men to move to the rear for food and a smoke, but for himself he had not left his post, doing without food or cigarettes, waiting for the German army to emerge from the woods.

"We will fight to the last man," said Hagenbeck when Felix reported the results of his conversation with the little subaltern. "It is true that they have the high ground, but they are only Russians and it is a well-known fact that one German soldier is worth ten Russians."

Pregnitz respectfully begged permission to point out that their losses had been so heavy they were nearly reduced to company strength themselves, but Hagenbeck silenced him by pointing out that at Thermopylae three hundred Spartans had held off nine hundred thousand Persians. Felix knew it was useless to point out to him that his numbers were wrong and every single Spartan had been killed.

The moonlit nights, which would have made it difficult for them to retreat (even if a German soldier could ever contemplate such a course), had also made it impossible for any supplies to reach them. On the third evening the sky clouded over and a few heavy drops of rain fell and cruelly ceased, as if in their terrible plight even the clouds could not resist mocking them. That night a supply party reached them, bringing stretchers, food and water, and, rumour instantly had it, a staff officer who wanted to get a personal view of the situation.

Hagenbeck's junior officers, who had borne with much, felt that this had gone too far. "They'll be bringing up journalists next," muttered Lieutenant von Kaunitz. "Who's he think he is?"

No one knew. He was conferring with Hagenbeck, it was said, and later, after the stretcher-bearers had gone back with the worst of the wounded, but without the mythical staff officer, word got round that he was going to stay to get a view of the terrain by daylight. The man was plainly a lunatic.

Dawn revealed him to be tall and very blond. His uniform, beautifully tailored, seemed at sunrise to consist mostly of a dazzling array of gold braid and medals. "Dear God," muttered Pregnitz to Felix, "I know him. That's Thor von Hagenbeck, Haggy's older brother."

"It's plain that the gods have forsaken us," said Felix, feeling that another Hagenbeck added to an already intolerable situation was distinctly too much.

"The thing is," Pregnitz whispered back as the dazzling vision approached them, "he isn't a bit like Haggy. I remember him from Lehzen."

"Attention!" snapped the adjutant and performed the introduction. Through a gleaming eyeglass Colonel von Hagenbeck surveyed the bearded, scruffy survivors of his brother's battalion. Despite his recent journey and a thick layer of dust on his boots, he looked very clean, smelling of expensive soap and Turkish cigarettes. He did not however use the occasion to remind his brother that the Spartans had at least troubled themselves to comb their hair before making their stand at Thermopylae. Instead he listened to their reports, commended Felix for bringing back a prisoner from his raid, and the rest of them for their splendid spirit shown in their headlong advance, though it was, he pointed out, the better part of wisdom to try and discover what one was advancing into. He delivered this last remark into the air, but it was plain that it could only have been meant for his brother.

"Well, Haggy," he said, "I think we'd better get you out of here. The sooner the better."

His younger brother respectfully asked that they might be allowed to stay and take the ridge. They were, Felix thought, as different as brothers could be. Thor von Hagenbeck, though very fair, had none of the washed-out guinea-pig look which characterized the rest of that inbred family. Had his mother by chance lapsed with the butler? If so, he must have been a very grand butler indeed. Being slight and dark himself, Felix considered those golden looks totally wasted on a member of the Hagenbeck family.

The colonel looked thoughtfully at his brother's request. The ridge, it was true, must be secured at whatever cost, and he could tell from the faces of the young officers that, having made fools of themselves rushing into a trap, they would like to fight themselves out of it with some credit. He said, "You will need reinforcements and artillery support. Thank goodness for that wood. It's just out of range of their machine guns. We'll lay on a solid barrage and see how they like that, sitting so pretty on their hill. Yes," he said courteously to Felix who had made as if to speak, then he remembered the protocol, "I should like to hear what any of you think. Please speak freely."

"Good Lord," thought Felix. "Haggy's brother! It must have been the butler." He told them about his talk with the infantry captain on the train and suggested that they might lift the barrage long enough for the Russians to bring up their machine guns and take their positions, then resume it for another five or ten minutes.

"Rubbish," said the younger Hagenbeck, who liked his junior officers to bring their bright ideas to him, so he could pass them along as his own. "All you'd do is give them extra time."

"I think it might work," said Colonel von Hagenbeck. "You have after all very little to lose."

For the rest of the morning he busied himself drawing maps of the terrain. Once he even stepped up on a rock and through his field glasses took a leisurely look across the plain. His brother made as if to pull him back; the others were too dumbfounded even to move. They concluded that their first guess about him had been true after all; the man was a lunatic. All the time they had been there the least movement, a bird landing on the parapet, the flies rising in a cloud, had brought an instant response from the Russian snipers. And here, in bright sunlight, medals and gold braid sparkling, the staff officer's tabs plainly visible, a German colonel stood well above the top of the parapet, taking a careful and interested look around. When he stepped down, his younger brother, forgetting rank and remembering only their relationship, said, "You bloody fool, you could have been killed. Do you know what their snipers are like? They can shoot the eye out of a bluebottle, those Russian sons of whores."

The colonel put an arm around his brother's shoulders. "Come, Haggy," he said, a note of amusement in his voice, "you know I'm not foolhardy and not even very brave. I can see," he said to the rest of them, "that you don't know how safe I was. No one in the world is as safe from being shot at as a German staff officer. They have orders not to shoot us." He could see from their faces that only politeness kept them from bursting into derisive laughter. "No," he said, "it's quite true. Several times when we've taken snipers prisoner we were told the same thing. You see, there is a bounty on soldiers; if they shoot a private they get one ruble. If they shoot a sergeant, five rubles. A line officer is worth ten rubles, but if they shoot a staff officer they get ten days' latrine duty. The way they look at it, if they manage to kill off the German general staff, we might win the war."

It seemed incredible, Felix thought, that a Hagenbeck should ever manage a joke against himself. Yet he plainly expected them to laugh and looked gratified when they did. Haggy's brother. How extraordinary.

It seemed that Colonel Thor von Hagenbeck was extraordinary in more ways than one. In an army where elephantine deliberation was usually considered a little headlong, he managed within days to have them covered by artillery, which kept the Russians from being a nuisance while supplies and reinforcements were brought up. The barrage did not trouble Captain Katiloff. He moved his company back to a second line of hills and watched with considerable amusement the German artillery smashing up positions where no one was at home. One night he staged a small and unobtrusive raid, capturing an artilleryman who, after being encouraged to do so by having a bayonet held to his jugular, told him the date of the planned attack. The bayonet was then withdrawn, or he might well have told the rest.

After this there was little to do but wait. Captain Katiloff found a rock to lean against, covered his ears, and read a French edition of *War and Peace* which he carried with him everywhere. His parents had always spoken French, and he felt more at home in that language than he did in Russian.

The night before the planned attack he moved his men and guns up again into the shelter of the rocks. "Messieurs," he said, saluting the dried riverbed. "we are ready."

The barrage lifted at dawn. The Russians, who had practised this many times, brought up their machine guns. Captain Katiloff waited, his eyes on his watch. When they saw him nod they knew they had done it in record time and that he was pleased with them.

He lifted his field glasses to his eyes and waited, as always during those final seconds, with that odd sense of excitement at the pit of the stomach, a wonder and a question, that men should, without the prod of bayonet or rifle butt, leave the shelter of a trench and surrender themselves to the tireless bullets. A last echo of the barrage rolled away into distant hills and faded, but no dark silhouettes appeared above the noisome parapet. Only the solitary kite still circled in the sky, patiently, as if it knew. And instantly Katiloff knew too, knew that over there, silent behind the parapet of rotting corpses, a mind which worked as deviously as his own had outwitted him. "Get back," he shouted to his men; "down, quickly, get down!" But this was not an order they were accustomed to hearing. They had never practised retreat, and in their doubt they hesitated one short moment to obey him. Then the howl and shriek and clatter of the barrage reached them at the same time as the searing rain of metal and the blast of high explosive which hurled them into the air and brought rocks crashing down upon them. Katiloff felt a great, burning hand lifting him, and then, carelessly, letting him drop against a rock. He felt no pain. When he looked down at his body, he saw that a shell had gutted him as with a disembowelling knife. Then pain and nausea fell upon him like beasts. The sky turned black with carrion crows.

When a water bottle touched his lips, he opened his eyes

and saw Sergeant Ivanov-Rinov, a bloody gash across his cheek, but seemingly otherwise unhurt. There were no crows in the pale sky; there never had been. He had merely fainted, and when he realized this he cursed himself as he had never cursed the rawest and clumsiest recruit.

Always he had maintained that a soldier must be able to look with indifferent eyes upon any sight, no matter how grisly, must endure pain—his own or that of others—no matter how unendurable. As a cadet he had stood at the windows of butcher shops and had studied the trays of flyblown offal, telling himself, like a monk reciting his *memento mori*, "You are the same as that stuff on the tray. Underneath that uniform with its gold fastenings, its tunic flung with such careful negligence over one shoulder, under the swirl and drama of your cavalry cape there is a sack of skin holding the things on that tray."

Out hunting he never averted his eyes from the hunts-man's knife as it slipped into the spread-eagled doe, with the delirious hounds falling upon the slimy ropes of intes-tines as they slid to the ground. "A boar's tusk could do this to you," he said austerely to himself. "This is what you are."

It was for a time like this that he had prepared himself, and he determined that he should not fail. He bent his ferocious will to keep from fainting again as he lifted himself on his elbow, roaring with pain, to look at what had to be looked at.

His men lay dead and dying, crushed under rocks, bodies ripped apart by shells, heads and limbs reassembled in grotesque combinations. The machine guns, those valued, cherished Landeck guns, docile to the hand, light to carry, held little reminder of what they had been. The one nearest to where he had been flung by the explosion, almost within his hand's reach, was invisible under a thick quilt of bloody flesh steaming in the morning air. Everywhere flies hovered and hummed.

He brushed weakly at them, raising a small black cloud. Flies, he thought; where did they hide until there was blood and carrion, and what instinct brought them so instantly to the place of carnage? There weren't any flies in *War and*

Peace. Books never mentioned such things. When Napoleon looks down at Prince Andrey and says, "That's a fine way to die," his boot does not stir up a cloud of bluebottles.

The water flask tilted at his lips again. He opened his eyes to see Sergeant Ivanov-Rinov, a quiet, circumspect man, quiet and circumspect even now. Katiloff realized that his mind had been wandering, he could not tell for how long. He must think clearly, put pain aside as irrelevant.

Small figures were moving across the plain; sniper fire held them pinned down many times, and there were those who, after flinging themselves flat did not get up again. That was good. The snipers had been hidden in the rear to wait for the Germans to approach closely enough to be easily picked off. They were good men, his snipers. He had trained them himself.

If only they had one machine gun left. But all those he could see looked damaged beyond repair. Only the one near him, which had been partially sheltered by an outcropping of rock, might still be able to be worked.

He said, "Are any guns still functioning, sergeant?"

"No, sir."

"What about this one?"

Sergeant Ivanov-Rinov was no fool. Though the small black figures were growing larger as they crossed the plain, he knew very well that not all the Germans were out there. Some had stayed behind, manning their machine guns. To get up from behind the rock to move aside the grisly covering was the same as committing suicide and he was not about to do it.

"It would be better to wait till they're so close their side can't shoot at us without taking a chance at hitting their own men," he said respectfully.

The calm with which the man disobeyed his order angered Katiloff, shooting a burst of strength down his right arm. Every move was agony, but he managed to get his revolver from its holster and point it at the sergeant. They had been together since Katiloff had been a second lieutenant and they thought the world of each other, but Katiloff was prepared to shoot and the sergeant knew it.

He began to prod away the bits of meat with the butt of his rifle, watching them roll down the hill.

The first wave was very close now. In their steel helmets the German soldiers had an archaic look. It put Katiloff in mind of medieval mercenaries. He realized that his mind was beginning to wander again and forced it back to the present.

"I think the gun might work, sir," said Sergeant Ivanov-Rinov, pushing aside the last dead man, who went rolling down the hill toward the Germans. The belt of bullets was twisted. The sergeant straightened it. Katiloff, finding the strap of his field glasses still around his neck, put down his gun and with infinite effort lifted them to his eyes. One lens had broken, but through the other he watched the grey figures at the bottom of the hill. A captain, a slight, slender man, looked up, and under the brim of his helmet Katiloff saw a bearded, dark face, which might have been handsome if the eyes had not been too close together. White teeth suddenly showed in the beard as the German captain laughed and shouted something, waving on his men. Katiloff could not hear him, but he had seen the lips move and knew what it was the German had shouted. *"Nach Moskau!"* Sudden fury gave him a last spurt of strength. As Sergeant Ivanov-Rinov engaged the trigger mechanism, he managed to put out his hand and pick up the belt of bullets to let it feed smoothly into the gun. He saw the earth spurt up, and, as the sergeant adjusted his aim, men begin to topple. He watched the smile disappear from the dark, bearded face, to be replaced by the look of indignant amazement he had seen many times before on the faces of men hit in battle. Then the German crumpled and fell, and did not move again.

Sergeant Ivanov-Rinov turned to look at him. He could not tell whether the sudden baring of teeth was a grimace of pain or a smile. "Got him," Katiloff began to say, but his mouth filled with blood and choked the words.

The last belt of machine-gun bullets was spent. In his quiet, circumspect way, the sergeant looked at the situation. Field-grey uniforms were scrambling up the rock. The snipers could deal with those. For him it was time to *filer*.

The expression was one he had adopted from Captain Katiloff, who tended to do most of his thinking in French. He looked down at the dead face, crusted with blood and flies. Though he knew that amid all this filth and blood a small decency could scarcely be of account, he knelt down beside his captain, brushed away the flies, and pulled the lids over the staring blue eyes.

Chapter 4

In April 1917, A Company had its first deserter.

The winter, which was drawing to an end, was said to have been the coldest in a hundred years. A bone-tired First Battalion, standing to at dawn and dusk, with the wind driving sleet like icy nails against their aching faces, did not need to be told.

It had been a winter of stalemate, mud, and exhaustion. The war had lasted, for some of them, more than three years. Once they would have been considered the lucky ones. Now they were too worn and cold to be sure.

Late in January they had a moment's cheer when a raid led by David on the kaiser's birthday managed to capture not only some very fuddled sentries and two Landeck machine guns, but as an unexpected bonus, a drunk German general who had convivially ventured into the line to drink the kaiser's health with his lads.

David was awarded a bar to the MC he had from the Somme, Sergeant Doolittle got the DCM, and the papers, picking up the story and dubbing it "The Kaiser's Birthday Raid," made a great play with it, knowing that in the winter of 1917 everyone, at home or at the front, needed a small victory and a good laugh. But one could tell by their tone of nostalgia that they knew that the kaiser's birthday raid, with its polish, dash, and good humour, belonged to a very different war.

The old war, the one the papers tried to pretend still went on, had ended for David, as it had for so many of them, on July 1, at the Somme, when First Battalion, eight hundred strong, had gone over the top in the morning and had straggled back that night, those who could still straggle, little more than two hundred men and three junior officers.

First Battalion, in its jump-off trench that morning, was to David the last moment of the old war. The officers had worn their best uniforms. Some had carried swords, one platoon commander had tossed a football in the air, which his platoon proposed to kick across no-man's-land. Colonel de Lacy, spurs gleaming, had stood by no. 1 Platoon's scaling ladder, for, in the gallant and wasteful Vickies' tradition, it was the colonel's privilege to be first in the field. He had worn a poppy in his buttonhole, and had carried his sword but no revolver, for he considered it an officer's duty to command, not to kill. The pet wombat had been considered too highly-strung to be brought into the line, but his Irish wolfhound bitch crouched at his heels, looking noble and heraldic, like a dog on a crusader's tomb.

The men, encumbered by sixty pounds of equipment, presented a less brave show than their officers, but they were cheerful, and with a tot of army rum still glowing in their stomachs, even eager for the moment when the officers' whistles would signal them over the top.

They had been promised a walkover. "I feel that every step has been taken with the Divine help," Field Marshal Haig had written the night before the attack, and the messages which had been read to the troops had taken an equally jaunty view of things. The German trenches had been demolished and the barbed wire cut by a seven-day barrage. They would stroll across no-man's-land, picking poppies along the way.

It had proved the bloodiest of lies. The first wave had scarcely scrambled up the scaling ladders and lined up to advance when the German machine guns—those light-weight, tractable Landeck guns—had begun their ill-tempered chatter. And only moments later the German artillery had opened fire, and the blue sky had turned to steel and fallen upon them.

Only David's platoon got even as far as the first line of trenches, for David's civilian mind distrusted army certainties. He knew they had been told the same tale before, and it had not worked then either. Survivors of the Neuve-Chapelle attack had told him how there a three days' barrage had been guaranteed to cut the wire and knock out the German positions. It had taken the English battalions, advancing in extended formation at a pace of a hundred yards every two minutes, very little time to learn that the wire was intact and so were the German guns. The newspapers had called it a victory, and those who had bought two hundred feet of churned-up mud with their lives could not contradict them. But David could not help wondering what commanders whose planning had resulted in thirteen thousand casualties on a three-mile front, could accomplish given a front stretching eighteen miles.

He had studied French small-unit tactics and had drilled his platoon in them against orders, for they were to advance at the Somme as they had at Neuve-Chapelle, in a deadly pavane of one hundred yards every two minutes.

Afterwards there was some debate as to whether he should be awarded the Military Cross for capturing a German trench, or court-martialled for not walking his platoon across no-man's-land at the prescribed sedate and murderous pace. By then he had been wounded and was very ill in a hospital in Amiens. This told in his favour, for a decorated dead hero looks better in the army lists than a dead felon. He was awarded the MC for gallantry in action.

The capture of the German trench had proved an idle success, for with no supplies or support able to get through the German fire, the position could not be held, and by early afternoon the Germans had reclaimed their property, while David, with what was left of his platoon, had hidden out in no-man's-land, waiting for darkness amid bloody mounds of khaki, which the swath of a machine-gun would at times twitch into a semblance of life.

Afterward he could joke about his *Boy's Own* defence of the German trench, but of the hours among the torn men, who had lain in the July sun, their water bottles shot full of holes, he never spoke to anyone, not even to Toby.

He was hit a week later during an attack on a wood surrounded by German machine guns on three sides. A piece of shrapnel severed his femoral artery, but luckily Sergeant Doolittle had proved to be quite good at tourniquets, and since the attack very quickly turned into a rout, he had been got back to the English lines and the casualty clearing station in a very short time. But he had lost a lot of blood, and his resistance was low. He caught a cold from the Church of England chaplain who came to visit him, the cold turned into pneumonia, and for several weeks he had been very ill indeed. Dreams, which had not touched his sleep, invaded his fever; A Company's dead, rotting in the Picardy sun, rotted again in his delirium. Night after night rats built a nest in Colonel de Lacy's ribs and cracked Andrew Fielding's bones with their strong teeth. He wept for them, but sensed that in those quiet watches he was healing. His memories were scabbing over like his wound. His scars would remain with him, but they would grow pale with time.

When he returned to First Battalion they were once again stationed back in the Salient, and, as it happened, were occupying the same stretch of trenches they had held before they had marched south to the Somme. Wearing his purple and white MC ribbon, and knowing from Toby that A Company was his to command so long as either of them should live, he felt a disturbing sense of homecoming as he made his way through the familiar warren of trenches—Primrose Lane, Piccadilly, Dead Man's Walk, and Little Venice, as always knee-deep under water. It was all so familiar. Nothing had changed. And nothing was as it had been.

The deserter's name was Wicks. Had he volunteered for the army he would, even as late as 1916, have been turned down. The draft was not so particular and chose to overlook his concave chest, flat feet, and bad teeth.

In training camp NCOs roared at him and fellow conscripts played jokes on him, but the food was better than any he had ever tasted, and for the first time in his life he did not go to bed hungry. Within the first four weeks of training he put on ten pounds and an inch around his chest. Once he heard his colonel say to a visiting officer that army training was a wonderful thing; you took spindly, whey-faced boys out of their slum environment, provided healthy outdoor exercise and decent food, and in a month their mothers wouldn't know them. Alfred Wicks squared his shoulders and felt proud of being a credit to his colonel. Then he overheard one of the sergeants muttering, "Fattening them up for the kill," and this gave him to think.

Everyone said his draft was lucky to be assigned to HRH Crown Princess Victoria's Own Yorkshire Rifles. He couldn't quite see why he should consider himself so very lucky. He didn't know much, but even he knew that the Ypres Salient was not a good place to be, and the Vickies had been there, on and off, ever since the beginning of the war.

Reality was worse than anything his fears had prepared him to expect. Mud, cold, rats, and worst of all, the unceasing sound of gunfire, the unending, ever-present danger, destroyed within one day the little heart his training in England had put into him. Even on quiet days men were killed or wounded at random, but in the Salient, where shelling was usually from three directions, there were seldom quiet days. Bloated, blackened corpses were everywhere to remind him of his mortality. A German sniper had their latrine in his sights, and this, since Private Wicks suffered from a weak bladder, added to his endless misery. Once he tried in the dark to relieve himself against the side of the trench, but a corporal had roared at him whether he thought he was a bloody Aussie, and had brought him up before the company commander. David had put him on a week's shit wallah fatigue.

There were, Wicks knew, ways out of this endless torment. There was first of all the self-inflicted wound. Then there was the story of the secret army. Of all the rumours bred by the war, this was the one which caught at his imagination. An underground army, he was told, deserters of all nationalities, English, German, Belgian, and French, lived in amity together in a warren of abandoned trenches. Like rats they survived by scavenging corpses. The idea of such a life did not repel Private Wicks.

When he was on sentry duty he stared out into the dark, wondering where this secret army might be hiding, where he could find them. One night he disappeared.

All his life he had never been good at anything. He was not good at being a deserter. At dawn he was brought back, and a court-martial awarded him a firing squad of his very own.

A grim end to a grim winter, thought David. A Company was lined up behind a destroyed farm, wearing battle order, as if they were about to go into action. In the exhausted light of early dawn their faces seemed grey and pinched. Wicks was their first deserter, and they were taking it hard.

It was a wonder, really, thought David, that it had not happened sooner. They had had their share of self-inflicted wounds, of course, over the last three years, and if Toby happened not to be paying attention, which was these days more often than not, the MO usually tried to pass these off as honourable blighties. They had all been so near to the breaking point so many times, especially during these last winter months, they knew it could have been any of them. A deserter was different. Private Wicks's escape had laid bare the rat and the cur that lurked in all of them; he embodied their most abject moments of cowardice, and therefore he had to die.

David doubted that among the worn and haggard faces belonging to A Company there was one who disagreed with the verdict of the court-martial. Not even the twelve members of no. 3 Platoon who had been chosen by lot to make up the firing squad.

"My platoon," David thought bitterly, though of course it was Basil Cobbleston's platoon now. He looked blurred and pale, but that might have been the fallow light of dawn.

Lieutenant Cobbleston had shambled into David's life to take over no. 3 Platoon. Tall, concave, spectacles slipping down his nose, puttees trailing, he had struck David—no spit-and-polish fanatic—as the most untidy officer he had ever seen. His batman had dragged a valise weighing considerably more than the permitted forty-six pounds because it was full of books. Upon this happy discovery David and Basil had instantly taken to each other, and no.

3 Platoon, once they had grown used to his peculiar methods and shambling appearance, took to him too.

In private life he had been a history don at Cambridge. He was a Kitchener volunteer, a survivor of that great New Army Field Marshal Haig had butchered so lavishly on the Somme, the best England had once had to give, just as with the draft they were now getting the worst.

Sergeant Doolittle was handing out bullets to the firing squad. Some of these were dummies. No one who pulled the trigger at sunrise would know whether he had killed or not.

There was a touch of relenting softness in the morning breeze, yet David found it difficult to keep from shivering. It was nerves, he knew, not cold. They were all drained of their last reserves of strength, patience, and tolerance, were reduced to nothing but bodies, lousy, filthy nuisances which daily had to be flogged, like an exhausted and recalcitrant animal, to their work. What kept them going was an old habit of discipline, and a bond of comradeship so strong they had not believed anything but death could break it. But Wicks, by deserting, had snapped it as if it had been no stronger than a spider's thread. For this too he had to die.

But not like this, thought David, not with all the panoply of a court-martial and A Company drawn up for witness. Someone should have taken him to the midden, shot him in the dark, and buried him without a word. Brave men died so horribly in this war; why should a coward like Wicks be allowed a ceremonial?

Not that he looked as if he were going to take the advantage offered him to redeem a squalid life with a decent death. David wondered whether he had been given a kindly tot of rum. If so, it had failed him. He had puked down the front of his uniform. His legs refused to hold him upright. Someone had brought a chair from a nearby farm. He had collapsed on it, weeping and begging for his life. The Church of England chaplain, paunchy with hospital visiting and easy living behind the lines, looking as pale as the wretch he had come to comfort, was reading from the *Book of Common Prayer*, promising no doubt, thought

David, jam tomorrow, since there was plainly not going to be any jam today. A Woodbine Willie was talking steadily and earnestly, pie in a nondenominational sky.

The horizon had lightened; the sky glowed as red as poppies in the east. The cough of anti-aircraft guns punctuated the sunrise with puffs of smoke. "I am the resurrection and the life," the chaplain read from the prayer book, and moved aside hurriedly as the command to fire rang out in the morning air, keeping his eyes on the book, reading falteringly on, flinching at the crack of twelve rifles, never looking at the bloody heap of khaki held by webbing to the kitchen chair. "Behold, I show you a mystery."

David dismissed A Company and went to report to Toby, who nearly a year after the Somme had killed most of First Battalion's officers, was still acting battalion commander. At first there had been talk of replacements, but there were few regulars left, and Toby was quite simply the most experienced officer they had. At twenty-five, he found himself in a position where in the very nature of his job virtually every order he gave was bound to maim or kill someone.

Battalion HQ was a farm kitchen. The farm's walls were so thick they had withstood days of shelling. No one knew where the owners were, but a few days before a pig had turned up, looking for its trough, and was even now being converted by Corporal Hamish into sausages and bacon.

Toby was seated at the kitchen table, drowsing over a stack of papers. A bottle of whisky stood by his elbow. Unlike David, who, like most line officers, had long since gone into other-ranks battle dress, Toby continued to wear the regulation uniform with its elegantly cut tunic and flared jodhpurs which had in the early part of the war made such an easy target of English officers. He looked up as David came into the kitchen. His eyes were bloodshot and blurred. He said, "Have a drink."

"Tea, please."

Toby poured himself another whisky and shouted for his batman. Holmes stuck his head around the door. "Bring some tea for Captain Harvey," said Toby. "And when I say tea I mean tea and not that tepid swill you consider tea.

260

If you can't learn to produce a decent pot of tea, you can go back into the line."

Holmes saluted and vanished. "Holmes doesn't like me,' said Toby. "He has a great talent for silent sulks."

"I don't wonder, the way you talk to him." Toby used up on the average one batman a month, and David had on occasion overheard the mutinous opinion that after four weeks of Major Strafford, being back in the line was a positive treat. What Toby needed, David thought, was a good, solid Blighty, one that would keep him in bed for weeks, and on convalescent leave for months. But no such good fortune ever came Toby's way. People talked of his incredible luck—in the worst of the fighting since the first days of the war and never a scratch. He was looked upon as very nearly miraculous, but David knew that such miracles exact a heavy cost. Toby had never been given time to rest, to mourn his many dead, to put aside his responsibilities. He continued safe in his horrible invulnerability, while the war ate away his nerve, judgement, and good temper.

Holmes came back with a teapot and two mugs. David drank a cup of it gratefully. It was hot, and if it tasted more of chloride of lime than Earl Grey, that was really not Holmes's fault. He said, "Thank you, Holmes, that's very good, quite like mother used to make. Oh, will you tell Pilkington to be sure there's some hot tea for Mr Cobbleston, and to put a big tot of rum into it?"

Holmes saluted smartly. "Yes, sir. Thank *you*, sir," and vanished before Toby could say anything.

"Poor Basil," said David, "he can't have liked it much."

Toby swallowed his whisky and said, "It all comes with the job."

"Yes, I suppose so."

David poured himself another cup and said, "Do you want some, Toby? It really isn't at all bad."

"Christ, David, you're such a bloody tart. Like mother used to make. How can you?"

"It gets results. Where's the writing paper?"

Toby pointed to the tin box which protected the regimental stationery from being eaten by rats. David took out one of the thick sheets embossed with a white rose, unscrewed his fountain pen, and began to write.

"Are you writing to Wicks's people?" asked Toby.

"Yes," said David without looking up.

"Then use the printed form."

Dismayed, David said, "Oh, Toby, no." The printed form, which simply stated, "It is my painful duty to have to inform you . . . ," with only name and rank to be filled in by hand, seemed to David so incredibly callous and insulting that, no matter how exhausted he was, and weary of writing such letters at all, he had always done it in person on their regimental paper.

"You know," said Toby, "the first two years of the war, when someone was shot for desertion, that's what their families were told. I've never had to do it, but I could have, more easily than writing a lot of cod's wallop."

"He's dead," said David. "Why distress his parents?" He wondered what they could be like. Wicks's face, the pasty skin and bad teeth, had told a life's history of growing up in a back alley unblessed by the sun. What had England given him that he should be willing to give his life for England? David put this question to Toby, who replied that England had given Wicks the same she had given all of them. David understood that he meant the privilege of being English. He supposed on the other side people felt as privileged being German. And they were every bit as right. It seemed a pity that they had to kill each other to prove the point.

He said again, "Why make his parents suffer?"

"I said use the printed form. That's an order, David."

David wanted to respond with a brisk, "Yes, sir," but looked at Toby's drawn face and bit it back. He took a form and filled in Wicks's name and the date of his death. He slid it across the table and said, "You sign it."

Toby picked it up, stared at it as if he had forgotten what it was, then tore it across. "Sorry," he said. "Go ahead and write a proper letter."

David smiled at him. "Stupid sod."

"Bloody civilian."

They quarrelled so rarely they scarcely knew how.

David had finished the letter, and was signing his name, when there was a knock on the door and Captain Strickland poked his head into the room, waving a sheet of paper. "I say, you chaps, we're going home."

"Oh," said Toby, "is the war over?"

David licked the envelope. "Who won?"

"Stow it, you two. I said we're going home. The leave roster's come down and you're both on it. Two whole weeks in blessed Blighty."

David and Toby looked at each other. "Home," said David. "I'd almost forgotten there was such a place."

Toby said, "Altondale," but he had a stunned and absent look as if his mind were saying something else. He had last been home in the autumn, while David was still very ill in the hospital in Amiens, and the Somme offensive, started with such high hopes of a breakthrough, was winding itself down, having achieved little but a few miles of churned-up mud and four hundred twenty thousand English casualties.

At Altondale late roses were blooming in the cottage gardens and spilling like a waterfall down the railway embankment. Against the station wall Mr Dobb's prize rose, *Gloire d'Altondale*, trembled and shed its petals. (Lady Millicent, Toby remembered, had needed all her tact to dissuade the stationmaster from calling it *Gloire de Dobbs*.)

Julian had been there in the pony cart, waiting for him, saying, in her cool small voice, "Hello, Toby, I'm so glad you've come," holding out a cool small hand for him to grasp.

His leave had gone, as home leaves always did, slowly the first few days, but during the second week gathering speed, so that it seemed he had scarcely put down his valise and kissed his mother's cheek, before he was picking it up again and kissing her good-bye. It was Lady Millicent's letter-writing day at the hospital, Augustus was out with the Home Guard, so it was again Julian who took him to the station in the pony cart. She said, "I somehow thought two weeks would be much longer."

"It always seems so at the beginning," said Toby.

The pony clattered into the station yard. Julian said, "I have a present for you, Toby." She felt in her coat pocket and held out her hand to him. On her palm lay a greenish gold pebble. "It's a cat's-eye," she said. "The old gypsy woman who lives up by High Fenton said a special spell over it, and it's supposed to be absolutely guaranteed to keep you safe. I know it's superstitious, but I do wish you'd wear it, just in case."

Toby took the greenish stone, touched at her thought of him. He said, "Thank you, Julian. I'll always wear it."

"I can hear the train coming," said Julian. "Toby, are there people on the platform? Is anyone looking?"

Toby looked along the platform, wondering why she wanted to know. Mr Dobbs's back was turned to them, his attention absorbed by a crate containing a far from amiable pig. A boy was down at the far end, sweeping. "No one's looking," said Toby. "Why?"

She turned to him, her smoky eyes uncannily attentive, as if she could see. She lifted her hands, finding his face, and said, "Good-bye, Toby." Her lips touched his. They were cool, like her hands. It was a very proper kiss, a young girl's kiss, lips closed, a sister's kiss. But Toby, muttering a hasty good-bye, and stumbling into the train just pulling into the station, did not feel as if a sister had kissed him.

"Good God," he muttered to himself, thankful to be alone in the compartment. He had kissed girls before on occasion, fast girls who giggled and didn't mind if you pulled their clothes about. They had made him feel excited and a little sick. But none of them had made him feel what the touch of Julian's cool, closed lips made him feel. "Good God," he said again. "She's only fourteen; she's practically my sister."

The word "sister" led him to another and worse reflection. Julian was David's sister. One knew, of course, of horrid old men who liked little girls and enticed them into carriages with offers of chocolates. It was disgusting and at the same time rather pitiful. But surely even they, poor perverts though they were, thought Toby, would draw the line at the sister of their best friend.

The train was nearing London before Toby calmed down enough to remember that he was on his way to the front, a world of mud and danger and rats and no women, where he would be too busy running First Battalion to worry his head about people's sisters. The cat's-eye was still in his hand. It had a small hole bored into one end. He unbuttoned his shirt, pulled out the leather thong on which he wore his identification disc, and threaded the cat's-eye on it.

Throughout that awful winter Julian had indeed seemed far away, though sometimes, as he moved, he felt the cat's-eye brush his breast like a caress. But his life was too harsh and burdened to dwell on thoughts so tender. Only now, when David said, "Home," and he had replied, "Altondale," the voice in his mind which could no longer be silenced, said, "Julian."

Chapter 5

Toby and David arrived at Victoria, feeling shabby and foreign. Soldiers, wearing their muddy uniforms, stumbled off the train, looking about them like sleepwalkers who have awakened, not knowing where they are. Then a voice in the waiting crowd would call out a name, a blurred face would become that of a son or husband, they shook hands—or far more rarely, kissed—and were at home. Those who had no one to meet them drifted past the buffet, which displayed cakes like grey india rubber, toward the exit.

Toby said, "Let's get a drink."

But of course there was no drink. While they had been away a spoilsport called DORA (Defence of the Realm Act) had closed pub doors, which had once stood hospitably open from six in the morning to eleven at night. Pubs were allowed to open only in the evening, so that munitions workers would return to work after lunch, instead of spending the afternoon boozing.

David would have been content to make do with tea and india-rubber cakes, but Toby said Strickland had given him the address of a private club in Soho where one could become a member by paying five shillings.

"It sounds rather foul," said David.

"Everything's foul. I noticed it on my last leave."

There were no cabs, so they took a bus. Things, David thought, had certainly changed. Penniless poets like himself had always taken buses, but a regular-army officer would before the war no more have been seen riding a bus than he would have walked down the street carrying a parcel.

Their fare was collected by a young woman. This too was new. She wore a smart blue uniform, with a surprisingly short skirt and leggings. "They're called conductorettes," said Toby. "Strickland told me."

Though it was a sunny spring day, London looked drab and down-at-heel. Many people were in mourning. There was a general air of shabbiness.

David knew his way around Soho, because Lucas had been fond of its foreign restaurants with their un-English smells of garlic and spices. He found the address Strickland had given Toby, and they both became members of the club by paying five shillings.

The room they entered was lit with coloured lights; its curtains were drawn against the sun and blue sky. There was very loud music. Young subalterns were dancing with girls in glittery rags of dresses. Toby and David assumed that they must be tarts, though neither of them had ever seen tarts quite so shamelessly dressed.

David looked around the room and quoted Carlyle. "Blackguards, improper females, and miscellanies."

Their drinks were served in teacups. "Good God," said David, tasting it, "what is it?"

"Cocktails," explained Toby, who seemed to have picked up a good deal of information from the knowledgeable Strickland.

One of the tarts, in a dress like a ragged dragonfly, was making her way toward them. David's previous encounters with Soho tarts had taught him that they summed one up with breathtaking speed and accuracy, going from, "Hello boys," to, "Well, you boys will be boys," without a second's hesitation. He did not mind for himself—it was no more than the truth—but could just imagine Toby's face should something of the sort happen. He said, "I think I'd better catch my train," but his retreat was cut off by the bedraggled dragonfly, who held out her hand to Toby and said in perfect Mayfair tones, "You're Toby Strafford, aren't you? I thought I remembered you."

Her hair was cut as short as a boy's. The dress, woven of some glittery stuff, left bare a great deal of back and more leg than David had ever seen outside a music hall. In the crook of her arm she carried a tiny, dejected-looking dog.

Toby, groping in the past, thinking, It can't be, but of course it is, said, "Miss Tremayne. We met at Camberley just before the war. This is Captain Harvey."

Miss Tremayne looked with interest at the MC with its small silver rose and said, "Can you tango?"

"I'm afraid not," said David. "We've just come from Flanders. We seem to have missed most of the fun."

"That's unkind. Isn't it unkind, Major Strafford? You can tango, can't you?"

"Sorry, Miss Tremayne. I've been too busy lately to keep up with my dancing."

"How stuffy. And sanctimonious. But you always were a bit of a prig, weren't you? I remember someone at Camberley saying, 'You must meet Toby Strafford. He's the most frightful prig.' Well, toodle-oo. I'm going to find someone who can dance."

"Goodness," said David mildly.

"Yes," Toby agreed. "I think you had the better idea. Let's go to Charing Cross and eat india-rubber buns till your train leaves."

"How do they do it?" said Toby, bemusedly to his cup of tea, which looked as grey as the buns. "I mean, how do they change their shapes like that? They all used to have—oh, you know"—he gestured —"hips and bosoms and things. How did they suddenly go all flat?"

"Perhaps she always looked like that," said David.

"No, I remember her very well. She definitely had a figure."

"Or padding," suggested David, who, having grown up with several sisters, had fewer illusions about female anatomy.

"Oh. Oh yes, I see."

They looked at each other and suddenly burst out laughing. "Oh dear," said David, "and I thought they were tarts. That poor dog. I wonder whether he can tango. Look, I really do have to catch my train."

"I'll see you to the platform. You know, I think it very odd that you aren't coming straight home."

"Yes. Well, lie for me, will you. I'll be there next week."

"All right. Lord knows, you've lied often enough for me."

"Lucas, how very nice to see you."

Lucas was at tea, a book propped against the pot. He looked up and said, "David! We didn't know when to expect you."

"I ought to have sent a wire. But I really wanted to walk in on you at teatime, just like that, as if I had never been away."

There was an empty cup on the tray. David poured himself some tea. "Are you expecting company?"

"No. Mrs Placid has sent up a spare cup ever since we heard you were getting leave."

David sat down across the table from Lucas and looked around the room. "It still goes on," he said with pleasure. "Tea, scones, honey in the comb. One dreams of it, of course, over there, but one no longer thinks of it as real."

"Isn't that what you went to France to defend?"

"Did I? I'd forgotten."

Lucas stretched his hand across the table and touched David's. "How are you, my dear? Really?"

"At the moment, extremely well and happy. You look tired, Lucas."

"Old, you mean."

"No older than usual. Tired was what I said."

"I don't sleep well. You can hear the guns, you know. Especially at night. I go for long walks on the beach and imagine that every single one is shooting at you."

David laughed.

"And of course all the fuss about *The Green Envelope* hasn't been much help," said Lucas, referring to his long antiwar poem, published in the *Cambridge Magazine* earlier in the year. "It may sound petty, but I don't enjoy being a pariah. It's a disagreeable feeling and I'm not used to it."

"You're lucky you're still alive. They used to kill the bearers of evil tidings."

The poem had caused a tremendous scandal. A public coddled by newspaper reports of constant victories and cheerful Tommies going over the top singing "Tipperary," was not about to accept what Lucas had to tell them. The very title of the poem, referring to the special kind of envelope which allowed a letter from the front to be sent uncensored, caused indignation, implying as it did that for the last three years the truth had been successfully withheld. This was not English, it was, if anything, German, and Lucas Ryder was a bounder if he thought otherwise.

Nor could his timing have been more tactless. For by 1917 the effects of the war were at last brought home to the civilian population who were asked to observe meatless days, not to clean their wallpaper with slices of bread, and to follow the example of the king and abstain from drinking spirits whose manufacture required grain. And no matter how cheery, even manic, the newspapers made life at the front to seem, they had also to print casualty lists and maps, and it had become difficult for the most optimistic not to notice that after every battle the promised breakthrough remained in the future, while the casualty lists grew longer. It was not very polite of Mr Ryder, with no loved ones at the front, to point out to those who had lost husbands and sons, that these losses were largely a waste.

Nor were Lucas's soldiers, foulmouthed, muddy, dog-tired, barely kept going by the rum ration, something the public was prepared to accept.

Then there was the poem itself, if poem one could call it. A jumble of army directives, soldiers' songs and jokes, doggerel, and lyrics mixed up with paragraphs of prose purporting to be quotations from the letters of an officer at the front; one hardly knew what to make of it. Bishops representing the Church Militant preached against it, and literary critics took it to pieces. The *Cambridge Magazine*, notorious for its antiwar sentiments, had its offices ransacked by patriotic civilians, someone threw a rock through a window of Lucas's Chelsea house, and the Duchess of Frome cut him in public.

Just when he thought he hadn't a friend left in the world, letters started to come from jubilant front-line officers, and soldiers who, for the first time in three years, read about themselves, not swimmers into cleanness leaping, not the smarmy neurasthenics which had made Robert Nichols's awful poems such persistent best-sellers, and certainly not the cheery, Jerry-bashing Tommies of the English press, but the muddy, cold, and lousy members of the poor bloody infantry. They found their jokes in the poem, their endurance, their songs, their endless slogging weariness, and the horrible, bloody ways in which they died.

"It's a very good poem, Lucas," said David. "Perhaps your best. I'm too close to it; I can't really tell. We all have huge chunks of it by heart. I'm sorry you've had so much annoyance about it, but if you didn't expect it you were incredibly naive. Do you know what I would like right now? A swim. Do I have time before dinner?"

"Yes, of course. But the water's still very cold, and you'll find some rather sad characters moping on the beach. Longacre Hall is a special hospital for shell-shock cases, you know."

"Good Lord. Well, never mind then." David looked out at the slope of the lawn. The tide was high and a silver edge of water curled at its rim. He caught his breath with pleasure. "Dear Lucas, this is extraordinarily nice."

He said the same thing over dinner and Lucas's excellent wine, and said it again in bed, stretching his naked body between clean sheets.

"It's what I dream of in Flanders," he said. "Probably a better and nobler person would dream of peace and universal harmony, but I dream of a hot bath and a clean bed."

"This bed?" Lucas could not keep himself from asking.

David smiled at him. "Yes, my darling, quite often, this bed."

He fell asleep easily. Once a nightmare caused him to cry out, but Lucas's touch turned it into something else without waking him. Rousing himself before morning stand-to was an agony. He struggled with his reluctant body until, between sleep and waking he became aware of smooth sheets, and realized that he was not in Flanders, but in a clean English bed. The sky outside the window shone like mother-of-pearl. There was a steady murmur in the air, setting the windows to vibrating gently, and it took him a moment to realize that it was the sound of the guns in France. Though he knew he was free to go back to sleep, he was suddenly restless. He got up, put on his British warm, and went downstairs.

He walked across the water meadow, startling the nesting birds with his footsteps, so that they cried out warnings. At the far end of the beach a man stood with a fishing rod in his hand. He made no acknowledgement of another presence. David wondered whether he was one of the shell-shock cases from Longacre Hall. He looked up at the smug, beautiful Queen Anne facade, then turned and walked away from the solitary fisherman. As the sky lightened he stared across the grey water, listening to the guns and thinking of his company.

As if he had been away from them a long time, he remembered the small ways in which they showed him they returned his affection; the slice of cake from home shyly offered, a joke kept against his rounds of the sentries on a foul night, the mug of stewed tea set aside and kept warm for him, the place nearest the fire which he never took, but which invariably happened to be vacant at his approach, not because he was their commanding officer, but because he was theirs.

He remembered Toby mockingly quoting a line from the marriage service in the letter he had written to tell him that he would be taking command of A Company. It really was something like a marriage, David thought, a bond indissoluble even in the most desperate and trying circumstances.

It was this bond which drew men who might have moved to staff duties or garrison service at home back again and again to the claustrophobic hell of the trenches. There was no explanation for it; it was a special grace not granted to everyone. Strickland, David thought, who was in many ways a bounder, had it; Toby, though an excellent officer, did not. Love, with its meaning, at one extreme of physical attraction, and at the other of the mysteries of sacrifice and Christian charity, was not too freighted a word to describe it.

He thought of all the early mornings when they had stood-to, staring across the mud and the splintered trees to the German trenches, where nothing ever moved. He thought of Toby, probably as sleepless as he, and of Felix, wondering whether he was standing, revolver in hand, in a German trench, the rising sun in his eyes. A wave nudged his foot. He bent and tested the water with his hand. It was horribly cold. All the same David took off his coat and walked through the shallows till it was deep enough to swim. If the solitary fisherman thought him a suicide he did not trouble himself about it, but continued to stare out toward the soft thrumming of the guns.

David swam until he was numb with cold. Then he snatched up his coat and ran across the water meadow, up the stairs and back into bed, so that Lucas woke with a shout of shock and indignation.

At Altondale Toby could find no rest. He slept badly, no longer being accustomed to sleeping at night at all. He missed the guns and he missed David, because he was someone who had shared his life. It was not that he wanted to go back to the fighting; he dreaded having to return, but that he realized that there was no other place where he still belonged.

"I've become war," he thought, horrified, as he woke from confused dreams of rabbit warrens before dawn. "There is no peace left in me, none at all."

Childhood habit and front-line experience combined to make him leave his bed before daybreak and drink a glass of milk in the kitchen. He would have liked to put whisky in it, but there was none in the house. Augustus had loyally stopped serving spirits when Their Majesties had announced that they were no longer offered at Buckingham Palace.

Toby did not linger in the kitchen, which was silent and warm and peaceful, but went out to prowl the wet spring-time woods with Hasselt or any accidentally met poacher. Odd, he thought, remembering childhood morning rambles through these same woods, how he had never once seen a poacher then. They had existed, of course. Hasselt had fought an unending war against them. But though he had been a small boy who neither would nor could have harmed them, they had silently melted into the thickets at his approach. Now they tipped their caps to him, showed him their bag, and treated him as one of themselves. They knew he no longer belonged to the world of peace and orderliness.

At other times he went ferreting with Hasselt. The feral creature stirring in its bag no longer frightened him, nor did the trap holding some poor screaming mangled animal. He had become at one with all of them.

Hasselt and the poachers knew, but no one else did. To his parents he seemed jumpy and restless, which was only to be expected. They did not look further, and had they done so, there would have been nothing to see. It takes more than three years of front-line war to break the crust of manners imposed by England's nannies and public schools.

He did what was expected of him. He walked around the place with his father, and approved the tennis court and croquet lawn dug up for a vegetable garden. He paid a long visit to Nannie in the day nursery, keeping an eye on his watch for pub opening time. Nannie clucked crossly at the state of his uniform, much torn by barbed wire and clumsily mended.

"It's my batman," said Toby. "He isn't much good at sewing."

"Fancy letting a soldier mend your uniform, Master Toby. You bring it up to Nannie tonight. I'll unpick it and do it properly. However did it get in such a state?"

"Barbed wire, mostly."

"That's those nasty French, I'll be bound. They've no

call to go putting up barbed wire all over the place. But at your age you should know better than to go crawling under wire, Master Toby, and you a major too. Just you use the road, even if it is the long way round."

Toby, who should have known better, tried to explain why it wasn't possible to use the road, but she only clicked her tongue about those nasty Huns, as if they were a nursery full of refractory children. "But there, you're teaching them a lesson, aren't you, Master Toby? It's one they've long deserved."

Toby was well aware that "teaching a lesson" was her euphemism for killing. When he reminded her that Master Felix, to whom she had always been shamelessly partial, was fighting on the German side, she grew wilfully deaf, so that Toby arrived at the Strafford Arms in a bad temper, which the watery beer did nothing to improve.

Lady Millicent, busier with the hospital than she had ever been in her life, consulted Matron about Toby's jumpy nerves. Matron, having taken note of the three red chevrons on the sleeve of his uniform, indicating a year each of active service, together with the lack of even a single wound stripe, had at once decided that his job must be a very cushy one, and had put him down in her mind as a malingerer. She said brusquely that long walks were the thing, but was not prepared to waste more time on someone who had no physical wounds to show her.

So Lady Milly said nearly every day at lunch, "Why don't you take Julian for a walk, Toby; it's such perfect weather," and Julian would put on her hat and coat and take his arm.

Every time she touched him, he felt as he had when she had kissed him at the station the year before but she was older now, fifteen, and so beautiful he could hardly bear the thought that she had never seen her own face. His heart wanted to cherish her with all the tenderness at his command, but his body wanted to have her as roughly as a soldier has an enemy woman.

In Augustus's victory garden the tendrils of early peas climbed the poles. The woods were full of primroses and cuckoo calls, and the hedgerows foamed with blossom. But Toby's mind was filled with hedges of barbed wire.

"You don't really want to go watch them ratting at the tithe barn, do you?" asked Julian. This had been Augustus's tactless suggestion for their afternoon's entertainment.

"No, I get quite enough ratting in France."

"Yes, that's what I thought. Let's go to the beech wood."

They climbed Hangman's Knoll and walked past the home farm and meadows full of sheep, still round and heavy in their winter coats. The beeches were pale green in new leaf; the ground, covered with last year's leaves, was golden brown. Mast crackled under their shoes. Toby had picked a branch of thorn on the way. He carefully cut the thorns off with his pocketknife before handing it to Julian so she could touch and smell the blossoms.

They stopped in a clearing so full of bluebells it looked like a reflection of the sky. Shards of sunlight fell through the furled leaves. Julian sat inside her darkness, leaning against a tree, her face turned to the dappling sun. Toby had found a robin's egg which he carefully put into her palm. He wanted to tell her what a beautiful colour it was, but of course it would mean nothing to her. He said, "Look, your braid's come undone. It must have snagged on a thorn. Let me do it up for you."

"Do you know how?"

"I think so."

Her hair was straight and silken—"Oh, such straight hair," Nannie used to mourn, braiding it. "Why couldn't it have a bit of curl?" It felt as pleasant as cool water on Toby's roughened hands. Instead of braiding it again, he was undoing it, his fingers tangled in its smooth strands, winding it like fetters around his wrist.

"Toby," said Julian, laughing, "what are you doing? I shall never get it untangled without a comb." Her laughter stopped as the first knell of the passing bell came across to them from St Michael and All Angels. They counted the strokes. "I wish they wouldn't ring it," said Julian; "I hate it so, especially when you're in France." But as it went on and on her mood lightened again. "Eighty-nine, ninety . . . It must be old Mrs Truscott; she did so want . . ."

Toby had not been listening to her. Now he said desperately, "I love you, Julian. I don't want to hurt you." But the hands knotted in her long hair were a soldier's hands, and they did want to hurt.

From the spinney by Hangman's Knoll a tireless cuckoo called and called. Toby, full of front-line superstition, counted the calls to see how many years he had left to live. He gave up when he got to forty-five, which would bring him up to seventy. Old enough. He stopped counting, though the cuckoo kept on calling.

Julian's light brown hair lay scattered among last year's leaves. Between the strands Toby noticed a tiny white flower, so little and starry that unless you were lying on the ground you would never, he thought, notice it. It was so small he could not imagine God creating it, for Toby, forgetting hummingbirds and wood violets, tended to think of God as given to grand effects. His hand, tangled in the long strands of Julian's hair, seemed coarse and brutal beside it, and he thought that if he had moved it so little as half an inch, the small white miracle would have been crushed.

Julian's hair smelled faintly of soap, like a clean child's. This innocent nursery smell robbed Toby of his peace. He lifted his head to look at her. She was looking up somewhere past him. A tear had dried on her cheek. It was his, not hers. He remembered it running down his nose and dropping on her face.

He licked the salt from her cheek, which made her smile. He thought how very rarely she did smile, having never learned from another's face that it is a form of human response. Or perhaps it was simply a family trait.

Her throat in the open collar of her coat was very smooth and white. He watched a pulse beat under the soft skin, just where the army instructor had taught them was one of the three best places to plunge a bayonet. He placed his lips against it and muttered, "I'm sorry I was so clumsy; I didn't want to hurt you." He felt the movement of laughter in her throat. She said, "Don't be silly."

He lifted his head and looked down at her, hardly able to believe that she could be amused. "Oh, Julian." Just to lie there and look at her—the never dulled pleasure of that beautiful face. Why didn't one tire of it? He had seen its male counterpart nearly every day for more than two years, had seen it grubby, unshaved, blind with exhaustion. Why was he never tired of looking at either David or Julian? The other vicarage children were as beautiful, but they did not have the power to move him as these two did.

The thought of David, Julian's brother and his own dearest friend, filled him with dismay. "Julian," he said desperately, "Julian, marry me."

She pushed him away and sat up, gathering her hair in her hand. "Oh, Toby," she said, like Nannie reproving a silly child, "we can't. We can't possibly."

"Why not?"

She began to braid her hair. "Your parents would never allow it."

"I'm twenty-five. I can marry whom I like."

"But I can't. Do be sensible, Toby. How can I marry you?"

"It's simple. One of my subalterns did it on his last leave home. You get a surrogate's licence and it only takes three days. You don't have to have banns read or anything."

"I don't mean that. What about our families? Think of Lady Milly. And everyone would say I'm too young."

"You are too young. It's all my fault. I should have waited."

"I didn't mean that," said Julian. "Do you think we might be secretly engaged?"

"It's not enough," he said, feeling desperate, wondering how he would ever face David again. "We have to get married."

To his consternation, Julian began to laugh.

"It's not funny, Julian."

"Well, it is rather, you know. You sound exactly like some poor housemaid who *has* to get married."

It shocked him that she should know about such things and make a joke of them. But he could not withstand the enchantment and contagion of Julian's laughter. In a moment he too began to laugh, lying back among the beech leaves. Julian let go of her half-braided hair, so that it spilled over his face, and laughing too, returned to his arms.

David sat in a dirty, crowded train compartment, noticing neither the grime nor the crowd, he was so deeply absorbed in reading a book Lucas had given him. Badly printed and bound in a cheap yellow cover, it was called *Prufrock and Other Observations*, and Lucas, handing it to him, had said, "A lion is in the streets."

"Anyone who's just written *The Green Envelope* is lion enough for me," David had said, but absorbed in *Prufrock* he saw what Lucas had meant, and loved him for the generosity that allowed him to rejoice in it.

Dusk had begun to fall when the train arrived at Altondale. David, still a little drunk with reading, nearly walked by Mr Dobbs, the idol of his childhood, without giving up his ticket. Mr Dobbs had been called back from retirement when younger men had deserted the station for the army.

He took David's ticket and said, "It's good to see you, Mr David. Captain Harvey, I suppose I should say. Your mother said you'd be coming home on leave, but she didn't know when."

"It's good to see you too, Dobbs. Do you remember the red, white, and blue flower bed you planted for Old Teddy's coronation? And how Toby, Felix and I all wanted to become stationmasters?"

"And now you're all in France shooting at each other. It doesn't make sense."

"No," said David, "it doesn't."

He walked down the village street, past the corpulent Britannia mourning Altondale's dead of the Boer War. How very long the list had grown since then. The windows of the vicarage were dark, except those of the nursery which shone like butter in the dusk. The stained glass of St Michael and All Angels was aglow with light. It seemed a long time to David since early communion and evensong had punctuated his day instead of morning and evening stand-to.

He knew the church would be nearly empty. Saturday night was scrubbing the floor night, and baths heating by the kitchen fire, getting ready for Sunday-best. A diehard spinster or two with an unrequited passion for the Vicar, old Mrs Spruce, who was nearly senile but dearly loved an outing, and whatever Harveys were at home, would make up what congregation there was. Nevertheless, David decided, church could wait for Sunday, when the avid eyes of the village would at least be shared between him and Toby. Just now he wanted the vicarage, empty and silent, with a fire glowing in the kitchen and a kettle spitting on the hearth, his own room steep-ceilinged under the roof, for a moment's quiet before his family returned from church.

As always when he had come back from school, the kitchen seemed larger, and his own room much smaller than he remembered. He put his valise on the bed and took off his trench coat. His body remembered, if his mind did not, to duck his head where the ceiling sloped down. It was a servant's room, really, with a rudimentary window and an iron bed which for the last ten years had been too short for him. He had moved into it his first vacation from St Dunstan's, wanting to have something entirely for himself, a room not shared.

He opened his pack to put away the books he had brought back with him. Those already on the shelf were like a diary of his childhood and school days. Grimm's *Household Tales*, Lamb's *Tales from Shakespeare*, never read as far as he could remember, the Aesop from which his father had begun to teach him Latin, *The Iliad*, but not *The Odyssey*, never as well loved, lent, perhaps, or forgotten at school. Virgil and Caesar with their grubby look of school texts, Horace, his grandfather's copy of *The Pilgrim's Progress* with its copperplate inscription: "To my beloved grandson David, on his tenth birthday," Fox's *Book of Martyrs* which Nannie had regarded as a suitable Christmas gift, and Shakespeare's *Sonnets*, bound in morocco, with Anthony Fielding's name crossed out and David Harvey written underneath in Anthony's hand. David had thought this romantic at the time but now found it merely embarrassing. He added *Prufrock and Other Observations* to the shelf and heard, before he was quite ready for them, his family return, and seeing the light in his room, call his name.

After the first exuberance of greetings they were almost shy with him. The twins, side by side on the sofa, kicked their heels. Mr Harvey said, "Are you well, David?"

"Yes, of course. It's a healthy outdoor life." He thought, Why am I talking to my father like that? We'll be discussing the weather next. He turned to the twins and said, "I've brought you a present, a souvenir from France." He gave Eve a cap badge embroidered with mountain flowers which had belonged to the sniper of an Austrian alpine regiment. "And a real German medal for you, Adam."

"Oh, thanks, David; that's splosh."

"It's what?"

"Splosh," said Mrs Harvey. "I forget what it was in your day. Ripping?"

"I feel a hundred years old."

"Did you take it off a corpse, David?"

"Adam!"

"No, a very live German general."

"I'll bet he was waxy."

"No. Only very drunk. He insisted on giving it to me. He'd been celebrating the kaiser's birthday too well."

"Is that what they gave you the bar to your MC for?"

"Yes."

"I think that's very splosh."

David caught a frown on the face of Fanny's captain. He knew what it meant. Don't make it sound attractive, it said. Don't let boys think war is a lark

"It only seems that way afterwards," David said to Adam.

"Can I wear the medal, David?"

"You have done nothing to earn it."

Agnes came down the stairs and hugged David. He said, "Can I come up and see all the new babies?"

"Better not. They'll be ready for bed and a stranger in uniform will only upset them."

"Yes, of course," David agreed, feeling very much like a stranger in uniform.

"Nonsense," said Mrs Harvey. "Come and meet everyone." She led the way to the day nursery, where

Fanny's Sabrina was splashing in a zinc tub by the fire. Fanny was kept busy retrieving the rubber fish and duck tossed on the floor with shrieks of delight. David, remembering another Sabrina, said, " 'Under the glassie, cool, translucent wave,' " and at once got a good deal of that wave over his uniform as Sabrina expressed her pleasure at having a new audience with a stout kick to the bathwater.

"Serves you right for being a literary prig," said Fanny, hugging him. "Dear David, it's wonderful to have you home."

Mrs Harvey picked Sabrina out of the tub and wrapped her in a large towel. Fanny said, "Come and meet Robin and Agnes's Verdun."

"What an awful name, poor kid." said David. Fanny laughed.

"It is very much in fashion," she said. "You can see it every day in the birth announcements: To General Marmaduke Birdwhistle a son, Verdun."

Fanny's Robin, aged nearly two, got up gravely to shake hands with David, but Verdun, aged practically nothing at all, was too busy sucking his thumb to take any notice. David said, "You might at least have called one of yours Wipers." Fanny laughed and said she would leave that for Agnes who planned to have five more.

David went back to the drawing room, where his father said gravely, "There is also a kindle of seven kittens in the washhouse, and three puppies in the coalshed, not to mention the new baby chicks."

"Yes, I can see you have been nice and busy."

"I cannot remember ever performing more christenings," said the Vicar. "Of course the gunnery camp at High Fenton has a good deal to do with that."

David grinned at Fanny's captain. "Yes, gunners are the very worst."

At dinner David once more encountered the grey india-rubber buns. "We do have bread," said Mrs Harvey, "if you want some. It's only that we're asked not to serve it unless somebody asks for it, because of the wheat shortage."

David said the buns were fine; he hadn't realized that wheat was such a difficulty.

"It's the German blockade; it's made wheat very scarce."

"We've been asked to read a proclamation from Their Majesties in church tomorrow," said the Vicar, "asking people to eat less bread, or anything made of wheat, really."

"I'd no idea things were so bad," said David. "I thought all those EAT LESS AND VICTORY IS SECURE posters were just propaganda."

The Vicar got up and went into his study. "If you're willing to pay for it, and don't have a conscience," said Mrs Harvey, "you can get all the food you want. That's the trouble with voluntary rationing. All the nice people go without and the hogs get more than their share."

"Here we are," said the Vicar, handing David the prayer book. The royal proclamation marked the lesson for the Third Sunday after Easter. "We do exhort and charge all heads of households," David read, "to reduce the consumption of bread, to abstain from the use of flour in pastry . . ." A glance at the lesson told him that he was also going to be asked to abstain from fleshly lusts, so that altogether it was going to be a dull Sunday.

At dawn David was awakened by Toby's familiar whistle below his window. It changed a confused dream of being lost in a warren of trenches to one of childhood summer mornings, rambles with Toby through meadows webbed with dew, and woods hushed in the moment before sunrise. Then Toby whistled again, and David awoke, not in a dugout, with a rat scampering across his blanket, but in his own, too short bed at home. He lit the lamp and went to look out of the window. There was a mist of rain on the air. Toby moved into the stream of light from the window.

"Hello, Toby."

"Hello, David."

"Hang on; I'll come down." He dressed and put on his trench coat. The third step from the top creaked as it had always done. In the kitchen he scribbled a note to say that he was out with Toby and would be back in time for church, then he went outside. St Michael and All Angels, which had not experienced war on its own territory since York had fought Lancaster, loomed stone-solid in the midst of its decently buried dead.

"Hello, David," Toby said again. "They said you were home. Did I wake you?"

"Not really. I've got out of the habit of sleeping at night."

"So have I. I have a trench clock in my head. I wonder whether it will ever run down."

There was no sunrise, only a thinning of the darkness under the rain clouds. "Let's go and see Hasselt," said Toby. "He's rearing grouse and pheasants, but they're not for shooting, only for the larder. He thinks it a sad comedown."

Hasselt joined them as soon as they entered the wood. He stepped silently from behind a tree, like a shadow breaking from its object. He did not speak, but simply touched his cap to them. He carried a gun, and dangling from his bloodied hand, two dead rabbits.

David, who had always envied Hasselt's way of moving through the wood without a sound, noticed that he and Toby too had now acquired this skill. Twigs no longer snapped under their boots, and the grasping branches of the trees did not scratch at their clothes. Two years of crawling in the dark through no-man's-land had been good for something, thought David, not gratefully.

The brooder shed was warm and alive with cheeping and flutter. A lantern hissed in the rafters. Hasselt fed and watered the chicks, then picked out two, as a gardener might thin seedlings, to give to David and Toby. They sat soft and warm in the palm, with racing hearts and panicky button eyes. Toby's settled down and cheeped to itself, but David's was a battler, attacking his fingers with its tiny beak.

"You've got a fighting cock there, Hasselt," said David, amused at the young creature's ferocity. Hasselt took him back gently and put him with his fellows.

Because he lacked the taste for shooting, it had always struck David as incongruous that so much gentleness and care should be lavished on creatures destined for August's guns.

"Food production," said Hasselt contemptuously. "No more shooting, no sport."

"Lucky little beggars," said Toby, and David knew he was thinking of the thousands of birds that had cowered with bursting hearts in the brush until the beaters and panic had driven them from shelter into the lines of the avid guns. Now it had become someone else's turn to cower in the earth and face the guns.

"Plenty of shooting where we are," he said.

"They're talking about shooting foxes," Hasselt said. "Not in my woods, I told His Lordship. I keep them out of *my* henruns; let others do the same. His Lordship agreed with me."

Now that it was daylight, David realized that Toby looked exhausted and harassed. He wondered what was wrong. Though it was a cold, wet day, he suggested a proper walk, right around the park, thinking that Toby might wish to talk. Toby readily agreed, but seemed to have nothing to say. They'd gone half around the lake in silence when David made up his mind to ask him directly. He said, "What's the matter with you, Toby? You look like someone who's spent a week in the Salient, rather than on home leave."

"I'm sleeping badly. Funny, isn't it? In Flanders I can settle down in a puddle of freezing water in the nearest funk hole and sleep with a barrage going on over my head. Why can't I sleep in a bed?"

"I know, I've got it too."

"When I go for a walk, I plan where to put my guns and my observation posts. The hedges look like barbed wire."

"Everyone does that. You know that from other people who've been home on leave. You remember Strickland telling us he dived into a rain puddle in the middle of Bond Street when a car backfired. I was sweating and shaking half a morning because a fool housemaid dropped a coal scuttle down the back stairs. And I thought I was doing so well. Do you want to hear something funny? I was handed a white feather."

Toby gave him one of the quick schoolboy smiles which had grown so rare over the past year. "You?"

"Yes. I was in Rye, doing some errands, and wearing a suit. And this woman in front of the post office handed me a white feather. I was rather stunned and didn't quite know what to do, so I just said, 'Oh, thank you very much,' or something idiotic like that. The really funny thing though is that I met her again that evening at a dinner at the Longacres'. I was wearing my uniform then, of course, and my MC ribbon."

"Did she recognize you?"

"Oh yes. She wasn't a bit embarrassed either. In fact she was quite smug about the whole thing, as if my transformation were all her doing. Instant cause and effect."

Toby laughed, and they walked on in a silence grown easier, though David did not think they had touched on Toby's real trouble. The rain, which had hung on the air in a thin mist, suddenly began to pour down. They sprinted to the far end of the lake and took shelter in a small Palladian temple. Over its entrance a carved owl, its head worn smooth by many rains, kept watch.

"We used to play with your trains here; do you remember?" said David. "What happened to them?"

"They're put away in the nursery with my other toys, to wait, like Nannie, for me to produce a son. I don't suppose he'd care for a clockwork train. They're all electric now, aren't they?"

"Save them for your grandson. By then they'll be valuable antiques."

"I don't think the chances of either of us having grandchildren are all that good."

"I don't know. We've lasted a long time."

"It can't go on forever."

"No, I don't suppose it can. Is that what's troubling you?"

Toby, who had been staring at the rags of fog drifting across the lake, looked up, startled. "No. Oh no."

"What then, Toby? Something is."

The church bells rang for early communion. Toby stared at his boots. He said, "It's nothing I can talk to you about."

"Why not?"

"Because I've done something I'm very ashamed of, and I don't want you to know."

David made a list in his head of things Toby would be ashamed of. He didn't shoot foxes, cheat at cards, or forge cheques. And he certainly was not guilty of cowardice in the face of the enemy. Which left exactly one thing. David said, "You're having an affair with the parlourmaid."

"Certainly not."

"The footman, then."

"Don't be disgusting."

David had far too many secrets himself ever to wish to force another person's confidence. But Toby looked so harassed and miserable that he said, "Come on, Toby, give. What have you done?"

"I can't tell you."

"Of course you can. I won't mind, whatever it is."

"Oh yes you would," said Toby gloomily. "This one you would."

David, who seldom gave much thought to his blind sister, got it finally. "You're in love with Julian."

"No. I mean yes. But that's not it."

"Oh," said David. "I see."

Toby stood and looked at his friend, feeling miserable but determined. David's next move would be to knock him down. It was under the circumstances the only thing an officer and gentleman could do. Toby, who had been Sandhurst's white hope at boxing, put his hands in his pockets, to show he wouldn't hit back.

David however did not appear to be aware of his brotherly duties. He merely said, "Well, the heavens haven't fallen, Toby. Are you in love with her?"

"Of course. Do you think I'd . . ."

"Is she in love with you?"

"I don't know; she never said, come to think of it. But she'd have to be, wouldn't she? I mean, girls don't . . ."

David was not sure. He knew Julian least well of all his family, but suspected her of being the one most like himself. He had watched her, so very much daughter of the house, Lady Millicent's exquisite shadow, butter not melting in her mouth. She must know that if Toby took a wife her days at Altondale would be numbered. David couldn't see a future Lady Altondale encumbering herself with so beautiful and enigmatic a succubus. He had little doubt that Julian knew this and had hit on the simplest of all expedients to prevent it. She would become the future Lady Altondale.

War and two weeks' leave did not allow time for subtle and ladylike stratagems. David suspected that if any seducing had been done, it had not been done by poor Toby.

But why poor? Julian had been trained by Lady Millicent, so she would undoubtedly act the part of Lady Altondale as well as anyone. The Straffords were rich enough so Toby need not marry for money. And Toby was in love with her. It doesn't matter, David thought, for what reason you get your heart's desire. What matters is that you get it.

He said, "Do you want to marry her, Toby?"

"Well, of course. What do you think I am?"

"What's stopping you? Are you afraid of your mother?"

"No. Well, yes, a bit. But that's not it. It's Julian. She says it's impossible."

Clever little Julian, thought David. She knows they couldn't stop him, he's of age, but they could certainly stop her. I wouldn't be surprised if she manoeuvred him into a secret marriage before his leave's up.

"She's only fifteen," said Toby. "That's the other thing. How could I have been such a rotter?"

Trying not to laugh, David said, "Julian was a little old lady when she was four."

" 'Older than the rocks among which she sits,' " quoted Toby, and seeing David's surprise, blushed and said, "One of the officers in the hospital said that about her."

"Do you know how that quotation goes on?" asked David. " 'Like the vampire she has been dead many times, and learned the secrets of the grave; and has been a diver in deep seas . . .' "

"Yes," said Toby. "It's odd, but there is something a bit scary about Julian sometimes. I expect it's just that she's blind. Because what she really is is a very proper English miss, who thinks these things ought to be done properly, an engagement, and bridesmaids and orange blossoms at St Margaret's, Westminster. But there isn't time. Supposing I get killed."

"Supposing something just as likely. Toby, did you . . ." It was now David's turn to be embarrassed. His own experiences had not prepared him for problems of this particular nature. "Have you thought that she might have a baby?"

As if presenting on cue a tableau called *Family*, two parent swans floated by them, conducting their grey fluff balls of cygnets to the other side of the lake. Even Toby, preoccupied with his worries, could not help laughing.

"I do hope that's not an omen. You're right, of course; we must marry. I've got the licence, you know. I got it from the surrogate in York. It was very simple. You pay two pounds ten and wait three days and that's all there's to it. We could get married this week, just to be on the safe side, in case she . . . well, you know. We needn't tell anyone. If nothing happens, we can still do St Margaret's, Westminster later on. Do you think my mother will cut up rough?"

"It's a little hard to imagine. But I don't think she'll like it much."

"She loves Julian."

"Yes. But she brought her up to be a companion to her, not the future Lady Altondale."

"I'm sure you're right. Well, we'll cross that bridge if and when we come to it. Look, it's stopped raining. I say, David, I do feel such a lot better. Thanks for putting up with me."

"We'll be brothers-in-law. Had that occurred to you?"

"Yes," said Toby seriously. "I shall like it of all things."

"What's all this about shooting foxes?" asked Toby at lunch. David had also been invited. "Hasselt seemed fearfully annoyed."

"It's monstrous," said Augustus, upset over a recent letter to *The Times* by a neighbouring Master of Foxhounds, suggesting that foxes should be shot in order to curb depredations on the nation's henruns. Augustus, who was himself an MFH, thought this a shocking sign of the decline of England, and went on about it at some length. "I'm an old man," he said finally, pushing away his plate of washy soup, "but I never thought I'd live to see *The Times* printing a letter advocating shooting foxes. Time I was dead."

David, who by taking great care not to meet Toby's eye, had got creditably through a prelunch interview with Nannie, looked across the table and realized that this was a joke Toby would not share with him. He probably didn't even see it as funny.

Matron, who was always invited to Sunday lunch, sat on his right, Julian on his left. He would have liked a chance to talk with his sister, but Matron, noting the gold wound stripe on his sleeve, extended to him the approval she had withheld from Toby, and asked him such searching questions of where, how and Dr Who, that he could only hope that in her enthusiasm she wouldn't ask to see his scar.

Julian had greeted him, holding out a shy, cool hand, but David wasn't having any of that. He'd said, "None of your Lady Milly la-di-da ways," had put his arms around her and hugged her. "This is how Harveys say hello." She'd laughed at that and hugged him back. He wondered about her now, while answering Matron's questions. Seeing her in her plain, expensive clothes, the shining plait of hair hanging down her back, he didn't wonder that Toby went about feeling as if he'd raped Kate Greenaway. Certainly she looked a good deal more Toby's proper English miss than Pater's diver in deep seas. And yet? Was it only her beauty and her blindness which made one wonder? After lunch Julian said she was going to the working party at Alison Grange. David said he'd come with her and then go back to the vicarage. Toby stopped him in the hall. "I meant to ask you before. Will you be my best man?"

"Of course."

Julian joined them with her coat and hat. David gave her his arm and they left.

"Alison Grange isn't a bit on your way," said Julian, "but of course you know that."

"I'm not in a hurry. And I think we ought to have a talk."

She did not ask what about, but turned her face to the warmth and said, "The sun's come out."

"Yes. Everything looks clean and shining after the rain. Let's talk about you and Toby, shall we?"

The tranquil face showed no change. "Toby?"

"You and Toby." A farm cart came up behind them, and David drew her aside to let it pass. As he put his arm around her he felt her trembling, though her face had remained so calm. The farmer touched his cap to them. David returned his salute. He had seen the names of two of his sons on the war memorial.

Until now, if he had troubled to ask himself (as he had as yet had scarcely time to do), what he thought of Julian's exploit he would probably have laughed and said that it was not bad for the local vicar's blind daughter. Yet, when he felt her trembling under his hand, he experienced for her the kind of respect and pity he sometimes felt for his men after they had been through an action too prolonged and brutal for human vulnerability to bear. She was a soldier, his little sister. Like a soldier she had put her body on the line to consolidate a position which had until now been hers only on someone else's sufferance. But unlike a soldier she had acted alone. She had had no one to talk to, and no comrades to support her.

He put both arms around her and held her until her trembling stopped. Then he said, "Don't be afraid, Julian. Not of me. Everything will work out all right. Look, do you have to go to this silly working party?"

"Yes. But it doesn't matter if I'm late. It's just important that someone from the hall should be there. It's what they come for, you know, so they can say that Her Ladyship had seemed to enjoy her tea, and how nicely Miss Julian did with her seaboot stocking seeing she's blind and all."

"Oh Christ, English village life. Are you sure that's what you want? Look, let's sit on the stile in the sun and talk a bit." He helped her up and sat down next to her. The air around them was ringing with bird song. David said, "I know there's no reason why you should trust me, Julian. We don't know each other well, even though we are brother and sister. But you badly need someone to talk to, and here

I am. I'm Toby's oldest friend, and we're both Harveys, even though you've been turned into some kind of a bogus Strafford."

"Is that how you think of me, a bogus Strafford?"

He saw that this had hurt her. "Only until you marry Toby. Then you'll be a real one. It's what you want, isn't it? To be Mrs Strafford?"

She nodded. After a silence she said, "It's what I have to want. It's that or the blind spinster daughter at the vicarage. Perhaps if I'd been brought up at the vicarage I wouldn't mind that, but I wasn't. Do you remember the story about the Princess and the Pea? Nannie used to read it to me, over and over. I'm like that, you see. Not a real princess—I expect that's why Nannie read it to me so often, so I shouldn't get ideas above my station—but I've been brought up to feel that pea under fifteen mattresses and wake up black and blue. So you see, marrying Toby is the only thing I can do."

"I suppose so. My poor Julian. Village working parties, the Christmas treat for the tenants . . . what about Toby?"

"How do you mean?"

"Do you like him? Do you love him, I mean. He's my friend and I would like him to be happy."

"I'm very fond of Toby."

It was what he would have said if asked his feelings for Lucas Ryder. He said, "Good. Fond lasts longer."

"I couldn't have done it without being fond of Toby."

"I daresay you could have. People do, all the time."

"Do you?"

"Not now. At school sometimes."

"I expect it's easier for boys."

"Don't you believe it." He began to laugh. "What an extraordinary conversation. What would Lady Millicent say?" He noticed a smile tug at the corner of a mouth that was not much given to smiling.

"I do wish you were home more often, David," she said. "It's such a relief to talk to someone who knows."

"Yes, I can see where having no one to confide in must have been absolute hell. I hope the whole business wasn't too nasty a surprise. Did you know what you were letting yourself in for?"

"Yes, I knew."

"Did you indeed. Not from Lady Millicent, I'll bet. Who told you, our mother?"

"Kitty, quite a long time ago. She thinks it's wicked the way girls aren't told anything and have to find out for themselves. She said the first time she . . ." Julian broke off, blushing.

"What?"

"It's so difficult to talk about these things because one never knows how much other people know."

"What do you want to know whether I know?"

Still blushing, she said, "Being unwell."

"Oh Lord," said David, laughing, "if you'd been brought up at the vicarage with three sisters instead of La-di-da Hall you wouldn't have to ask."

"Well, Kitty said the first time it happened to her she had absolutely no idea. She thought she had some awful disease and was going to die, and she was too embarrassed to tell her mother. So she decided that if she ever had a daughter she'd tell her everything. She doesn't have a daughter, but she very kindly told me."

Christ, thought David, women and their bloody plumbing, their whole lives tethered, except for the few years of childhood and old age, to breeding and feeding. And if they weren't doing one or the other there were cramps and bloody rags to remind them to get back to their proper work. Poor sods, no wonder they cried so much at weddings. He felt suddenly very conscious of his own body, lean and unencumbered under the khaki uniform, and scarcely aware that he was doing so, moved a little away from Julian. She was usually very sensitive to other people's feelings, often more so than they were themselves, but she paid no attention to David's slight withdrawal. Instead she held out her hand and touched his face. She said, "Do we really look as much alike as everyone says?"

"Yes. More so than the twins even. Funny, your not knowing what you look like."

"I do know, by touch. But I don't know what it means."

"You're a bit weird at times, Julian. I do hope you'll be good to Toby."

"Oh yes," said Julian. "It will be much easier than being good to Lady Milly."

They were married on Friday at the registrar's office in Dewsbury. There were several other couples waiting on line. In fact the registrar was doing a brisk business.

Julian had put up her hair and wore her Sunday silk dress and her most grown-up hat. But David doubted that it would have mattered if she had come dressed in a pinafore. The registrar was far too busy to bother about her age. He read at tremendous speed through an abridged form of the marriage service, congratulated them briskly, and said, "Next!"

"Oh Julian," said Toby, a little dashed. "We'll have a bang-up wedding at St Margaret's, Westminster when I come back, with bridesmaids and flower girls and everything handsome about us." He had remembered to buy her a ring. She put it on a thin gold chain she wore around her neck and said, "I'll never take it off, Toby. I don't mind a bit about the wedding. But if you want to do it properly next time, of course it will have to be at St Michael and All Angels."

David took them both out to lunch and even managed to get hold of a bottle of passable champagne. Then they took the train back to Altondale, trying hard to give the impression that they were people to whom nothing interesting had happened.

Dawn took Julian from Toby in sleep. He begged her to stay with him—it was his last night at home—and she said, "I'm not a bit tired, really," but sleep loosened her arms almost as soon as she spoke, leaving him only her beauty for contemplation. Yet he felt her scarcely more remote from him in sleep than in love's embrace. It was a feeling for which he had no explanation. She had not withheld from him anything that he had asked. Had he not asked enough? Or the wrong questions? Was the possession of a body not the answer? Could one ever possess more, another mind or heart? If he had said, "Who are you really," would she have told him something that he did not know? What would he have said if she had asked the same question of him? But then, she never did ask questions.

He looked at his watch. Nearly time to go. His kiss did not rouse Julian. She sighed and turned away, but did not awaken. He got up and dressed. He did not really want to say good-bye to her. It would be easier to leave her like this, as he had done all the other mornings, before the housemaid came to light her fire, as if he would meet her again at breakfast.

Nannie, in a quilted dressing gown, her braided hair like a grey rat's tail down her back, awaited him in the kitchen. He had said good-bye to her the night before, hoping—though not with much hope—to avoid this encounter. The rest of the family had accepted his wish not to be seen off, but Nannie was, as she had always been, a law unto herself.

"I've made you a cup of tea, Master Toby," she said, making him feel ten years old, off to school.

"You shouldn't have got up, Nannie."

"Nonsense. I always saw you off to school. I'm not letting those nasty Huns stop me from seeing you off to the war. Now mind you, Master Toby, you're not to go crawling under the barbed wire again, now that Nannie's mended your uniform."

He promised recklessly that he would not. Because her beady eye was on him he gulped down the tea, which was real nursery tea, weak, more than half milk. "Thanks Nannie, that was splendid. I've got to run or I'll miss the train." He put his arms around her and kissed her cheek. Her old body was very soft. It occurred to Toby that this was probably the first time that he'd ever hugged her when she hadn't got her corsets on. Usually it was rather like embracing an oil drum. "Good-bye, Nannie."

Nannie looked as if she might cry. Her hand was halfway to her pocket for her handkerchief. But she pulled herself together and said, "Mind you behave yourself, Master Toby. Such a worry you always were, tearing your clothes and getting yourself dirty."

Toby said, "I'll be good, I promise, Nannie," and went

quickly out the door. Like Nannie he hardly knew whether to cry or be stern.

He arrived at the station out of breath and nearly late, and flung himself into David's compartment.

"This is all so Romeo and Juliet," said David. "Secret marriages, partings at dawn. I do hope you'll end more happily than those two silly squits."

"I expect we will. Mummy will go all Montague and Capulet about it, but Dad will simmer her down." He yawned hugely, burrowed down into the collar of his British warm, and was soon asleep.

David was glad to see him so cheerful. Apparently, he thought, it hadn't been the secrecy of his affair with Julian which had made him unhappy, but the illegitimacy. Now that he had a piece of paper from the surrogate, it was right as rain.

The next time Toby opened his eyes they were in the London suburbs, passing houses of stockbroker Tudor and gardens patriotically planted with vegetables instead of flowers. David said, "I'm having lunch with Lucas Ryder. Won't you come too?"

Toby, looking embarrassed and shifty, said, "No, I . . . thank you, David, but I . . ."

David, who could not imagine why Toby was so evasive, said, "You have to see a man about a dog."

"If you must know, I want to see a man about some whisky. They're only allowed to sell it between noon and half past, and I'm told there's always a hell of a queue."

"So I should imagine. Come along for coffee if you have time. If not I'll meet you at Victoria."

They found First Battalion well behind the lines quartered in a nearly undamaged village. In weather as pleasant as could be, Vickies' Own bathed, got their uniforms deloused, sang endlessly their own version of a hymn which began: "Just as I am, without one flea . . . ," bore with kit inspection, rifle inspections, foot inspection, rejoiced in small things such as clean straw to sleep in, and flowers growing in gardens, and tried not to think beyond the day.

The officers were busy licking into shape the new replacements, conscripts unpromisingly described by Sergeant Doolittle as "hold men and hinfants in harms," and getting up rugby and cricket games, for it was considered essential, when out of the line, to keep the men busy at all times and so out of trouble. David, who had never changed his opinion about organized games, said to Toby that war seemed at times to be merely an extension of public school by other means, but had to admit that the hard outdoor work was exhilarating, and that, lunatic as it assuredly was, he was happy to be back with his company.

The same could not be said for Toby, whose temper these days was very ragged. David put it down to drink, and it was not till they were back in the line that he was forced to admit to himself that Toby had arrived at a state of nerves and exhaustion for which two weeks' home leave was about as much use as a sticking plaster is to an amputee. He took over as many of Toby's duties as he could without being obvious about it, and said nothing about his worries even to Basil Cobbleston.

He was moving down the trench leading to Toby's dugout late one afternoon when a 5.9 fell short and was almost immediately followed by one which fell rather long. It was not difficult to guess that the next one would accurately hit the trench, and David, forgetting that air of nonchalance which was at all times to be worn by the officers of Victoria's Own, dived down the dugout steps with more speed than elegance. Toby was sitting on his cot, the whisky bottle by his side, muttering: "The little dogs and all, Tray, Blanch and Sweetheart—see they bark at me."

"What?"

He shook his head at David. "Mastiff, greyhound, mongrel grim, hound or spaniel, brach or lym . . ."

"Toby, why are you reciting *King Lear*?"

Toby turned on him a face white with fury. "Shut up, damn you."

"Sorry," said David, surprised. "Were you trying to remember? I think it ends, 'Or bobtail tike, or trundle-tail.'"

"Thanks, I know. We did *Lear* my last year at Eton."

He tried a grin; it was rather shamefaced. "Sorry. I didn't mean to shout at you. It's just something silly I've got into doing when they're bracketing. I have an irrational feeling that if I can finish the verse before the next shell comes over I shall be all right. Do you think I'm going mad?"

"I doubt it," said David with an ease he'd had ready for weeks in case Toby should ask this. "Everybody's madly superstitious out here. Sergeant Doolittle carries a rabbit's foot, and our snipers waste endless ammunition shooting at single magpies."

"It's not the same, David."

A very large shell said Whump and landed somewhere behind them. David looked at his watch. "That's the last. Turnip time in the Jerry trenches. I do like that about them; they're so punctual."

Piper, the latest in the long series of Toby's servants, came in with two mugs of tea. Toby poured his on the ground and filled the mug with whisky. "Do you want a drink?"

"Thanks, this is fine."

Toby stared at the pattern the spilled tea had made on the mud floor. "Do you know how much I'm drinking, David?"

"What's it matter?" said David. "It's not as if you'd ever exactly been a byword for sobriety."

Toby stared at him with strained, red-rimmed eyes.

"I mean," David went on a little desperately, "if I were looking for someone to give an inspirational talk to the Temperance Society, your name wouldn't at the best of times have come into my head."

Toby managed a very small grin at this, but shook his head. "It's not the same any longer."

"Nothing's the same. Look, lie down and get some rest. I'll take stand-to for you and come back afterwards and we'll have dinner."

"All right. Thanks, David."

David walked along the trench, receiving reports of casualties and damage. It had not been a good day. He stopped in the RAP, where the wounded were being got ready to be moved to the casualty clearing station. "One of these days," said the MO, "the Jerries will change their dinner hour and smash us to bits. Meanwhile, bless their regular habits."

"Yes. I was just saying the same to Strafford."

"Oh. How is he?"

"All right. Why?"

"He's seemed a bit under the weather lately."

"Is that surprising?"

"Not at all," said the MO urbanely. "What a very splendid sunset."

The western sky was so deep a red that even the east had caught fire. As they stood-to, staring across no-man's-land at the line of German trenches, the colours faded in plumes of red and gold. David went back to Toby's dugout, thinking about the MO's remark. He knew it would not have been made, even in so mild a way, if the subject of Toby's drinking and nerves were not causing general comment. He wished the MO had been a little less urbane and had suggested a remedy as well. He was like someone who is awaiting disaster, but does not know in what shape it will arrive.

The level in the whisky bottle had gone lower and Toby had fallen asleep. David sat down at the table and went through the papers piled there. He had fallen into the habit of doing as much of Toby's work as he thought he could get away with without rousing comment.

Piper put his head around the gas curtain and said, "Shall I bring your dinner here, sir?"

"Will Major Strafford sleep long?"

Piper's eyes slid to the bottle. "He won't wake again tonight, sir."

"I see," said David, hating him for that look. "No, don't bother with dinner, Piper. I'll just finish up this bumf and get along to my dugout. Goodnight."

When next they were in billets, Toby handed the battalion over to David and went to see General Molyneux. He returned, cheerful and fairly sober, but said nothing about his meeting with the brigadier.

The good temper and sobriety continued throughout the weeks they were out of the line. David, a little suspicious of this new Toby, could not help wondering whether he had asked General Molyneux for a staff assignment behind the lines. It would have been a reasonable thing to do, yet so unlike Toby that David could not bring himself to believe it.

When they went back into the line Toby was still with them, a little less sober, very quiet, still cheerful.

For weeks, ever since they had returned from their leave, David had lived with constant fear for Toby, wondering at what point he would decide to slow down at a traverse a German sniper had in his sights, or show his head above the parapet, so removing himself, reputation intact, honour satisfied, from a job he could no longer do. Every time a runner brought a message to his dugout, David had prepared himself to hear that Toby was dead. But this new, almost sober, very calm Toby showed no inclination to slow down at dangerous corners or show his head over the parapet. David supposed he ought to be grateful, but he continued to worry.

On a beautiful summer morning, soon after stand-to, a dogfight broke out over their heads. The PBI considered these aerial performances part of their perks; a show put on to relieve the monotony of their claustrophobic lives. All work came to a standstill while officers and men put back their heads to watch the sky.

In the early part of the war these encounters had usually been between two planes, who, like knights jousting in the blue, circled around each other, trying to get on each other's tail, to settle in the other flyer's blind spot. Watched from the ground they presented a pretty picture, and the muddy moles who watched them from their trenches might be forgiven if they saw it as a spectacle and gave little thought to the pilots inside those planes until at last one of them hurtled to the ground, trailing a plume of black smoke, erupting into a rose of flame.

It was a long time since any of them had seen such solitary and knightly combats. Now flights came out in squadrons and fought by numbers. The battle which whirled over their heads this morning involved at least twenty machines, funnelling like pigeons in flight, the trail of their tracer bullets punctuating the blue sky.

A German plane with black Maltese crosses painted on the wings spun out of control and crashed in no-man's-land, and in another moment two machines locked wings and came spinning down like demented dancers. The others moved on toward Zonnebeke, but three suddenly turned back, two Albatrosses painted red, and a Sopwith Triplane they had managed to cut out from its flight. The English pilot, being outnumbered, resorted to trickery and let himself go into a spin, shamming dead, pulling out at the last possible moment, so that the German who had followed close on his tail, left it too late and smashed into the ground. The second German machine screeched down in a dive, while the English pilot struggled desperately to gain altitude. Perhaps his petrol tank had been hit, thought David, watching the machine hanging like a deadweight from the propeller. He thought of petrol sloshing around the pilot's feet in the cockpit, where a bullet, any spark would ignite it, and shivered in the cool morning breeze. The men were shouting, "Go, Tripe!" as if it were a football game, but the unwounded Albatross had closed in and machine-gun bullets were ripping apart the Triplane's fuselage. Spitting castor oil, trailing black smoke, she came hurtling from the sky directly over their part of the trench. Scattering down the traverses, heading for the shelter of the dugouts, the men ran cursing. David, running too, turned back from an old habit of responsibility to make sure everyone was safely out of the way, and saw that Toby had not moved, but was standing where he had stood, watching the falling plane, an arm held up to shade his eyes from the sun. David froze for a moment while a wing tip ripped open the sandbags, then, shouting Toby's name, he raced back toward him as the nose of the plane burrowed into the parapet and flame, transparent in the sunlight, clawed at Toby's face.

The hospital was called Notre Dame de Pèlerinage. A former convent, it had been ceded, with its contingent of nursing sisters, to the French government for the duration of the war.

David thought he had seldom seen a grimmer looking place. The fact was that he was badly frightened. In all the two years of fighting behind him he had not been as terrified as he was now.

The sister who took him down the corridor, though a nun, was not immune to so handsome a face. Noting his pallor she said in gentle schoolgirl English, "Please, do not worry. There is nothing terrible to see. He is all bandaged up, you know." She opened the door and stood aside.

Somehow the bandages made it worse. Whatever David had nerved himself to confront, it was not this head mummified in gauze, with a slit left open for the eyes and a small round hole for the mouth.

From the hole came a voice he had known all his life. "Hello, David."

With a rush of relief David said, "Your eyes are all right, then. I worried about that more than anything else, somehow."

"Yes," said the familiar voice behind the white mask. "I suppose me and Julian both would have been a bit extra. I must have thrown up my arm to shield my eyes. I don't remember."

David, knowing he would never forget that khaki figure standing still, its arm uplifted against the sun, said, "Yes."

"It's rather embarrassing," said Toby's voice. "I believe they're going to give me a medal. Some bloody fool told them I got this"—a bandaged hand pointed to a bandaged head—"trying to pull out the pilot."

"It was the most obvious explanation," said David.

"So it was you. I suspected as much. I never asked you. Did you get hurt?"

"Nothing that a bit of sticking plaster couldn't cure. It wasn't much of a conflagration, you know. I expect his petrol tank was very nearly empty."

"That's good. I shouldn't have wanted you to get hurt on my account. It was very good of you," said the voice, and added, as if David had brought flowers or chocolates, "You shouldn't have bothered."

His back to the room, David looked out the window at an avenue of poplars where men were walking on crutches, or being pushed in wheelchairs by the nurses. Toby said, "How's everyone? Or wouldn't it be wise to ask?"

"No, it's all right. We had very nasty fighting in August, but we've been out of the line since then. Nobody's lunatic enough to start anything this late in the year. The good old Flanders rains will be starting up any day now. It was a bloody monsoon all August. Toby . . ."—David's voice sounded suddenly constrained in an effort to hide strong feeling—"did you know they've given me the battalion?"

"Yes," said Toby. "I know."

"I don't mean acting colonel, I had that coming, being senior after you. I mean they've given me First Battalion. I'm the CO."

"I know," said Toby, sounding amused behind the bandages.

"Did you have something to do with it?"

"I told Molly, that time I went to see him, that if anything ever happened to me, you'd be the best person for the job."

"I can imagine what he said to that. The Vickies' death-and-glory battalion in the hands of a chap who's never been to Sandhurst. Whatever next?"

"Well, there was that, of course. But he loves First Battalion, you know, as much as we all do. It used to be his, after all, and he wants it properly looked after. Uncle Peregrine saw to all the rest."

"I see," said David, his voice not quite steady. "I wondered how it happened. Thank you, Toby. I promise I'll take great care of it for you."

Chapter 6

"We must hate," announced the Bishop of Eschenbach from the Romanesque chancel of his cathedral. In spite of the many years he had preached there, he still sometimes forgot the treacherous acoustics of the nave. The word "hate" rolled among the pillars like a name shouted in an echo cave.

Angelika turned to Frido and made a face. Frido, looking very dashing in his Hungarian cavalry uniform, smiled at her and shrugged. "I come not to bring peace but the sword," had been used as the text for so many Sunday sermons it was worn to rags. Frido doubted that even the Bishop of Eschenbach, an ardent hater, could wring anything new from the subject.

Frido's left sleeve was turned under and neatly pinned to the side of his tunic. Angelika, who had done Red Cross work since the beginning of the war, and had seen many broken bodies returned from the front, took a practical rather than a romantic view of wounded heroes. Though she did not say so to Frido, she considered the loss of an arm a small price to pay for having him back alive.

The bishop gave his Bible a smart slap with the flat of his hand, rather as if he suspected Lloyd George to be lurking somewhere within its illuminated pages. "We must hate," he said, "not only the English people, but the very spirit of England itself."

Sophie, who had sat quietly, wearing her church-going expression of attentive rapture, at this gathered together her gloves and prayer book, climbed across Frido's legs, curtsied to the altar, and walked quietly down the aisle toward the door. Frido and Angelika, hardly knowing what to do, followed her out.

Pale green leaves trembled in the spring breeze, which tugged at Angelika's veil and bellied out Frido's cavalry cape. Sophie was put together as firmly as a statue; no spring wind dared unbind her hair or ruffle her skirts. She looked pale but composed and even managed a smile as Angelika joined her.

"Dear Mama, did you feel faint?" In the bright sunlight the Baronin's face, worn to the bone with prayer and good works, seemed very frail.

"I'll get the carriage," said Frido. Hesso's motorcars were these days used mostly to transport wounded soldiers and take convalescents for rides.

"I am quite well, dear, thank you," said the Baronin. "I merely felt that our Lord, who especially enjoined us to love our enemies, could not possibly approve a sermon about hating not only a people but the very spirit of that people. And neither, of course, can I."

"Well, he is an old bore," said Angelika, "and you were quite wonderful, Mama, but why today? He's been maundering on about hating the English for three years."

"I know, and I blame myself very much for not having made my feelings plain sooner. I have prayed and prayed, but until today I simply had not enough courage."

"Well, I think you were jolly brave," said Frido. "Personally I'd rather face a charge of demented Serbs again than walk down that cathedral aisle with every eye on me. That bishop's probably reading a commination service over you this very minute. You ought to be a general, Mama."

"Don't be an ass, Frido," said Angelika. "Of course Mama is brave. Mama's the bravest person there ever was. Look how she stood up to the town when she opened up the day nursery for those itty-gitties and everybody said she was encouraging immorality."

"You're not to call those unfortunate children itty-gitties, Angelika. It is the war, not I, that encourages the lax morals, but it would be most unfair and unchristian to make those unfortunate children suffer for the sins of their parents."

"Poor little bastards," said Frido kindly, a remark which the Baronin, equally, kindly, pretended not to have heard.

Sunday lunch at the abbey was these days only the poorest shadow of what it had once been. There was tuna fish disguised as pork cutlets, turnip purée disguised not at all, and artificial lemonade. Of course Hesso could have afforded to buy everything he wanted on the black market, but both he and Sophie would have felt this to be wrong.

Over the last year food had become an almost insoluble problem. At the mills, which were running on two twelve-hour shifts a day, accidents had grown frequent, and the rate of production was down.

Sophie sent every scrap of produce from the Landeck home farm to the works canteens, but the farm, begun as a hobby by Hesso's grandfather was not really very productive. It had been run by the same manager for nearly thirty years on the principle that what was good enough for his father was good enough for him. In the days when it had existed largely to provide the nursery with new-laid eggs, or to make a pleasant destination for the children on their walks to visit baby ducks or watch a new foal try to stand on its stalky legs, this had hardly mattered. But when the rate of accidents in the works went up weekly, while efficiency decreased, the problem became so serious that Sophie, who seldom addressed her prayers to the highest authority directly, preferring the diplomatic intervention of saints and the Blessed Virgin, went straight to the top and asked God for a miracle. It was sent to her in the form of Frido, missing a hand. That was the trouble with miracles, they almost always arrived with a catch to them. However, when Providence threw in Felix with a shattered knee, she repented her critical thoughts and donated a large sum to the cathedral for the renovation of a side altar.

At first no one looked upon Frido as an answer to prayer. In fact, no one quite knew what to do with him. Unlike Felix he couldn't be put in charge of a steel mill; he hadn't the brains and was in any case not the kind of person who would allow himself to be confined in an office. He'd once confided to Angelika that, had he not been born so terribly rich, he would have loved to be a peasant, and on this flimsy qualification it was decided to put him in charge of the home farm.

Here, squelching about in gum boots and a blue smock, Frido proved to be what Sophie often called him, a perfect godsend. He was a natural-born farmer. He had the patient kind of temperament which is content to stand and scratch a pig's back for an hour, or sit up all night with a cow about to calve. The only thing he had no patience with were methods of farming which should have gone out with the old century. The former manager, who had been forcibly retired but had been allowed to keep his cottage, stood daily in the doorway, watching Frido and prophesying ruin, in spite of which the farm flourished as it had never done before. As if to show Frido that they appreciated his interest, the hens laid double-yolked eggs, the cows gave top milk, and the pigs nearly burst through their sties in their eagerness to grow more ham and streaky bacon. For Frido early peas podded earlier, late beans bore later. His little army of landgirls, old men, and disabled soldiers sowed, tilled, and harvested with the very latest in up-to-date farm machinery. Here Frido was lucky, having a father-in-law who was a steel baron, and could provide him with anything he asked for. If very little of this bounty reached the Landeck dinner table, the food in the works canteens was greatly improved, accidents decreased, and production went up. What was left after the works canteens were supplied went to the cottage hospital and the day nursery Sophie had started so that mothers, married or not, could be free to take the place in the mills of men fighting at the front.

One thing which gave both Sophie and Hesso the greatest satisfaction was the fact that they had nearly all their family seated around the table. Only Marit still lived away from home, in her small, cold room over the sooty yard, where the pig—long since transformed into sausage and eaten—had once grunted beneath her window. She continued to cherish, patiently and tenderly, the most undeserving poor of Eschenbach, and seemed to Sophie hardly to be aware that her fatherland was fighting for its life.

Felix's war had ended the day his battalion had taken the ridge near Kovel. He had been hit in the knee, an excruciatingly painful wound which had reminded him of a story he had once read, in which a sadistic duellist always aimed for the knee rather than the heart, this being supposedly the most painful wound that could be inflicted on human anatomy. Felix did not know whether this was scientifically accurate, but he had been very ready to believe it while he was lying in the shelter of a rock watching his company storm the ridge, and it had not been until he had been given a large dose of morphia that he had been able to share in Pregnitz Minor's laughter at the fact that the machine gun which had hit him bore on its underside the crossed rapiers which were the trademark of the Landeck Stahl Fabrik.

His had been a good war right up to the end, a war of

movement and victories, of hardships shared with good friends, riotous parties and victory celebrations. Felix had never had to endure the murderous stalemate which broke body and spirit on the Western front, and if he was not overwhelmingly sad at having to leave his regiment, it was simply because the war had gone on too long. No war, Felix thought, ought to last more than a year. You'd squeezed out the best and the worst of it by then. The rest was merely repetition.

When the surgeon had told him that he would never again walk without a limp, and that his military career was at an end, it had seemed to him in some way that he did not entirely understand, that this information signalled an important transition in his life; that his wandering, idle years were past, that with the end of his life in the army, where decisions were made for him and responsibility always rested with someone of higher rank, had come the end of a rather protracted youth. He was twenty-five and had never given his future serious thought, living for the day and hoping in a general way that his father would go on forever as the head of Landeck Steel. Lying in his white hospital bed in considerable pain, he suddenly felt himself ready to assume the responsibility of being a Landeck, to be prepared to accept his inheritance.

It was a very different Felix who returned to Landeck, though he seemed to his parents, apart from the limp and the cane, quite unchanged. Instead of spending happy, languid hours deciding whether to buy a painting, finding a pretty widow in need of cheering up, and sampling a variety of expensive wines, this new Felix went to the office with his father in the morning, put in a twelve-hour day of work, and returned as soberly and sedately as any book-keeper, to his family in the evening.

"You'll never guess what Mama did today," said Angelika, who had quickly lost interest in the tuna cutlet. "She brawled in church."

"Angelika," said Sophie, "how dare you. This is entirely untrue."

"I don't know what you call it, getting up in the middle of the sermon and walking out, followed by your devoted daughter and loyal son-in-law. I call it brawling." She started to laugh. "Poor old bishop, what a trial he must find us. First my wedding and now this."

"Children, this is hardly a subject for laughter," said Sophie reprovingly. "You behaved very badly, Angelika, and it is only by God's mercy that everything turned out well in the end. And now I'm afraid I've behaved badly too."

Hesso and Felix, the two Protestants of the family (it had been part of the marriage agreement that Hesso would get the boys and Sophie the girls), looked at each other, quite unable to believe that Sophie would be able to bring herself to commit even the smallest impropriety in the house of God.

"What on earth is Angelika talking about, Sophie?" said Hesso. "What did you do?"

"I'm afraid I walked out, right in the middle of the sermon. It was a dreadful thing to have to do, I know, but I'm ashamed I did not have the courage to do it sooner."

"Was he on about hate hate hate again? You'd think he'd get bored with it."

"It was wicked, Hesso. I know one shouldn't call a bishop wicked, but it was. He said we must hate not only the English, but the very spirit of England. Just think of it, Shakespeare and William Wordsworth and Mr and Mrs Browning."

"I thought we were supposed to hate the English," said young Frido. "Fräulein Wesendonck says we should."

Sophie, with Frido and Angelika's agreement, had taken the revolutionary step of letting the Porkers go to the Eschenbach grammar school instead of having them tutored at home. Fräulein Wesendonck was their teacher. She wore her sleek black hair cut short, rode a bicycle to school, and had a pince-nez pinned to the front of her shirtwaister. She was young and fierce and unusually pretty, and both boys were secretly in love with her.

Sophie explained that they might hate the sin but never the sinner.

"But they invaded Belgium and bayoneted babies and

burned old people in their houses and hung priests up in bell towers."

"Fancy Toby behaving like that," said Felix to Angelika.

"It's dreadful to think that the English could have been so wicked and misled," said Sophie. "I suppose they are told to hate us too. But to say one should hate the spirit of a people, why, it's like saying you must hate Beethoven and Goethe, for we must never forget, little Frido, that Shakespeare was very nearly as great a poet as Goethe. I know it's not easy to love one's enemies, in fact it's one of the hardest things a Christian has to do. But if we pray for grace every day, God will help us to do it."

"Does that mean I can't hate Golo?" asked young Frido. "He glued my socks together and I was late for school and Fräulein Wesendonck made me write I MUST LEARN TO BE PUNCTUAL a hundred times and I hate Golo."

"That's all right," said grown-up Frido. "There is nothing in the Bible about loving your brothers. In fact the very first brothers, Cain and Abel, got along every bit as badly as you two, until Cain finally hit his brother on the head and killed him. No one minded very much. It's true Cain had to emigrate, but he founded the first city and became the patriarch of an extremely talented and clever family. Isn't that so, Mama?"

"Your father is teasing," said Sophie to the Porkers, remembering with some dismay that it was indeed so. "You two must learn to love each other like . . ."—she tried to think of two biblical brothers who could serve as a good example, but could remember only Castor and Pollux, who, being pagan, wouldn't do. "Drink up your milk, my darlings, so you can grow up big and strong."

"And shoot French and English soldiers," said Golo. Sophie with a sigh changed the subject and asked what everyone had planned for the afternoon. It was a sign of the times that she should ask this at all. In peacetime she had spent her Sunday afternoons taking tea with the Mother Superior of the local convent, discussing various charities, and attending vespers in the visitors' section of the chapel. She expected the rest of her family to spend Sundays in activities equally beneficial for their souls, which had made

Sundays rather a bore at the abbey. When the mills had gone into full war production, Sundays existed only on the calendar. Sophie, who, though her Christian principles kept her from hating the enemy, was as fully convinced as the bishop that Germany's was a holy war, had taken her doubts to the Mother Superior, who had said, "The Sabbath was made for man, not man for the Sabbath," for she was a very reasonable woman and only incidentally a mystic. Felix and Hesso had not waited for permission from the Mother Superior. The week was never long enough for all that had to be done.

Their long-standing competition with Krupp was for the moment at an end; enough orders were placed by the government and its huge war machine to keep both firms working around the clock. Krupp was still the giant, and always would be. To be a giant, reasoned Hesso, meant to be large and strong, but also cumbersome, muscle-bound, and inflexible. Landeck Steel strove to become all the things Krupp was not. It was Landeck which had invented lighter, more flexible steel, but Krupp won out over Landeck in the matter of submarines, which Hesso had viewed as an underwater vehicle for two men, while Krupp submitted designs the approximate size of the Titanic, and got the contract. Big Bertha ruptured the military and crushed its cement emplacement, but Landeck invented the most reliable, and most portable machine gun of the war. Landeck designed the first synchronizer to enable pilots to shoot their machine guns between the blades of the propeller. And Landeck designed aeroplanes which could outmanoeuvre, outclimb, and outlast anything the English or the French had as yet built.

The flying field, where Toby and David had lunched on the oily grass the year of Angelika's nonwedding, had grown into a new industry. The single canvas hangar, which had flapped in the wind while they had eaten chicken sandwiches, had grown into a village of workshops and hangars, and instead of the single flying machine put together by an obsessed young man from balsa wood and piano wire, there stood now a row of planes waiting for their final tests before being sent to the front.

Here too had gathered a group of test pilots, ex-cavalry officers, who rode their machines with whip and spur, and younger men, who had never found their feet on the ground. Small and neat, like jockeys, they swore and drank prodigiously, and had already managed to get the better part of the female population of Eschenbach in trouble. For all their rowdy pleasures it seemed to Felix that they were never quite real until they were in the air. Like eagles and archangels they had made it their own. A hair's breadth from disaster, they took their frail machines to the very edge of the possible, testing struts and wires, and sometimes, having gone beyond the possible, hurtling from the sky like Lucifer, trailing a cloud of oily smoke and flame.

Hesso said that he and Felix were going out to the airfield, where the Libelle was going to be put through her final paces that afternoon. She was their latest darling; a miracle of speed and manoeuvrability, which could climb to ten thousand feet in less than ten minutes, could turn on her own axis, was an abstemious drinker of petrol, as sweet of temper as a dove but a panther in a fight. Her black and white wings and black flat rudder, rather like a dragonfly, had given her her name. While Sophie could hardly approve of testing a plane on a Sunday afternoon, she also knew that no protest on her part would stop them. Where the Libelle was concerned, both Felix and Hesso were like parents with a new infant.

The Libelle being tested was a speck no larger than a fly among the clouds when Felix and Hesso arrived at the airfield.

"Went up like a rocket," a mechanic said to Hesso. Quite a party was watching the test; the pilots and engineers, as well as the townspeople, who found that these days the airfield provided them with free entertainment while they worked up an appetite for their afternoon acorn coffee and rubbery cakes.

The fly grew into a bird, swooping out of the clouds. "Who's flying?" asked Hesso.

"Wirtz," said Felix.

Hesso remembered him for his remarkable clumsiness on

311

the ground, a lad straight from the farm, his feet and hands finding obstacles wherever he turned. But once in a flying machine he was transformed; the large hands moved like a harpist's amid the instruments of flight.

They watched him through field glasses standing the Libelle on her tail, stalling her and letting her go into a spin for the sheer fun of practically grazing the ground before levelling her off, climbing steeply, putting her head down, gathering speed and looping once, twice, each time coming so close to the ground the watchers had consciously to resist the impulse of throwing themselves flat. Finally he brought her down, in spirals as tight as a corkscrew, levelling off in graceful S-turns, to a perfect three-point landing. Then he climbed out of his seat and tripped over his own feet. The burghers of Eschenbach, though sorry they had not been treated to a flaming crash, applauded and cheered.

The engineers, ignoring Wirtz, swarmed over the plane with magnifying glasses, checking struts and nuts and bolts, while Wirtz shyly mumbled to Felix, not daring to address Hesso directly, that he thought she would do. The engineers, not shy at all, thought so too, and Hesso, exchanging with Felix the look of a parent whose son has successfully graduated from kindergarten, said, "We'll go into full production tomorrow."

Felix said, "I brought champagne."

"To christen her?"

"Yes. And to drink to her future."

This was all the test pilots needed to hear. They ran to fetch the hamper from the back of Hesso's motorcar. "What shall we call her?" said Hesso.

"The Landeck Libelle."

Hesso broke a bottle of champagne over the machine-gun mount, which he considered the least fragile part of her. "May nothing worse ever hit you," he said and they all drank the toast, except Wirtz, in whose red hands the champagne glass had disintegrated like a soap bubble.

Felix and his father touched glasses and smiled. Hesso, who was easily moved, had tears in his eyes.

Chapter 7

"His Majesty the King has been graciously pleased to approve of the award of the Distinguished Service Order to the undermentioned officer.

Major David Harvey, MC and bar,
H.R.H. Crown Princess Victoria's Own Yorkshire Rifles.
For conspicuous gallantry
and devotion to duty
in the attack
on the Passchendaele Ridge,
9th of October 1917.

"Despite intense enemy fire and heavy losses, Major Harvey succeeded in capturing a fortified German pillbox, thus enabling the rest of the battalion, under covering fire, to capture two more pillboxes and take numerous German prisoners. Though gravely wounded, Major Harvey refused to leave his battalion until it was relieved that night.

"In all, this officer has consistently displayed exceptional courage and skilful and devoted leadership."

Matron was on the warpath. The white wings of her veil were almost horizontal, so rapid was her advance through the intestinal convolutions of the hospital hallways. In front of her she held a wastepaper basket, and the expression on her face led the nurses she passed to conclude that it contained something very nasty indeed.

"May I speak to you for a moment, Doctor?"

"Yes, Matron," said Colonel Hilton. "Come in. Please sit down."

Matron ignored this invitation. She put the wastepaper basket on the desk in front of the doctor. "Look at this, if you please, sir. One of the charwomen found it and very properly brought it to me."

"What is it, Matron?"

She brought out a piece of paper which had been crumpled and smoothed out, and put it in front of the doctor.

" 'His Majesty the King has been graciously pleased . . . ,' well, I'm damned. Sorry, Matron."

"And here is his DSO."

"Major Harvey's, of course."

"Of course."

"What a careless fellow. It must have fallen out of his locker."

"That is what I told the charwoman. I don't think she believed it, and I don't think you do either, sir."

"No. But we must pretend to do so."

Matron sniffed. "He is a very unsatisfactory patient, Doctor."

"Oh, really? The ward sister seems to think rather highly of him."

Matron acknowledged this remark with a minimal smile. They both knew that the sister in charge of David's ward rated her patients according to their visitors, and on that count David scored very heavily indeed, what with the Provost of Oriel, the Duchess of Frome, Lucas Ryder, Lord Altondale and Lady Millicent, and best of all, Jago Portman—the actor manager, my dear—who had staged one of his celebrated entrances in her ward. He had been on his way to the theatre, and had worn, to Sister's intense satisfaction, a cloak lined with crimson silk.

"Why do you say Major Harvey's unsatisfactory, Matron? He seems such a very quiet patient to me."

"Too quiet. He doesn't eat his food, he doesn't sleep at night, and VAD Ledwidge tells me he doesn't read his mail."

"Perhaps it's all bills." Colonel Hilton smoothed the citation and folded it. He put the medal in the pocket of his white coat. "Thank you, Matron, you did quite right to let me know about this."

"Thank you, sir." It was unsatisfactory, but one never did get satisfaction from Colonel Hilton. He was a very good surgeon, Matron freely admitted, but he had a regrettable tendency of siding with the patients.

"Aren't you going to read your letters, Major Harvey?"

asked VAD Ledwidge reproachfully. "You've got a nice lot."

She was new to the job, and still found young men in pain intensely attractive, and David Harvey easily the most attractive of all.

"Anything good, do you think?"

"I can't tell. Would you like me to open them for you?"

"No, thanks. I'm getting quite handy again."

This, VAD Ledwidge thought, was a lie. A piece of shrapnel had smashed his right elbow. The wound was taking a long time to heal; shattered bits of bone continued to work their way out and he had had to have surgery three times. But it was also a fact that he was not trying to use his hand, and seemed relieved not to be able to write letters. Other people had managed to learn to write left-handed, but he had never tried. She had several times offered to do his letters for him, and once he had accepted, dictating something like, "Dear—. It looks as if my right arm is going to be out of commission for a bit, so do forgive me for not writing. Thank you for your letter (card, flowers). Best love." He had given her a list of names and asked her to send a copy to each.

"All right, VAD Ledwidge," said Colonel Hilton who had a disconcerting way of coming upon VADs unawares. "I think Sister is looking for you. How's the arm, Harvey?"

"Splendid, thanks."

VAD Ledwidge put down David's letters and went away. Colonel Hilton sighed. "I never know when they're less use, when they're new and think wounded soldiers are romantic, or when they've been here three weeks and think they're nothing but bags of tripe and offal. Well, she's a very pretty girl, so I daresay you don't mind if she's a bit of a nuisance."

David said she had been very kind. Colonel Hilton put his hand in his pocket and brought out the DSO. "I'm really here to return some lost property," he said. "It must have fallen off your locker. You are a very careless fellow, Harvey, and Matron is seriously annoyed."

"You'd think she'd have something more interesting to do with her time than nose through wastepaper baskets."

"One of the chars found it. I'll put it inside your locker, shall I? It will be quite safe there."

"Thank you."

David was wearing khaki, and Dr Hilton, noticing this, said, "Good Lord, I nearly forgot; it's your board today. I'd better have another look at that arm before you go up."

He gave David a hand with his tunic and shirt. Sister hurried up, but Colonel Hilton, who never played by the rules, said, "Thank you, Sister, this is just a friendly visit. We needn't disturb you." He gently moved David's arm, flexing the joint. David made no sound, though he had turned very white around the mouth.

"That elbow is beginning to look rather nice. If there aren't any more splinters to come, I think I can recommend to the board to let you go home in a few weeks. I expect you'd like that."

"Yes," said David indifferently, "thank you."

"Matron says you're not sleeping. Do you want something for the pain?"

"No, thank you, I'm fine."

"I'll have something sent round for you all the same. You needn't take it unless you want to."

David thanked him, knowing that he would never want to. Pain was what kept him safe; his vigilant sentry on guard against sleep.

It was sleep he dreaded, the inattentive mind which let in the ghost battalion that stood in wait for the first careless moment of drowsiness, ghosts, most of them now in fact, but ghostly even then, ranged in the dawn and slashing rain behind sandbags scarcely two deep, while enemy fire flickered blue from the Passchendaele Ridge. They had drowsed on their feet like horses, exhausted past caring that they stood thigh-deep in water and stinking mud, that there was no English barrage, that guns had not been brought up and could not have been emplaced in the mud if they had been. Their march to the jump-off trench had been calculated to last four hours. This would have allowed them five hours rest before going into the attack at 5.30. But they had not marched; they had floundered through mud and poisoned water, on duckboards submerged in the morass. It had taken them the full nine hours simply to reach the front-line trench, and none of the company commanders knew how many of their men had drowned in the mud on the way.

As he had stood with his eyes on his watch, David had felt the deadweight of the men's exhaustion. Only a few days ago he had promised Toby to take great care of them. Now he was about to order them into an uphill attack against fortified pillboxes. The wounded would be left to drown in the mud. There was no way stretcher-bearers could reach them in time and carry them back. It was not a military operation but murder. David, watching the seconds tick away, was in no doubt about that.

At 5.29 he had lifted his eyes and had seen Captain Cobbleston, in command of A company, look at him and smile.

It was all right to think about Basil Cobbleston; he was not a ghost. In fact a letter from him lay on the pile by David's bed, unopened like the rest.

That morning they had not entrusted each other with their final letters home as they would normally have done. Without discussing it they had left them with the transport officer. Neither had expected to survive the day.

Then it was 5.30 and David had given the order to advance.

His Majesty the King has been graciously pleased . . .

Christ, thought David in sudden panic, don't let's start while we're awake. Let's have a game of patience. It'll take what's left of our mind off our thoughts.

He spread the cards on the counterpane. It was one thing he had learned to do well with his left hand. He had had a great deal of practice.

Red queen on black king; it looks rather good, it might come out . . . I killed those men as surely as if I'd gone up to each one with my revolver and put a bullet through his head. Black ten over here; good boy, you're doing fine. It would have been kinder to do it that way. Much kinder. Here's a red four; that's very good. You do see, Matron dear, don't you, that's why I threw away my DSO. Do you think all the people I drowned in the mud that day appreciate my gesture?

It was a cold day. In the morning a few snow flurries had shivered across the estuary, but after lunch the sun came out and the grasses and trees shone with the hard glitter of frost. David sat by the window, playing patience. He had done so for an hour, and not a single game had come out. Finally he grew bored and began to build a house of cards. His hands were not really steady enough to make a success of this, but he was very patient. As often as the cards collapsed he gathered them together and began to build again.

Lucas, who sat reading by the fire, tried not to look at the khaki figure in the window. David always wore his uniform now, even in the house. Lucas did not think that he had reached some conscious decision about this. It seemed rather a submission to something inevitable, like a felon who has been given a life sentence and knows that he will wear prison uniform for the rest of his days.

The endless card-playing set Lucas's teeth on edge. He told himself that he was being unfair, that if David had spent his days reading Edgar Wallace he probably would not have minded, and the waste of time would have been the same.

David's arm had healed as much as it was going to. It would never again straighten entirely, and it still hurt, but it was basically all right. Lucas could not say as much for the rest of him. Apathetic and restless at once, he passed his days in stupid card games and his nights in desperate stratagems to keep from falling asleep. Lucas wondered whether he had done well to have him at the Dower House. Perhaps it was too quiet for him here, perhaps his large, noisy, loving family would have helped his mind to recover better than one loving, worried old man.

"The sun's come out," he said. "Would you like to go for a walk?"

David's house of cards collapsed. He gathered them up and began to rebuild it. "Yes," he said, "let's go for a walk. Let's walk along the beach and listen to the guns."

Lucas sighed. "I've been wondering whether I wasn't rather lordly, carrying you off to the Dower House for your convalescent leave. I can't now remember that I actually ever asked your opinion. I think I just assumed you wanted to come here. Would you be happier with your people? You must go where you like, David."

David looked up from his cards. "Poor Lucas. You're sick of me. I can't say I blame you. Of course I'll go home if you want me to."

"I'm not sick of you. I never meant that. I only want you to do what will make you happy."

"Let me know if you find out what it is, will you?"

Lucas went for a walk by himself and was joined along the beach by Dr Aitken from Longacre Hall. "How is your problem child?" he asked, having heard a good deal about David and his troubles.

"I wish he were a child. You can take a child to the pantomime and buy it a cake, and whatever its grief was, it will be forgotten."

"Grown-ups take more time," said Dr Aitken peacefully. "Still, in more cases than not, with patience, the pantomime and the cake will do their work."

"Would you come and meet him? As a friend?"

"With pleasure. I'll come to tea, shall I?"

"Yes, do. I believe Mrs Placid is making scones."

Lucas was carefully casual when he mentioned to David that Dr Aitken had invited himself for tea. "We've become rather good friends over the last year, and he has a weakness for Mrs Placid's scones."

"The loony doctor?"

"He's an alienist if that's what you mean. I'm told he's done extremely good work with those shell-shocked officers at Longacre Hall."

"Neurasthenic, Lucas. Other ranks get shell shock. Officers suffer from neurasthenia. As a word it doesn't mean a thing, but it sounds much more polite. What will he do? Will he take me back with him?"

"It's not a professional visit, David. I told you, he's a friend."

Dr Aitken, perhaps in contrast to his fidgety patients,

had developed a manner of almost elaborate calm. Surely no one, thought David, could by nature be quite so tweedily, pipe-stuffingly boring. He made much of Mrs Placid's scones and talked about the weather until David, who knew that Lucas did not usually suffer bores gladly, wondered how they had ever got to be friends.

"You'd think days like today, all crisp and frosty, would exhilarate people," he said, "but not my patients. They're much happier when there's fog, or a nice, blowy gale. It's very odd."

"Not a bit," said Lucas, since David made no comment. "Weather like this always makes you feel you should be doing something brisk, like going for a walk, when all you want is to stay home by the fire with a book. It's the same in summer. I can't think of anything more delightful than a rainy Sunday afternoon. You can stay in with the Sunday papers and not feel you ought to be playing tennis or sitting on the lawn in one of those folding chairs that always collapse."

"You're right of course," said Dr Aitken, noting, without seeming to pay attention, the untouched food on David's plate. "As a nation we're far too strenuous. It's our public-school upbringing, I daresay, all that filling of unforgiving minutes."

Lucas smiled, and avoiding David's eye, said, "I'm afraid that's exactly what I must do now. I have to write a letter to catch the afternoon post. Please excuse me for a few minutes."

When Lucas had gone, David pushed the tea things away and reached for his playing cards. Dr Aitken stuffed his pipe and watched him. He felt his judgement confused by David's extraordinary good looks. Once or twice he had noted in Lucas's study a pen and ink drawing of a remarkably beautiful young man seated on the balustrade of an Italian villa, wearing a peasant's wide-brimmed straw hat far gone in dilapidation. He had taken this to be an artist's ideal of youth and careless happiness and found it disconcerting to encounter the reality in this hag-ridden young officer wearing shabby khaki and wire-scarred boots.

When David had laid out the cards, he looked up and

said, "You'd think someone who's written as many plays as Lucas Ryder could have staged this scene a little more convincingly."

"Staged?"

"My friend Dr Aitken, who just happens to be a loony doctor, has invited himself to tea to meet my friend David Harvey, who these days happens to be a bit of a loony. So I shall go and write a letter, leaving my friend Dr Aitken to study David and see if he qualifies for Longacre Hall." He covered a two and a nine, then, finding himself with three fives, cheated, turned up a six, and won.

"What is it you're playing?"

"A very dull kind of patience. The ward sister taught it to me. You lay out three rows of three, cover all the cards that add up to eleven, and that's it. It doesn't take any brains and nearly always comes out."

"Do you really believe you're a bit of a loony?"

David looked at his hands. "I'm not in very good shape."

"That's not the same as being a lunatic."

"Does Mr Ryder expect you to cure me?"

"I doubt that he has such an exalted opinion of my powers. I'm not even sure there's anything to cure."

"You think I'm malingering?"

"No, I didn't mean that. How long is it since you've slept?"

"Last night, I suppose. Why?"

'I don't mean catnapped, sitting on a hard chair alert for bad dreams." David looked at him sharply, then returned to his cards. "Do you think I don't know? That's how they sleep up at the hall, my shaky patients. Let me rephrase my question. How long since you've slept properly?"

"Infantry officers don't need proper sleep. That's the first thing they teach you out there."

"Why won't you let yourself sleep?"

"Same reason as Macbeth," said David lightly. "I've killed too many people."

"Germans?"

David looked up again. A line of secret amusement creased the corners of his eyes. He said, "If I'd killed as many Germans as I've killed Englishmen they would have given me the Victoria Cross."

"You are speaking about the men under your command, I take it. Surely such responsibilities go with being an officer."

"Yes."

"Then isn't it rather sentimental and self-indulgent to keep brooding about what cannot be changed?"

"You're a very rude doctor," said David, relaxing a little. "Is that how you talk to your shell-shock patients?"

"When I think they're ready for it."

"That sounds encouraging. You think I'm ready for it?"

"You know, the best way to get rid of nightmares is to have them. It sounds like a paradox, but it quite often works."

"You mean, go to sleep properly, in a bed, and see what happens?" said David, interested. "What if I turn into a raving lunatic instead of nice, quiet neurasthenic with a nervous titch or two?"

"That is a chance I am prepared to take."

For the first time in many weeks, David laughed. "That's very good of you." He was not himself aware how much he had relaxed during their talk, but Dr Aitken missed neither the easier set of shoulders, nor the quick laughter and the fact that David was no longer playing patience and his hands were still.

"Of course if you like yourself in your present state, there is nothing to stop you continuing in it," he said, having sized up his new patient as someone who could accept a good deal of rough handling. "I know what I'm asking of you. Facing the kind of nightmares people bring back from the trenches takes a great deal of courage, but then, judging from your military record, you have plenty of that. Why not give it a try? No one will give you the Victoria Cross for it, but you may find yourself sleeping again."

When Lucas joined them he found them drinking sherry and being boring about the weather.

"What did you think of Aitken?" Lucas asked at dinner that night.

David started to laugh. "Oh Lucas, you think you're so devious, and all the time you're more transparent than a child. Could you really come up with nothing more convincing than having to write a letter?"

"I did have to write a letter. Several, in fact. I get a good deal of mail now that I'm back in the country's good books again."

"The one good thing Passchendaele accomplished."

"Nothing good was accomplished at Passchendaele," said Lucas, but it was true that the news from Flanders in October had restored his popularity. Though the papers had valiantly attempted to keep things cheery with such headlines as BATTLE RAGING AT PASSCHENDAELE—RACING AT GATWICK, the casualty lists told another story, and reports of the conditions on the battlefield had trickled back with the wounded. The bungled attack, during the heavy autumn rains, on a terrain all of whose dyking had been destroyed by three years of artillery barrages, could not be kept secret for long, and there was considerable indignation when General Robinson, asked why he had ordered it, had replied that he had to do *something*. With this indignation came the recognition that *The Green Envelope* had been trying to tell them all this the year before. Without the inconvenience of having to die first, Lucas achieved the romantic aura of prophet and martyr. If his name was not on the next honours list, those who had thrown bricks through his windows would want to know the reason why.

"Was Aitken helpful at all?" asked Lucas, thinking that David was looking more cheerful.

"He was rather rude as a matter of fact. He said I was being sentimental and self-indulgent, refusing to accept my responsibilities. He also thinks I ought to go to sleep and have my nightmares and get it over. It might of course drive me round the bend, but he seemed to be prepared to take that chance."

Lucas wanted to say how good it was to see David at last regain a sense of humour about himself, but decided to keep this observation for Dr Aitken. He said, "You mean you plan to go to bed, pull up the covers, and turn out the light?"

"I may not go so far as to turn out the light," said David.

"Would you like me to come with you?"

"If you want to," said David indifferently. "It isn't any good, you know."

Lucas smiled. "I didn't expect Aitken to cure all your problems in one afternoon. I merely meant you might like someone to wake you if things got too rocky."

"Bless you, Lucas, that would be nice."

By confronting the problem of sleeping as if it were a dangerous but interesting military operation, David found that he could begin to deal with it. But though he taught himself, with many setbacks and difficulties, to sleep again, and though this took care of most of his nervous symptoms, the pain in his heart and mind did not ease. Dr Aitken, who often joined him on the long walks he took to be able to sleep at night, thought he saw a man deeply divided between his loyalties and his will, but hesitated to speak of it. Once, on their walk, David said, "You know, when I commanded a platoon, and even a company, I enjoyed soldiering. It's when you take over a battalion that it gets so difficult, because it's your orders that are killing people, yet you aren't removed from them like a brigadier or a divisional commander. You live with those people every day. It nearly broke Toby, who was a professional, so it's no wonder it broke me."

As spring arrived, and with it the great German March offensive, which drove the English from their intricate system of trenches and swept them back to the Channel ports, Dr Aitken, watching the outward signs of the struggle he knew was tearing David apart, and undermining all the ground he had gained, decided that not to speak would be an evasion of his responsibility. He said, "Luckily for me most of my patients will never be fit for front-line duty again. I don't know if I could cope with patching people up simply to send them back. I'm glad you're not my patient, though it hardly makes it easier."

David looked curiously at him. It was one of those days

when the wind blew from France, carrying with it the sound of the guns. "I don't like days when the wind is from the south," said the doctor. "It fusses my patients."

"I don't wonder. Are you saying you think I ought to go back?"

"I'm not sure," said Dr Aitken. "I wish I were. Both morally and physically there is of course no earthly reason why you should. Your arm will pacify any medical board, and you've had far more than your fair share of the fighting. Only, I get the feeling that when one has said all that, one hasn't said much. And now I wish I hadn't said even as much."

"You think I owe it to First Battalion to go back?"

"Oh no. I think *you* think you owe it to them. And perhaps until you do your mind will never be at rest, and if you do you may get killed or go mad, so that you would have done better to stay home with a divided heart."

"I don't know if I can go back," said David. "In fact I'm almost sure I can't. I have a medical board next week. Perhaps I'll toss a coin."

In the train to London, David took a letter from his tunic pocket and read it for the fourth time. It was from Basil Cobbleston, and said, "I'm glad your arm's healed. Now take my advice, find a good friend and have him break it for you again."

The medical board was a monthly routine which in David's case lacked even the charm of suspense. With his stiff elbow there was no question of his being assigned to anything more serious than garrison duty at home. He'd had the same doctors last time he'd been up, a fat one, a thin one, and a superannuated colonel who had a tendency to fall asleep between sentences.

"How's the arm, Major Harvey?"

"Splendid, sir. Good as new."

"That's good news. Everything fine?"

"Top-hole, sir."

"You feel fit enough for garrison duty at home, then?"

"I'd like . . ." He felt very sick. The room was chilly, but his shirt was wet and stuck to his shoulder blades. He could feel a cold trickle of sweat run down his ribs. "I'd like to apply for an A1 classification, sir, to rejoin my battalion."

All three looked surprised. "There's no need for that," said the fat doctor. All the same, there was such a shortage of experienced officers at the front, they had been told not to be too fussy in passing people as fit. "Let's have a look at the arm." David took off his tunic. "It's still a bit stiff, isn't it?"

"Not to notice, sir."

"No pain?"

"None at all," David lied.

"Eh what?" said the old colonel, suddenly waking up.

"Major Harvey wants to rejoin his regiment."

"Good lad, good lad," said the colonel. "Get a bash at the Boche, what?"

"Permission granted."

They had guests for dinner that night, some convalescent officers from Longacre Hall, Dr Aitken, and several of his prettiest VADs, so that it was very late before David was able to tell Lucas his news.

"I suspected it was coming," said Lucas, "but I wish it hadn't. Why, David? There's no need, surely."

David held up his right arm against the pale loom of moonlight in the bedroom window. "My passport to Blighty. Why indeed?"

"Because you want to go."

"There isn't a more hateful prospect. No, I don't want to go."

In the silence of the night they could hear the thrumming of the guns from France.

"Is it because of Captain Cobbleston?" asked Lucas, who could scarcely have failed to notice the frequent letters from Flanders.

"He said I ought to find a kind friend to break my arm for me once again"

"For tuppence," said Lucas, "I'd do it myself."

David, restless, got up to find a cigarette. For a time he sat silently in the window seat, smoking. Then he said,

"You've no need to be jealous of Basil. He's a friend, that's all. The kind one makes out there, very close, very quickly—Andrew's gone, Basil walks in with a valise full of books, yours among them—we discovered we think alike about a lot of things, even trivial things like liking Perrier water better than wine. It's a very uncomplicated friendship, and there is truly nothing in it for you to be jealous of. No one's ever been a better friend to me than you, Lucas. But ours is a much more complicated relationship. You were my employer, we were lovers, you're older, and then, of course, you're Lucas Ryder, which makes an enormous difference. There was always a lot of respect, even awe, if that doesn't sound too pompous, in my feelings for you. I really meant it when I said I was honoured that you should want me. It wasn't a pretty speech."

Lucas, his eyes on the dark outline of David's body against the window, said, "That's very flattering, David. I just wish it weren't all in the past tense."

"I didn't mean it that way."

"I think you did. It's funny, I used to worry so about losing you, but I always thought of it in terms of wounds or death. Not like this, with you here with me." He sensed in the dark the movement of David shaking his head, and said, "Oh yes, I've lost you. I've known since last summer. Those letters you wrote—I shouldn't have been surprised to get a Field Service postcard next. That's how I knew."

David shook his head again. "That had nothing to do with you and me. It's just that there aren't any words for the way things were. One would have had to invent a new language which nobody could understand. I don't think the filthiest animal, not even a hyena, would live as we did. If I've any human feeling left it's because through it all there was Basil. But I'm not sure I have anything left. Mostly I just feel numb. Here," he said, touching his head and heart and groin, "and here, and here."

The windows vibrated softly with the pressure of the wind and the sound of the guns. "So there it is," said David. "Not much left, you see. What there is, is yours, just as it's always been."

"It's more than I dared to expect," said Lucas. "I can make do."

It seemed to David there could scarcely be less, but he said nothing.

Chapter 8

Armistice Day found Toby in Charing Cross Hospital, looking in the mirror. He had trained himself to do this quite steadily for five minutes at a time. It was only when he accidentally caught sight of himself that he still felt shock. He wished the surgeons would call it a day. Everything they did to him hurt, and it served only to rearrange the hideousness in new patterns. He was very tired. He wanted to go home and bury his pain and betrayals and cowardice in Julian's tender body, and let the fields and woods of Altondale heal as much of him as might be healed. The Quasimodo mask of his face seemed to him to mirror very accurately the state of his soul. He still found it hard to cope with the shock and polite blankness on the faces of those who caught sight of him unprepared. At Altondale everyone would quickly grow used to the way he looked, and Julian, blessedly, would never have to know.

Eleven o'clock. The last shot of the war had been fired. He thought of David and wondered where the armistice had overtaken him. He had not heard from him for many weeks, but did not worry that he might have been killed in the final fighting. Those who command men in battle develop a sixth sense for knowing who will survive and who will not. David was a survivor. Though he too was still alive, Toby did not count himself one as well.

For David the war ended where it had begun, on the battlefields of Ypres, which were peopled for him by the very worst ghosts of all. They had fought, this last month, in rain and an insatiable mud, which clutched at their boots like an importunate beggar. It might by now have been sated with English dead, but four weeks before the end it had swallowed up Basil Cobbleston. After this David did not feel that anything mattered anymore, nor could he imagine that it ever would again. His nightmares returned, worse than they had been after Passchendaele, but even this seemed to take place in another man's mind. He led his battalion in the endless, familiar fighting against an enemy unfamiliarly ready to retreat. The armistice surprised First Battalion while they were waiting for the lines of communication to catch up to their rapid advance. No one had told them peace was coming.

At eleven o'clock on the eleventh day of the eleventh month, they were called out on parade by General Molyneux, who happened to be in the vicinity and wished to mark the day by addressing what was left of his command.

They ranged themselves in the square of a village just far enough behind the lines to have been scarcely damaged. Its houses had roofs and windows, and chrysanthemums survived in the cottage gardens.

General Molyneux arrived punctually at eleven o'clock. After the formalities of greetings were over, he stepped on the running board of his staff car to address his troops. They could hardly, David thought, fill him with much satisfaction, being a ragbag, barrel-scraped lot, patched together over and over from the survivors of other, even more mortally wounded battalions, and consignments of reluctant conscripts.

"There are very few regular-army survivors among you," said General Molyneux, and David wondered if this reflection was inspired by the want of spit and polish among the disgraceful remainder. But it seemed not. The Brigadier was paying them a compliment. "You are a citizens' army," he informed them, "who have left your peaceful pursuits and loving families to come to the aid of your country."

"Yus," David heard a mutinous mutter from the ranks, "we 'ad a fuckin' choice." That would be Private Peeve, the scruffiest and most reluctant of recent conscripts, living up to his name. For the one moment David liked him so much he did not have the heart to tell his platoon commander to take his name for talking on parade.

Now, the Brigadier told them, they might return to a grateful country, the proud and fortunate survivors of a great and terrible adventure. As for those who would not return, the many whose bodies, buried in Flanders and Artois and Picardy, had made of these foreign fields shires forever English . . .

"Hullo, Rupert," said David to himself, wondering whether the peasants of Flanders would be grateful for all that fine human fertilizer, or whether they would spend the next hundred years cursing their ruined dykes, the barbed wire, and the rusty debris of battle littering their fields.

"They are dead because they did their duty as citizens of a great and free nation. Every one of you, I know, would willingly have done the same.

"Like 'ell," came the mutinous mutter of Private Peeve.

David said, "Take that man's name, Mr Garlis."

Since, said, General Molyneux, it was every citizen's duty and privilege to defend his country with his life, nothing was owed to those who had done so. Nothing, that was, but loving memory and the obligation never to forget what it was they had died to preserve.

David withdrew his attention while the General cotinued to extol the heroic dead. He wanted someone to take away all those loving memories, blot them from his mind and nightmares, that long list which had started with Andrew Fielding and had ended, last and hardest of all, with Basil Cobbleston, who had, during that whole fiendish summer been more than his good angel, drowned in Flanders mud.

"The time has come," said General Molyneux, "to put behind us the duties of war . . ."

"The time has come," David thought in a panic, not wanting to remember, " 'the time has come, the walrus said, to talk of many things, of shoes and ships and sealing wax, of cabbages . . .' "

He was suddenly aware that General Molyneux had finished. He had missed the Brigadier's peroration, and the end of the address had taken him by surprise. He found himself at a loss. Was he supposed to call for a cheer? Hip,

hip, hurray for what remained of Vickie's beautiful First Battalion? There were no jolly good fellows left.

Cheer the silent guns then. At least it was over.

Unless someone's watch was slow. Or he simply wanted the distinction of having the last word. A single bullet whip-cracked past their heads and embedded itself in the thick wall of a house.

"Now 'oo done that?" Sergeant Doolittle asked reproach-fully. "The bloody fool might 'ave killed somebody."

This broke the stiff embarrassed silence. The realization that after four years of sniping, shelling, and barrages they were once again living in a world where a single shot was an anomaly and had no rightful place, caught them up into jubilation at last. They shouted hilarious, obscene advice at the solitary sniper who did not know the war was over.

David said, "Fall them out, sergeant, and give everyone a double ration of rum to celebrate."

The officers' billet was an old, whitewashed farm, shel-tered by bare, unwounded trees. Great drifts of autumn leaves were piled in the yard. A large table in David's room was covered with papers. He looked at it wearily, and sat down in the deep window embrasure. The leaves drifted and circled under the rakes of a working party.

One of them began to sing.

> *Far, far from Wipers,*
> *I long to be . . .*

The others took it up mournfully.

> *Where German snipers*
> *Can't get at me . . .*

A curl of smoke rose from a mound of leaves being burned David opened the window to breathe the acrid blessing of moist, clean air.

There was a knock on the door and Strickland stuck his head in. "Are you busy?"

"No," said David with a disgusted look at the table. "But I ought to be."

Strickland grinned. "A paper war. Well, it's over." He

joined David at the window. Together they watched the whirling brown leaves.

> *Damp is my dug-out,*
> *Cold are my feet . . .*

Strickland began laugh. "They've forgotten it's over," he said. "They've forgotten they're going home."

"They have the habit of war," said David. "It won't be easy to break."

"I'm rather looking forward to breaking that one," said Strickland. "A new suit from Kilgour and French, dinner at the Café Royale, an expensive tart to take back to my expensive hotel room—I don't think it will be all that difficult. What about you? Are you going to resign your commission?"

"I don't know," said David. "I haven't really thought about it. Perhaps I never quite expected the war to end, or perhaps I'm like them." He nodded at the working party piling up mountains of leaves. " 'Far, far from Wipers I long to be,' but I can't picture myself anywhere else anymore. You know, when I first joined up it took me ages before I stopped feeling like a civilian dressed up in a soldier suit. But now it's the other way round. When I'm home on leave I feel like a soldier masquerading as a civilian. Last time I simply didn't bother anymore, I just wore my uniform all the time."

He felt odd, talking so intimately with Strickland. They had been fellow officers for more than two years without ever becoming friends. Strickland was a good officer, and a courageous one; he was loyal to the battalion to the point of having asked to be sent back to it after being offered a staff appointment, when anyone looking at him would have assumed that staff and red tabs were exactly his kind of thing. Behind the lines he was a great frequenter of officers' brothels and expensive restaurants. His men called him Tarts-and-Tarts. There was about him an air of sleekness and sharp practice which derived from his peacetime occupation of stockbroker.

"Yes, I know what you mean," he said, not because he did but because he regarded everyone as a possible client who must be humoured into confiding his money to him. "But it will pass as soon as we get home, I expect. Which reminds me why I came. The chaps are having a booze-up tonight to celebrate. You'll come, won't you?"

"Yes, I suppose so. Thanks."

"You might sound a bit more enthusiastic. It's something to celebrate, isn't it, having survived the war."

"Yes, of course."

"You sound as if you weren't entirely sure you have survived," said Strickland.

"Sometimes I'm not."

"I don't know what you mean by that. We're here."

"We? Who is that? The people who left England three years ago?"

"Oh, I see. No, of course not. I feel changed too. For the better, I think. I feel tougher, better able to cope. Even less of a bounder, possibly, and aware that only a bounder would say so. I've learned a lot from people like you and Strafford. But then I hadn't it to lose."

"Sorry," said David, "you've lost me now. Hadn't what to lose?"

"The thing you've lost. You and Strafford and all your sort."

"And what was that?"

"Innocence."

David laughed, though he was not amused. Strickland said, "You know what I mean. I'm not talking about the fact that people like you and Strafford never set foot inside a blue-light and wouldn't if the war lasted another hundred years. That's not the kind of innocence I mean. The kind I'm talking about was the exclusive property of your sort—which means there were only about five percent of you who had it to lose."

"You keep saying Strafford's and my sort. I'm not Toby Strafford's sort. I haven't a bean except what the army pays me. There's a considerable difference between Toby Strafford's sort and mine."

"Only where money is concerned."

David laughed. "That I should have survived the war to hear a stockbroker say, 'only money.' "

"Look," said Strickland, "I know I can buy you ten times over, and give me a few years and I'll be able to buy Toby Strafford and Altondale as well. Money's got nothing to do with what I'm talking about. When I say your sort I'm talking about people who until 1914 woke up every morning of their lives knowing that God was in His heaven and all was right with the world. Ninety-five percent of us knew it wasn't so, even then. Now you know it too."

"Yes," said David. "Thanks. I'd like to come to your party."

Part 3

A GAME OF GHOSTS

Chapter 1

The steel mills stood silent. The heart of Eschenbach had stopped beating.

To the workers standing idly in the street, it had seemed at first as if their own hearts had stopped, but as they lived through the first winter after the war they grew accustomed to the silence, and the days which stretched ahead of them, empty and without purpose.

The cast-steel statue of Maximilian Landeck still stood in the town square, but in the last days of the war, as revolution had spread throughout Germany, radiating from the mutiny at Kiel to its industrial centres, someone had torn the crossed rapiers which were the trademark of the family, from the entrance gates to the mills.

There was no revolution and no strike at Landeck Steel. The Polish workers, who had been brought in when the mills were running on two twelve-hour shifts a day, had talked a lot, had demanded a workers' council and a strike, but the foremen of the mills had been able to keep order without great difficulty. Landeck workers knew what they owed the family. How should they not? From the day they were born in the Landeck Cottage Hospital to the day their bodies were buried by the Eschenbach Benevolent Burial Society, they lived under the family's protection and care. Even when the Polish labourers pointed out that it was this very philanthropy which had kept them from forming unions, getting a better wage, sick benefits, and a pension plan, they put it down as revolutionary nonsense. They felt themselves to be members of the Landeck family. Like well-behaved children they owed it loyalty and obedience.

Had the Poles been allowed time to spread their theories, such loyalty and obedience might well have been eroded as it had been in other parts of Germany. But sensing the danger, Felix had seen to it that it was removed. In the tradition of family benevolence, he had offered a free railway ticket and generous severance pay to all those who wished to return to their homeland. Workers who had been employed by Landeck Steel before the war were put on half pay while the mills were idle. No one knew how long things could go on like this, but for the moment Eschenbach was a quiet, if uneasy, town.

At the abbey the great beating heart of the mills had never been more obtrusive than the beating of a pulse, and was not consciously missed. The silence of the family around the lunch table was of a different nature.

Sophie, making an effort at conversation, talked quietly to Frido about a sowing of early peas. Hesso ran his fork through his food, pretending to eat. Felix stared at his plate, not bothering to pretend. They were, thought Angelika, like a family who at any moment expects a death to be announced from the next room. All that fuss over a few planes no one needed now, she thought, impatient with the sentimentality of men, and said, "Who is going to represent the family?"

"I will," said Felix.

Hesso said, "I think I had better."

Felix looked at his father with affection and irritation. During the last winter Hesso had grown old so quickly that no one was as yet accustomed to it. A minor stroke had for a brief time slurred his speech and made him unable to use his left arm, but he had recovered, and the doctor had pronounced him as good as new. The deterioration which had set in since then (and for which the doctor could not account) was far more shocking to his family than the stroke had been. His robust frame appeared to have shrunk, flesh and skin hung from him like putty, not live tissue. He grew careless at table, spilling food, and if Sophie and his valet had not constantly looked after him, he would have been not just untidy but actually dirty.

The stroke had not affected his memory. His speech was once again clear and his recollections accurate, but his thoughts seemed to have come to a standstill with the end of the war, as if by refusing to acknowledge recent events he could undo them.

The mill stood silent by his orders. Landeck was a maker of munitions. Swordmakers to the Crowned Heads of Europe, said Hesso, do not manufacture cooking pots and plumbing pipes. When Felix pointed out that even a concern as rich as Landeck Steel could not continue to pay wages without producing, Hesso merely said that the wages must be paid.

About the millions owed Landeck Steel by the German government at the end of the war, Hesso refused to worry. Such a debt was a debt of honour, he said, and he had no doubt that the kaiser, in his exile in Holland, was bending every effort to discharge it. Meanwhile he agreed that they might sell the hunting lodge in Bavaria to tide them over.

No one much minded about the lodge, which was an enormous castle built to celebrate Germany's victory over the French in 1871. Its exterior was imitation Gothic, the interior genuine Wilhelm I. Hesso's father had had a great love for hunting, but not much taste. There was a buyer, one Herr von Lenz, who had made his fortune during the war manufacturing army boots.

Felix knew those boots; he had seen them in Russia, dissolving like cardboard in the snow. He had witnessed the cases of frostbite and gangrene which paid for the medieval castle and the *von*, one as fake as the other.

At each meeting with Herr von Lenz Felix wanted to plant one of those shoddy boots in that gentleman's backside and kick him downstairs, but Lenz was prepared to pay cash, and Landeck Steel needed ready money desperately. Felix forced himself to swallow the familiarity and oily confidence, playing a game of his own, holding out for the sum he wanted, bluffing and lying like a trader in a Levantine bazaar.

Compared to the hours spent with Herr von Lenz, Felix told himself, this afternoon should be child's play. An Allied commission was coming to burn the last consignment of the Libelle flying machines which had never reached the front. The pain of it was a purely personal one, such as one might feel at the loss of a child or a lover, not the public humiliation of having to be polite to the likes of Herr von Lenz. Felix was mainly concerned with sparing his father.

"I'll go," he said. "The presence of the head of the firm would be making too much of an occasion of what is really nothing but an act of spite and vandalism."

"Can we go?" asked the Porkers. Though they were almost constantly at war with one another, they usually thought, and often spoke, in unison.

"No you cannot," said Felix in a tone of voice which allowed no further discussion.

The Porkers sighed. The end of the war had proved a sad anticlimax for them. They were too young to remember what peace had been like, and their expectations of an armistice had mostly centred around food—they had expected a sudden pyramid of oranges in the window of the greengrocer, great haunches of beef materializing in the butcher shop. Since the English blockade had not been lifted, however, the only way in which they could tell war had ended was by the ringing of the passing bell of the cathedral, which had interrupted Fräulein Wesendonck's history lesson.

She had taken off her pince-nez and had waited in silence until the bell had stopped. Without the barrier of her spectacles her deep violet eyes had seemed unendurably sad and fierce. Her dark hair was cut as short as a boy's, framing her face like a cap. From the moment she had entered their lives, every single boy in her class had been in love with her. They formed a secret society, paladins who dreamed of rescuing her from shipwreck or fire, witchcraft and dragons. Only the Porkers held themselves aloof, not because they were less infatuated than the rest, but because they felt they had more truly apprehended her essential being. Fräulein Wesendonck was not a soppy girl waiting for rescue from shipwreck or dragons. She was a heroine, Pallas Athene in her winged helmet, Penthesilea challenging Achilles to armed combat, Joan of Arc defiant at the stake. Only a true hero could ever deserve her regard, and in a hundred secret ways the Porkers were preparing themselves to become heroes.

For Fräulein Wesendonck they fasted secretly, bathed in cold water even in winter, and in the coldest weather never slept under more than one blanket. They inflicted pain on each other, boxing and brawling, and on themselves, experimenting with the lash of a leather belt on a bare back, and the heat of a candleflame held to an unflinching hand. Had Fräulein Wesendonck asked them to die for her, they would have done so with exaltation and no hesitation.

She demanded, however, nothing so extreme. When the bell from the cathedral had stopped ringing, she had put back her spectacles, and had spoken to them of the meaning of that bell, and of what it commemorated. Today meant not the end of the war, she had told them, merely a temporary laying down of arms, a pause in a conflict which had not ended. "Remember always," she said, while they gazed at her, raptly, "that Germany has not lost this war on the field of battle. Why, only a short time ago our soldiers were at the gates of the Channel ports." There was a map on the wall of their classroom, with little coloured flags denoting the German positions at the time of the great spring offensive. Of late the flags had not been moved, so that the German army still stood, undefeated, where it had stood in June.

"There is no army finer and braver than ours," she had told them, "and I want you to remember as long as you live that it was not defeated on the field of honour but betrayed and stabbed in the back by socialists and Jews."

The Porkers did not exactly know what Jews were; there were none in Eschenbach and Herr von Lenz, much as he longed for it, had never been invited to the abbey. The word called up, vaguely, Jesus and his apostles, which they knew was not what Fräulein Wesendonck meant.

"None of us knows when we can resume the fight," she said, looking at them with her fierce, alight eyes. "But you are young; you are the future of Germany. While you wait you can be a secret army, an army without uniforms and guns, an army that may have to suffer humiliations, perhaps for many years. Use your time well, study your enemy, learn all you can, discipline yourself when no one else will do it, and when the day comes you will be ready."

The Porkers rarely needed to talk to one another, their minds ran so much on the same track. While they ate their dessert—a powdery pudding made from synthetic mix—they thought about the humiliations Fräulein Wesen-donck had promised. Today humiliation was coming to Landeck Steel. This afternoon an Allied commission was coming to pour kerosene on those fragile, graceful black and white birds of death which had not been delivered to their aerodromes in France by the end of the war. Whatever their Uncle Felix had said, even (and especially) if it got them a beating afterward, they would do what Fräulein Wesendonck had told them to; they would ride their bicycles to the airfield to study the enemy and experience humiliation.

Felix went out without saying anything, and put on his coat. His fingers touched the rectangle of a white envelope in his breast pocket. It had been there, unopened, for more than a week.

There was no return address, but the writing was David's and it had been posted in Cologne.

Felix knew that David was with the Army of Occupation, for very shortly after the conclusion of the armistice Algy Strafford had turned up on their doorstep, wearing impeccably tailored khaki with the green tabs of Army Intelligence on the collar. Normally the association of Algy and any form of intelligence would have provided Felix with a hearty laugh, but he found little to move him to laughter these days.

Hesso had been delighted to see his cousin; they had both behaved as if the war had been a cricket match at Lord's which in the nature of things one side or the other had got to lose. Felix had been happy to learn that both Toby and David had survived the war; statistically it seemed almost impossible that the three of them should have come through alive, and he had often dreaded news from England.

Algy had brought no news from Kitty, except that she was still in London and had not remarried. What her feelings about Felix were, in what frame of mind she remembered (if she did) their brief and clandestine engagement on the night when the North Sea had turned to gold, Algy naturally had no way of knowing. No letter came from her, nor had Felix expected one. If one of them made a move it would have to be he, and he did not know what move to make. He was not even certain what he felt about her; at twenty-two he had been a very different person from the crippled veteran of twenty-six. Only face to face could they possibly discover what they felt about each other, but even if their love had remained constant, what would be the good of finding it out? What had he to offer her now: a nearly bankrupt munitions empire with no prospects of recovery. He had schooled himself not to think of her, but could not school his dreams; she persisted like a succubus to haunt his sleep.

Shortly after Algy's visit he had a letter from Toby, which he had read, though not yet answered. Toby had spoken quite as much of David as of himself, and Felix found it very difficult to come to terms with the beautiful dandy in the velvet coat transformed into Major David Harvey, DSO, MC with bar. At one time it would have made him laugh, but now it only made him sad, as if his friend David had indeed been killed in the war, and had substituted a stranger who walked as a conqueror in the streets of a defeated town.

He did not hold it against David and Toby that they had fought and won. They had done their duty as he had done his. But that David should have come to Germany with the occupation army, to help preside over its subjugation, he could neither understand nor forgive.

At the airfield the machines were lined up in front of the sheds. The townspeople had come to gawk, as they had in the days when the test pilots had put their planes through their spectacular paces. Felix was angry with them, but knowing how drab their lives were, could not really blame them for having come to watch a bonfire.

Wirtz, the test pilot, had taken up one of his beloved machines for a farewell flight. He was just coming down in long S-curves for a landing, bumping across a tarmac which had been neglected all winter since there was no further use for it. "I couldn't resist it," he said a little shamefacedly to Felix. "Silly, isn't it?"

"It only makes it harder," said Felix. "Still, I know how you feel."

"Would you like to take her up? There's plenty of petrol. I didn't fly her long."

In the course of his love affair with the Libelle, Felix had learned to fly, discovering that as long as he was at the controls he did not get sick. He said, "You know, I think I would."

Wirtz handed him his leather coat and helmet, fur boots and goggles. Jackdaws scattered like black rags from the wash of the propeller. The Libelle had a lovely, gentle way of taking off; you scarcely knew you no longer touched ground except that the earth began to float away under you. Felix banked her over the hangars and began to climb. It was a dreary day with a low cloud cover. Soon he found himself flying through brown murk, which at once caused him to lose his sense of direction. Wirtz had told him that this happened even to the most experienced pilots, instancing the case of his own flying instructor, who, coming out of a bank of fog, discovered that he had been flying upside down and had lost his observer. Felix did not entirely credit this story, for fliers, in his experience, were much given to telling big lies. "Just keep on climbing." Wirtz had told him. "Sooner or later you'll find God or fine weather."

The Libelle could climb ten thousand feet in less than ten minutes if she was in a good mood. The brown murk changed to white. Felix couldn't so much as see his wing tips. Then, suddenly he was out of the clouds, flying in the pure light of a summer day. The sky was like a bell jar, speedwell blue and so clear that Felix thought that if he could touch its rim with a wing tip, it would chime like crystal. There was no sound up here except the breath of the wind in the wires, and the smooth clicking over of the engine. Only a few mountain climbers, Felix thought, had ever seen the sky like this, had touched these heights. And even they had been burdened by their own bodies and the weight of their packs. Only birds and angels had ever known such freedom.

He felt exhilarated and happy, until he remembered that

within an hour this beautiful, docile creature he had helped design and build would be burnt.

He shut off and let her fall through the clouds, through milky whiteness and brown murk, coming out above the aerodrome and seeing the motorcars of the allied commission. Faces turned up at him like white ovals at the sound of the engine.

Tail and landing gear touched down together, and Wirtz ran up with Felix's coat. The Allied commission consisted of three officers, French, English, and American. The Frenchman wore a colonel's stripes on his sleeves, a pencil line of a moustache on his lip, and was quivering with rage. How dared he, he asked Felix, mistaking him for a test pilot, it was an outrage, strictly against the regulations of the armistice . . . serious consequences . . . stealing aircraft which was the property of the victorious powers . . .

Felix waited till he should have talked himself to a stand-still, taking in the English major, rosy, a little piggy, with red tabs on his collar, and the American, a captain, young and very large, with cheerful blue eyes which rested with amused contemplation on the explosive little colonel.

When the Frenchman had at last to pause for breath, Hesso's secretary, who had stood patiently at Felix's shoulder, said, "Permit me. Baron von Landeck, may I present Colonel de Vergennes, Major Hepplewhite, and Captain Brandt." Felix's heels touched; he bowed mini-mally. Major Hepplewhite fixed him with a pale stare and pointed out that they had been kept waiting for quite ten minutes. Before this could set the French colonel off again, the secretary held out a piece of paper and a pen, and said, "Will you please sign this receipt?"

"Sign?" asked Major Hepplewhite in very bad German. "Sign what?"

"The receipt for the machines of which you are about to take possession," said Felix, speaking English. This might have been a courtesy to a stranger in his country, but sounded as if he could simply not bear to listen to the major massacring his mother tongue.

"We sign nothing," said the French colonel. "It is not part of the procedure."

344

"*Mon colonel*, I must insist." If Felix's English had been polished at Oxford, his French had been brought to perfection in the Touraine, which claims the purest accent in France. The colonel, who had the misfortune to hail from Marseilles, was not pleased.

"Sorry old boy," said Major Hepplewhite, "but I'm afraid you're in no position to insist on anything. You lost the bloody war." He waved to the driver of the staff car, who had stood by, petrol tin in hand. He and another driver set to work, drenching the first of the frail machines, setting a match to it, then moving on to the next. The canvas and struts caught flame quickly; one could see the skeletal structure through the trembling heat as it collapsed into ashes.

Felix felt the townspeople of Eschenbach like a wall at his back. He wondered what they were thinking. Wirtz looked angry and miserable. It was all over very quickly. The Allied commission got back into its cars and drove off.

"Get someone to clean up this mess," said Felix to the secretary, and turning sharply to Wirtz, added, "Go and get drunk, for God's sake. Get some more Eschenbach girls into trouble. Just don't stand there looking like that." He turned and walked off. At the back of the crowd of townspeople he caught sight of the Porkers. He said, "Have you been watching?" Despite the look on his face they knew he was not angry with them. They said, "Yes, Uncle Felix. We know you told us not to."

"You were right to watch. Always remember that to destroy what you cannot build is the act of a vandal. But vandals know only how to destroy. We can rebuild."

Wirtz, still holding Felix's coat, came up and handed it to him. "I'd forgotten," said Felix, though it was a chilly day. "Thank you, Wirtz." His fingers touched the white envelope in the pocket. He took it out and walked over to the blackened heap of burnt planes. In the centre of one of them a cyclops eye of flame continued to smoulder. He held the edge of the envelope to it. It caught quickly. For a moment the writing of the address stood out clearly, then it turned grey and a gust of wind took the ashes and blew them away.

Chapter 2

"You do look awful, Lucas," said Jago.

Lucas, cheered by his friend's want of bedside manner, said, "You must make allowances. I am dying."

"Nonsense."

"Don't be bracing, Jago. Sit down."

Jago pulled up a chair and looked critically at Lucas. "You look a fright," he conceded. "I didn't even know you had been ill."

"Neither did I," said Lucas, "until I broke two ribs. Not doing anything, you know, just breathing in a perfectly ordinary way. It felt a bit like being assassinated. James taped me up, but I could see he didn't like the sound of it, so he sent me to London to have some tests."

"James is an old woman. What does he fancy you've got?"

"Something called osteosarcoma. Cancer of the bone to you." Lucas did not share in the prevailing notion of his generation that to mention cancer was akin to discussing syphilis in mixed company. Nor did Jago appear troubled by his solecism. Jago's concerns rarely went beyond the limits of his own person. "Is it catching?" he asked anxiously.

Lucas could not help laughing at this typical reaction. "My dear Jago," he said, "if it were, they would never dare tell us. Just think of the consequences. Doctors would refuse to treat us, hospitals would shut their doors in our faces, like lepers we would have to ring bells in the street, and when we came to die, we would have to depend on the mercies of bevies of penitential nuns."

In spite of their long friendship, Jago was never sure when Lucas was being funny. "My dear," he said, "I am deeply distressed."

Lucas did not doubt it. He did not know whether Jago regarded him as his oldest friend or his oldest enemy, but he knew that Jago would be most unwilling to lose either. Nor did it surprise him that Jago's distress, honest as it undoubtedly was, should quickly give way to curiosity. The actor's magpie eye quartered the room and searched Lucas's face. "What's it like?" he asked. "Actually knowing?"

"At first it was rather nasty. It's not so bad now. At least not in the daytime."

Jago pointed his chin at a Douay Bible on the table. "Is it as nasty as all that?"

Lucas followed his glance and smiled. "The Duchess of Frome heard I was ill and sent her monsignor. He left me the Bible. He also asked me whether I had made my peace with God. I told him if one of us was entitled to a grievance it was surely me, and I would therefore wait for God to make his peace with me."

"A good point," said Jago approvingly. "What did the monsignor have to say to that?"

"That suffering prayerfully undertaken is pleasing to God. Isn't it a monstrous idea? God as a kind of divine Marquis de Sade who must have his daily ration of screaming and tears to keep him in good humour. Do help yourself to a drink, Jago."

"What about you? Or is it bad for you?"

"Nothing is bad for me. That's one of the more agreeable aspects of my position."

Jago handed Lucas a drink. They sat silently for a few moments, enjoying the sunlight on the estuary. The day was glassy and warm, the town on its hill very near. There would be rain before long. Jago said, "Where is David? Why isn't he here to look after you?"

"He is with his regiment in Germany."

Something in Lucas's neutral tone told Jago that he had inadvertently drawn blood. Not bothering to hide his satisfaction, he said, "My dear Lucas, can there be trouble in paradise, a rift in the lute? I thought you two were so endlessly devoted." His expressive voice classed devotion among the dreariest of virtues.

Lucas, who would not for the world have deprived his friend of whatever pleasure he could derive from his malice, said, "There will be a rift in your head if you don't stop, Jago."

"I'm sorry, my dear. But really, what can have happened?"

"I'm not sure. The war, I suppose. It was all over last time he was home; I really knew it then though I tried not to admit it."

"My poor Lucas," said Jago with considerable satisfaction. "Do you ever hear from him?"

"Well, of course. All the time. Can you imagine David, with his beautiful manners, just dumping someone? He writes a very nice letter once a week, just as he wrote a letter home from school every Sunday. And now tell me about yourself. How was America? Are they as taken with you as ever?"

It took Jago a good half hour to tell Lucas exactly how taken with him America was. When he had finished saying every single thing there was to be said on the subject, he remembered that Lucas too had enjoyed a recent success and said sourly, "Oh, by the way, congratulations," for Lucas's name had been included in the latest Birthday Honours. Jago thought it most unfair that writers, who were after all no better than anyone else, should so often become Sir Somebody, while the taint of rogues and vagabonds still clung to actors, keeping them among the common misters.

"It will look very nice on my tombstone," said Lucas to cheer him up.

"How did they come to pick you? I heard somewhere that the king said he would never knight a bugger," said Jago.

"I lead a very quiet life. He probably doesn't know. I don't think he really knows much about it. Dorian Hope told me that once, when the king discovered one of his best friends was one, he said, 'Good God, I thought people like that shot themselves.' "

Jago laughed, and hearing the chime of the quarterboys in the church tower, said, "Heavens, is that the time? My dear, I shall have to run. I'm dining with Lady Parsons."

"I was rather hoping you'd dine with me."

"I wish I could. Lady P's getting up some ghastly charity matinee or a bring-and-buy, I didn't quite take it in, and she wants me to do something, recite *Mandalay* I shouldn't wonder."

"Poor Jago."

"Well, she always buys five boxes for my opening nights, so I can't very well refuse. Good-bye, my dear. I'll come again soon." He bent down to kiss his friend, and recalling Lucas's mocking comments on the possibilities of contagion, gave an impromptu and hilariously funny imitation of a penitential nun kissing a leper.

When the door shut behind his friend, Lucas sighed, half in relief, for Jago could be an exhausting companion, half in regret at having to spend the evening alone. He picked up a book which had lain face-down on the floor—not the Douay Bible, which despite his extreme position he had not yet troubled himself to read—but soon his eye was drawn from the page to the estuary, mantled in gold by the setting sun. In the glassy air the town on its hill had an unreal look, like a mirage, David had said, seeing it at that hour. It was Lucas's favourite time of day. He watched the sky fill with colour, and the trees grow dark and two-dimensional.

It was astonishing how well and happy he felt at this hour every day. He had not expected dying to be in the least like this.

At first of course it had been horrible. From the wild indignation at learning the nature of his illness, to the nausea and malaise of a stay in the hospital for radiation treatments, no consolation had seemed possible, and nothing had given him cause to think that a sense of well-being, even cosiness, could grow from it. Absurd as it might sound, cosy was the word. Every day at this time he felt like a precious piece of china wrapped in cotton wool.

Of course he paid for it in the wakeful small hours and the knowledge of what lay ahead, but none of this counted in the early evening, with the marine sky darkening outside the window, and a night heron taking wing across the watermeadow. "Look," he said, as if David were in the room with him, "just look at the sky."

Very cock-a-hoop because *he* at any rate was not going to die, Jago got off the train at Charing Cross and hailed a taxi. "Upper Cheyne Row," he told the driver, having resolved to do a good deed for once in his life. Nearly forty years after their affair had ended, he still had a latchkey to Lucas's house, for Jago did not believe in ever giving anything back. He told the driver to wait, and let himself in. There was a musty smell of rooms kept closed, and though darkness had not yet taken possession of the streets, it was very dim inside, and full of the crepitations of a house settling in for the night. Jago lit a lamp and carried it upstairs to Lucas's study, where he rifled through the desk until he found David's letters. Full of curiosity he unfolded them and began to read, but soon grew bored, they told so little. It was commendable of David, thought Jago, to write at all, since he so obviously had nothing to say. He copied down the address, returned the letters to their drawer, and went home to dress for Lady Parson's dinner. The doing of a good deed, he discovered, had given him a terrific appetite. For the sake of his figure he resolved never to do another.

The parlourmaid who opened the door of the Dower House to David was new and did not recognize him. She said Sir Lucas was on the terrace. David gave her his cap and stick and told her not to bother to show him the way, he and Sir Lucas were old friends. He did not know how their meeting would turn out and wanted no witnesses.

The parlourmaid, whose standards of propriety were considerably higher than David's, looked shocked, but David had already crossed the drawing room and had stopped by the French windows to look out at the terrace. The parlourmaid, who had followed him with the firm intention of announcing him properly whatever he said, stopped too, struck by something odd in his silence and stillness.

It was a beautiful day, the kind that sometimes comes to the south coast even after the autumn gales have stripped the trees of their leaves. Lucas sat in a chair out of the wind, surrounded as always by a jumble of books and papers. He looked to David diminished, old, and unbearably alone.

It had never occurred to David to think of Lucas as being

any particular age. Both the formidable public person, and his private paganism had made him seem to belong to neither youth nor age. David would as soon have thought to ask Zeus how old he was.

But mortality had touched Lucas, and David, who had over the last four years lost so many dear friends and comrades to death, did not know how he could bear it. Tears pressed against his lids as hard as pebbles. He blinked them away. It wasn't fair to Lucas to stand spying on him like this. He turned to the parlourmaid, still hovering, and said, "On second thoughts, please do announce me."

Relieved to be able to do the proper thing, she went to the terrace and said, "Please, Sir Lucas, it's a Major Harvey to see you."

He had claimed to be an old friend, but Sir Lucas did not seem particularly pleased, as he looked up frowning and said, "Why the devil can't you ever send a telegram to say you're coming, David? You know I don't like surprises."

Major Harvey, who, to the parlourmaid's dazzled eye, looked barely old enough to be a captain, said, "I'm sorry. I was in such a hurry to get here I forgot, and you're a bloody liar, Lucas, you love surprises," at which point Sir Lucas said, "That will do Hopkins; we'll ring for tea," and she had to leave, dragging her feet, hoping to hear more, for life at the Dower House, she thought, lacked drama. But they said nothing more until she had shut the door.

With Hopkins gone and no need for pretences, they looked at each other for some time in silence. Then David crossed the terrace and knelt down by Lucas's chair. He said, "My dear, this is the first time I have ever been deeply angry with you. Why didn't you let me know?"

"How did you find out?"

"Jago wrote to me."

"How very unlike him."

"You should have been the one to do it, Lucas. At once, when you first knew."

"It would have worried you to no purpose. They don't have compassionate leave for the likes of us in the army."

David said, "I could have got out any time after the war was over. You should have let me know."

Lucas thought this over in silence. "I see," he said. "Or rather, I'm not sure I do."

"I'm not sure I can explain. It wasn't that I wanted to be away from you, not really. It was more—I don't quite know—not feeling civilized enough to become a civilian again, or to be with other civilians . . . it sounds like great nonsense, I know. Like those stories one used to read in the papers about prisoners let out of jail who ask to get taken back inside. Something like that."

Lucas said, "You were looking for a hairshirt."

"Yes, perhaps. I hadn't thought of it that way, but Germany under the occupation and the blockade certainly proved to be one."

They watched a formation of wild geese flying past the estuary. "And what are your plans now?" asked Lucas, sounding very casual and careless.

"Just now I'm on my way to Altondale for a few days. Toby and Julian are getting married and I'm to be best man. Toby's mother dying of influenza slowed them up a bit, but the wedding is the day after tomorrow. After that, if you'll let me, I'd very much like to come back here and ask you for my old job back."

Lucas thought, I shall never know now whether he would have come back on his own. It's not important, not compared with the fact that he has come back. I must concentrate on that, not on the other. David has come back to me. Why do I feel so sad?

St Michael and All Angels looked as festive as could be managed at a time of year when chrysanthemums, always a depressing flower, are bound to predominate. Two large tubs of white cyclamen had been sent over from Altondale Hall, and the altar was alight with candles.

David had never been best man at a wedding before, except at the hurried ceremony before the registrar in Dewsbury, and had not realized what a good view the best man has of the congregation.

The vicarage pew was full. The twins, Agnes's children,

Jenny and her captain and their little boy, even Sabrina, aged two, staring at the candles with wide eyes. Mrs Harvey, notorious for always starting to cry at the first *Dearly Beloved*, held her handkerchief ready. She had grown very stout, and her gilt hair had faded. One morning, David thought, it would be pure white and she would look in the mirror and think herself old.

His father seemed to him entirely unchanged, as was Nannie, seated upright as a bolster in the Strafford pew, sending out waves of disapproval of candles and the High Church marriage service.

Augustus, standing prepared to give away the bride, also seemed to have weathered the war without appreciable change. David reminded himself that the four years which had changed him and his contemporaries so completely that they were like ghosts looking for their former selves, had for those at home been nothing worse than a few years of bad food and mild discomfort.

Only Toby was changed outwardly as much as David felt changed inwardly. David had dreaded their meeting. He had known burned pilots at the hospital, and it had always cost him an effort of will not to let his eyes flinch from their ghastly faces. Having failed to allow for the passage of time, and the advances of wartime surgery, he had prepared himself to confront a charred mask, but Toby's face was a mask of a very different kind. Crosshatched with scars which had begun to fade and would fade more, skin was stretched, smooth and polished, across the framework of bones. It was a face completely without expression or personality, not unhandsome in a chilly way, but not Toby's. Had he passed him in the street, David doubted he would have recognized him.

After the first shock he had made a brave attempt to smile, and some of the tension had left Toby's eyes—the steady, blue Strafford eyes, which were still his own. He said, "I used to force myself to look into a mirror a certain amount of time each day. I started with two minutes and worked up to a quarter of an hour. Now I'm fairly used to it except when I come upon my reflection unexpectedly in a window or a looking glass in a shop. Then I always catch myself thinking, Who the devil is that?"

David wondered how long it would take him to get used to this smooth-faced imposter who used Toby's voice and tricks of speech. He said, "It's rather handsome, I think."

"They take bits of skin from elsewhere on your body, your stomach or your thigh, whatever looks most suitable, and patch your face with it. It's got to be your own skin, you see, or it won't stick." The macabre enormity of this appeared to amuse Toby; he spoke in such an earnest, yet comical way that David could not help laughing. Then Julian had come in, arm in arm with Kitty, and soon Augustus had joined them and Toby had sent for champagne and they had grown cheerful and nonsensical.

It was not till dinner that anyone mentioned Felix, and then it was Augustus, not Kitty, who asked David whether he had seen anything of him while he was in Germany.

"I wrote him a letter and said I'd like to come and see him," said David, "but I never had an answer."

"I wrote to him too," said Toby. "He didn't answer me either."

"I didn't really expect him to," said David.

Still Kitty said nothing. It was Julian who asked, "But why not? You were all such good friends."

"Oh, Felix is fearfully proud," said Toby, turning to her. "He'd only have answered if he'd won the war."

"Do you mean," said Kitty, drinking a lot of wine at a gulp, "you just left it at that?"

"Yes. We must wait till Felix is ready to make a move."

Kitty thought about this, meditating over her empty glass. "You're like those people in Henry James's novels," she said finally. "So full of sensibilities you never get anything done. Why didn't you just bang on the door and see if he'd throw you out? That's what I would have done."

"You could have," said David. "You wouldn't have been wearing the uniform of a country that had not only defeated yours, but was leaving your children starving in the street. We're doing awful things in Germany, Kitty. They call rickets *die Englische Krankheit*, you know. It's not exactly how one would choose to be remembered. I really don't

354

expect to hear from Felix until things are going well in Germany again, and that will take years." With a sigh Kitty put her empty glass on the table, letting Toby refill it. David wondered whether she could still be in love with Felix. He had never been able to take Kitty and Felix entirely seriously; there was always something invincibly comical in Felix's enthusiasms. The thought that one of his musical comedy romances should be capable of giving pain to someone as nice as Kitty for so many years was a daunting one.

"Who giveth this woman to be married to this man?"

With a sudden access of best-man panic David made sure of the ring in his pocket. Kitty caught his gesture and smiled. Augustus handed over the bride to her real father. David wondered whether they felt this to be as strange as he did. Altogether it seemed a very strange wedding. When you considered that most of the principals were going through it for the second time, it was almost farcical. Yet it lacked the raffish good humour of the first occasion.

He gave Toby the ring. Toby endowed Julian with his body and his worldly goods. The Vicar said, "Let us pray."

Julian, wearing Lady Millicent's wedding veil, looked enclosed in a secret, and very beautiful. There had been an audible intake of breath when she had come down the aisle on Augustus's arm. A fairy tale had come true, the blind beggar maid was about to become a local princess. Did she see herself like that, David wondered. He doubted it, remembering how coolly she had planned her future. There was nothing of the romantic in Julian. At an age when other girls giggled and exchanged confidences she had prepared a trap with her body as bait, and her future as lady of the manor as prize. No romantic could have done that. David hoped that what she had achieved would make her happy, but he hoped so mainly because he wanted Toby to be happy. He found he did not really much care whether Julian was or not; in fact at that moment he found himself not liking his little sister very much.

He reminded himself that he was the very last person to sit in judgement on Julian's behaviour. And there was no reason why she and Toby should not be happy; such arrangements often worked out better than fecklessly romantic ones; look at himself and Lucas.

The Vicar besought the Lord to bless Toby and Julian that they might both be fruitful in the procreation of children. David's mind, once snagged on the thought of Lucas, stayed with him, much preferring the memory of the night they had spent together (rather more circumspectly than was their habit, out of respect for Lucas's damaged bones, but talking as easily as ever) to the prayerbook's embarrassing insistence on heterosexual copulations.

"I was so angry at first," Lucas had said. "Poor James. He hadn't wanted to tell me, and when I dragged it out of him I wanted to scream at him, 'Why me, you bastard, why not you?' Can you imagine it? Dear James, we'd been friends for years. Afterwards I wrote a poem about James dying ahead of me and me going to his funeral and being nice to Molly—not a good poem, needless to say; you can have a look at it tomorrow. What time's your damned train?"

"Early. I'm sorry, Lucas. I don't very much want to go. I'm terrified of seeing Toby for one thing. I expect the family will want me to stay on a few days, but I'll come back as soon as I can."

"It's all right. I don't mind waiting, now that I know you are coming back."

"What did James say, exactly?"

"Exactly very little. You know how one can't pin doctors down. I asked him how long I'd got, and he made one of those infinity gestures with his hands and said his heart wasn't in the best of shape and for all he knew I would outlive him. That's what set off the poem, I suppose, because I thought he was lying and I wanted it to be true. How easily we turn into fiends."

"There's no need to tell *me*."

"I stopped being angry after a time, and then it got really bad. I just sat there sweating and shaking for ages, but I expect you know more than I do about that kind of thing."

"Oh yes."

"Do you want to know what I did then?"

"Well yes," said David, "of course I do."

Lucas began to laugh. "I called a taxi and went to a pub someone had told me about and picked up a soldier and brought him back to Chelsea. It's not something I'd ever done before, but it was perfectly simple, a pint and a quid, just as they said. Amazing, isn't it? For one pound and the price of a drink you can buy human companionship and sex both."

David wasted a smile on the dark. "Was it good?"

"Well, no. You wouldn't expect it to be, would you? But it got me through a very nasty night. Nothing's ever been as bad since."

"I wish I'd been with you."

"I think just that once a stranger was better. But David, can you imagine my embarrassment when Molly called the next day and said James had had a heart attack and was dead. And I went to the funeral and I was nice to Molly and it was all exactly like my poem."

David laughed. "You're like those witch doctors who stick pins into dolls and kill people by remote control."

"I know, it's awful. And what's even more embarrassing is that it all worked out so nicely for me, because James's partner, who took me over, is a much better doctor. He's a Canadian who was an MO in the war and a patient up at the hall for a bit. That's where James met him. They struck up a friendship and James took him into his practice. His name's Timberlake and I find myself liking him very much indeed."

"Kindly remember that I am back."

Lucas laughed. "Nothing like that. It's just that James was old and old-fashioned, while Tim's up on all the latest dodges and takes chances."

"With you?"

"Well yes, of course with me. Those radiation treatments are very experimental; nobody seems to know much about them. I was awfully sick at the time, but I've been fine ever since, so I'm glad I took the chance. James would have prescribed morphia and told me to prepare for a holy death."

"Amazement," said the Vicar and the wedding was at an end. The frog prince could sleep in the princess's bed and eat from her plate. To seal his bargain he bent to kiss his bride. If there was anything redemptive in the kiss, there was no outward sign. Toby's face remained the scarred, smooth mask of a stranger, the frog prince was a frog still. David, suddenly sad, thought that as surely as if he had died, he would never see the real Toby again.

Chapter 3

Lucas looked well when David returned to the Dower House. He had got his appetite back and appeared to have put on a little weight; in fact he seemed now very much the Lucas Ryder David had always known; the vision of him old and diminished on the terrace no longer seemed quite real.

But mortality had entered their lives, and even when things were going well they could not entirely forget it. It was like a game of grandmother's steps, David thought. You looked behind you and the players stood frozen into statues, a foot caught in midstep, a hand raised, scarcely breathing. You looked away, counted, turned back to find the players once again frozen into stillness. Yet they had come closer. The raised foot had touched ground, the hand was lowered. Did Lucas turn suddenly at times, David wondered, to find death striking an attitude, never seeming to move, yet always nearer?

One night after Lucas had fallen asleep, David went down to the library and searched among Sir Noel Ryder's medical books until he found the one he was looking for, which was not difficult, for the page was marked with a jamspoon with some of the jam still clinging to it. Lucas too had been reading his father's books. With an apologetic glance at the hanging judge in the portrait over the chimneypiece, David removed the spoon and carefully separated the sticky pages.

Sir Noel's medical textbook could not have given Lucas much comfort. Its description of the illness was so bleak, so devoid of hope, that David had to force himself to finish reading it. He thought of Lucas, sitting over his lonely tea, the book propped against the teapot, reading this sentence of a slow and cruel and humiliating death. For the first time in his life David wanted to destroy a book. It would have given him the greatest satisfaction to break the heavy binding, rip out the pages and throw them on the fire, to watch the bleak words writhe in the flames. The hanging judge's dispassionate eye made him realize the fatuity of his anger. He wondered what Sir Noel had died of. Had he realized the futility of medicine at the end?

He went quietly back upstairs in case Lucas should wake and miss him, but he knew he would not be able to sleep. How could Lucas, knowing what lay ahead of him? There was something very admirable, David thought, in this domestic act of courage, so very different from its military counterpart, and surely much more difficult.

He would have liked to talk with Dr Timberlake, but there seemed little chance of that, for the young Canadian had taken against David on sight, sensing, correctly, not so much a rival for Lucas's attention, but someone in total possession of it. All the months that he had looked after Lucas there had never been a mention of anyone else in the household, then suddenly Lucas had said, "My secretary is out of the army and will be coming back to live here," talking a little about David's background, of what he had done in the war, sounding oh so pleased as he said, "You must come to tea and meet him."

It had been a very sticky tea party. Dr Timberlake had greeted David and thereafter ignored him as if he were a social solecism. Surely, his pained and surprised expression seemed to say, secretaries, like parlourmaids, had no business in a drawing room once the tea had been poured.

David, always ready to like anyone Lucas thought well of, managed to keep a straight face until Dr Timberlake had been shown out the door by Hopkins, then he and Lucas burst out laughing. "I can't think what was the matter with him," said Lucas. "He's never behaved like this before. We must make it a sherry party next time. Perhaps drink will thaw him out."

359

"I expect you've been leading him on," said David.

"I have not. Really David, just look at me. Am I in condition to lead anyone on?"

"You do it like breathing. In Athens they would have fed you hemlock long ago for seducing the young, like Socrates. You'll be doing it when you're ninety."

"Elsewhere alas," said Lucas, sighing. They talked about death easily and without constraint. David had lived with it too closely throughout the war to have many reticences left and Lucas had always deplored the suburban hush surrounding the subject. "As if," he said, "dying were something one caught in a brothel."

"You'll go shouting for Alcibiades, I've no doubt," said David, "the moment you get to wherever-it-is."

"Do you believe there is a wherever-it-is?"

"Not really. During the war I used to wish sometimes that there might at least be such a place as hell so some of our generals could roast in it, but on the whole, no."

"Nor do I."

"I think," said David, "I'm like Marlowe's Mephisto-pheles when Faust tries to pump him about hell and he says, 'Why, this is hell, nor am I out of it.' Only it's not quite so bleak as all that, because at other times it can be heaven and of course one is in that too."

It was not done to talk religion in front of the servants, so they discussed the possibility of rain while Hopkins cleared away the tea things. Lucas wondered whether he had just been told that it was he who made David's heaven and hell, but again it was hardly something that could be talked about with Hopkins in the room, and by the time she had finished he had thought better of asking. He said, "I had a secretary once who believed in reincarnation."

"The one who wouldn't swat wasps? I remember your telling me about him. Does that idea appeal to you?"

"If I could come back as me, yes, I think so. But I shouldn't like to be sent back without guarantees."

"Pythagoras says our souls choose what we come back as."

"In that case a good many souls make remarkably bad

choices. No, the whole thing's far too risky. Perhaps I'll become a ghost."

David smiled at him but his eyes were grave. "In that case," he said, "please come and haunt me. I'm going to miss you dreadfully."

It was nearly a week after their difficult tea party that David, returning from doing errands in Rye, met Dr Timberlake on his way to visit the Dowager Lady Longacre, who suffered from gout. The doctor greeted David and would have passed him, but David, knowing that Lucas liked the people he was fond of to like each other, planted himself in Dr Timberlake's path and said, "What's amyloidosis?"

Dr Timberlake came to a halt. He had nothing against David except his looks, his war record, and his position in Lucas Ryder's house.

Had he met Lucas in London, he would from the first have had to share him with his other friends and worshipful young disciples. But in the isolation of illness and country life, he had had Lucas very much to himself, and it had not occurred to him that he was only one in a long line of charming and handsome young men who had begun to enjoy Lucas's attentions almost from the moment Jago Portman had found his neatly packed bags awaiting him outside the locked door of the house in Upper Cheyne Row. It was not in Lucas's nature to be long alone, and since young men were flattered by his attention (this had been particularly true of Dr Timberlake, who in his provincial fastnesses had thought that famous poets talked only to other famous poets) and Lucas, valuing companionship, took trouble with them, they often got themselves more deeply into emotional tangles than Lucas had intended. In the long run it did them no harm; Lucas was neither a Don Juan who valued conquest by numbers, nor a seducer, and took into his bed only those who already shared his tastes.

While David had been living with him, Lucas had felt no need of anyone else, but David had stayed away a long time. The others could not in any case affect his feelings for David, whose place was unassailable. Timberlake knew none of this. All he did know was that he had had Lucas Ryder to himself long enough to have grown proroprietary about him, only to be asked to tea to meet a usurper claiming a place which the doctor had thought to be his. Coldly he stepped aside and said, "I'm afraid I cannot discuss my patients with you, Major Harvey."

David was determined to win over this prickly young Canadian, if only to please Lucas. "Of course," he said. "I shouldn't have asked. And please, do drop the major. The only thing I want to do about the war is not be reminded of it." He looked up at the beautiful, smug facade of Longacre Hall and added, "I very nearly ended by being a patient up there once during the war."

Dr Timberlake, who had tried and failed to bring medical detachment to his own nervous breakdown, found himself disarmed by the easy admission of a flaw in that dazzling war record he had heard so much about.

"I was up there for a bit myself," he said, feeling that to confess so much was only fair.

David, who knew this from Lucas, thought it more tactful not to say so. "Did you know Dr Aitken?" he asked. "He was a great help to me."

"Yes. He was a great help to me too. I was there as a patient, you know, not a doctor."

David held out his cigarettes to him and sat down on a fallen log by the roadside. Dr Timberlake might have pleaded an urgent engagement, but found himself, still a little reluctantly, accepting the cigarette and sharing the seat on the fallen log.

"You were an MO, weren't you?" asked David. "I used to think that must have been the most hellish job of any in the war. When I was hit at Passchendaele they took me to a farm without a roof. It was far too near the front and shells kept falling quite close. The surgeons were working on kitchen tables and there was a horrible smell of blood, and human limbs stacked like firewood against the wall. I was full of opium or morphia, whatever they used, so I can't be sure how much of it was real and how much nightmare, but I remember wondering why the doctors didn't all go round the bend."

"Quite a lot of us did. Or took to drink or drugs." All the hostility had gone from Dr Timberlake's voice. He spoke easily, as if to an old friend. The shared experience of war, David knew, could do this every time. That was why he had used it as a short cut, though he hated his memories. Even now, after nearly a year at peace, he could feel a muscle tighten and twitch in his cheek, and a trickle of sweat run down his ribs. He said, "I hope I'm not keeping you from an urgent case."

"Not at all. I was going to see the Dowager. When the wind's in the right direction you can hear her bellowing all the way into town."

And this, thought David, from someone who ten minutes ago said he couldn't discuss his patients with me. He said, "That's one I do know. Hyperuricaemia."

Dr Timberlake laughed. "You've been reading Sir Noel Ryder's medical books. I do wish you wouldn't. They're about a hundred years out of date."

"Are things so much better now?" David asked, and added at once, "I'm sorry. You told me off for trying to discuss your patients with you. It's only . . ." and Dr Timberlake thought he heard in that momentarily unguarded voice a note of grief which made his own jealousy and resentment seem petty indeed.

"I think," he said, "you're more of a friend than a secretary. Otherwise you wouldn't mind so much."

David, thinking with some amusement that it would have taken an Englishman three years to ask that question, and then he probably wouldn't have done it, skated serenely over thin but familiar ice. "I was Sir Lucas's private secretary before the war. I don't know what I'd call myself now. General dog's body, secretary; yes, I think friend. And I do mind, very much."

"I know. Doctors are trained not to take things personally, but I mind too. But truly, things are not as hopeless as they must have seemed from Sir Noel's books. I admit that radiation is still at a very experimental stage but we have had some remarkable results."

"Cures?"

"It's too soon to tell. Some fairly decent reprieves at any

rate." His voices was confident, but David did not seem much cheered by his words. Fat drops of rain began to fall, and over the estuary the gulls wheeled and screamed in the sudden gusts of wind. The two former soldiers paid no attention to the weather. "I wish I hadn't read all those horror stories," David said. "I wish *he* hadn't." It was the first chance he'd had to speak with anyone about the things that had been tormenting him, and his voice was unguarded and desolate.

Dr Timberlake, after a long moment's hesitation, said, "This is really unethical, but I'll tell you, because you'll have enough troubles without worrying about things that will never happen. Knowing Sir Lucas as well as you do, hasn't it occurred to you that he's the last person to drag things out and wait around for the end?"

It was odd, thought David, that in fact this had not occurred to him. He even felt a little resentful that Dr Timberlake should know it and not he. "Has he discussed it with you already?"

Dr Timberlake stood up. "I think you're trying to get me thrown out of the BMA. Conversations between patient and doctor are privileged and you know it. I've been unethical enough for one day. And now I'm going to visit the Dowager."

"Stop by for sherry later," said David.

"Thank you," said the doctor, "I would like that very much."

All that winter and throughout the spring there seemed little reason for gloomy plans. Lucas was well. At first he and David rejoiced in their reprieve like children let out of school, but presently they grew used to it and began to take it for granted. Nothing so dramatic as the broken ribs of the first time came to warn them that their time of grace was at an end, merely Lucas's movements grew more cautious, he seldom put his arm out for an object past his reach. Though the summer was more beautiful than either of them could remember since before the war, with roses flung over every wall and clouds like bundles of clean washing bustling across the deep blue sky, Lucas preferred

364

to watch it from his seat on the terrace and no longer went for walks. When he said cheerfully one morning that he was feeling too lazy to get up and would spend the day in bed if David would fetch him some books, David, who had until then watched in silence, said, "Don't you think it's time you stopped play-acting?"

"I'm not play-acting," said Lucas. "I'm sticking my head in the sand. It's not an elegant position, but it's remarkably comforting." He looked out at the rain which had followed the long sequence of perfect summer days. "Well," he said, "I've had almost a year. Time for some more of Tim's disgusting treatments, I suppose."

"The sooner the better," said the doctor who called round at the Dower House nearly every day.

"I'm not going back into the hospital," said Lucas. "That I have definitely decided. I'll stay in my own house and go there every day if you insist, but I will not go into a hospital ever again."

"As you like," said Dr Timberlake. "Though you'd be better off in hospital. But since you are well known to be more stubborn than an an army mule, I won't waste my time trying to persuade you."

"Will it work a second time?" asked David, as he saw him out.

"No reason why it shouldn't. We'll have to see. You'll need a nurse if he insists on staying at home."

"I can look after him. I'd like to."

"You'd be the last person."

"Why, is it something you need a licence for?"

"It's not that. It's just that under the circumstances he'll be better off with a professional."

"I still don't see why."

"Look David, I've watched you with Sir Lucas all this last year. Have you ever, since you've known him, refused him anything?"

David thought back and said, "I've never wanted to. I could if I had to, I suppose."

"Have you ever been seasick?"

"Yes, once. Why? When I went back to France after Passchendaele. I hadn't even a cat's-paw of wind for an excuse. Just poor neurasthenic Major Harvey, hanging over the rail from Folkestone to Boulogne."

"Well, then you'll know what Sir Lucas will be feeling like much of the time. Could you stand over him at a time like that and bully him into eating because somebody will have to."

"I don't know," said David. "I could try."

"I'll get you a professional nurse."

They went up to town a week later. Lucas drove daily to the hospital for his treatments, which made him every bit as sick as Dr Timberlake had predicted, but left him enough energy to carry on a spirited battle against his nurses. Whether it was their cheerful habit of treating all patients, no matter how old or distinguished, as if they were imbecile children, or whether it simply fussed Lucas to have women so constantly about him, David did not know, but Lucas, usually the easiest of employers, went through nurses the way Toby had gone through batmen the last year of the war.

"Let *me* look after you," said David, after having dismissed the fourth nurse in as many weeks. "I'd like to."

Lucas shook his head. "If this were one of these ailments people get in novels, where they lie about looking pale and romantic, I'd say yes at once. But not while I'm feeling so squalid."

"My dear, that's just silly. I do assure you, after three years in the trenches I haven't a fastidious bone left in my body."

"No," said Lucas. "If you're not fastidious, I am. And so should you be. The war's over."

"Well, that leaves us with St Jude, I suppose."

"Why?"

"Patron saint of lost causes."

"Yes," said Lucas, who was having a week's rest between treatments and was feeling rather cheerful in consequence, "I should say I definitely qualify for that."

After tea David went to Lucas's study to answer some letters, and noticed that a leak in the skylight, repaired barely a week ago by Mr Chantry (Odd Jobs Expertly and Cheerfully Done) had begun to drip again. He put a celadon vase under it and with murder in his heart set out for Fulham to bespeak the cheerful expert's services yet again.

Mr Chantry was a well-known local character who did patching and glazing. He was shifty and incompetent, but much employed by Chelsea writers, who treasured his extraordinary gifts of invention when he either failed to turn up or did a job so badly it fell apart again two minutes after he had pocketed his payment.

After he had told Mr Chantry exactly what he thought of his work, David walked back along the Fulham Road. It was raining heavily. The pubs were just opening, and in the light of the window of the King's Head, David saw a man dressed in shabby uniform selling pencils. There were far too many men like that, and David had already far too many pencils, but he stopped and bought another dozen. The soldier looked up at his face in the light and said hesitantly, "It's Major Harvey, isn't it?"

"It used to be. Do I know you? You weren't in my battalion or I would remember."

"Base 'ospital, sir. 'ow's your elbow?"

"Of course. You were an orderly. I do remember now. Robinson, wasn't it?"

"You have a good memory, sir."

"Well, I was going to try Smith next."

Robinson smiled. He had the peaky, washed-out look of someone who lives on bread and dripping. David said, "Look, it's just opening time. Come and have a pint."

Robinson picked up a stick from the ground and David saw that he walked with a limp. "What will you have?" he asked.

"Mild and bitter if it's all the same to you, sir."

David got their beer and brought back a plate of bread and cheese as well. Robinson had taken off his wet coat and was putting his cane carefully on the floor by his side.

"What happened to your leg?" David asked.

"It's gone. We were in the ambulance bringing in some of the wounded when a Jerry plane dived straight down on us. He must have seen the Red Cross, sir."

"Yes. The problem is, when you start painting red

crosses on ammunition trains, you declare open season on ambulances as well. I'm sorry about your leg."

"Oh, I manage. The army gave me an artificial one. It's very comfortable, sir."

David had spent enough time in hospitals to appreciate this brave lie. He said, "Have some of that cheese. It's not at all bad."

He noted the nice manners, how he tried not to snatch at the food and had waited to be invited to help himself. It was Robinson's hands which brought him back most vividly among the other orderlies; large, awkward-looking hands which had nevertheless, David remembered, always been patient and careful. He said, "I've been doing your kind of job myself lately, in a way. I've been trying to look after a friend who's been having treatments that seem to make him sicker, though the doctor says they'll do him good in the long run."

"Like medicine doing the most good if it tastes nastiest."

"I keep trying persuade myself of that. Have another."

"It's my turn, sir."

"Thanks," said David, not wanting it, but unwilling to hurt Robinson's pride. Just what percentage of the day's takings would buy two half-pints, he wondered.

"Why the pencils?" he asked when Robinson got back. "You surely have a pension."

"It's not very much and everything's got so expensive. I've got to look after my mum—she isn't well."

"Are you married?"

"No, sir. There was a young lady, when I first went into the army. But there, you can't blame them, can you? They like the uniform but they want two arms and two legs stuck inside it."

"I can. I can blame them very easily," said David. "But it's probably a waste of time."

"I never thought you'd get to keep your arm, sir, if you don't mind my mentioning it. I remember to this day when you came in, all covered with mud and blood and a big white splinter sticking out through your sleeve."

"Yes, I remember that bone," said David. "I had to keep myself from looking at it because it made me sick to my stomach. I kept telling myself it was *my* bone, but it made me sick all the same. You were very good about it, I remember now. I always hoped I'd get you when it was time to change the dressings. The other orderly was much rougher."

"Charley that was. Not a bad sort; he just didn't have much imagination. It's all a question of hempathy, Colonel Young used to say. Putting yourself in the other châp's place; that's what that means."

"Yes," said David, looking at him. A face like a Bath bun with raisins for eyes, and those big, clumsy hands and delicate feelings. He made up his mind. "That friend I was telling you about," he said, "we did try nurses, but they were awfully cheery and would say things like, 'We haven't eaten our custard,' and it just didn't work out. We really do need someone, though. Do you think you'd like to give it a try? If Sir Lucas Ryder approves, of course. He's the friend I was telling you about."

Robinson said, "Oh, sir," and buried his face in his beer mug. David said, "Come back with me now if you have the time. I live in Chelsea; it's not far."

"Yes, sir," said Robinson enthusiastically. "I have to go home to fix Mum's tea in a bit, but she never minds when she gets it."

David suspected that there wasn't enough to the tea to mind about. Thinking of the cane and the missing leg, he looked for a taxi, but it is a fact well-known that London taxis melt in the rain, and by the time they saw one they were in the King's Road and it was no longer worthwhile. Robinson seemed in any case to manage very well with his cane. David had noticed it in the pub where he had carried their beers without a spill. "Here we are," he said, unlocking the door. "Make yourself comfortable; I'll just go up and tell Sir Lucas about you."

Lucas was in bed reading. "How are you feeling?" David asked.

"Better, thank you. You smell uncharacteristically beery."

"I ran into a man I knew in the army and we had a few in the Fulham Road."

"What on earth were you doing in Fulham?"

"Looking for a new lover, what do you think?"

"In Fulham?"

"I went tell Mr Chantry the skylight he mended last week is leaking again. He won't have a telephone in the house, you know."

"I do know," said Lucas, who had heard this story many times. "It's because his auntie was struck by lightning in 1901—'no, I'm telling a lie, Cap'n; 1902 it was, coronation year.'"

David laughed. "That's Mr Chantry exactly. I suggested he might have a telephone and use it when there weren't any thunderstorms, but he appears to think residual electricity might lurk there, waiting to rush into his ear. 'Runs in the family, see wot I mean, Cap'n, what with auntie being took and all.' Lucas, St Jude may have come up to scratch. The man I ran into used to be an orderly at the base hospital they sent me to in France after they demolished my elbow. How would you feel about a male nurse?"

"What's he look like?"

Amused, David said, "He squints and his teeth stick out. If you think St Jude and I are going to find you a gorgeous male nurse you're a lot sicker than I think you are. But I remember him as being very gentle. He says it's all a matter of hempathy. Will you see him?"

"Yes, of course."

"I'll send him up to you."

The interview lasted such a short time that David thought they hadn't hit it off. But Robinson's face told a different tale.

"Sir Lucas says I was to go home and give Mum her tea and come back tomorrow."

"Good. I'm glad. Listen, Robinson; I don't know about you, but I'm awfully tired of uniforms." David gave him an envelope. "Go and buy yourself something unmilitary to wear."

"Thank you, sir." He could hardly wait to get outside the door to see what Major Harvey had given. Five pounds! Why, it was sinful. People spent five pounds on a suit! In his street he could get one with two pairs of trousers for a quid and a half. And Mum could have a proper tea with an egg and a sardine and everything.

"I do like your Robinson," said Lucas a few days later. "He is very pleasant. The only thing is, I sometimes get the feeling that he'll end by bringing me a bottle and putting me over his shoulder to burp me."

"He's rather touching. I gave him five pounds to buy a suit with. He tried to give me back what he'd got left—three pounds and change."

"Five pounds does seem rather a lot."

"It was my five pounds, not yours."

"That's a pointless remark."

"Why? I'm not careless with your money. With my own I do what I like."

"You can do what you like with mine too, you know that. I merely meant that five pounds seems a lot of money to hand to what is after all a comparative stranger."

"Robinson seems to have agreed with you. I do hate money having so much power in people's lives. I wish there were some other way."

"Socialism?"

"Making everyone equally drab? I don't know. I don't have any answers, only half-baked questions. We must ask Toby. Now that he's going in for politics, he has an answer for everything."

The constituency comprised of the villages of Altondale, High Fenton, and Fenton St Bury was traditionally represented by a member of the Strafford family. If by chance there was no Strafford of suitable age, or, as in Toby's case, he was away at war, one of the Lappiters or Molyneux would hold the seat in trust, but it was clearly understood that this was a temporary expedient. The latest incumbent, Sir Carnaby Lappiter, had upon Toby's return from the war politely vacated the seat by dying, and there was to be a by-election.

Toby had rung up David, explaining that he had to come to London to see some people, that he was lunching with Old Bingo, but would like to have dinner with David at his club. David did not ask who Old Bingo was, in case he should be someone frightfully famous like the prime minister. He had a vivid memory of the food at Toby's club, so he suggested tea at Upper Cheyne Row instead, thinking that it might amuse Lucas to meet Toby after so long. "I'd like to make it dinner," he said, "but Sir Lucas is usually too tired to see people by then."

Toby accepted a little reluctantly. Eton had instilled in him a low regard for people who frittered away their lives writing poetry, and at the time of *The Green Envelope* he had thought horsewhipping too good for Lucas Ryder.

"Fancy Toby a politician," David said to Lucas, telling him about the telephone call.

"I think it's a very good thing," said Lucas. "I should like to see Parliament and all the cabinet posts filled with ex-soldiers. Perhaps then they wouldn't be so eager to rush into wars."

Toby, remembering both *The Green Envelope* and Lucas Ryder's position in the world of letters, was shy and stand-offish at first, but Lucas was always very good with the shy and young, and by the time the second cup of tea was poured Toby was talking as easily as if Sir Lucas had been a celebrated cricketer instead of a poet.

Lucas was always curious about how things were done, and asked Toby how one went about becoming an MP.

"That's easy," said David. "You see to it that you are born in Altondale a member of the Strafford family. Altondale must be the last of the rotten boroughs in England. As far as we are concerned, the Reform Act never happened."

"It's easy for you to laugh," said Toby, "and I daresay it was true in Uncle Peregrine's day, but things have changed, you know. Fenton St Bury has put up a Labour candidate. So I want you to come home and vote for me."

"But I've mever voted," said David. "I wouldn't know how."

"It's perfectly simple," said Lucas, smiling at him. "Especially when you've already been told whom to vote for. Who is Fenton St Bury?"

Toby explained that it was not a who but a what, a small mining village hidden from the fastidious eyes of High

Fenton and Altondale by a green fold of hills. The miners living amid its slag heaps had seemed to someone like Toby scarcely more human than their pit ponies, and before the war it would as soon have occurred to a pit pony to vote as to a miner. But the war had taught them their power. They could supply or withhold coal, the very lifeblood of the struggle, and all through the war they struck, long and repeatedly, sending their wives to work in a nearby munitions factory and their daughters into well-paid whoredom at the gunnery camp outside High Fenton. The organizer of those strikes was now standing as Labour candidate, contesting a constituency which had been the Straffords' ever since there had been Straffords at Altondale.

"There's nothing for it but to woo the miners," said David with affectionate malice. "I believe you go into kitchens and talk to their wives, kiss their babies, gruntle their cats, and drink tea with condensed milk. Then you head for the pub and tell the men how they helped us win the war, and promise them lots of jam tomorrow and plenty of pie in the sky. That is what politicians do, isn't it?"

"You might ask Mrs Snow to vote for you," suggested Lucas. "Think of what she went through for women's suffrage."

"That's all very well," said Toby, "but the fact is that now women have got the vote they none of them want to use it because it means admitting they're over thirty. Besides, Kitty's American. How is she, anyhow?"

"You ought to stop in to see her," said David. "She's always complaining that she leads such a dull life. Personally I think she misses the good old days of window smashing and being had up before the magistrate"

When he saw Toby to the door, David realized that Julian's name had not been mentioned at all. Cautiously he asked whether everything was well at home. Toby said yes, very well, his smooth face incapable of conveying joy or grief. But looking into his eyes, David knew that his marriage was still a wonder and a miracle to him, and that he would have been embarrassed to tell even his oldest friend of the degree of his happiness.

Chapter 4

Even as David was speaking to Toby, Kitty's life was on the point of ceasing to be dull. She was drinking sherry and looking in a melancholy manner at the fog gathering outside her window when Annie announced a caller. Kitty was quite used to people coming to see her for music lessons, and said a little impatiently, "Well, show him in, Annie."

Annie still looked hesitant. "Please, miss, it's not a gentleman, not a real gentleman, if you see what I mean."

"I guess he's a parent. Let's hope he's a rich one. If his money's good, we won't mind if he isn't in *Debrett's*. Show him in."

On either side of the drawing-room door narrow panels of coloured glass were set into the wall. Through these Kitty watched the gentleman who was not a gentleman, bathed in purple and pink, divest himself of an astrakhan coat and a tightly curled bowler. Annie opened the door and said, "Please, miss, it's Mr. . . . ," but the visitor, hand extended, was already in the room. "Popkin's the name, nightclubs's the game," he said, shaking Kitty's hand heartily.

"How do you do, Mr Popkin," said Kitty. He was a very little man. Everything about him was round; his stomach, his face, his button of a nose, and his merry blue eyes. Even his mouth was pursed in a perfect circle; Kitty guessed that it usually held a cigar. There was an air of Havanas, old brandy, and ready money about Mr Popkin which was very pleasant and made her hope that he was indeed the parent of a future pupil.

She offered him a chair, into which he plopped with a great sigh of relief. "New boots," he said, stretching his legs so that she could admire their high polish, pointed toes, and elastic sides. "What a time I had to track you down, Mrs Snow. I finally had to make a donation to the Hospital Comforts Fund before that old dragon, Sister Wigham, told me where you lived."

"Oh," said Kitty, enlightened, "were you at the

hospital?" She had often had letters from men back at the front, and even later, demobilized and home, to thank her for singing for them. No one had ever before called on her in person, and she thought it very nice of Mr Popkin to do so.

"Yes indeed. Had a bit of shell in the old tum-tum." He caught a look of doubt in Kitty's eye and began to laugh cheerfully. "You think I'm too short for the army, eh?"

Kitty, who had in fact been thinking this, hastily denied it.

"Well I was in, all the same. Bantam regiment. No one above five foot three, except the colonel. He was six foot seven. You should have seen us marching—laugh? I'm five two and three quarters."

"Why, so am I," said Kitty, feeling, however irrationally, that this fact cemented a sudden friendship.

Mr Popkin explained that he was the owner of a number of picture palaces; the Cadiz, the Escorial, and the Alhambra. Kitty nodded. She had visited one of them, she couldn't remember which. It had been very grand, in a Spanish style of architecture which might have surprised the Moors, and had boasted the mightiest of mighty Würlitzers. He was, Mr Popkin said, even now in the process of building a picture palace which would make all the others look cheap, but the fact was he was getting tired of the whole business. He couldn't even think of what to call it, which was a sure sign he had lost interest. Did Kitty have any ideas?

Kitty suggested the Vatican.

"There, I knew you had a head on your shoulders," Mr Popkin said delightedly. "Or do you think the pope could sue me? I'll get my lawyers onto it."

Kitty offered him a drink and asked him to smoke if he cared to. With the cigar his face suddenly looked complete. He explained that he had not come to discuss his picture palaces with her, that they were, so to speak, credentials to attest to the fact that he was a serious man of business, not a fly-by-night enterprenoor. What he really wanted to talk to her about was a nightclub he was thinking of opening.

Kitty could not imagine why he would want to discuss

this with her, but his presence had done so much to brighten what had promised to be another dull evening that she said, "A nightclub?"

"Yes. A place where people can drink after hours. Very popular these days. But what's wanted is something special. Young people are bored with dancing at the Savoy. Look how they're flocking to the Tottenham Court Road. Tottenham Court Road, I ask you. If I couldn't do better than that I'd cut my throat. So, what I've done is, I've bought a synagogue in the East End, just off Commercial Street." It was no longer used as a synagogue, he explained; it had been properly deconsecrated or whatever they called it, and the building was up for sale, so he had had the splendid idea of buying it for a song, and was even now remodelling it to emerge from its present derelict state as the Temple Bar Club.

"I think that's an excellent name, Mr Popkin," said Kitty. "But will people go all the way to Commercial Street just to get a drink after hours?" She suspected from his accent that his own origins were rooted in that cheerless neighbourhood, and wanted to be tactful, but she had in her suffragette days attended some of Sylvia Pankhurst's East End rallies and was full of doubt.

"Lord bless you, yes. They'll come anywhere so long as it isn't Mayfair and Belgravia. And I want you to come too, Mrs Snow."

"Well, thank you, Mr Popkin. That's very nice of you."

"You see," he said, "I need a singer."

"A singer? Oh, I see. But I'm very sorry, Mr Popkin, I don't think I can help you. I do have pupils, but to be perfectly truthful, they're none of them very talented, whatever their mamas may think."

"Pupils," said Mr Popkin with the utmost contempt. "Mrs Snow, you're not getting the idea at all. I don't want your pupils; I want you. I said to myself when I heard you at the hospital, there's a voice with a future—struth I did."

Kitty began to laugh. He was obviously a crook, but such a nice one, she couldn't help liking him. "If you really heard me sing, Mr Popkin, you must know have no voice at all. I used to, a little, enough to sing in church on

Sunday, but these days I simply give a good imitation of chronic laryngitis."

"But don't you see, Mrs Snow," said Mr Popkin, stubbing out his scarcely begun cigar in his eagerness to explain, "that's what I'm looking for. I don't want an English virgin singing 'Fairest Isle.' I want a voice for a smoky, boozy nightclub, a voice that sounds right with a nigger jazz band, and believe me, Mrs Snow, you're it." He suddenly stood up on his pointy little boots, did a shimmy, and sang in a tuneless tenor:

> Hello! ma baby, Hello! ma honey,
> Hello! my ragtime gal . . .

His notion of an American accent and his shimmy were so droll that Kitty laughed till tears ran down her cheeks. "I'm sorry, Mr Popkin," she said at last, mopping her eyes with her handkerchief, "I didn't mean to be rude. I just couldn't help it."

"Do you good to laugh," said her guest, laughing himself. "You always had a bit of a sad look at the hospital, I thought."

"It was all those soldiers being patched up just to be sent back where they'd get shot all over again," said Kitty. "I couldn't help thinking about it."

"You don't have to tell me. I was one of them, remember. And now, Mrs Snow, what I'd like you to do—you're not busy, are you; no more piano lessons? Good. Then what I'd like you to do is to come with me to Aldgate and have a look at the place. See what you think of it."

"What, now? Just like that?"

"No time like the present. Got the Rolls waiting outside."

Kitty liked Mr Popkin, but she did not entirely trust him. Still, it seemed hardly likely that he was going through all this trouble to abduct her for either immoral purposes or ransom. She looked out the window and saw very grand Rolls, exuding an air of the utmost respectability. There was a very grand chauffeur as well, and if worst came to worst, Kitty decided she could always lean out the window and scream. The truth was that she had been having a very dull time lately, and was longing for an adventure.

The Rolls floated along the Embankment; it was like riding a magic carpet made of eiderdown. In the financial district the traffic of late afternoon slowed them down. Or perhaps, thought Kitty, the Rolls merely felt comfortable surrounded by so many banks and so much money, and wanted to linger. They passed St Paul's, looking like a ghost ship in the fog, and presently entered meaner streets where the rich car itself seemed like a phantom. Men wrapped in shabby coats and layers of shawls sold winkles from barrows. "My dad did that," said Mr Popkin.

Commercial Street stretched dank and endless, with the bloom of riverdamp on its stones. They turned a corner, there was a blaze of light, the cheerful sound of hammering and sawing, and they drew up in front of what had obviously been a synagogue.

"The boys are working overtime," said Mr Popkin, ushering her in. "I'm excited about this place. Listen to those acowstics! Come in, Mrs Snow."

Kitty had never before been inside a synagogue. This one, she judged, must have been a very small and poor one. Over the clatter of hammering, the shouts of the workmen, and the scrape of a saw, Mr Popkin conjured up a dance floor the size of a dinner napkin and a raised platform for the band. It would be just big enough, Kitty thought, to accommodate one very emaciated saxophonist.

"Jazz band," shouted Mr Popkin, "piano—upright of course," reluctantly conceding that the space would probably not hold a concert grand, "and you, Mrs Snow. How do you like it?"

There was a trestle table where the workers had taken their tea. Mr Popkin pushed their stained cups and crumpled newspapers to one end, spread a handkerchief over a barrel full of nails, and with a flourish begged Kitty to sit down.

"Isn't it a little small?" said Kitty. "You won't be able to get too many people in here."

"That's right," said Mr Popkin, seemingly pleased with this criticism. "Got it in one. I said you had a head on your shoulders. We'll keep it exclusive, see. Not everybody gets in. That'll make them want to. At the same time, you know, they like being jammed together. Never ask me why, but they're happiest packed so tight they can't move. Here you," Mr Popkin shouted to one of the workmen shifting a ladder, "mind that window. That's art, that is."

Kitty looked up at a stained-glass depiction of what appeared to be Moses expressing his low opinion of the golden calf. "We're keeping that. I want a bit of a religious look. That window, menorahs for lights, use the altar for a bar. And then a Negro jazz band and you singing blues—it's the contrast, see. It'll make them feel wicked."

"Sacrilegious, you mean."

"That's it, that's the word. It's the way these young people like to feel nowadays. Give them no end of a kick. As for you, Mrs Snow, we'll get you clothes from Paris—short skirts, all spangles and beads; you'll look a proper smasher. You've got the figure for it. I used to think you were too skinny back in the war—you don't mind my saying that, do you?—but now all the girls are trying to look like boys, so you're ahead of the game."

Kitty, who had been enjoying her visit, having almost forgotten why she had been brought here, grew thoughtful at these words. She said, "You know, Mr Popkin, I'd love to do it. I really would. But I don't see how I can. I'm a respectable widow with a son at Eton, and to be perfectly frank, I don't have any money at all except what I earn giving music lessons. Lord Altondale, who is a very distant cousin, is kindly paying for Oliver's education, or he'd have to go to a board school. So you see, I can't suddenly put on spangles and beads and show my knees in a nightclub. I'd lose all my pupils and starve to death."

The workers were by now packing up to leave and the room had grown much quieter. Mr Popkin caught hold of a carpenter's apprentice and said, "Here you. Go out front to my motor and tell the chauffeur—he's the one in the gaiters and peaked cap—to bring us some champagne. It's in the hamper in the boot. You'll have a nip, won't you Mrs Snow? It'll keep us bright while we talk."

The boy ran off on his errand. "Goodness, Mr Popkin," said Kitty, "do you always travel with a bottle of champagne?"

"Yes," said Mr Popkin simply. "You never know when it'll come in handy."

Kitty, who was extremely fond of champagne, found herself liking her peculiar host more and more. She wondered whether he was married. He might be only five foot two and three quarters and perfectly spherical, but she could imagine life with Mr Popkin as being very pleasant indeed. As if he had read her mind, he said, "I hope you like your champagne dry. Mrs Popkin likes hers sweet, but I like it so dry you can blow the dust off it. Paul Roger do for you?"

By this time the chauffeur had brought in a bottle of Pol Roger packed in ice, and two glasses. It was a pity about Mrs Popkin, Kitty thought. This man was obviously a treasure.

They touched glasses and drank. The small cave of the synagogue looked dim and cheerless in the sparse lamplight. Yet here they were, Kitty thought, drinking champagne, as merry as a pair of grasshoppers.

"Something the war taught me," said her host. "Always be comfortable when you can. You'll be uncomfortable again soon enough. Now you listen to me, Mrs Snow. When I built the Alhambra everyone thought I was barmy. Until then they sat in a draughty church hall on a wooden bench and thought it was the treat of the century. Well, it stood to reason at first, moving picture being a novelty. But novelty wears off, and that's when people start to expect a bit of posh. 'You'll have to charge too much admission,' they said to me; 'people won't pay for it, it's too grand.' Well, that's true enough, it was grand. Plush seats, Moorish screens imported from Spain, no expense spared. You go any night, to the Cadiz or the Alhambra or the Escorial, and see if they don't pay admission. Never an empty seat in the house; doesn't matter if the film's good or not. People like a bit of swank, especially after the war. So what with one thing and another I've made my bundle and if you come to work for me, Mrs Snow, you can tell all those squeaky sopranos and all your da-de-dum-dedum piano and students to go find themselves another teacher. You'll be the toast of London or my name's not Abednego Popkin."

Kitty choked into her champagne. "It isn't. I don't believe it."

"Well, it is. My friends call me Pops mostly; you can see why. I hope you will too.'

"Yes, of course. And I'm Kitty."

He poured them each another glass of champagne to celebrate the christening. Kitty gazed pensively at the bubbles as they rose in the glass. "No more 'Happy Peasant,'" she said. "No more 'Für Elise.' Never again 'Let the Bright Seraphim.'"

"That's right," said Mr Popkin. "It's Hello! ma baby from now on. Have you got a solicitor, Kitty?"

"No. Well, Lord Altondale's, I suppose. He drew up the lease for the house where I live."

"Good. I never talk business with a lady. Their minds aren't made for it, bless them. You give me his name and I'll call on him and we'll draw up a contract. Twice what you make now and all the champagne you can drink. What do you say?"

Amused at this peculiar way of doing business, Kitty said, "You don't know what I make now."

"Oh, all right, three times, but that's my last offer. Now, is it a bargain?

She wondered what Felix would say to her dressed in spangles and showing her knees in an East End nightclub. But Felix seemed very remote these days. Though he was less than a day's journey away from her, he seemed far more removed than during the years of war, when she did not know whether he was alive or dead. She sighed. Mr Popkin, seeing her look sad, quickly poured her more champagne.

"Drink up, Kitty, old girl. What do you say? Is it a bargain? I promise you, you'll never regret it."

Kitty held out her hand across the trestle table and said, "You may regret it, but I don't think I will. Yes, Pops, it's a bargain."

Chapter 5

Revolution came to Eschenbach on Easter Sunday, 1920. Hesso and Felix were in their offices in the administration building, putting in a few melancholy hours with the account books while the cathedral bells called the faithful to Easter mass.

Landeck Steel was once again in partial production, turning out cooking pots, cutlery, typewriters, lampstands, whatever anyone wanted to buy. The noisy clatter of machinery was cheering, like the clatter of coins in the cash register, but with each pot and each fork coming off the assembly line came the reminder of how far down the former swordmakers to the crowned heads of Europe had come in the world.

Those workers not busy making pots were employed in dismantling mills and workshops, for under the terms of the Versailles Treaty half of the Landeck Steel empire was to be pulled down. The workers hated the job, though they were paid their usual wages for it by Hesso. They goldbricked, scrimshanked and malingered to a degree that had until then been unknown in the industrious town of Eschenbach. Felix, who had taken over the supervision of this mandated destruction to spare his father, knew that they were behaving like this out of loyalty to the family and was touched, but it made his days twice as long and his work twice as hard.

Sometimes he wondered why anyone still bothered about anything. Was there a future in which hard work and productiveness would once again benefit a country bled white by war and so demoralized by defeat that it seemed beyond the hope of recovery? The government sat like Job atop the dungheap of a beaten country, scratching its boils and listening to bad advice. In such a vacuum it was no wonder that hardly a week went by without a political faction declaring itself to be in charge, only to be bloodily put down by the *Reichswehr*, or by another faction which in its turn proclaimed itself the government. Chancellor Ebert was often a fugitive. Only last week the ultraright had taken over Berlin, the chancellor had fled, first to Dresden, then to Stuttgart, while the army had watched which way the pendulum would swing. There had been a general strike, and now the Red Soldiers' League, with captured arms, was taking over the steel mills and foundries of the Ruhr.

They had moved into Eschenbach under cover of night, and had gone from house to house in the working quarter of the town, talking, reasoning, quietly, convincingly arguing with the Landeck workers. Despite their name they were not Communists; they were mostly former soldiers, nearly a hundred thousand of them spreading through the industrial heart of Germany, fighting if they had to, taking possession quietly when they could. Their leaders were former noncommissioned officers, quiet, competent men, accustomed to command, but among their following there were many who cared nothing for the rights of workers, who simply missed the excitement of war and liked the feeling of power that comes of a pocket dragged down by the weight of a revolver.

By the time they had occupied the mills and posted sentries, and had assembled in the Maximiliansplatz, they were an orderly but rough-and-ready, impatient crowd.

Hesso's office faced the square. He liked to sit behind the great gold-inlaid desk which had been a gift of Napoleon to his great-grandfather, Maximilian von Landeck, to be able to see, as he lifted his head from his papers, his huge and ugly cast-iron statue in the square outside. As the sound of voices grew louder, he got up to see what the commotion was, and found the square filled with several hundred men, many of whom were strangers to him.

"What is it?" he said to Felix, who had joined him at the window.

"I think it's the revolution."

Someone had jumped on the pedestal of Maximilian's statue, and was making a speech. "I think you're right," said Hesso.

The crowd was listening to the speaker. Most of them cheered him, some seemed hesitant. Almost everyone appeared to be armed.

Hesso's secretary entered the office. "What is to be done, Herr Baron?" he asked. "I have locked the doors and I've tried to telephone the police, but the lines appear to be cut."

"We must put a stop to this," said Hesso. "There are too many guns about. Someone will get hurt."

Felix kept his army revolver locked in the drawer of his desk. He went to get it, but Hesso said, "No. This must be done quietly."

Felix opened the window a crack. The crowd, roaring approval at something a speaker had said, was still orderly except at its fringes, where small knots were gathering, each being harangued by a speaker of its own. The April wind snatched their words and blew them away, so Felix could not hear what they were proposing, but they looked as if at any moment they might turn ugly.

Hesso took his coat from its hook, picked up his hat and his cane, and began to walk out of the office. Felix had never been so proud of him; his back, frail and rather bent since his stroke a year and a half ago was straight now, his blue eyes seemed suddenly young again in the slack face.

Felix shut the window and said, "I think we'd better go out the back way, Papa. You don't know what the sight of a bloodsucking capitalist might do to a crowd like that. And there's only three of us against a lot of them."

"Quite a lot are our men," said Hesso, sounding a little sad at having to admit it. "I shall come to no harm."

"That's probably what the tsar of Russia said. Come upstairs, Papa, please. I'll talk to them if you like."

Hesso paid no attention. He unlocked the main entrance doors and opened them wide. As the crowd grew aware of him, with his son at his shoulder and his secretary behind him, a total silence fell. No one had thought that anyone was in the administration building on a Sunday.

From the back of the crowd there were shouts about the factories belonging to the workers. Someone threw a rock which hit a window, but Hesso stood clamly, surveying the crowd.

In the very front line Hesso recognized the foreman of one of the rolling mills, a quiet, steady man called Borchert.

384

He looked embarrassed to be found in the forefront of a revolutionary mob, had indeed been pushed there by the surge of the crowd rather than his own will. When he caught sight of Hesso and Felix he took off his cap. Other Landeck workers followed suit.

The revolutionary spirit has quite a long way to go, thought Felix, amused.

"Borchert," said Hesso, speaking to the man, but loudly enough to be heard by the crowd. Those in the back stopped shouting. "It's Easter Sunday. I am going home now. But if you elect a delegation I will be back here at nine o'clock on Monday morning and hear what you have to say."

Someone shouted, "You don't give orders here anymore, Gramps," and Felix noted the face; a good-humoured soldier's face, which disappeared from sight as the huge paw of a Landeck steelworker covered his mouth. Hesso seemed not to have heard. He went down the steps and a path opened for him. His motorcar stood by the side entrance he always used. A rock flew out from somewhere, shattering the wind-screen. Hesso kept on walking, his back straight, his steps unhurried. The secretary opened the car door and swept glass shards from the front seat into the street. Felix took the wheel. They drove slowly, almost as slowly as they had walked, through the crowd which opened a path for them.

On the other side of town the cathedral doors opened to the sun and people in their Sunday best were pouring into the street. Felix drove carefully; it was difficult to see through the starred windscreen. They had turned onto the road to the abbey when there was a strange sound in the backseat, something between a cough and a cry, and the secretary said, "Herr Baron." Felix looked in the rearview mirror and saw that his father had slumped forward, his head on the secretary's knee.

Toward dawn Felix was able to persuade his mother to lie down for a few hours. He had not slept, though she had insisted he and Angelika go to bed, but he told her he had and she believed him.

Hesso lay so still that Felix several times got up and checked his breathing. His face, with its drawn lip and staring eye, seemed to him pitiful rather than grotesque. He had always been very close to his father; none of those great rifts which give so much material to novelists and alienists had ever opened between them. As he watched by that large, vigorous body, lying as if poleaxed, he remembered mostly Hesso's kindness and good humour, how he had left him with such obvious reluctance at Lehzen, had extricated him with tolerant amusement from his amorous tangles, had waited so patiently for his only son to put aside his irresponsible games and enter upon his great inheritance. He thought that since he had returned from the war, so much more serious and responsible, Hesso had been pleased with him, and for this he was grateful. Once again he got up and touched Hesso's wrist, and carefully dribbled some drops of water between his dry lips.

At his touch the other eye, which had been closed, opened and recognized him. The left hand, which could move, fumbled weakly across the blanket and grasped Felix's arm. Breath shivered in his throat and he made a sound, a croak, a groan, Felix did not know which, but understood that his father was trying to speak to him.

"What is it, Papa?"

Again the shivery breath, the croak. Felix sensed the effort behind it and said soothingly, "Yes, Papa, of course." But this did not satisfy the stricken man. Again and again he tried to speak and failed.

When the door opened and Angelika came in, Felix said desperately, "He's trying to say something and I can't make it out. I can't stop him. He'll wear himself out trying."

Angelika knelt down by the bed and stroked her father's hair. "Rest now, Papa dear. You can tell us later."

"I've tried that," said Felix. "It doesn't work. I'm not even sure he can hear us."

The left eye blinked. "Does that mean you can?" asked Felix. The eye blinked again.

"We'll get Mama," said Angelika.

"She's only just gone to bed. She watched with him all night."

"She's probably in the chapel, praying. I'll go and see. Don't talk for now, Papa. We'll get Mama."

Sophie, wearing a dressing gown, returned with Angelika. She was pale, but showed no resentment at being awakened so soon after going to bed. She bent over Hesso and wiped his forehead with a cloth wrung out in tepid water and said, "Sleep now, my dear. We can talk later."

Did he know that there could be no later, Felix wondered. Again there was that shivery, hoarse breath, that awful croaking sound which conveyed no syllable of human speech. Twice more he repeated it and at last Sophie said, "Can it be something about an appointment, Felix? It sounds like appointment. Did he have an important one for today?"

Felix had almost forgotten that his father had agreed to meet with a delegation of the Red Soldiers' League. From the doctor, who had visited the abbey on Sunday afternoon, and again late in the evening, he knew that Eschenbach was quiet. Hesso's unexpected appearance in the Maximiliansplatz had evidently led many of his workers to have second thoughts about taking over his mills by force. The quiet reminder that it was Easter Sunday had also not been without its effect. Fortunately it was a sunny and warm day. Most of the revolutionaries had retired to the town's outdoor beer gardens to continue their endless debates, and had been invited to share Easter dinner with the millworkers.

Felix knelt by his father's bedside and said, "Don't worry, Papa. I'll see them. Everything will be all right."

The eyelid which could still move, closed. The other eye remained open, staring at the ceiling. Hesso drew a shallow breath, a breath with no effort behind it. "He'll sleep now," said Sophie. "I'll stay with him."

Angelika went downstairs to make sure there would be breakfast for Felix, while he went to his room to dress. At the back of the drawer where he kept his studs and cufflinks lay the bundle of letters he had written to Kitty during the war, and had never sent. They were dirty, ragged at the edges, torn where the piece of string which held them together had cut into the paper. He often looked at them and held them in his hand, but he never untied the string. Sometimes he dreamt that he had gone to London and knocked on her door until a neighbour came to tell him that no one lived there now, that the house had stood empty for years.

He ate his breakfast resentfully, cursing the Red Soldiers' League and the Landeck Steel workers impartially. He would not have cared if they had stood waiting in the square until they grew whiskers to the ground. Meeting them meant that he might never see his father alive again. But he had promised, and of course he must go.

It was a beautiful morning, with a gentle breeze from the south. The trees stood in a green haze, their leaves still in bud.

"Nice day," said the chauffeur as they drove down the straight avenue lined with poplars. Felix was about to agree, but shouted instead, "Look out!" as a muddied and blood-stained figure stumbled in the way of their car. The brakes screeched and Felix was aware of the chauffeur's curses and the dazed figure in the road whom it seemed they must hit. The wheels locked, the car skidded, and the man put out his hand as if to ward it off. They stopped less than an inch from where he stood. He staggered, leaned across the bonnet, and his hand left a damp palm print on the windscreen.

"Here, you stupid sot," the chauffeur cursed, thinking of having to clean up the mess.

Felix got out of the car and caught the man who seemed about to faint. There was no smell of drink about him.

They eased him into the back seat. The chauffeur produced a flask of brandy from the glove compartment, saying that the Herr Baron kept it there in case of accident. Felix did not believe it; it had a cheap, raw smell and was probably the property of the chauffeur.

The man gulped the brandy. He looked familiar, though Felix could not put a name to him. "Brauck," he said. "Foreman, Number 2 rolling mill." He seemed dazed, but though he was spattered with blood, Felix could not see a wound. He wondered where the man had been going; the road led nowhere but to the abbey.

"Were you coming to see me?" he asked.

"Yes," said the man, taking another gulp of brandy and leaning his head against the back of the seat. "They've closed the town, you know. All the roads are blocked. Somebody had to come and tell the Herr Baron what was happening."

"My father is ill," said Felix. "I was coming in to meet with the workers' delegation in his place." He had been too preoccupied before to notice that the road was empty. Easter Monday was by tradition a holiday, and normally it would have been full of people taking picnics to the woods. "What do you mean the town is closed off. Who has closed it?"

"The *Reichswehr*, Herr Baron."

"Are you sure?" Under the provisions of the Versailles Treaty the Ruhr Valley was a demilitarized zone, closed to the German army as well as to the occupying powers.

The brandy seemed to have done some good. A little colour had come back into the man's grey face, and he told his story clearly. The *Soldatenbund* and the steelworkers had elected a delegation as the Herr Baron had suggested, and they had assembled early in the town square in front of the Landeck administration building. Many of the workers not in the delegation had come also, not to riot, simply to be there. Some people had climbed up on the pedestal of Maximilian's statue to make speeches; it seemed, said Brauck, that the members of the Red Soldiers' League simply couldn't see a crowd without at once wanting to make a speech. But it had all been orderly and peaceful. Then the trucks of the *Reichswehr* had rolled into the town, the soldiers had jumped down, and seeing the large crowd had asked no questions but had opened fire at once.

Here Brauck's orderly tale came to an end. Speaking of what those guns had done to a tightly packed crowd at point-blank range, he began to gasp for air as if the memory were snatching the breath from his throat.

The Red Soldiers' League, being armed, had returned fire as long as it could. But the *Reichswehr* had machine guns. "I was in the war," said Brauck; "I thought I'd seen it all. But I've never seen anything like what that square looked like when they stopped shooting." The *Reichswehr* had made wholesale arrests among the survivors, taking even the wounded who could still walk. Brauck had got away through a back garden and a little wood behind the town known as Rehlingwald because of the mushrooms which grew there so plentifully.

"Here," said Felix, "drink the rest of the brandy. I only wish it were a better brand."

At the entrance to the town a truck was drawn across the road and members of the *Reichswehr* stood with drawn revolvers. Felix's chauffeur came to a stop and they surrounded the car. Felix had been in the Prussian army quite long enough to acquire the correct tone for dealing with such things, and it took him no time at all before they backed their truck onto the grass and let him proceed.

The cobbles of the square were red and sticky with blood. The dead lay in the ungainly poses Felix recognized from the war. Women wearing their holiday best were walking among them, staring into bloodied faces, looking for their own.

The cottage hospital had never been meant to cope with a disaster of this size. Supporting Brauck, who could barely walk from shock and brandy, Felix found that he could not even get near the entrance. Wounded men lay or sat in rows amid the primroses and hyacinths of the hospital garden. Some were screaming, some sobbing, but many, though horribly torn, were silent, staring at the blue sky, as if their bodies had ceased to hold any interest for them. Felix had seen such men often in the war and knew that most of them would not live.

He found a spot against a tree for Brauck, moving a dead man to make room for him, then told the chauffeur to hurry back to the abbey to get Angelika and let Felsen, the butler, choose such of the servants he thought might be of use. Blankets, sheets to tear for bandages . . . Angelika would know; she had trained with the Red Cross during the war. It came to him that Angelika too would now not see their father alive again, but he knew well enough from the war that disasters never come singly. "Don't tell my mother," he remembered to say, certain that if Sophie knew what was happening in town she would leave her dying husband in the care of a servant and come to give aid.

Inside the hospital men were packed tightly on every inch of floor, leaving scarcely a passage for the nurses and stretcher-bearers. There were not nearly enough beds for even the most severely wounded. Dr Huch was at work on the operating table; old Dr Mond, so covered with blood as to be nearly unrecognizable, worked on a kitchen table which had been carried into the operating room. "Good God," thought Felix, "I remember his retirement party. I was only a boy." But he could see that the old man's hands were steady and his face calm.

Marit was already there, a drawsheet pinned over her darned, grey dress. She looked up at him with the peculiar, sweet smile which always gave him the creeps, because he knew that she smiled like that at everyone; her family, a dog run over in the street, a drunk vomiting in the gutter. As she bowed her head and resumed her bandaging Felix saw that she was smiling at the bloody hole where a face should have been.

Eschenbach ladies who had nursed with Sophie and Angelika during the war were beginning to arrive. Urchins stood gawking, getting in everyone's way. Felix didn't blame them; at their age he would probably have done the same. All it needed, he saw, was organization. With the phone lines cut the urchins were a positive godsend. He sent them on errands, to the Hill where most of the firm's directors lives, to requisition sheets and blankets and motor-cars; to the Eschenbach Female Academy, which had been used for a hospital during the war, to ask the headmistress to accept the less seriously wounded.

As help arrived Felix was able to set up a proper transport system, put the urchins to work as stretcher-bearers (a task they performed with breathless pride and caution), saw to it that food and coffee were set out on a table where the nurses, and eventually even, he hoped, the two doctors might take a moment's rest and have a bite to eat.

Though all the windows stood open, the place stank like a slaughterhouse. Presently Felix saw Angelika come into the ward, carrying a pile of blankets, followed by the chauffeur with the huge coffee urn they used for parties at the abbey. Behind him was Sophie with an arm full of towels.

He came to the door, took the towels from her, and said, "I so hoped no one would tell you." She smiled at him. "If Hesso knew, he would want me to be here."

"I know," said Felix. "That's why I hoped no one would tell you."

She set to work at once, calmly, as if she had done this kind of thing all her life. Looking up from papers and lists, Felix would catch sight of her and his sisters, snipping sutures, praying with those who had no more use for medical skills, holding bleeding limbs for the searing iron.

As the awful day wore on, seeming to be without end, gifts of food, coffee, and lemonade arrived from the town, and, as the news of the shooting spread, ambulances and doctors came from the city hospitals of Düsseldorf and Cologne, and with them tales of terror from nearly every town of the Ruhr Valley. The *Reichswehr* had fought pitched battles with the Red Soldiers' League, had shot indiscriminately into crowds, and in Essen had opened fire just as churchgoers were coming out into the street after Easter services. Everywhere they made wholesale arrests and were trying the members of the Red Soldiers' League. Executions had already begun.

Like the potbellied, starving children, like the planes burned and the mills pulled down, thought Felix, this too was defeat, but it was worse, for it was not a punishment imposed by a foreign conqueror on a helpless nation; this was German turning on German. No humiliation imposed by outsiders was worse than what they were now doing to themselves.

It was very late before the Landeck family felt free to leave the hospital and go home. Marit proposed to visit the families of the dead, but Felix, his temper wearing thin, reminded her that her own father was dying and suggested she start her charities at home.

Hesso was as they had left him. Frido, who was celebrated for always fainting at the sight of blood, had watched by his bedside, and Felsen had seen to it that a hot meal was waiting. Sophie had hers off a tray by the bedside, but insisted her children eat properly in the dining room and then go to bed.

Felix reminded her that she had not slept for two days and nights, but she waved this aside as irrelevant, as he supposed it was. They knew it was no use arguing with her, so they kissed her and went away. Sophie ate a little of her dinner and drank half a glass of wine, but when Felsen announced Pastor Möwe, she told him to take the tray away.

The pastor apologized for the late hour; he had not felt free to leave the hospital before. Might he say a few prayers? Sophie indicated Hesso with a gesture of her hand. The pastor stood by the bedside and took Hesso's hand. Sophie withdrew to a dark corner of the room, letting the beads of her rosary slip through her fingers, trying not to listen to the Lutheran prayers which were all that would see Hesso into the next world.

She doubted that Hesso could hear them. He had given no sign of recognizing her when she had spoken to him. Only his shallow breath and pulse showed that he was still alive. A priest could have given him absolution and the last rites so long as a flicker of breath remained in his body, but Hesso, despite his wife's unceasing prayers, had never joined the one true church, and now it would be, Sophie feared, very much a matter of sink or swim.

She had done him a great wrong there, she thought. She should have insisted that he become a Catholic on their marriage. But the fact was that he had come into her life like the hero of a saga, with his red-gold hair and laughing blue eyes, and she had fallen in love as foolishly as a shopgirl with a lord, and had been afraid of losing him if she insisted on his joining her church. The match was such an advantageous one that her parents too had been willing to make concessions; the church, perfect as a divine institution, but administered by fallible men, had accepted benefactions and granted concessions as well.

Pastor Möwe finished his prayers, and after a few kind words to Sophie said he must go back to the hospital, but she was to send for him if she needed him, not matter what the hour.

393

Sophie returned to the bedside. The circle of light shone on Hesso's distorted face. Her golden-haired hero. She remembered how, when she had first met him, she had tried, on the advice of her confessor, to remind herself of the skeleton under the smooth, ruddy skin, the hollows in the grinning skull, to remember that beauty is the most transitory of our possessions and only the soul lives forever.

He was so still she could not tell when he stopped breathing. When next she held a mirror to his lips the glass did not cloud over. She touched his wrist but could feel no pulse. She closed the lid over the staring eye, smoothed the distorted lip. In death the face regained its seemliness. The hands she was about to fold on his chest lay cold and limp in hers. She held them for a moment, then placed them in an attitude of prayer. She stood, thinking that as soon as she called her children and the servants, the doctor and the pastor, all would be public ritual and she would never have Hesso to herself again. But though he and she were alone in the bedroom they had shared for so many years, she knew that her own Hesso was gone. A dead body, she thought, ceases to be private the moment its breath stops. The pious disposition of the hands, so very unlike the real Hesso, made the man on the bed seem no longer hers. She rang the bell for a servant to stay with the body and went to wake Felix.

The king was dead. Long live the king.

Chapter 6

Toby returned to Altondale and set himself to woo the miners of Fenton St Bury. The advice had been given in mockery by someone so apolitical he could not be trusted to know the prime minister's name, but Toby recognized it as being good. For the first time in his life he visited the dark part of his future constituency. Once he got started, he found that he had a natural knack for kissing babies, talking to housewives in their kitchens and men in their back gardens. He even began to enjoy it.

His opponent, a sincere but limited man, was disturbed to observe these Tory inroads on his territory. He grew blustery and short-tempered, and tried to bully. The miners, an independent lot, thought he was getting above himself, which did him more harm than all Toby's baby-kissing. Who did he think he was, they asked, looking all the more favourably upon Toby, who had never shown any side at all. He simply reminded them, day after day, of their great contribution to England's victory in the war, and promised them so much jam tomorrow and pie in the sky that he grew afraid of catching sight of his face in the mirror lest he should find the word LIAR stamped on his forehead.

The results of the election proved perhaps only that there are as many dupes among miners as among the rest of the population, but Toby's encroachment on what had been considered a Labour stronghold was noted among the elder statesmen of the party, and he was marked down as a young man to watch.

Toby and Julian moved into the family house on Chesterfield Hill. Julian, who took no interest in domestic arrangements, left the running of the house to the servants, and very poorly run it was. It could not be expected that she should notice the smeary windows and unpolished silver, but surely, said David to Lucas after he had dined with them, she must be aware of the terrible food. Toby was very busy at the House and felt the discomfort of his home only vaguely, without being able to put a finger on what exactly was wrong. His political life absorbed him completely. In his maiden speech he dealt with the disgraceful manner in which England had received back its veterans, instancing a London newspaper of immense circulation, which had not taken back a single one of its employees who had followed their country's call and enlisted in the army. He named no names, but everyone knew that he meant the *Afternoon Clarion*, whose immensely rich and powerful proprietor, Justin Hogg, had written the most fervently patriotic leaders in all of the British Isles throughout the war.

Unless it was a question of bribery or corruption, Mr Hogg's paper did not normally concern itself much with politics. His speciality was the moral lapses of the upper classes. He was of low birth himself, and deeply resented those who found a comfortable place in life awaiting them merely because they had been born into the right cradle. Every day the *Clarion* tattled on duchesses having affairs with butlers, scout-masters falling victim to charming scouts, Mayfair abortionists and embezzlers in fashionable legal offices. He did not mind being sued for libel. His circulation was such that he could well afford the occasional fine, and the fact was that very few people ever did sue Mr Hogg, for fear that additional skeletons might fall from the opened closet door.

When word reached Justin Hogg that a young MP from some Yorkshire village no one had ever heard of had taken him to task in his maiden speech, he sent for the most intrepid of his gossip writers, who signed his column with simple vulgarity: Nemesis.

"Who is this Strafford chap?" Mr Hogg asked. "Anything against him?"

"If there is," said Nemesis, "we shall soon know."

But after several weeks of the most exhaustive research, Nemesis had to admit to his chief that Toby had proved to be that most frustrating of a gossip columnist's nightmares, a man against whom nothing is known because there is nothing to know. He was a *bona fide* war hero, his marriage to the local vicar's blind daughter was the very stuff of romance, and he was rich enough not to be tempted by shady financial transactions.

"I hear the wife's a looker," said Justin Hogg.

"Smashing," Nemesis agreed. "But she's a kid, little Nell from the country. He must have snatched her out of her cradle."

"No sign of a baby?"

"If it was that she'd have had it by now," said Nemesis, understanding perfectly well what was meant by the question.

"Sometimes those sweet young things from the country go on the razzle-dazzle faster than their city sisters," said Mr Hogg hopefully. "Meanwhile you keep an eye out."

"There's her brother, of course. Sir Lucas Ryder's private secretary. Private secretary can mean all kinds of things."

But Justin Hogg shook his head. "We'd better leave that happy pair alone for now. I hear Sir Lucas is in a bad way. If we stir up a hornet's nest and he dies on us, it wouldn't sound too good, hounding our uncrowned poet laureate to death. Besides, it's nothing to do with Strafford. You stick to him and his little country mouse. Nobody is without an Achilles' heel. Something will develop."

Nemesis hoped so. Though he did not tell Justin Hogg, he had a personal reason for getting back at Toby Strafford, for they had met during the war, and it had been an encounter Nemesis had neither forgiven nor forgotten.

Despite a clubfoot Nemesis had been Justin Hogg's most brilliant war correspondent. Wearing a uniform tailored by Kilgour & French, tailors to the Prince of Wales, and staying at a comfortable hotel in Cairo, he had covered the Gallipoli landing with such eyewitness immediacy that he had been rewarded with an even more comfortable hotel room in Paris, from which he and other correspondents were on occasion taken in luxurious staff cars to villages well behind the battle lines to see what war was actually like. On one such occasion he had watched First Battalion, muddy and exhausted after three gruelling weeks in the line, about to move into billets. Nemesis, seeing the opportunity of getting some firsthand accounts of the fighting to pass off as his own experience in the trenches, had asked the staff officer who was shepherding the correspondents for an introduction to their ranking officer. Toby, red-eyed, hardly able to keep on his feet, with all the work of seeing his men fed and housed before he himself might eat and sleep still ahead of him, had looked at the reporters in their gorgeous, clean uniforms as if they were beings from another planet. Then he had begun to laugh. "Oh, it's very jolly," he'd told Nemesis. "Up and over the top, jerry-bashing all day, madmerzell-bashing all night. We like it, don't we, lads?"

The comments made by the "lads" in support of their commanding officer were not something which could be printed in a family paper, and Toby had afterward been severely reprimanded, as had the unlucky staff officer who had let him loose on England's intrepid working press.

Though he practiced a profession which took little account of people's sensibilities, Nemesis was sensitive on his own behalf, and had not forgotten the encounter. He was not an impatient man: no one who lives for spite can afford to be. Keeping in mind his chief's words about country mice going on the razzle-dazzle, he settled back, watching both Toby and his wife, waiting for things to develop.

Julian was lonely and bored in London. Political wives, she quickly discovered, came in two categories, the Lady Bountifuls and the Socials. The Lady Bountifuls knew all about malnutrition and slum-bred diseases. The Socials knew to the last degree who could be helpful to their husbands' careers, who could be used as a stepping-stone, and who, having been of use, could be kicked aside. Julian thought them hateful, and their dinner parties made her jaws ache with an effort not to yawn.

But she soon renewed her friendship with Kitty, which had never entirely lapsed. Kitty had often visited Altondale during the war, and twice Julian had been allowed to stay with Kitty in London, though the permission had been most reluctantly given, for Lady Millicent had found the days when Julian was not with her very long.

As always when Kitty and Julian met, they felt that they had never been parted at all, and at once fell into their endless talks over cocoa or sherry, gossiping and giggling like schoolgirls. The twenty years difference in their ages, which had not troubled them when Julian was ten and Kitty thirty, counted even less now that Julian was eighteen and a married woman.

Kitty introduced her to Popkin's, where Julian found her feet at once, falling in with the crowd the gossip columnists had dubbed the Bright Young Things, who had made it the fashion to take the last tube to Aldgate East, make their noisy way down Commercial Street to the club where they drank very bad, very expensive champagne (not a drop of Pol Roger was wasted on the likes of them), listened to Kitty sing the latest in American songs, and squeeze onto the tiny dance floor to dance the "Camel Walk" and the "Elfreda."

Kitty Snow and Popkin's (somehow the name Temple Bar Club never really caught on) had been an instant success. Mr Popkin, who had a flair for publicity, had found a preacher to work himself up against the desecration of the temple, and had induced two journalist pals to be in the congregation, though they had not been inside a church for so long they nearly forgot to take off their hats.

It was the silly season and their reports were printed; there was a flurry of letters to the editor pro and con, and the night Popkin's officially opened, there were so many Daimlers and Hispano Suizas blocking the narrow street that Mr Popkin had to send out two waiters to direct traffic.

Kitty, suffering from terrible stage fright, but sustained by many glasses of Pol Roger, sang in her husky, broken voice, and her American accent, spidery legs, and flat chest, her short hair and expensive, sleazy Paris rags, were so much in fashion that she soon had her photograph in *Vogue* and her name mentioned regularly in all the best gossip columns. Sons of the peerage (and often their fathers as well) bribed the waiters for a table near the band, and the Bright Young Things, forever in search of something new, imitated her voice, her accent, and even, by dint of Spartan starvation, her figure.

With the Bright Young Things Julian felt at once happy and entertained. They took her up as they took up any novelty. They were puzzled as well as charmed by her, for her blindness set her apart, as did Lady Millicent's formal manners which she never quite managed to shed, so that she seemed always a little distant from them, someone to be made a pet of, to be courted, cajoled, and pleased.

Julian liked their untiring quest for amusing things to do, from the time they dragged themselves from their beds for a cocktail and a late lunch to the small hours when they piled into their fast and expensive sports cars parked outside Popkin's and roared through the early dawn as sleepy navvies were making their way toward the docks to begin their day's work.

Their amusements, recorded in minutest detail by Nemesis and his fellow columnists, were innocent enough; paper chases across London at midnight, pyjama parties, baby parties, the latest in nightclubs, cocktails, and American jazz. But at the time of Julian's arrival their pursuits changed. It was probably a coincidence and mostly due to the fact that Popkin's had made them free of the East End; certainly the suggestions never came from Julian, yet it was at the time that she joined them that it became smart to explore the small foreign restaurants of Soho, their flavours of spices and garlic strange on English tongues, to buy winkles and eels from the costermongers after a night at Popkin's, and to venture into the pastimes of the lower orders, to attend prizefights, cockfighting, and greyhound racing. This last gave Nemesis the opportunity to headline one of his columns: BEAUTIFUL YOUNG WIFE OF TORY MP GOES TO DOGS. Toby, reading it, felt that in coming to London he had left the dear and familiar Julian behind and was now married to someone entirely different and strange. It was exciting, but he was not sure he liked it.

Like the rest of London, David and Lucas followed Julian's progress in the pages of the *Afternoon Clarion*.

"'Beautiful wife of Tory MP goes to dogs,'" David read out loud. "I can't get over it. My little sister."

"I can't wait to meet her. Let's ask her to tea."

Lucas had had a bad winter. His resistance was so low that he seemed scarcely to be recovering from one attack of influenza before beginning another one.

But with spring and warmer weather Lucas began to feel stronger and was once more in a mood to see people. So David rang up Toby, who brought Julian to tea the very next day.

Lucas was startled, almost disconcerted, to find her such a female replica of David. She had cut her hair short since coming to London; it was scarcely longer than David's.

When a strand of it fell over her forehead, she put it back with a gesture that was a duplicate of his.

"How can two people ten years apart in age and not even of the same gender be so much like twins?" Lucas said to Toby.

"It's uncanny, isn't it? I've known them both all my life, and I've never got quite used to it. They're much more alike than Adam and Eve who are twins." He picked up two Greek dictionaries and a number of scraps of paper from a chair and sat down. "What are you working on?" he asked David.

"It's not work; it's a game. We're amusing ourselves by trying to translate bits of the *Greek Anthology*," said David, "and quarreling like Billingsgate fishwives in the process."

"David's an incurable pedant," said Lucas.

"And you think the Greeks were born too long ago to have much notion how to write poetry, so you keep trying to improve on them."

"Are you such a pedant?" Julian asked her brother. "During the war, when we were saving paper, Adam used an old copybook of yours in which you'd translated the *mutis* in *sonum cygni mutis piscibus* as referring to the swan instead of the fish."

"I couldn't have," said David indignantly.

"Adam said you did."

"Then you should know enough not to wash the family dirty linen in public."

Toby, who was munching his way through a slice of Madeira cake, looked up as surprised as if Julian had suddenly spoken Chinese. He knew of course that she had done lessons with her father, but he had never given much thought to the scholarly side of her nature since it meant nothing to him. Lucas too was surprised to find this pretty creature quoting Horace like any bluestocking.

"I like the *Greek Anthology*," said Julian.

Thinking of its pungent graffiti and unabashed sexuality, Lucas said, "Do you know it well?"

"He means," said David, "that it is not a suitable book for a proper young lady."

"I meant nothing of the sort."

"I don't know all of it," said Julian. "Since it had to be read to me, I daresay they left out all the improper bits. What I like best in it is the epitaphs."

Toby, who had seen enough of Lucas Ryder by now to know that there were no forbidden subjects in his presence, emerged from a second slice of Madeira cake and said, "The best epitaph I ever saw was at the Somme. Only it wasn't in Greek, of course. This was near Mansel Copse, David. The Devonshires there defended their trenches to the last man. When our side retook them, somebody put up a board and wrote on it:

> *The Devonshires held this trench,*
> *The Devonshires hold it still.*"

They were all silent for a long moment after Toby finished speaking, then Lucas said, "I don't think even the Spartans at Thermopylae could have asked for a better epitaph." He turned to Julian. "All the same, you seem a bit young for a preoccupation with such gloomy things."

Julian said, "I don't think they are gloomy. They're bleak, because there is no hope of an afterlife in them, but that's what I find so admirable, that they had the courage to face the fact that eternity is nothing, just emptiness. I don't know any other people except the Greeks who didn't invent some kind of a heaven, happy hunting ground, Mohammedan brothel, Tir nan Og, like an eternal consolation prize for having to die. Well, the Greeks faced what they had to face, that when you're dead, that's the end. I think that's admirable."

Toby looked at her, shocked by what she had said. Toby was an empire builder at heart and knew that he had been born into his particular place and time for a specific if as yet undisclosed reason. To believe like Julian was to cut oneself adrift in the universe. He said, "If what you say were true, Julian, why are we here at all?"

Julian did not bother to answer a question so vast and vague. It was Lucas who said, "To create a corner of order in a disorderly universe."

Toby, as an empire builder, felt this to be by no means

402

too large a task for him. "How?" he asked, almost as if he were expecting specific instructions.

"You might learn to write poetry like Sir Lucas," David mocked him. "Art is a supreme agent of order."

"Kindly don't burden me with quite so much responsibility," said Lucas, "though you're right about art, of course. But there are many other ways. You can plant a garden, or make laws. Politics, Strafford, can be an agent for creating order, though it does more often seem to be a great muddler and stirrer-up of disorder." He smiled at Julian. "Marriage—though I speak as an outsider—the founding of a family . . ."

"Which like politics results far too often in muddle and disorder," said David, "though it probably isn't for a chronic celibate like me to cast stones."

It suddenly came to Toby that he was the only married man in the room. There was nothing out of the ordinary about this, yet it made him feel like an impostor, a member of a club, which, if the truth about him had been known, would have blackballed him. The free days of his bachelorhood were past, and for a moment he felt middle-aged and heavy. Then he looked at Julian, who had drawn him away from the easy and familiar life of male companionship, and he recovered his happiness. Julian said, "If I were a man, I would never marry."

Toby was as startled as when he had heard her speak Latin or put forth her views of an afterlife. But now he was hurt as well.

"Dear Julian," said David, noting the look on Toby's face, "you mustn't say things like that in front of your husband." When everyone laughed Toby decided it had all been a joke and laughed too. "It can have its disconcerting moments," he agreed. "This being one of them."

"What would you do with your bachelor freedom if you were a man?" Lucas asked Julian.

"Explore," she said without hesitation. "Walk off the map. Meet cannibals and people who shrink heads . . ."

"Anthropophagi and men whose heads do grow beneath their shoulders," said David, amused. "Why, Julian?"

"Because they aren't suitable," Julian said, and David

knew she meant that they were as unlike Lady Millicent as anyone could be.

"I'd go along with that," Toby agreed, "but as an explorer you wouldn't be meeting them socially, so suitability would hardly come into it."

"Oh, but it's socially I'd want to meet them."

"Really, Julian!"

"I know exactly what Mrs Strafford means," said Lucas. "In fact when I was a young man, I used to travel precisely for that reason."

"I think it was your travel books that corrupted me," said Julian. "Lord Altondale used to read them to me. We both adored them."

"Thank you. But, you know, books were all I ever got out of those journeys. Because the disappointing thing about natives is that they are really very dull."

"Oh please don't say that," Julian said; "I shall have no illusions left."

"Well, I don't mean dull for anthropologists," Lucas explained, "or for missionaries, but dull for people who travel for the reasons you've mentioned, to indulge the anarchic side of their natures. I used to wonder why it was that whenever I finally got to where I'd wanted to be—up the Amazon or in a Bedouin tent, I'd suddenly be so bored there was nothing left but to write a book. Then it came to me. It's because the more primitive a tribe is, the more structured and hedged about is its social life. People tend to think because some natives don't wear clothes they don't have restrictions, but it's really a matter of climate, not of morals. People in primitive tribes lead lives infinitely more circumscribed than any monk's. It's civilization which permits variety."

"From the way you describe them they sound just like us."

Toby protested that modern Londoners were not subject to fetishes and taboos and primitive superstitions.

"Of course they are," said Julian. "Only they call it etiquette. Look at all the fuss that's made about which fork, and who sits where at dinner parties, and all the things you can't say in front of servants. And servants themselves. Why should one class of people have to pick up after another?"

"Someone has to," said David. "You'd soon complain if they stopped."

"Yes, but why not change about every now and then? I used to think at Altondale sometimes what fun it would be if the servants got to sleep late and we brought them tea in bed and made up their fires and cooked for them—perhaps take it turn and turn about by the week."

David, with a mental vision of Lady Millicent emptying slops, said it was a splendid idea. Toby, remembering that he and Julian were going to a dinner party where there would doubtless be a large number of forks and a great fuss would have been made over who got to sit above or below the salt, rather reflectively took Julian home.

"What a surprising sister you have," Lucas said after they had gone. "And what an odd wife for Toby. How did she come to marry him?"

"I don't think she had much choice. Julian should have gone to a university. I know the problems were nearly insuperable. There's her blindness, and there was hardly enough money to educate the boys, but all the same, it's a pity. She had lessons with my father, of course, but I don't know that a purely classical education is enough for a girl. So now she's a little provincial in the big city running around with the most incredibly silly people and imagining that she is seeing life."

"I expect they're the closest she can come to anthropophagi and men whose heads do grow beneath their shoulders," said Lucas.

"I hadn't considered that."

"But really, David, what a wife for Toby! I foresee trouble."

"Yes. He hasn't a clue."

"Perhaps his simplicities will keep him safe."

"They so rarely do that."

That night a very polite young man in most beautifully cut evening clothes appeared at Popkin's, sipped a glass of champagne, and looked about himself with detached interest.

"It was the mercy of Providence," Mr Popkin said afterward to Kitty, "like a voice going off inside my head saying to give him the Paul Roger and not the plonk, because not one minute later our Len—he used to wait tables at Ma Maybrick's so he knows about these things—told me who it was."

The very polite young man had sipped his champagne and had bespoken a table for a party of friends for the next evening. It was against every rule of the club to accept reservations. The competition for tables, and the chance of being stranded in the East End, was part of the excitement of going to Popkin's. The very polite young man, however, was promised the best table near the band without demur.

"A party of friends," said Mr Popkin to Kitty. It was their habit to have a final glass of champagne in Mr Popkin's office after the place had closed for the night. "No names, no packdrill. That's class that is. That's haristocracy for you." Mr Popkin had long since taught himself not to drop aitches, but when excited he sometimes added them where they had no business to be. He poured them both another glass of champagne. "We're going right to the top, old girl. There'll be no stopping us now."

"Our Kitty has danced with the Prince of Wales," said Toby, stopping in at Upper Cheyne Row around teatime. "It says so in the papers."

"Goodness," said David, "there'll be a fearful fuss at the palace. You know how he always fancies older women. And now an American widow singing in an East End club. Can you imagine it?"

"I do hope she'll stop by to tell us all about it," said Lucas.

"I expect she will. We shall feel quite shy." David gave Toby a cup of tea. "I met him once," he said. "The Prince of Wales, I mean. He and the Royal Mum were visiting the hospital when I had my arm bashed up. They used to hide all the really horrid cases in a back ward and put the presentable ones out front. You'd never have done, Toby, with your face done up in bandages, but I, with my arm in a sling and otherwise not visibly damaged, was the ideal wounded hero."

"Did he talk to you?" asked Toby.

"Oh yes, he had a bit of something ready to say to everyone. So did the queen, of course. It was in fact supposed to have been on that very visit that she was said to have asked a man where he was wounded and was tactfully told, 'Mum, if you'd been wounded where I've been wounded, you wouldn't 'ave been wounded at all.' Unfortunately I don't think it can really have happened, because a case like that would definitely have been hidden away in the back ward."

"I heard that story in every single hospital I was in," said Toby. "I wonder if it ever happened."

"Oh, I do hope so," said Lucas. "What is all that noise in the street, David?"

David looked out the window and said, "It's Kitty trailed by the English press."

Hopkins, looking quite addled at being so near someone who had recently danced with royalty, showed Kitty in. They gave her the best chair and a large cup of tea and stood looking at her as if she were made of sugar icing.

"Well, come on, tell."

"Oh, those awful journalists. They're camping outside my door. I'm practically a prisoner."

"David, tell Hopkins to bring up some champagne," said Lucas, feeling that tea was perhaps not festive enough for one who had danced with bachelor royalty.

"Oh no, please, this is fine. I had too much champagne yesterday. Ever since the equerry came to look the place over, Pops was all excited and kept the Pol Roger flowing, and then when *he* actually arrived with his party I thought I was going to faint I felt so nervous, so I drank some more, and then, after I finished singing and the equerry came and said the prince wanted to meet me and would I care to join their party, I drank another glass to make me feel less wobbly, so I'm not going to touch anything but tea all day today. You know how when you're full of champagne you talk a lot and think you're the life of the party and then when you wake up the next morning you wonder?"

Toby said he had often had the feeling.

Kitty, recalling far too clearly regaling the royal party with stories of her suffragette days with Mrs Castlemain, and doing a killing imitation of a singing pupil never quite managing to hit the high note in "O, For the Wings of a Dove," blushed at the memory.

"I'm sure you were wonderful," said Lucas. "After all, he did ask you to dance."

At this a dreamy look came into Kitty's eye. As they had moved to the tiny dance floor and she had placed her hand into the royal palm, she had become as one with every English debutante and shopgirl who had ever pictured herself standing at the altar in Westminster Abbey taking Edward Albert Christian George Andrew Patrick David for better or worse. To her rapt audience she described in some detail the royal ease of his manner, the princely charm of his smile, and the wit of his conversation. He did not sound very much like the vapid young man who had compared the names of French villages with David in the hospital, but David would not for the world have disillusioned her, and when she left them, followed by her tireless journalists, she was still walking on a cloud.

"Goodness," said Lucas, "what an apotheosis."

"Yes. That's something I've never understood," said David. "What is it about royalty? I mean the dull kind we have nowadays. I can quite see being impressed by the ones they used to keep around, like Henry VIII and Elizabeth; there's something fascinating about people who can have your head cut off at a moment's notice. But why are we so taken with these playing-card characters who're no earthly use except to sell Sunday papers? It was just the same when they visited the hospital, and it wasn't just the nurses. The doctors were every bit as smarmy. And really, you know, he's a squit. A nice squit, but a squit all the same."

Toby, who felt that this was not the way to talk about England's future king, refused an offer of sherry to show that he disapproved of David's lèse majesté and said he must go. "I wonder where Julian is," he said. "It's just occurred to me that she said she was going to visit Kitty, but then she would have come with her."

"Perhaps she has a secret lover," suggested David, to punish him for having been stuffy. But Toby only laughed at this.

"You won't get a rise out of me that way," he said. "If Julian had a secret lover, we'd long since have been told all about it in the *Afternoon Clarion*."

Chapter 7

When he waited on her in the restaurant, Danilo called her Signora, but when she came to visit him in his room she was Giuliana, though even this was not really her name.

He wished his room were not so awful. It was directly above the restaurant kitchen, small and hot, and smelled of stale grease. When Giuliana came to see him, Danilo always put an extra lot of scented brilliantine on his hair to hide the smell. This day he had two roses as well. The old woman who hawked them from table to table in the restaurant had given them to him because they were too overblown to sell. "For your pretty signorina," she had said, cackling like the toothless bawd she was. Danilo knew she thought he was Giuliana's lover. So did the other waiters, who laughed approvingly and slapped him on the back, for it was a strongly held belief among them that all English husbands were cold and that it took an Italian to awaken an Englishwoman to the joys of love. Danilo's brother Carlo, who had worked in Soho before him, had told him that Englishmen took no interest in such matters and their wives were starved for love. A warm-blooded Sicilian, Carlo had said, could make a lot of money that way in England. But when Danilo had fallen heir to Carlo's job, he had discovered quickly that in England not only the husbands and the weather were cold, but that the women were very, very ugly.

The Tiberio restaurant was not nearly so grand as Carlo had led everyone to believe. It was in fact a typical small Soho restaurant, with check tablecloths and a very dirty kitchen. Its clientele consisted largely of medical students from a nearby hospital, and Soho tarts, all of whom were too hungry to be fastidious and asked only for large portions at small prices.

Then it was suddenly taken up by a group of fashionable young people who made a lot of noise, left most of the food on their plates, and called everything from the candles stuck into Chianti bottles to the waiters too divine for words, my dear. Danilo knew all about them, for they appeared frequently in the gossip columns of the *Afternoon Clarion*. Danilo, wishing to perfect himself in the English language, read the *Clarion* every day and looked up all the words he did not know in a pocket dictionary. The paper was excellently suited to his purpose, for on the *Clarion* only Nemesis ever used words of more than one syllable.

It was among this group of pink young men, and girls as pretty and vapid as spun sugar, that he had first seen Giuliana. She had turned to ask him for some soda water and the grey eyes in the exquisite face had struck him with a sense of magic and mystery, until with a shock he had realized that she was blind.

For a week or two they came nearly every day, and Nemesis's mention of the Tiberio in his column made it fashionable. The greasy, handwritten menus gave place to large sheets of parchment bound in imitation leather. The price of the dishes was raised twice in one week, while the size of the portions grew smaller by the day. The dishes themselves, however, remained very much the same. White cloths now covered the tables and candles were no longer stuck in empty Chianti bottles but in silver-plated candlesticks. Just as all this was accomplished the Bright Young Things, disappointed in their nostalgic search for something that would shock their nannies, moved on to the Ponte Vecchio down the street, while the whores and medical students, unable to afford the new prices, ate at the Vesuvio. The blind signora came back a few times with her husband, who always asked suspiciously whether a dish had garlic in it, which was silly of him, because all the dishes at the Tiberio had garlic in them. He had a smooth, strange face and cold blue eyes and Danilo did not like him. The blind signora always spoke to him very pleasantly, but though Danilo was ready enough to believe that the husband (a member of Parliament and some day to be a lord, as Danilo knew from his study of Nemesis) was as chilly as an icicle, he was not fool enough to think the signora was shopping for a gigolo, until one afternoon, after she had not been in the restaurant for weeks, one of the other waiters told him she was in a taxi outside and had asked to see him. Lunch was just over, and the waiters had settled down to their own meal. Danilo suspected a joke, but the waiter, smirking, swore on the soul of his mother, and Danilo left his lunch and went outside. She was sitting in a taxi and asked him to join her for a moment. She wore a very plain grey dress, too plain for so rich a lady, Danilo thought, not recognizing the elegant cut of Paris. His heart pounded a little with excitement and curiosity.

"I want you to do me a great favour, Danilo," she said. "I'd like you to come to Popkin's with me tonight. It's a nightclub, and I'm desperate for someone to take me. Can you get off? We don't usually go till quite late. Do please say you will."

Distracted by the clicking of the meter—such a wicked waste of money—wondering what an evening like that might cost, wondering too whether Carlo had after all been right and a whole new future was opening up for him, he said he would be honoured to take the Signora wherever she said. At least, he thought, he had a good suit to wear. His whole family had clubbed together to buy him a suit fit for London. It was a very bright blue with white pinstripes, heavily padded shoulders, and a smartly nipped-in waist.

The blind signora gave him an envelope with an address written on it and said, "Can you come at eleven?"

It was not till the taxi had moved away from the kerb that Danilo realized that the envelope contained a bank note. Stunned, he looked at it. It was all true then. An Englishwoman, not an old or ugly one, but one who was young and very beautiful, wanted him, Danilo, enough to pay for it. It was just as Carlo had promised. England was a country of unlimited opportunity.

The evening itself proved disappointing. He was introduced to those of Giuliana's friends he had not already met. There were the usual pink young men with no chins wearing impeccable evening dress. The most chinless and impeccable was escorting a young woman whom Danilo recognized because she plied her trade on the streets of Soho. Tactfully he pretended not to know her, but she said, "Wotcher, Danny," very loudly and everyone agreed that Mavis was a scream. There were others who seemed not to be part of the group, though it was difficult for Danilo to be certain, except for a pallid man whose escort claimed he was a burglar, and one other who was American and black.

Danilo, who had dreamt of an evening of guilty splendour among the rich, was disappointed when they suddenly went off in a great rush to fling themselves down the steps of the underground and into the last train of the night. They got off at Aldgate East and piled into a taxi which took them down a street of warehouses and riverdamp, to turn the corner into another street, equally desolate, though given an air of spurious wealth by the many expensive motorcars which were parked along its kerb. A dim light hovered in the window of the Temple Bar.

The doorman, greeting most of them by name, admitted them, and Danilo looked around with a feeling of profound disappointment. He had read in Nemesis's column that the Prince of Wales often came here, and had expected something more palatial. They were all jammed around a small table, from where they could watch through dense cigarette smoke the dancers crowded on the floor. Three blacks on a platform played what Danilo respectfully guessed to be American jazz. A waiter brought them sweet champagne, which Danilo innocently enjoyed.

Then the band stopped, the dancers applauded and returned to their table, waiters hurried round with champagne as if to resuscitate them, and there was a great burst of applause. The band began to play again, and a red-haired lady Danilo had not noticed before began to sing in a voice as smoky as the room.

She seemed to be the main reason why they were all here. The club, which had been so noisy only moments ago, was hushed. Danilo did not know what to make of it. He had sometimes gone to the Palermo Opera and knew what singers should sound like. The red-haired lady either suffered from laryngitis, in which case she ought to rest her voice, or she was chronically afflicted, in which case, as far as Danilo was concerned, she should remain chronically silent. In addition to her flawed voice she had neither hips nor breasts, and everyone in Palermo knows that only witches have red hair.

He looked to see what the blind signora made of her, and she, perhaps sensing his bewilderment, leaned toward him and said in a whisper, "That's Kitty Snow. She's a great friend of mine. Don't you think she's wonderful?"

Several people said "hush", as if they had been talking in church.

After the ugly lady had finished, everyone applauded for a long time and said, "Isn't Kitty divine; don't you absolutely adore Popkin's?" and crowded back on the dance floor. Julian said, "Do you like to dance, Danilo?" and put her cool hand in his. Feeling both shy and very happy, he put his arm around her waist and led her into the dance. Danilo loved dancing and spent most of his free evenings with London shopgirls and waitresses in the Empress Rooms or the Kensington Town Hall. He's met some very good dancers that way, but never one who followed him as lightly and sensitively as the blind signora.

"Oh, I love dancing," said Julian when he had hesitantly told her so. "But if you call me signora once more I shall have to call you signor and that would be silly. My name is Julian."

"Giuliana?"

"Close enough. You're a very good dancer yourself, Danilo."

He told her about Saturday nights at the Empress Rooms, and she said, "It sounds marvellous. I'd love to go there. Would you take me one night?" but he could not believe that she meant it.

Later the ugly signora sang again and afterward she came to their table and was so unaffectedly friendly to Danilo that he forgave her for having no hips and breasts.

Though Giuliana had said they were great friends he was not himself sure about that, for he overheard her saying quite sternly something about scavenger hunts and it not mattering when it was things but being wrong to use people. He did not know what she meant, but Giuliana kissed her very affectionately, and said, "Don't be cross, darling. Philippa gets the prize tonight anyhow, with her nice Negro, or do you think Baby Pettifoot's burglar? Of course it's very unfair, her father being a prison governor. Not even a cat burglar, he says. Just smash and grab."

A sooty dawn seeped into the streets when at last they climbed into their marvellous two-seaters, yawning and cross, until someone suggested coffee and scrambled eggs in an all-night ABC. When Julian's taxi left him outside the Tiberio, trucks were watering the streets.

Danilo brewed himself a pot of strong Italian coffee on the gas ring in his room. He could not say that he had particularly enjoyed the evening, though at least it had cost him nothing. The envelope Giuliana had given him was still in the pocket of his suit. The suit, at any rate, had been a great success. All of Giuliana's friends had complimented him on it.

But why had she asked him to the party? She had been very pleasant, but it had been an almost impersonal pleasantness, and at no time had she indicated that she expected anything in return for the money. Still, Carlo had said that English ladies often hid the heats of Vesuvius under an iceberglike exterior, so perhaps she would melt by and by.

"Human scavenger hunt in East End," read Toby out loud. "Julian, what does it all mean?"

She stirred under the silk counterpane embroidered with hundreds of tiny flowers, which always made Toby think of spring meadows at Altondale. "What time is it?"

"Past twelve."

She yawned as daintily as a kitten. "I feel as if it'd only just gone to bed."

"Tell me about this bloody article. Human scavenger hunt. 'Not content with outraging the silence of nighttime

414

London and disturbing the well-earned sleep of its hard-working citizens with their noisy motorcars and screaming brakes, as they scour the town on their childish midnight treasure hunts, the Bright Young Things have now begun scouring London's underside for a human scavenger hunt.' "

"Good Lord," said Julian.

"You may well say so. 'The beautiful wife of our favourite Tory MP arrived at Popkin's escorted by the son of one of Sicily's famous banditti families. Much as we would like to award the prize for the evening to our favourite lady, it must in justice go to the charming daughter of a lady-in-waiting (you will not read about *this* in the *Court Circular*), who came accompanied by an unemployed Negro clarinettist, while the runner-up is without doubt the present-day Lucy Lockit who arrived with a recently paroled burglar in tow.

"'As so often before we note the inventive ruthlessness of the gentler sex, as compared to the pedestrian efforts of the men, who for the most part got no further than escorting members of the oldest and most overworked profession.'"

Business at the Tiberio was slow these days. Two couples made up the lunchtime crowd. At one table two fat women seemed determined to eat their way methodically through the prix-fixe lunch, at the other a pair of lovers held hands and gazed at each other while the spaghetti grew cold on their plates. Danilo, waiting for them to get on with it, retreated behind the coatrack and turned the pages of the *Afternoon Clarion*, which despite its name usually managed to get on the street about noon, so the joint-and-two-veg crowd could enjoy the sins of society with its lunch.

HUMAN SCAVENGER HUNT.

Danilo read it through, a little indignant to be called a member of a banditti family, for his people were, by Sicilian standards, honest. He did not know the meaning of the word "scavenger," and turned the pages of the pocket dictionary he always kept with him in case of emergency. "Scavenge," it said. "To scrape dirt from the street."

He read the article through again, very angry now. The

beautiful, blind signora had regarded him as street scrapings. He looked up and saw that the two fat ladies had finished their meal and were casting longing glances at the *zuppa inglese*. He cleared the table and brought them dessert. His pride throbbed like a boil, and a great feeling of sadness settled inside him. She was the only person he had grown to like since coming to England. Almost, he had dared to think, he might have found a friend.

"Kitty, are you awake?"

"No. Go away, Julian."

"Darling, you must come to lunch with me."

"It's much too early for lunch."

"It's a quarter past one. I heard the church clock strike as I came down Tite Street

"Don't be silly."

"Kitty, please, please wake up. I must see Danilo. If you don't come with me, I'll go by myself and that will cause more talk and Toby is already so cross with me."

Kitty sat up and rubbed her face. "What's the matter?"

"Have you read Nemesis yet?"

"On an empty stomach? Are you crazy?"

Julian handed her the page she had torn from the paper. Kitty read it, getting out of bed and drawing back the curtains.

"It doesn't sound as if he likes you very much," she said. "I'm not sure I do either."

"I don't like *me* very much," said Julian sadly. "It sounds awful, the way he puts it. It wasn't meant to be like that, it was just a silly bet that we could all bring someone—well, someone not quite our sort. It was just meant to be a lark."

"It was a very cruel lark."

"Do you think he's read it?"

"Very likely."

"Oh, Kitty, you do see, don't you, that's why we must go to lunch there. If he looks cross you can tell me and I'll grovel or whatever one does. I do feel awful."

"He may not be eager to see you, Julian."

"Oh dear." She looked so dejected that Kitty hugged her and said, "I'll tell you what, I'll make us a cocktail. It'll

416

make you feel better. Though I frankly don't think you deserve to feel better."

"Oh bless you, Kitty."

"Do you think it's true?" asked Kitty, rattling the shaker. "About the banditti family, I mean."

"I don't know," said Julian, beginning to giggle. "Wouldn't it be absolute heaven if it were?"

Of the two couples in the Tiberio, the fat ladies had departed. But the lovers were still sitting over their coffee, gazing into each other's eyes. The waiters were yawning, wishing they would go too, so they could have their own lunch. Then the door opened and Kitty and Julian came in. The headwaiter slapped a welcoming smile upon his face and escorted them to a table in Danilo's part of the restaurant. Danilo, who had not thought Giuliana would have the gall to come to the Tiberio again, traded his table with the waiter who had the young lovers and owed him a favour. He took from his pocket the envelope with the bank note Julian had given him and said, "When you bring them their change, give the blind signora this."

The waiter went to take their order and returned shortly to tell Danilo that the blind signora had asked for him. He could not refuse the direct request of a customer. Very well, he would hand her the envelope personally. "Signora," he said, his voice as cold as any English milord's.

Julian at once told him how very sorry she was, and he could tell from the look on her face that she meant it. She looked so lovely and so dejected that he could not go on being angry with her. But he did not quite know what to say to her either, especially with the red-haired signora present. Julian, made reckless by his silence, said, "What time do you get off here? Let's meet somewhere. I want to explain properly and I can't do that here."

The red-haired signora looked as startled as Danilo felt. It occurred to him that Giuliana might be mad. In Sicily one knew of course when people were insane: they behaved in a definite and recognizable manner. But in England this might very well not be so. The English were very deceitful, he had been told, and it might be only by such indications as a lady asking a waiter for a rendezvous that one could tell at all.

He looked for help to Kitty, who smiled and shrugged, refusing to take any further part in this particular comedy. It was up to him, and customers being always right, he said, "I shall come to the little cemetery by St Ann's," feeling that the presence of a church might lend respectability to what was not a respectable proceeding. "It is very pretty," he added, forgetting that she would not be able to see it. "Like a garden. There are benches and many people go to sit there in the sun."

They ordered lunch. A gentleman with a limp and a cane came in and was seated, so that there was a sudden air of busyness about the place, a shaking out of napkins and the sound of corks being pulled.

"I will be there," said Julian as they paid their bill, but he still did not quite believe her. When the gentleman with the limp left and the restaurant was empty, Danilo told the other waiters that he did not want lunch and hurried upstairs to put on his good suit. After he had changed he remembered that Giuliana would not be able to see it, but he kept it on nevertheless. He found her waiting for him in the little cemetery, under a flowering bush which dappled her with light and shade. The gentleman with a limp was there too, on a sunny bench on the other side of the cemetery, smoking a cigarette and reading the papers, but Danilo made nothing of this, for Nemesis, for every good reason, never had his picture in the paper.

"I thought you might not come," said Julian. "I thought you might still be angry."

He said politely that he was not and found that it was true. Soon they were talking easily despite his halting English. She asked him questions about his job and he made her laugh with funny stories about his customers. She asked him what he usually did with his free hours in the afternoon. He told her that he went to his room to make himself some Italian coffee—"real coffee, very bitter and strong. Then I read the English newspapers and look up all the words I don't know. You have never tasted such

418

coffee," he boasted. "No one in England has, unless they have visited Italy."

"I'd love to taste it," she said. "I want to taste lots of foreign things."

"I will make you some next time you come to the restaurant."

"Make me some now."

"Here? In the cemetery?"

"No, of course not. Invite me to your room."

Now he was certain she was insane. It was bad enough that an English lady should be sitting on a bench talking to a waiter like any shopgirl, but that she should suggest coming to his room was so preposterous that there could be no other explanation.

"Certainly not," he said.

"You are still angry with me."

"I am not angry. It is only that it is not proper."

"Oh, proper," said Julian, sounding suddenly weary. "If you only knew how tired I am of being proper, Danilo. I've been proper all my life. Can you believe that I spent all my time in a house with a front door for the gentry, a side door for the tradespeople, and a back door for the servants. And no one ever went in or out by the wrong door. I was a lapdog in that house, such a well-trained one. They taught me all the things they thought important, that you may never take a bite out of a fruit, but must quarter it and eat it with a knife and fork, and that if you put the milk in the cup first and then the tea, the heavens will fall and a lightning bolt with smash the family Spode. And of course all one's friends had to be proper. Suitable, they called it. Only there wasn't anyone suitable, just farmers and tradespeople, and my brothers and sisters, who didn't much care to have a lapdog for a friend." She sighed. "You can't think how dull suitable people are. Now that I've got away from Altondale, I want to know all kinds of unsuitable people, and never be proper again."

Danilo had not understood much of what she had said, and for himself he wanted more than anything in the world to be proper, suitable, a gentleman, but he had caught the forlorn sadness in her voice, and because he was often, in

England, forlorn and sad, he stood up and put her hand on his arm. "Come," he said. "My room is very poor and dirty and it smells of cooking oil, but I will make you the best coffee you have ever tasted."

Nemesis put down the paper he had been holding in front of his face and followed them as far as the back door of the Tiberio. He took out a pocket diary and scribbled a note to himself. Not that he intended to make immediate use of what he had seen. This was one pot he would allow to simmer until a suitable moment should present itself to upset it and spill the beans.

In Italy it would not have occurred to Danilo that he could have a simple and uncomplicated friendship with a young, very beautiful woman of so different a class. Yet not since he and his cronies had dived off the quay for tourist pennies had he felt so at ease with anyone. Neither the difference in social class nor in gender seemed to matter when she sat in his one easy chair, sipping the strong, bitter coffee from its tiny cup. Like children they exchanged stories and laughed at nothing very much. They were both, in fact, still very young—barely eighteen—their grown-upness seemed to them scarcely more than children masquerading in their parents' clothes on a rainy afternoon. He was often homesick and found comfort in telling her of his large family; his mother, who moved in a delectable aura of garlic and red wine, for she was a professional cook, his father, who took her wages and beat her, and her many children, whom she berated day and night for being lazy, ungrateful, dirty, worthless, all except the latest, the baby, who was an angel, a cherub, and, naked as a cherub, was permitted to crawl on the kitchen floor wherever she was cooking, piddling like a puppy.

Julian could not picture such a household any more than he could understand life at Altondale Hall or the vicarage, no matter how often she described it to him. The very notion of a priest with a wife and eight children was incomprehensible to him. Julian said, "You are like the Irish-woman in the joke. When she heard an Anglican clergyman addressed as Father, she said, 'Imagine calling the likes of him Father, and him a married man with five children.' "

Julian's friends were devoured with a curiosity as consuming as it was idle to know where she spent so many afternoons. They accused her of having a lover, and when she laughingly, silently, shook her head, they said, just like Toby, "Never mind, I expect we shall read all about it in Nemesis presently."

"I have very special news for you today, Danilo," said Julian, refusing, as she had done for several weeks now, the strong, bitter coffee. Danilo had not grown up in a family of fifteen without having a good guess at what the special news might be, but he was too polite to do her out of the pleasure of surprising him.

"I suppose you guessed when coffee started to make me sick. I know I did. But this morning I went to the doctor and it is now official. Isn't it nice?"

He congratulated her warmly, for he had grown up in a family where, no matter how much the older children were scolded and deplored, a new baby was always a joyous event.

"I think it's nice too," Julian said. "And Toby is absolutely blissful. He bought me a delicious lunch and I couldn't eat a bite of it I was so sick. Of course he wants an heir for Altondale. Oh, but the doctor was horrible, Danilo. How do they stand doing such things every day? How can they bear to get married?"

Danilo considered this. It did not seem to him decent for a doctor to attend pregnant women; it was a business for midwives. Still, this was England, where nothing was ever done properly. "Maybe they don't marry," he said. "Maybe they are . . . "; he made a very Sicilian gesture with his hands, forgetting, as he so often did, that Julian could not see. "Palermo is full of English milords like that."

"Like my brother, you mean. Yes, that would be much nicer for them, poor things. I'd have preferred a woman doctor, I must say, but this one's a Sir Nigel and he's supposed to be frightfully good, so I expect it's all right, really. Anyhow, I don't have to see him again for four heavenly weeks."

When she left he took her, as he always did, down the back stairs, making sure there was no one about to see her. In the street he whistled up a taxi for her, and gave the driver her Mayfair address. On an impulse, because he was so happy for her, he put his head inside the cab and kissed her cheek. *"Felicitazione, Giuliana,"* he said. *"Ciao."*

This, thought Nemesis, was almost too good to be true. The visit to Sir Nigel, *accoucheur* to Mayfair and Belgravia, the celebration lunch at Boulestin's with the husband, the visit to the lover. The beans had been simmering for a long time. They were ready to be spilled.

"Kitty," said Toby, "is Julian with you?"

Kitty, wearing a ratty kimono with a dragon writhing down the back, was only half awake. "No," she said yawning. "Was she supposed to be?"

"Yes." To tell you our news, he almost added, when he remembered.

Kitty looked at the clock on her chimneypiece. "Oh, God, I had no idea. It's awful. I never seem to see daylight any more." For the first time she looked attentively at Toby. "You look sort of rotten," she said. "Are you okay? Don't worry about Julian. She gets around so well, I'm sure she just ran into a friend or the phone rang just as she was on her way out. She'll turn up."

Toby put his hand in his pocket and gave her a strip of newsprint, Nemesis's column, clipped from the *Clarion* and delivered to him by hand at the House of Commons.

Kitty read the first few lines, said, "Oh no," and sat down to read the rest. It was a typical Nemesis production. He began by taking his readers into his confidence, asking them why a beautiful young woman, at the centre of everything smart and fashionable in London society, with a devoted husband who was a rising young MP, should pay frequent visits to the back door of a sordid Soho restaurant. A vexing question, was it not? Lest his readers should be vexed as well as he, Nemesis had undertaken to discover what lay concealed behind the dirty stairs in a room above the kitchen. He described the room, smelling of grease, with no furniture but some wicker chairs, a wobbly table and a bed covered with grey tangled sheets. He had never been inside the room, but he was a good guesser, and the description was close enough.

His description of Danilo was close too, tilted just enough to make him appear a greasy gigolo instead of the nice, shy young waiter who sent home half his wages to his mother every week. On at least one occasion he had publicly escorted the lady in question, and Nemesis did not fail to remind his readers that they had read of this notable event in his column and no one else's. He rehashed a good bit of it, then proceeded to the visit to Sir Nigel, obstetrician to the beau monde, the celebratory luncheon at Boulestin's, the visit (celebratory as well?) to the dingy room in Soho, the kiss in the taxi. He added some moral reflections about the postwar generation's *nostalgie de la boue*, and concluded: "Or is that giving it too much psychological importance? Is it perhaps simply, to coin a phrase, a case of love being blind?"

"Why, the filthy, rotten . . . someone ought to knock his block off," said Kitty, becoming very American in her indignation.

"I did. At least I tried to," said Toby.

"Do you know who he is?"

"Oh yes. I made it my business to find out when he started sniping at Julian."

"I wish I knew. He must have been at Popkin's a dozen times. You describe him to me, Toby, and I'll make Pops take him to the men's room and wash his filthy mouth out with soap. What did you mean, you tried to knock his head off? Why didn't you? Wouldn't he see you?"

"Oh yes. He was very polite, opened the door himself, asked me in, all very proper."

"He's got a nerve."

"He didn't need it. He's a cripple, you see. He wears a shoe with a thick sole on it and walks with a limp. He knew I couldn't hit him. So I just left. I couldn't have brought myself to talk to him."

Kitty was upset by the vile gossip and desperately sorry for Toby, but at this she could not help laughing. "Oh, Toby," she said, her voice shaking, "when will you grow up?"

"I don't see that it's funny," said Toby stiffly.

"No, of course you don't. I think you'd better have a drink."

"Thanks."

She poured him a large double, adding very little water. He drank it straight down and accepted another. She doubted that he was even aware of what he was doing.

"Poor Toby."

He looked down into his second drink, emptied the glass and got to his feet. "Kitty?"

"Yes, Toby."

"All those afternoons, those other times, was she here?"

It had not occurred to her until he asked that he doubted Julian's innocence. Yet the moment he did ask she too began to wonder. "Yes," she said quickly. "Yes, of course she was here."

Even in his distress Toby had to smile. "I hope you never have to lie for a living," he said. "You do it so badly. Thanks for trying, though. That was nice of you."

She began to say, "Oh, but Toby, you can't . . ." but he had already picked up his hat and was on his way out the door.

"Where are you going?"

"Home," he said. "To wait for Julian."

He walked against a strong stream of people returning from work, newspapers under their elbows. He pictured them settling down to their tea, flipping open the *Clarion* to Nemesis's column, reading it to their wives between gulps of tea and chews of bloater paste sandwiches. "Rising young MP. Who do you suppose . . ."

Toby hailed a taxi. He had to get out of the crowd.

The afternoon post still lay on the mat on the floor. A housemaid hastily bundled it together as she heard Toby's latchkey and put it on a tray. The house had a neglected, makeshift air, as houses do when left to the care of servants. Toby had never noticed it before.

No, said the maid, Madam wasn't home yet; no, Madam hadn't said when she would be back, she couldn't say, she was sure. Her eyes never once met Toby's. Of course, he thought, they'd have read it in the servants' hall.

He took his letters to the drawing room and poured himself another drink. The level rays of the setting sun lit up the smeary windows, showed dustmotes dancing in the air. All afternoon, like a man stumbling through a wood filled with traps, Toby had moved a step at a time, not thinking ahead. The drinks he had had here and there had helped keep his mind numb. He read his mail, had another drink, and went upstairs to dress for dinner. He heard the door open downstairs, Julian come into the bedroom, the gush of bathwater. When she did not knock on the door of his dressing room or call out to him he knew that she knew. He wondered who had read it to her.

He heard her say to her maid, "I was sick three times this afternoon, Agnes. Will it just keep on like that?" and the maid's comforting, "Oh no, madam, it's only the first three months they say," and with this his numbness left him, not gradually, as an anaesthetic does, but all at once, so that he doubled over and retched as if he had swallowed poison.

The baby! His mind flinched from the thought as his hand would have flinched from red-hot iron. The baby. Oh Christ Almighty, whose? He thought of the lunch at Boulestin's; it seemed incredible that it had only been yesterday, how happy they'd been, how they'd laughed because Julian hadn't been able to touch the delicious food and Toby, very hungry with all the excitement had eaten it for her, happy, loving, secretly touching hands, touching glasses, Julian saying, "It's funny, but champagne's the only thing that doesn't make me sick," and he'd said, "You shall live on champagne from now on," and she'd gone from that to the greasy room in Soho, to him, to tell him her news. Toby gulped the rest of his drink, which helped a little.

Julian was at the table when he came down. He took his seat and a maid served the soup. She was well trained and self-effacing, but if she had handed the plates walking on stilts her presence could not have been more obtrusive. Julian said, "Did you have a good day, dear?" which had been Lady Milly's unvaried opening of the dinner conversation, and was singularly inappropriate on this particular day, Toby thought, though he took it up gratefully and told her about a debate in the House which had been held weeks ago but gave him something to talk about while the maid removed their untouched soup and served the fish. Toby tried to eat for appearance's sake, but the bite of fish was as dry as paper in his mouth. He poured himself a whisky to wash it down. Julian began to talk about the weather while the maid brought in the meat course. Toby told her they would help themselves and ring when they were ready for the savoury. She said, "Very good, sir," and closed the door with ostentatious caution, as if on the bedroom of someone mortally ill.

Toby said, "Where were you this afternoon, Julian?" His heart pounded in his throat. He caught at a breath. Julian was silent for so long that he thought she would not answer him at all and was at a loss as to how to go on. Then she said, as if she was teasing a child who has asked a silly question, but with a note of threat in her voice she would not have used to a child, "Where did I tell you I was going to be?"

He grew angry at this but only said, "At Kitty's."

"Very well then," Julian said, still with that note of threat, "I was at Kitty's."

"I went there to find you. She hadn't seen you."

"Why did you want to find me?"

He took the strip of newsprint from his pocket and laid it on the table. She put out her fingers and touched it.

"Was that where you were this afternoon, like all those other afternoons when you said you were going to Kitty's?"

He could not read her blind face, but the threat was very clear in her voice when she said, "You must not ask so many questions, Toby. Other faithless wives can say they were at an art gallery or a dress show or at the cinema. But none of those will serve me."

"You admit then that you were faithless."

"You've never put me to the test, Toby. I should have thought today it's for you to have faith in me."

As she spoke he found himself overcome suddenly and very strongly by a conviction that if, even now, he said he trusted her, if he asked her pardon for having for a moment believed Nemesis's foul slander, love would be born between them—not the kind he had felt for her till now, which was only a mixture of lust and pride of possession—but another kind, the kind that is spoken of in the marriage service, full of fear and amazement.

And let her make a fool of me over and over again, he thought, the complaisant husband, always the last to know, and with this pain overwhelmed him and he said helplessly, "Oh, Julian, why did you do this to me? I loved you so much, more than my life."

"But not quite enough to give me the benefit of the doubt," she said and stood up. "The smell of this food sickens me. Let's go into the drawing room." It was, Toby thought, as if she had said, "You sicken me," as if he had failed some secret test, and judgement had been passed upon him, which was ridiculous. It was not he, after all, who was the guilty party.

She lay back on the sofa, and when she spoke again he knew from her quiet voice that she was very angry now. She said, "What now? Have you already made plans of how to dispose of me? Do you want to divorce me?"

He had thought about this during the afternoon and had his answer ready. "I do want it, more than anything in the world. But I never shall. I could never bring myself to name your lover in open court."

"'A perturbation of scullions,'" she said. "That's really what's bothering you, isn't it, Toby? If it had been someone of your own sort, an old Etonian, a member of your club, it wouldn't be nearly so bad. It's your pride that's hurt."

He was about to protest that it was not true when she got up and said, "I feel so sick," and quickly left the room, giving him time to reflect on her last remark, and in the silence of the empty evening, have to admit that it was true.

When she came back she said, "Sorry, it couldn't wait." He helped her to lie down again and offered her a drink from his glass. She shook her head. "It makes it worse."

"Who told you about it?"

"David. That's where I was this afternoon, being lectured and reproved for my sins. Odd, really, coming from David with his lover dying upstairs. One wouldn't think he'd be at all the person to defend conventional morality. And all the time he wanted to be with Sir Lucas. I could hear him thinking, Oh the wicked waste of time, but he did his duty as my brother and your friend."

His mind was worn with running in circles, and drink had slowed him down, so it was a moment before he took in what she had said. Then it made him blindingly angry. "Julian," he said, "you are never to say that about David again. I know that crowd you run about with thinks its smart to make remarks like that, but it's not true and if you ever say it again . . ."

"Say what?"

"That Sir Lucas is David's lover," he said, reluctant even to put it into.

Julian could not help smiling. She said, "I'm sorry, Toby. Of course I won't say it again if it upsets you. It simply never occurred to me that you didn't know."

"There is nothing to know."

"Oh, Toby, how can you say that? How can you be in the same room with David and Sir Lucas and not know they're lovers? How do you manage not to feel such things? If you walked into this room tonight, wouldn't you sense anger and hate and violence? How can you not sense what is in Sir Lucas's house? The air is filled with it, tenderness and attention and pain, all the things that make up being in love."

"Don't be vile, Julian. You are talking about your brother and my best friend."

They heard the maid clear the table in the next room and were silent until she had gone away. Then Julian said, "All right, Toby, I won't talk about them any more. But how can you say that you love people, David or me, when you never take the trouble to know who we are?"

"I certainly didn't know who you are," he said bitterly.

"You still don't."

She looked so frail and beautiful, and he suddenly felt that he could not bear to be in the same room with her another moment. Every word she spoke was a toad leaping from her mouth. He said, "I'll ring for your maid. I think you'd better go to bed. I'm going out for a bit."

He drank in various pubs till closing time, and after that in those clubs where one could buy membership for a few shillings after hours. Drink, he knew from the war, would blunt the pain, and there was nothing like a hangover the next morning for taking one's mind off one's troubles.

The faces around him were growing blurred. Soon, he thought, he would be able to sleep. Yet he had a sense of something incompleted, a duty left neglected. David, that was it. Julian had insulted David. It was vile, what she had suggested. Just because she herself was vile she could not see anyone else . . . it wasn't true about David. And yet, a thought wriggled like a worm in his brain; there was that friendship with Lord Anthony. Everyone at Eton had known about Anthony Fielding; he was practically the school whore. He had spent holidays at the vicarage and David had stayed at Frome; they had shared a house in their last year at Oxford. And what about the week's leave David had spent with Lucas Ryder in '17 before going to Altondale? He had not told anyone, and had asked Toby to lie for him. Would one do that if one was just someone's secretary?

He began to laugh, or perhaps he was crying; he couldn't be sure which. This day had certainly made a clean sweep. He had lost Julian and David both.

He ordered another drink. Might as well get blind. David would see to the battallion. Good chap, David. Sober chap. Doesn't get squiffy. Does other things though. Disgusting things.

"Hold on," said Toby to his empty glass. Odd that it should be empty; he'd only just ordered it. "Waiter, here, let's have another, a double." Not fair, accusing a chap, not giving him a chance to tell his side. Innocent till proven guilty. Go see David. Give him a chance to exonerate himself.

Drink always brought out the prefect in Toby. He put money on the table and staggered out into the street. The cool air made him feel drunker at first, the it blew away the fumes. A taxi slowed down beside him, but he waved it away. He would walk to Chelsea and arrive with a clear head.

It was a long walk and sobered him somewhat, though not quite enough to cause him to abandon his errand. A clock struck two as he reached Upper Cheyne Row. The street was silent, but in Lucas Ryder's house the lights were still on, shining through a second-storey window.

David himself answered the door, and stepped aside when he saw it was Toby. He took Toby's coat, saying the servants had gone to bed, except Robinson, who was with Sir Lucas. Toby looked around a little dazed and said he hadn't realized it was so late; he was sorry.

"It doesn't matter," said David, who had seen Toby like this before.

"Do you want a drink?"

"Please. Anything."

That David should be so unemphatically the same seemed strange to Toby. Indeed this particular David was a very familiar one; he looked as he had in the trenches when he hadn't slept for a week. Toby, who had not thought he would ever be able to bring himself to mention the name of David's lover, said, "How is Sir Lucas?"

"Very bad."

"I'm sorry."

It seemed even to Toby, who had had a good deal to drink, that this was not the time to confront David with what he knew. Instead he said, "David, is there much gossip?"

"Gossip? Oh, about Julian. I don't know, Toby. I haven't been out in some time."

"I'm sorry. One forgets other people have troubles too."

"They seem to be piling in on us rather. Ask Kitty; she's very thick with Julian's crowd."

Robinson came into the room. David looked up. Robinson said, "I'm sorry to disturb you, sir, but Sir Lucas is awake."

"Thanks Robinson. I'll be right up." He looked bleakly at Toby and said, "I'm so sorry, Toby, but I have to go. I shouldn't worry about the gossip too much, you know. That crowd has a mind like a mayfly. Everything is a one day's wonder. Tomorrow someone will find a dismembered body in a trunk or an actress will elope with a duke, and they will have forgotten all about Julian."

It seemed to Toby, in his maudlin state, very touching that David, in his own great distress, should try to console him. He would have said so, but stumbled over a word, and David stopped him, saying. "I'm sorry, Toby, I must go. Come back soon and we'll have a proper talk. Or if you don't want to go home, you could stay here. Robinson'll look after you."

"No, thank you," said Toby, very stiff and dignified. He might be drunk, and he might be maudlin, but he was not about to be a guest in a household where unnatural vices had been practised.

Robinson brought him his coat and held open the front door. Toby turned to say goodnight. David was standing on the half-landing, where the light threw his face into vivid relief. Toby saw that like an actor preparing for an entrance, he had, going up the stairs, put on a new face. It was another face with which Toby was very familiar, and knew it to be, of all David's faces, his most mendacious. He had worn it always as he had turned from the top of the scaling ladder to wave his platoon into the fire of the German guns. It was a face which said that God was in his heaven and David Harvey hadn't a care in the world.

"That was Toby," said David, seeing Lucas awake. "He wanted to know if there was much gossip. He can be extraordinarily naive at times."

Lucas, whose eyes had been on the clock, looked away. It was nearly an hour till his next injection, and he did not like to be caught watching.

At first he had approached the necessity of morphia injections with his usual interest in any new experience. He and David had read *Les Paradis artificiels* and De Quincey's "The Pleasures of Opium," and for a time the pleasures had been very real. The days had slid in and out of one another with gorgeous reveries hidden in their folds. Lucas had dreamt of balancing without anxiety on catwalks ending in mid-air, bestriding mountain crags as if he were held aloft by wings, and loveliest of all, riding among boys cantering their horses in the spray at the edge of the sea, watching him with smiling, welcoming eyes. At such times he had been overcome with a memory of sensual sweetness he had not known since an impudent boy-actor dressed as Romeo had laid a painted mouth on his.

But the drug was of dreams and the disease was real. Soon he was again mere sinew and gristle of pain, and his dreams were of voracious rats in an agony of starvation gnawing his bones.

"Do you want your injection now?" David asked, seeing Lucas's eyes return against his will to the clock.

He nodded, watching David's preparations with impatience and a terrible sense of irritation. When the pain had eased enough to allow him to talk, he said, "Why have I left it so long?"

David had no need to ask what he meant. "Because," he said, smiling, "you have more curiosity than the elephant's child and cannot bear the idea of not being around to see what happens next."

Lucas managed a smile. "True. No longer true. I think I am at the end of my curiosity. I have the answer to my final question at any rate. I used to wonder how brave I'd be when it came to the point. Well, now I know."

"Purely physical courage," said David, who happened to have a great deal of it, "is the most valueless of qualities. On a matter of principle I can see you put your hand in the fire more readily than most."

"Can you? That's generous of you after these last weeks with me. But there's no principle involved here. There is no point in hanging on. The only thing is—I've been thinking about it, David—I don't want to die here. I want to go back to the Dower House. I want to look out the window over the estuary once more and watch a gale sweep in from the sea."

David could not imagine how Lucas could possibly survive such a journey, but he only said, "Of course, my dear. I can't guarantee a gale, but we'll go back to the Dower House if that is what you want."

For several weeks Toby was incapable of thinking about the future. He had had a great shock and went about protected by a numbness that almost made him feel as if he had died and the nightmare of Julian's infidelity was happening to someone else. Julian, with one swift cut, had severed him not only from herself, but from his daily manner of filling his time. He avoided old friends, the House of Commons, and his club. For the first time in his life he was without props. The clocks in his house ran down and he did not wind them.

Julian's life seemed scarcely to have altered at all. She did not go out as much as before, for she still felt sick much of the time, but her friends proved surprisingly loyal and spent hours in the house on Chesterfield Hill, chatting, playing bridge or the gramophone, rolling back the rugs to dance. If Toby happened to come home while they were there, he entertained them with scrupulous courtesy, making a fourth at bridge, mixing cocktails, winding up the gramophone. It was, Julian thought, as if they were a hair shirt he was making himself wear, and once she said to him, "I do wish you wouldn't behave as if my friends were the labours of Hercules."

She waited for him to say, "Cleaning the Augean stables," but he did not answer her. He only spoke to her when there were other people present, and except for the fact that in all that time he was never entirely sober, he gave no sign that he was in pain. Nannie and Eton, Sandhurst and the army had trained him well. He was safe inside his carapace of manners.

Julian thought, If I live to be seventy, will it go on like this for another fifty-two years? For at eighteen she had not yet had the chance to learn that nothing goes on for very long.

She had been angered and hurt by his readiness to believe Nemesis's accusations, playing judge and jury with no presumption of innocence for her. But she was not in love with him and was therefore not hurt nearly as much as he;

she was willing now to stop punishing him, to tell him the truth, but he gave her no chance.

Still, there was one way she had always been able to get around Toby, ever since the first time in the woods of Altondale, she had only to put her lips in his palm or stroke up the short hairs at the back of his neck, and he would whimper to have her like a puppy locked out of doors.

He had not touched her since the day he had read about her and Danilo, but she did not think she had lost the power to trouble him. Her pregnancy had not yet begun to show, and though she had enough sense to put little trust in her friends' lavish and constant compliments, she trusted the authentic note of envy in their voices when they told her she had never looked more beautiful.

She was not much in the mood for it—she rarely was. Since she had been pregnant, she felt less like it than ever, but the prospect of going on with Toby in this awful, polite silence was even worse. He was sitting by the fire, a little muzzy with drink, and she could hear him turn the pages of a newspaper. She went up behind him and slid her arms around his neck. For one moment he sat perfectly still, his breath caught in his throat, then he got up and put her aside, slowly and carefully, his arm trembling with the effort not to thrust her across the room. She understood then that she had become his Augean stables, and that he would not trouble himself to clean them.

Judging by the letters from home, no one in Altondale was aware of the gossip about Julian. The *Clarion* was not the kind of paper either the Strafford or Harvey families would read, and none of them moved in the kind of social circles where such gossip would be a staple of conversation. Algy must have known, though he gave no sign of it except to say to Toby that the weather had never been worse and Julian was looking pale; why didn't Toby take her away for a bit to the Montefiore's little villa on the Riviera.

Toby, who had been too numb to take any action, accepted this solution gratefully. He had not the making of a hermit and knew he could not go on forever without his background of clubs, the House, and old boys, and that the best way to stop gossip is simply to remove its object.

Julian did not protest. She said, "I am your wife. You may move me about, like a parcel." This was true but he wished she would not say such things to him.

The villa was not little, but like all Sir Abraham's belongings was lavish and beautiful. The weather unfortunately was as cold and damp as it had been in London, and the chimneys smoked. It was not very comfortable or interesting for Julian, but she did not complain.

Toby was scrupulous about visiting her whenever the House was not sitting, but bored and lonely as she was, she could never decide whether his visits were any better than being left to the conversation of French servants.

The baby came several weeks before it was expected, and Toby was not there the night his son was born. He arrived two days later with an English nursery nurse and Nannie. Nannie had not been his idea; she had been a terrible nuisance on the journey, and without speaking a word of French managed to set Julian's servants by the ears in no time at all, but Toby knew that Nannie with her mind made up could not have been stopped by a regiment of dragoons, and resigned himself to a force of nature he could not alter.

Julian had had a difficult birth; the French doctor had been gallant but not very competent, and Toby, looking in on her, saw that she was too exhausted and feverish to talk and left her alone.

He would have liked to put off seeing the baby. For eight months he had wondered what the child would look like, or whether he would even be able to tell at first glance. He had never mentioned these thoughts to Julian, who could have reassured him, but when the French nurse Julian had hired pulled aside the blanket, Toby laughed out loud with happiness and relief, for there, like a wrinkled and angry orange, with fuzz as pale as old-man's-beard plastered to his pulsing skull, lay an unmistakable Strafford baby. "He is very ugly now," said the nurse with the realistic detachment of the French, "but that proves nothing. Many ugly babies grow up to be very handsome men."

"What did she say?" asked Nannie suspiciously.

"That he is very ugly."

The baby appeared to resent this. He screwed up his face, showed his toothless gums, and began to yell.

"Well, if that isn't foreigners all over," said Nannie. "He's a beautiful baby, and just like you, Master Toby. I had you from the month and I remember it as if it were yesterday. Such a trouble you always were."

"Do you think he's hungry, Nannie?" asked Toby anxiously. "Shouldn't he be fed?" He put his finger into the baby's palm. As if soothed at the touch, the gaping dotard's mouth closed, the lids grew smooth and he went to sleep.

The next day Toby visited Julian. She was better then, though her breasts were swollen and ached. She asked to have the baby brought to her. Toby said a trained nurse was looking after it.

"Why won't they bring him? Is something the matter with him? Is he deformed?"

"No. He's a healthy, fine baby. But I think it will be easier like this."

"How do you mean easier?"

"For you. Like this, with a nurse looking after him. Otherwise you might grow fond of him and miss him when we take him home."

She would not have believed it of him. Not the cold, patient cruelty which had planned this punishment for her during all the months of her pregnancy.

She did not mind very much about the baby itself. When she had first discovered that she was pregnant, it had seemed exciting, and she had been pleased because Toby had been so happy. But in her exile, as her waist thickened and she continued to be sick straight through the nine months, she had grown resentful of this usurper of her body, and after the long and agonizing birth, when the midwife had said, "It's a little boy," she had turned her head aside, thinking only, "Well, Toby's got his heir."

"You're taking away my baby?" she said, but it was his cruelty which made her throat and eyelids ache with tears she had never learned to shed.

"It is my baby too," Toby said.

To ease the pain in her throat she became cruel as well. "Oh, is it?" she said lightly. "I didn't quite like to ask.

436

But I might have known. If he'd been born with a head full of black hair scented with grease, and a little black moustache, he would hardly qualify to be brought up at Altondale. And how do you plan to dispose of me, Toby? Am I to return with Nannie and—what's his name, by the way?" During their celebration lunch at Boulestin's, Toby had said that David must of course be godfather.

"Augustus, I think."

"Not David?"

"Certainly not."

At this Julian began weakly to laugh. "Oh God, Toby, you *are* funny."

He did not reply to this. "Algy and Rachel have asked me to tell you that you can consider this your house as long as you like. But I think it would be best if we found you one of your own. We can say you are staying on for your health. There are some very pretty houses here. There is one I particularly like except that it's painted a ghastly shade of cyclamen, but that needn't bother you."

"It would, now that you've told me. So you mean for me to keep away from England."

"I think it would be best."

"What if I simply buy a train ticket and come home?"

"I'm sorry, Julian; I'm afraid I can't afford to have you do that. Your behaviour in England has not been exactly a help to a rising politician."

"I don't think I care very much about your political career, you know."

"You've certainly demonstrated that. If you don't care about my position, you might think about yours. If you come back to England, I will be obliged to divorce you. It would be a great scandal, which would do neither of us much good. On the other hand my father's not going to live forever. Perhaps you would prefer to be Lady Altondale with a good allowance on the Riviera rather than a divorced vicar's daughter living in a dingy room in Earl's Court."

"A remittance woman," said Julian, amused. "That really is funny. I'm afraid I shall be a very expensive one, Toby."

"The lawyers will arrange all that. I don't think we'll

have occasion to meet again, Julian. I'll find you a house and a reliable staff before I leave. Good-bye."

She said, "Good-bye, Toby." A strand of hair had fallen over her forehead, and she pushed it back with the gesture that was David's. Toby left the room, shutting the door quietly, then quietly went to the lavatory and was sick.

Chapter 8

A gale had stripped the garden of the last of its autumn flowers, but David found two overblown roses still dangling from the bush in the sheltered corner of the kitchen garden. He broke them off to take to Lucas.

They had been at the Dower House for more than four weeks, ever since the day after Toby's drunken visit to Upper Cheyne Row. The journey from London, over bad roads, had been worse than anything David had imagined. He still could not bear to think of it; it was as if Lucas's pain had left a bruise on his mind. But the moment Lucas was installed in the dowager's great bed, with its view of the estuary, and gulls tossed on the autumn winds, everything had suddenly come right.

Lucas had slept all that night and had awakened to see David sitting on the windowsill, looking out at the sunny tide. "What time is it?"

"After nine."

"Good heavens. I haven't slept like this in months. When did I have my last injection?"

"Yesterday evening, around seven," said David, who had checked Lucas's breathing many times that night, fearing that the trip might have been too much for him.

"I don't feel any pain," said Lucas, puzzled. "I ought to be screaming the roof down. In fact I don't feel anything at all."

David came to the side of the bed and touched Lucas's knee through the blanket. "Can't you feel that?"

"No. Nothing."

"I daresay it's temporary," said David, not knowing what to make of it.

"Good God, I hope not."

Dr Timberlake, who came in shortly after this, did tests with pins and patella hammers, and assured Lucas that his paralysis was indeed permanent. The disease had begun to attack his spinal cord.

"I knew something marvellous would happen," said Lucas, "if I came back to the Dower House. This place has always brought me luck." And though both knew that it must be the last step of his physical deterioration, David and Lucas had embraced, half laughing, half crying with relief.

The sudden freedom from pain was so exhilarating that Lucas scarcely resented the humiliations of a body which had to be handled and cared for like a helpless infant's. Though he would never allow David to be in the room when Robinson bathed him and changed his linen, he was in a good enough humour to see the joke in his present condition.

"You always make me feel like a roast being larded for the oven," he told Robinson, who was rubbing his heels and elbows with oil.

"Not larding," said Robinson. "Larding is weaving suet in and out of the meat with a big needle. You wouldn't like that."

"The things you know. Has Mrs Placid been giving you lessons?"

Robinson turned red. "Slim pickins you'd be," he said, "suet and all."

Lucas, looking at his body with a mixture of disgust and detachment, thought that in the manner of medieval monks who had slept in their coffins to remind them of their mortality, he these days had the reminder of it by inhabiting his skeleton. No one had been careless enough to leave a mirror near him for a long time now, but he could guess what he looked like; a shrivelled old ape, compounded of curiosity and rue.

"It's odd," he said to Robinson; "I look at myself and

think, this isn't me, when after all, what could be more intensely me than my own skeleton."

"Bones last longest," said Robinson, mistaking the remark as a request for reassurance. "'undreds and 'undreds of years." He shook several books out from the covers and stacked them within arm's reach on the bedside table.

Free from pain, Lucas had been able to stop taking morphine, and though this had made him for a time extremely cross with anyone who did not have the wits to keep away from him, his mind was once again clear, he was able to read, and spent his days happily going through all his favourite books. When his eyes gave out he and David played cribbage, a game to which Lucas brought the ethics of a Mississippi riverboat gambler and a talent for addition which left David thousands of pounds in debt.

"You're as bad as Quilp," David told him once, after Lucas had achieved a very unlikely score by adding his cards backward and upside down as well as forward. "I'm obliged to tell you that he died by drowning in a very dirty part of the Thames and was buried at the crossroads with a stake through his heart."

When it turned out that Lucas had never heard of Quilp, David fetched a copy of *The Old Curiosity Shop* and read him the description of Quilp's cribbage party.

"I had no idea it was such a funny book," said Lucas, laughing. "I thought it was all treacle and the death of Little Nell."

"Well, the death of Little Nell is fairly funny too."

"Yes. Oscar used to say you had to have a heart of stone not to laugh at it."

Dr Timberlake, coming up the stairs and hearing their laughter, wondered how long it could go on, for he was of a cautious temperament and believed that laughter in the morning is inevitably followed by tears before bedtime. Once, when David had said to him, "It's like a miracle," he had looked so grave that David had added, "I realize that it's bound to be a very temporary one. What do you expect next?"

"I don't know," said the doctor. "Any number of things

can happen. If he lasts till winter, which I doubt, it will be worse than last year because his resistance is even lower. He'll get pneumonia where someone else would get a mild cold. That would be the kindest way."

"What are the unkind ones?"

"One can't tell. His heart's sound; that's the devil of it. It might attack anywhere, kidneys, lungs, brain . . ."

"Yes," said David, "I see."

Yet, in spite of everything, their sunny mood continued. Lucas, like a miserable scholar left behind in class, embraced the freedom which comes when there is nothing left to be done. It was not, he once said to David, a situation which would yield to an earnest approach, so why bother? David, drawing on the discipline he had learned in the army, living a day, even hours at a time, agreed and did his best to match Lucas's mood. But his insomnia came back as bad as it had been after Passchendaele. Once again he could not trust himself to his dreams.

When Lucas started to have headaches, ran sudden high fevers with exhausting fits of vomiting, David remembered Dr Timberlake's warnings, but it took him nearly a week to gather up enough courage to take down Sir Noel Ryder's book entitled *Diseases of the Brain*. When he reached for it with a hand that was not quite steady, he found the pages marked with a piece of dried-up orange peel. He rang for Robinson and showed it to him. "When did this happen?"

"Thursday, sir. When you went to Rye to the dentist. Sir Lucas told me to bring him the book."

"And you had no more sense than to do it! Bloody hell, Robinson, can't I even have a toothache without something like this happening? Why didn't you simply refuse? He couldn't get out of bed and chase after you, you know."

"Yes, sir," said Robinson, his aggrieved look seeming to add, "How often have you refused him anything?"

"Sorry," said David. "It's not your fault, I know. Here, get rid of that damned orange peel. I suppose you've read it all too."

"Very long words, sir," said Robinson, refusing to commit himself further.

Dr Timberlake had no more to say than Robinson, which

David understood to mean that there was nothing to be done and nothing to be gained by talking.

Yet, in the unpredictable way things happened now, the fever went away and for the last week Lucas had felt well, so well that he had suggested they ask Jago Portman, who was riding a great wave of triumph for his recent production of *King Lear*, with himself in the title role, to come to tea and tell them all about it. Jago accepted and promised to bring them all his press clippings. "He says," David told Lucas, coming back from telephoning, "that it is a *succès fou*."

"The English language is plainly inadequate to express just how *fou* it is," Lucas had said, amused at his old friend running so true to form.

David carried the two wind-tossed roses to the kitchen where Mrs Placid was baking scones for Jago's tea. She looked at the roses and said, "Who'd have thought it, after last night's storm," and wiping her hands on her apron went to get a vase for David. He gave her the roses and saw that his hand was sticky with blood where the thorns had made deep gashes in the palm. He had felt no pain. This kind of thing happened to him constantly these days; he often found cuts and great bruises on his body without knowing how he had come by them.

Lucas, who had felt well all day, with only a slight headache to remind him of his condition, was looking out over the estuary. A copy of *King Lear* lay on the counterpane. "Roses?" he said, smiling at David. "After last night's storm?"

"I expect they're the last. A bit blowsy, but yes, roses." He put them where Lucas could see them easily and picked up *King Lear*. "Act I, Scene II. You didn't get very far."

"I can't keep my mind on things the way I used to. When I made that very injudicious remark about wanting to be a chronic invalid, I thought how nice it would be to lie in bed and read all day without being accused of sloth. It didn't occur to me that I might ever have trouble with my eyes. The lines run into each other."

"I expect you need new spectacles," said David easily.

After having been open with one another for so long, they had arrived at evasion at last.

"Or else it's *Lear's* fault. It's not an easy play to like. That nasty old man does so richly deserve every beastly thing that happens to him, it's hard to feel sympathy for him. Besides, you know, Shakespeare doesn't matter. The important thing is, have you studied the press notices?"

"Yes," said Lucas, "I think I've got those by heart."

The West End had not seen a Shakespeare production since the end of the war. Popular sentiment held that after four years of squalor and fighting, people wanted to enjoy themselves. Jago, taking serious counsel with himself and his looking glass, and coming most reluctantly to terms with the fact that his days as a perennial and melancholy under-graduate had best become a thing of the glorious past, decided to take the horrible plunge into old age by acting the nastiest old man of them all.

Everyone who knew anything about Shakespeare, the West End theatre, or the spirit of the times, had prophesied disaster, and the end of Jago Portman's career. Like someone planning to leap off a bridge to make everyone sorry, Jago would have half welcomed a debacle, but the other half was too professional, talented, and ambitious to permit it. The doubters and prophesiers of disaster were confounded by Jago's triumphal entry into senility. His *Lear* became the play to see; it was the high point of the London season.

"Such a pity men don't do women's parts in Shakespeare anymore," he said to Lucas after having repeated every single rapturous press notice he had received. "I'd adore doing one of the wicked sisters. Goneril, or better yet, Regan." The actor's eye devoured the mise-en-scène; the dying man on the bed who could still laugh wholeheartedly at the feat of memory which allowed his old friend to recall every favourable notice he had received since he had toddled on stage disguised as an elf at age three; the way everything in the room was placed within the eye's and hand's reach of the man on the bed, who had no need to reach for anything, his every wish being anticipated with unfussy readiness by David and Robinson.

No amount of money, only love, Jago thought, could command such unfailing unobtrusive attention. For himself he had early in life opted for the chillier winds of public adulation and had never regretted his choice, but a good deal of that adulation had come Lucas's way as well, and Jago could not help thinking jealously that it must be very nice to be unfailingly able to eat your cake and have it.

"I think you would make an excellent Regan," said Lucas, a comment Jago chose to take as a compliment. "Do please eat those scones. Mrs Placid made them especially for you. With *Lear* it won't matter if you put on a few pounds."

"Alas," said Jago, who had persuaded the costume designer to dress him in very exiguous tatters for the scene on the blasted heath, thus allowing him to show, even in an old man's part, a generous amount of the legs which had been celebrated since he first put on Romeo's doublet and hose. "Well, to keep Mrs Placid happy. I won't eat dinner tonight, and if I rumble on stage, I will pretend it's thunder."

David handed him the plate, and thinking that the two old friends might want time alone on what might well be their last meeting, said, "Will you both excuse me for a half hour? I want to finish some letters before the evening post."

There were indeed a good many letters waiting to be answered. Word of Lucas's illness had spread, and friends and admirers wrote from all over the world to ask after his health and offer good wishes. David answered these letters the same way he had written condolence letters during the war, routinely, mind averted.

When he heard the door to Lucas's bedroom shut, he got up to see Jago out. Jago was very red about the eyes, which did not prevent him from saying, "This must be frightfully dull for you, David, dear. Why don't you come and spend a few days in London with me? You could see my *Lear* and I could give you an amusing time."

David said, "You know, I learned some very offensive language in the army, but none of it seems entirely adequate to this occasion."

Jago was unperturbed. "How unfailingly you run true to form, my dear. It's rather nice, if a little boring. But then it doesn't bore Lucas, and that's the main thing, isn't it?"

Lucas looked flushed and feverish, but said he felt fine except that Jago's effervescent personality had made his headache worse. "We had such a farewell scene," he said. "The death of Little Nell is nothing to it."

"I'm sorry I let you in for that. It all comes of exercising tact."

"Oh no, I wouldn't have missed it for the world. Only it was rather an effort to keep a straight face. Well, now that that's out of the way, it's time I was too."

It was said so casually that David, who had been gathering up the tea things, was a moment taking it in. He put down the cup he had been holding, and looked at it in surprise when it shivered into pieces on the tray.

"My dear," said Lucas, "did you think it was never going to happen?" and watched the man in khaki, the one who hadn't a care in the world, take control.

"On the contrary," said David; "I expected it every day. Which comes to much the same thing." He came to the side of the bed and took Lucas's hand in his. "Did Jago by any chance hint that you were getting to be a nuisance to me? Because if so, you can forget all about it. It's not true."

"He did rather more than hint, but I promise that had nothing to do with it. I'm getting to be too much of a nuisance to myself. I've had these four extra weeks here with you; it will have to be enough. Let's not discuss it, David."

"We won't." The man in khaki was now completely in charge. "It's your show, my dear. How do you want to do it?"

"Oh, just take a lot of pills," said Lucas, who had been planning it ever since he had sent Robinson downstairs to find his father's medical books and had confirmed his suspicions of what the headaches and fevers and vomiting meant. "Intravenous is quicker, but I'm not in a tearing hurry, and I doubt I've got a usable vein left anyhow."

David looked at him and smiled, his face the serene,

mendacious mask Toby had seen so often. He said, "Do you want a drink?"

Lucas thought this over. "I suppose it does call for something more notable than a cold cup of tea."

"Brandy and soda?"

"Yes, that would be nice."

When David had gone Lucas lay still, looking out over the estuary, feeling no fear, only a deep sadness at leaving this place he so loved, and most of all David.

It had been from this very window that he had watched him walking across the meadow nine years ago; a wind-blown young dandy in brown velvet coming to offer his person and calculating heart. Lucas could not remember what he had thought, watching him approach. No doubt there had been some excitement inherent in the possibility of something new, but since the novelty consisted of exchanging one Bunny Trevelyan for another, it would hardly have seemed new at all. That from such trivial and shoddy beginnings had grown love and absolute devotion seemed to Lucas, looking back, a gift beyond price.

There was, it occurred to him, one small thing he could do for David in return. He could get on with what he proposed to do. He would have liked David to be the one to hand him the pills, one by one, between sips of brandy. David would do it if he asked him. But some day if not now that formidable vicarage conscience would begin to trouble him for his part in his lover's death. That much at least he might spare him.

The pills were in the drawer of his bedside table, which he could reach easily, and there was tea left in his cup. By the time David came back with the brandy and soda, Lucas, with the jaunty mood that any finished action, even a disastrous one is apt to produce, took his drink and said, "Cheers, David."

David looked at the empty phial of pills and said, "You might have waited."

"I thought of it, but I decided it was better this way."

"I wish you'd sometimes resist those awful impulses of yours to be noble and generous. You'll be making a speech about swans next."

Filled with chemical well-being compounded of brandy and morphine, Lucas said, "Certainly not. I've always thought the Greeks appalling gasbags, expecting everyone to sit around and sob while they made endless speeches. The Romans did that kind of thing with much more style."

"I don't know," said David—how curious that they should be arguing amiably as they had done thousands of times on their walks or across the dinner table; "cutting your wrists in the bath. I've always thought it left an awful mess for someone to clean up."

"I've never taken so much of the stuff before," said Lucas after a while. "I feel very curious, as if I were floating above the bed. It's a strange feeling, but not unpleasant."

"If you could actually manage to levitate we might have you declared a saint," said David. He had caught Lucas's note of jaunty irresponsibility now; it was not after all very different from the wartime—"You've got a Blighty, you lucky sod," said to someone whose intestines were spilled on the ground.

Lucas laughed. "That would be very nice. St Lucas Ryder." His voice was growing drowsy. The light was fading from the estuary, and the bedroom had grown dim. The reading lamp beside the bed cast a shaded circle of light. David stood by the window, looking out over the water meadow, from which came the first forlorn calls of night-hunting birds.

"David?"

"Yes, my dearest."

Lucas sounded very sleepy. "You won't go away?"

David turned from the window and went to the bedside. He seated himself with his shoulder against the headboard and carefully slid an arm under Lucas's head. The once bulky, familiar body had grown so light and strange, it often seemed to David like a well-known field over which a battle has raged, leaving few landmarks.

He said, "I'll stay right here. Are you comfortable like this?"

"Yes, thank you. It's funny, you know; I don't feel anything in particular. Just sleepy."

"That's good," said David. "Go to sleep then."

Lucas was silent for so long David thought he had dozed off. Then he said, his voice blurred, "Do they still bury poets in Westminster Abbey?"

It seemed to David a pleasant thought for a poet to cast himself adrift on his final sleep. He said, "Would you like that?"

"Not sure. All those tourists trampling on top of one." He spoke less drowsily, as if the notion had pulled him back from sleep. "I shouldn't have minded being a bust glaring down at everyone."

"It's a pity you never had one done," said David, gently tracing the line of Lucas's forehead and nose. "You'd have made a wonderful bust. Very Roman and grand."

Lucas was drifting off again. "I must say," he said, as politely as any parting guest, "it's all been great fun."

David held him, listening to the call of the nightbirds outside the window. Lucas's breathing was shallow and slow. His head grew heavier on David's shoulder, and David began to think of other dying heads he had held, his tunic at times splashed more crimson than any staff officer's. A gust of wind came down the chimney, blowing the fire into a brighter glow. A filament of words formed itself in David's mind. It had been so long since he had written a poem that he did not at once recognize it for a line of verse. Another followed—an experience long forgotten demanding to be given shape—another dying head, whose? A man from his platoon, a fellow subaltern? No one he could now remember, holding on hard, dying hard. And all that time the sun had glinted on the precise hub and spokes of a spiderweb strung between the insane tangle of barbed wire.

"Damn," thought David. He had four lines. The first quartet of a sonnet?

Cautiously he groped in his pocket and found a pencil but no paper. There was always a notebook somewhere among Lucas's blankets and sheets, but he couldn't see it and didn't want to move and perhaps waken him. The octet was completing itself irresistibly in his head. He carefully moved his hand and picked up *King Lear*. Taking care not to disturb Lucas, he drew up his knee and propped the book, open to the flyleaf, against his thigh. Even now his mind rebelled against defacing a book, but this one was one of Lucas's, stained and tattered, and he must get the octet down.

He wrote quickly at first, then went back to tinker with a word here and there, changing a rhyme, afraid of coming to a dead stop before the sestet, which he wanted to be as orderly and sunlit as the remembered spiderweb.

He completed the octet, and the sestet was there, waiting for him with an appropriate metaphysical conceit, its rhymes falling easily C-C-D C-C-D, so that he did not even have to cheat with a quartet and a rhyming couplet. He read it over, first with the exultation a completed poem will bring even to the writer of doggerel, then critically, as Lucas had taught him, picking apart his metaphors. "If they come too easily," Lucas had once said, "they're either obvious or someone else's." He had been pleased with "hedgerows of barbed wire"; now he remembered that it had been Toby, that unpoetic clot, who had first used the comparison, and drew his pencil through it. On second thoughts he decided to let it stand. He read it all through once more and was pleased with it. It was minor, of course, but good.

By his side, but already out of reach, Lucas slept.

Chapter 9

"You must take Fraülein von Cremmen to the home farm after lunch, Felix, dear," said Sophie. "Everything is so lovely just now. I've always liked spring best of all the seasons." She turned to their guest. "What is your favourite season, dear Fraülein?"

It would have to be the home farm, thought Felix, accepting the unspoken rebuke in his mother's suggestion. Spring—meadows and ponds, sties and cribs filled with calves and foals, ducklings and goslings, shoats and baby chicks. Trees in blossom promising fruit, seedlings thrusting toward the sun in the vegetable garden. Only he, the heir, a mere month away now from his thirtieth birthday, was celibate and sterile.

He knew his mother wanted proper grandchildren, by which she meant those born to the Landeck name. The ones she had, the Porkers and Zia (named for her grandmothers, Terezia Sophie) counted for nothing, since they were called von Au and not Landeck.

Now that some of life's former ease had returned to the abbey, Sophie had set herself to matchmaking. Angelika, who was so happily married that she often found it in her heart to pity the pope, entered enthusiastically into her mother's plans; resumed neglected friendships with old schoolmates who had suitable younger sisters, while Sophie turned to friends and acquaintances busy marrying off their daughters. A steady trickle of Fräulein von Tin Mines or Baroness von Coals appeared at the abbey to be taken to visit the home farm or the conservatory, in a punt on the river, for a walk through the woods, only to be replaced by another Fräulein von this and that.

Felix knew that his mother was bewildered by his persistent bachelorhood. He was bewildered by it himself, for he had no excuse for not marrying any longer. Three years after the end of the war, Landeck Steel was once more in full production, manufacturing everything from pots to railway tracks. German politics, it is true, continued in a turmoil not easily grasped by the casual onlooker, but Felix troubled himself little about what went on in Berlin. Even a child might realize, he thought, that if you inflate currency to pay your war reparations and sell German goods cheaply abroad, your money will be worth less and less. But inflation hurts mostly those on fixed incomes and pensions. For a concern like Landeck Steel, with many customers abroad, it actually proved to be an advantage. Landeck could pay its debts with worthless German money, while selling its goods outside Germany for sound foreign currencies. In a company town like Eschenbach the threat of inflation was far less noticeable than in large cities; there was food in the shops and if prices had risen deliriously, so had wages, and Felix was a considerate employer who always gave his workers half an hour to shop as soon as they had collected their pay. There was full employment, and during the last year he had been able to reinstate the apprentice programme which had been so dear to Hesso's heart. Once again Eschenbach boys came to work at the age of fourteen, to rise through the various departments at the mills to whatever levels their abilities allowed.

Thinking of their alert, eager faces, their cheeky curiosity, Felix smiled to himself. His own generation of young men who should have worked their way up in the firm, had been cruelly winnowed by the war; the workers and supervisors at Landeck were old or middle aged. But now there was youth again at Landeck Steel, and schoolboy devilry and laughter.

"What are you smiling at?" asked Angelika. "You've been miles away."

"I've been thinking of the next generation. I hear good reports of them."

"Yes," said Angelika, misunderstanding him and smiling at her own two Porkers. "They are good boys. And they admire you so much."

It was true that the Porkers had a great admiration for Felix, not so much Uncle Felix who worked long hours at the mills and had little time for them, but Felix the war hero, with a drawer full of medals and a silver knee cap. Amid the general effort to find him a wife it had occurred to the Porkers that he would be the perfect mate for their heroine, Fräulein Wesendonck. They had managed to contrive a meeting—not an easy thing to do since the young schoolmistress did not, of course, move in the Landeck social circle—and Felix, casting his eye over her with appreciation and prompt stirrings of lechery, had declared himself delighted to make her acquaintance. Five minutes of her conversation had quenched both lechery and appreciation.

The Porkers were disappointed, but their admiration for their uncle did not diminish. After all, some of the greatest knights of legend had opted for celibacy and chastity.

Chastity was a virtue Sophie too admired, in its proper place among the saints. It was a virtue totally useless for the heir of Landeck Steel, and completely unnatural for Felix, whose amorous career had caused her much worry in the years before the war. Had he kept a mistress in an apartment lined in pink satin (it was thus Sophie pictured all irregular unions), she would have prayed earnestly for the salvation of his soul, but she would have found it reassuring.

She wondered at times whether Felix could still be in love with that very unsuitable American widow. If so, he gave no sign of it, and that lady would by now in any case be approaching her fortieth birthday and would be useless for the purpose of breeding Landeck heirs.

But just in case the memory of that unsuitable widow (whose name, if not age, Sophie had long since forgotten) should still linger, she had invited Fräulein von Cremmen, a skinny child with spidery arms and legs, red hair, freckles, and tawny eyes like a lioness. She resembled the Munch drawing which still hung in Felix's bedroom, and if she was also wonderfully silly, Felix would probably not mind that.

She had prattled away for a good ten minutes about her favourite season, which was that of balls, opening nights, and dress shows, and Felix, gathering up his thoughts, which had been far away, thought how pretty she was, and if she was a twittering idiot, how much nicer that would be than Fräulein Wesendonck, who had firm, well-thought-out opinions, and a firm, terrifying way of imparting them.

Besides, there was much to be said for an alliance with Cremmen Coal GMBH, so he took her away to visit the foals gambolling in the pasture, the ducklings exploring the joys of a very muddy pond, and a kindle of pure white kittens in the barn. Fräulein von Cremmen, pretty as a pure white kitten herself, was enchanted with all she saw, and managed to make it quite clear that this included the owner of Landeck Steel. But when Felix returned her to his mother and sister, she had got nothing from him except the gift of a gardenia blossom from the conservatory.

To escape Sophie's reproachful eyes—all that coal, all those grandchildren—he went to his room to dress for dinner. In the drawer with his studs lay the bundle of letters he had written to Kitty during the war. It had become an almost daily ritual to take them out, to weigh them in his hand—will I, won't I—and put them back.

The red-haired muse of the *Ninth Symphony* over his bed had become confused in his mind with the real Kitty, of whom he had not even a photograph.

Was he still in love with her? It was a question to which he had no answer, no matter how often he asked it of himself. If he was not, why did he not marry someone else? The celibate life did not suit him; he was often lonely, he wanted to be married, he simply could not find a woman he wanted to be married to. Had falling in love with Kitty had the same effect as vaccination? Was he, even if he was no longer in love with her, immune to all others?

"Enough," he said to his face in the mirror. That was another thing; he often found himself talking to himself out loud, surely not a good sign. "You are nearly thirty and grow more idiotic with the years, not less so. Make up your mind once and for all. Either burn those letters or send them."

"Why should they interest her after all this time?" said the face in the mirror. "She's probably forgotten all about you. She may be married again; it's more than likely. She may have gone back to America."

"Then," said Felix, "the envelope will come back stamped REMOVED and no harm will have been done."

The narrow face, its dark hair sleek, its eyes a little too close together, said, "You'll feel a fine fool."

"Very well, I'll feel a fool."

"Why don't you toss for it?" said the face in the mirror. "Heads you send, tails you don't."

"Cad," said Felix to the face which had made the suggestion.

"Coward," taunted the face.

Felix put a hand in his pocket and brought out some change. He spun a coin in the air and caught it. "Heads," he said to the face in the mirror.

"Cad," said the face.

The manila envelope with German stamps plastered all over

it was so fat that it would not go through the letter slot in Kitty's door. The postman, who knew that she was on holiday and that her maid was away as well, took it back to keep until she should return.

Kitty sat in the sun on the terrace of a house whose cyclamen colour clashed badly with the bougainvillea cascading like a waterfall down to the sea, which was the kind of blue you could never really imagine until you saw it. David had once described it as being as blue as ink, if ink were transparent, but that seemed to Kitty not to allow for its brilliance and luminescence.

On the other side of this incredible blue was Africa, which Kitty pictured as an ocean of sand, where bedouins, on swift camels, carried off a blameless English housewife to a life of opulent humiliation. In principle Kitty was a feminist, but she was not immune to popular fiction.

"I can't get used to everything being so sunny and bright," she said. "London was foggy and cold, and I felt so smoky."

"Your voice still sounds smoky," said Julian. "I like it like that."

How terrible, Kitty thought, to live among so much beauty and not to be able to see it. And since to think a thing and to say it were usually the same thing with her, she said, "I do wish you could see the flowers, Julian."

"I can smell them. There are hundreds of different scents here. And the sounds. Listen."

Kitty, her ears far less sensitive than Julian's, heard a bumblebee in the oleander making a noise like a small sports car, the never-ending scratching of the cicadas, the clink of glasses and talk of Julian's friends, and dance music from the gramophone. Something, she thought, was missing. It suddenly came to her that there were no birds.

"I know," said Julian. "It took me ages to figure it out. I like it like that. Bird song is the one thing that might remind me of England."

This seemed to Kitty a very odd remark, for everywhere around them was the high-pitched English chatter of Julian's friends. Kitty, who had expected to find Julian lonely and homesick, felt rather a fool.

At the beginning of her exile, pregnant, sick, even perhaps panicky, Julian had in fact written several times to Kitty, begging for a visit. She had never complained, but her loneliness seemed to seep through the unformed writing of her maid. Then Toby had come back with the baby and Julian had stopped writing, and Kitty, never a great letter writer, had a little guiltily stopped writing too. Then Mr Popkin had decided to renovate the Temple Bar. Religion was out, gangsters were in, and Popkin's was about to be transformed into a speakeasy, with bathtub gin and waiters wearing fedoras like Chicago gangsters. Meanwhile he suggested to Kitty, "Why not have yourself a bit of a holiday? Go somewhere sunny, eh?"

Kitty thought about this without enthusiasm. Holidays alone weren't much fun. She'd as soon stay home and put her feet up. Then she remembered those lonely letters from Julian and the silence since. "I might visit Julian," she said to Mr Popkin. "I think she may be lonely."

"That's the ticket," Mr Popkin had agreed enthusiastically. "Have yourself a bit of spree and cheer up an old pal at the same time. That way you can let yourself go a bit and still feel you're doing something for the good of your soul. I always liked Mrs Strafford. No side to her, not like her husband. Maybe she didn't ought to have done what she did, but what I say is we're none of us perfect."

Kitty was having a very nice holiday, though she could not feel she was doing very much for the good of her soul. She lived like a lotus-eater, amid oleander and umbrella pines, bathed in the blue sea, ate ices and drank cocktails with Julian's friends, drove at top speed in little sports cars along the Corniche, and won a shocking amount of money at Monte Carlo. Everyone made a tremendous fuss over her. It was known, of course, that she had been asked to dance by the Prince of Wales, and sang in an East End nightclub. These things made her a celebrity among Julian's friends, who seemed to Kitty to be very nearly indistinguishable from the crowd she'd run around with in London; younger sons who had just missed the war and could find no footing in a world at peace, ex-officers with brilliant war records, gentlemen by virtue of their commissions but lacking that other attribute of an English gentleman, a settled income, remittance men without remittances, and a few rather dubious French and Italian counts. The women were pretty and amusing, but Kitty never could work out which of them belonged to any particular one of the young men, perhaps because they themselves were not at all clear about this.

Lilies of the field, they existed lavishly on very little, drove racing cars, coached tennis at the big hotels, or lived on their wits, which mostly seemed to mean they gambled and sponged on their friends.

As in London their days were spent in an arduous and never-ending pursuit of amusement. Lunches, dinners, drinks, bathing, parties on someone's yacht, gambling at Monte filled their hours agreeably if a little frantically. Kitty enjoyed them very much, though in the long run, she suspected, they might make her feel as if she'd eaten too many cream puffs: stuffed, but not fed.

It was only late at night, getting ready for bed, that she and Julian had time to themselves. They would sit on her bed, yawn, drink hot cocoa, and talk for hours.

"Does it mean you've forgiven me," Julian asked the first night, "your coming here to stay with me?"

"You've done me no injury, Julian; there's nothing to forgive. I only wish you hadn't been so cruel to Toby."

"I never meant to be," said Julian, and it was plain to Kitty that she was speaking the truth. "He somehow managed to back me into a corner and I couldn't get out of it. It was extraordinary, when you come to think of it, how everyone just assumed it was true about Danilo and me. Toby never even thought to ask me, you know. Neither did David. I don't mind so much about David; he hardly knows me, after all, and with Sir Lucas dying I couldn't expect him to have much attention to spare for me, but Toby has known me all my life, and yet he never, for a single moment, hesitated to believe someone who never once told the truth about anything."

Kitty would have liked to say that she had never believed it, but it would not have been true. It had not occurred to her any more than it had to Toby and David, to doubt Nemesis's story. "Julian," she said, "was none of it true?"

"Are you good at keeping secrets?"

"Nobody's good at keeping secrets."

"Well, you must keep this one. Promise."

"All right."

"None of it was true. Well yes, the bit about him kissing my cheek in the taxi. It was the first time he'd done that; it was only because he was so pleased about my having a baby."

Kitty felt tears spring into her eyes. "Oh, Julian, we were awful to you. But you should have told us."

"I don't think anyone would have believed me. At first I didn't defend myself because I was too angry with Toby, but I always meant to tell him later, when he'd calmed down a bit. Of course when he'd calmed down he made it impossible; it would have felt like going up to a total stranger then. I suppose I should have told him about the baby. He never asked, you know. It must have killed him, wondering, but in eight months he never once asked."

"He has his pride, Julian."

"Oh pride. Toby isn't a real person at all. He's just a lot of attitudes he was taught, Nannie attitudes, Eton attitudes, army attitudes, English gentleman attitudes. He isn't even grown-up enough to have attitudes of his own. And he was fairly cruel too when he took the baby away."

"Poor Julian. Did you want it very much? The baby, I mean?" Kitty found it difficult to see how motherhood would have fitted into Julian's racketing life.

"I don't know. They never gave me time to find out. Poor little baby, has Nannie got him?"

"Body and soul. David says she's like Faust after he sold his soul to the devil; she has gained eternal youth."

Julian laughed. "Well, heaven help him. Is he a nice baby?"

"Yes. Very much like Toby. Not like you at all."

Julian put down her empty cup, stretched, and dropped her head against Kitty's knees, rubbing her cheek against the soft stuff of her ratty kimono. "You think that a good thing, do you?"

"It's a very good thing for Toby," said Kitty. "It would be so cruel if every time he looked at it he were to be reminded of you."

"Has my memory been blotted out so completely. Have they erased my name from the family Bible?"

"No, of course not. The story is that your health keeps you in the South. Toby's always inventing letters from you when people ask after you. It's not easy for him."

"What a pity my health is so good," said Julian bitterly. "Just think how much it would simplify everything if I could just quietly and politely be dead."

By the next morning Julian was gay again; their talk might never have happened. Yet Kitty could not forget that moment's bitterness. Through all that happy holiday it came between her and the sun.

When she returned to London, Kitty went to have tea with David, whom she had not seen since the memorial service for Sir Lucas in Westminster Abbey.

"What a nice tan," he said. "It's done nothing but rain here since you left. Did you have a good holiday?"

"Yes, it was beautiful, almost unreal, like a dream. Everything except Julian's house. I can't imagine how Toby could have brought himself to buy it. It's painted cyclamen, and there's all that crimson and orange bougainvillea . . ." Kitty shuddered at the memory.

"It's a mercy Julian can't see it. How is she?"

"Oh, much the same as she was in London. The same crowd, a little older, fewer rich young men-about-town and more gigolos. At least they say they're tennis professionals at the big hotels, but I suspect gigolos is what they really are. Lots of drinking, gambling and playing musical chairs with each others' lovers—not Julian, of course, she doesn't do any of those things, just eggs on the others and sits back being amused. I don't think I was much use to her, David."

"Is that why you went? How very nice of you. But I really don't think one can be much use to people like Julian except in practical ways; money, and letting them know they can have your roof over their heads when their own comes crashing down on them."

"Does she ask you for money too?" asked Kitty. "She told me she often gets double cheques out of Toby by threatening to turn up in London."

David laughed. "How does she manage to get through it all?"

"Oh, gambling, and then those friends of hers—they're very nice, but they never seem to have any money of their own, so they borrow Julian's. I think she rather enjoys spending Toby's money on them."

"I see. Tell me, did she by any chance borrow from you?"

"Certainly not."

"How much?"

"I told you she didn't."

"Don't be silly, Kitty. She's my sister. Besides," David added sadly, "I've got such a lot of money now."

For several weeks after Lucas's death, David had stayed on at the Dower House. He was like someone recovering from a long and draining illness. He slept a lot at odd hours of the day and forgot mealtimes, though when Hopkins looked reproachfully at the congealed food on his plate and said, "Oh, sir, you haven't touched your dinner again," he would suddenly find himself ravenous and eat it cold rather than wait for her to bring him something hot.

Letters from all over the world had come at Lucas's death. David sat down to answer them, only to find that hours had passed and he was still staring at the blank page. "I feel so strange," he said to Dr Timberlake. "I can't read, I can't concentrate on anything. Do you think I'm going mad? It doesn't feel at all like the last time."

"I don't think you're going mad," said the doctor. "I don't think you were mad last time either. You've let the well run almost dry, that's all. It takes time to fill up again."

"Do you think it will? Wells don't, do they, when there's no water left in them."

"I'm sure it will," said Dr Timberlake, looking at the beautiful, worn face and wondering just how sure he was. "How old are you?"

David had to think for a moment. "Twenty-nine. Funny.

During the war I wouldn't have given you tuppence on the odds I'd live to see thirty."

"What do you plan to do with the forty you've got left of your threescore and ten?"

"Go back to Oxford," said David. It was a plan which had been in the back of his mind ever since he had learned that his days with Lucas were numbered. On the way back from his last visit to Altondale he had stopped off to lunch with his former tutor—now Provost of Oriel—to discuss the work he planned to do. Oxford was a far quieter place now than it had been in his own undergraduate days. The battered survivors of the war had brought to it a note of seriousness and purpose which David felt suited Oxford very well. "My father once said that Oxford grows on one like a shell on a snail," he said to the doctor. "I didn't know what he meant then. I think I do now. I'm beginning to feel like a hermit crab looking for a shell, and that shell is Oxford."

They went up to town for a memorial service at Westminster Abbey. Mr Pym, who had been Lucas's solicitor, approached David afterward and said, "Shall I find you if I come to call on you within the next day or two?" David said yes, and Mr Pym, who had expected David to suggest a specific time, frowned a little. Young men ought to be about and busy. But so many of them seemed vague and without direction nowadays, especially those who had been through the war. Mr Pym had no patience with them.

David went to stay in Upper Cheyne Row. Robinson lit fires in all the rooms to air them, but it still felt damp and cold. David did not notice. He asked Robinson to find him some empty boxes and began to pack his own things; books mostly, and some clothes. Mr Pym, when he arrived at the correct time to be offered a drink (remembering that Lucas had always had a very good sherry) looked at the boxes in some surprise. He was a small man, very neatly dressed, with a face like a buttonhole.

He said, "I have come to discuss certain bequests in Sir Lucas's will which concern you, Major Harvey."

David was not at all the kind of person who attends a

deathbed with dreams of legacies dancing in his head. Had he been asked to choose a keepsake from among Lucas's things he might have taken a favourite book or two, or, for reasons of sentiment, not monetary value, the Whistler drawing. The idea that Lucas might leave him money had scarcely entered David's head.

When Mr Pym, looking more than ever like a buttonhole, primly mentioned the large sum Lucas had left him, David was touched by Lucas's thought of him, but in terms of cash it meant very little. He had grown up in a family which muddled along happily on practically no money at all, and thus had never acquired a serious and responsible attitude toward financial matters. When he had money he spent it, or just as likely gave it away to someone who had none. When he was the one who had none, he let other people spend theirs, or did without. He had enough saved from his army pay for a frugal year at Oxford while he worked for his fellowship. Further than that he had never troubled himself to think.

"You are a very fortunate young man," said Mr Pym, who did not approve of sums of such size being left outright to beautiful young men. "If you take my advice you will leave the money invested as it is at present. My father had occasion to give the same advice to Sir Lucas when the money came to him on the death of his father, and I do not think he ever had cause to regret taking it. Sir Noel Ryder was an excellent judge of investments. It is a gift I have often noticed among the members of the healing profession, though why this should be so I cannot tell. Now, as for the houses, you know that the Dower House is leasehold. The Longacre family is very eager to buy back the lease to use it as a residence for old Lady Longacre."

David was aware of this, for the Longacres had scarcely been able to bring themselves to wait till the blinds were drawn before touching on the subject, and their kind inquiries after Lucas's health had never quite veiled the fact that they were eager to be rid of the dowager, her gouty toe, her yapping Pekingese, and her quarrelsome companion.

The Chelsea house was freehold, owned outright by Sir

Lucas. "He told me," said Mr Pym, "that you always preferred it in any case, though, since he was himself so very fond of the Dower House, you were too tactful to say so."

It took David a long moment before he took in what Mr Pym was saying. His voice a croak, he said, "Do you mean he's left it to me?" He looked so white Mr Pym wondered whether he ought to ring for brandy. Still, it was gratifying to see some emotion from someone who had accepted the legacy of a very handsome fortune as if it were a child's box of playmoney.

"The house and its contents. Do you mean to tell me Sir Lucas never mentioned this to you?"

David shook his head. Some colour had come back to his face. "We never talked legacies at all."

Mr Pym looked at the high-ceilinged room with its white walls and many books, and said, "If it were mine I would sell it. I consider Chelsea a very uncertain quantity where property is concerned. Think it over and let me know. And now," he said, draining his sherry, "it only remains for me to congratulate you."

David thanked him and saw him out. After he had closed the door behind him, he stood a long time, looking up the flight of stairs dimly lit by the window on the half-landing. He had fallen in love with this house the moment Lucas had unlocked the blue front door and handed him the key (Bunny Trevelyan's key, no doubt), saying, "Yours."

He touched the banister and it occurred to him that in all his life he had never owned anything but his clothes and his books. Now he owned this banister. He put his face against the smooth wood, and wept.

A few days after Mr Pym's visit, something had come his way which just then he needed more than money or a house, a job of work. Philip Goldenrod had called on him, suggesting that David should edit a complete edition of Lucas Ryder's poems. "I should like to get it underway at once," Philip Goldenrod had said. "There is so often a slump in a poet's reputation after he dies, and I should like to get this into the bookshops before it happens to dear Lucas."

David, thinking that here was something he could do in return for Lucas's generosity to him, had agreed without hesitation.

"Had I but known," he said to Kitty, who'd asked him what he was working on. "I thought it would just be a question of arranging the poems from his various books, and tracking down the ones that were in magazines and for some reason never got published in book form, and that would be the end of it. I suppose I should have known better, but somehow I was never with Lucas when he had one of his poetry-writing fits. From what Mrs Placid tells me, he simply couldn't catch sight of an empty sheet of paper at times like that without at once beginning to scribble on it—like a boy with a coal and a newly white-washed wall, she said. We even found a poem in the back of the butcher's order book. And Robinson keeps finding scraps of poems in the pockets of his clothes as he's getting them ready to give away. And then there are sometimes as many as twenty versions of a poem with nothing to say which is the final one. I seem to have got the entire household involved; it's like a paper chase."

Over tea Kitty told him about her holiday, while David scarcely listened, preoccupied with the preface he was writing for the *Collected Poems*. He had loved Lucas's poetry ever since he was a schoolboy, and had a good deal he wanted to say about it. He hoped that Kitty would not, as was her usual habit, stay talking until teatime imperceptibly merged into the hour when she would have to be offered sherry.

Fond as he was of Kitty, he saw her out with relief and returned at once to the study to work on his preface. He was not at all pleased when the telephone rang ten minutes later and Robinson came up to say that it was Mrs Snow and that she sounded extremely upset.

He picked up the telephone. "Yes, Kitty."

She was all out of breath, as if she had just had a fright. "David, could you come over here? Are you very busy? Please . . . I . . . please come."

"Right away."

She was waiting for him by the door, the freckles like

dark moles on her white face. He could feel her hand shaking in his as she led him to the drawing room. "There," she said, pointing to letters scattered beside the sherry decanter and an empty glass. The letters looked grubby, as if they had been carried in someone's pocket for a long time, and David recognized them instantly as letters from the front.

"Felix?" he asked.

She nodded. "They came in that big yellow envelope. It didn't fit through the letterbox, so the postman held on to it till I came home. That's why it wasn't with my other letters this morning. He wrote to me all the time, right through the war." Tears were spilling down her cheeks. David, staring at the letters, absently handed her his handkerchief. She blew her nose and poured herself another sherry. "Do you want some?" He shook his head. "Of course he couldn't send them during the war," she said, much interrupted by sobs and hiccoughs, "but he kept on writing. I didn't, you know. I couldn't think of anything to say."

"Why now, three years after the war's over?"

She gave a final, noisy sniff, poured herself another sherry, and picked up a letter written on Landeck writing paper. David recognized the crossed rapiers in its upper corner. "Read it," she said.

"Are you sure?"

"Of course I'm sure. It's not a love letter."

He took it from the clean, crisp envelope. It was a long time since he had seen Felix's spiky German writing. "Dear Kitty. These letters have lived at the back of a drawer for three years. It seems presumptuous to think you might want to have them after all this time, throw them out unread if you like. I've thought about sending them to you so often—it seems strange not even to know whether you still live at the same address. It's a long time since we got engaged so recklessly on the beach at Fallon. The war, and all that followed have made those seven years seem more like seventy.

"I fought in Russia mostly. I never thought of them as enemies any more than I did of the English. The French

464

are something else; we're brought up to think of them as the *Erbfeind*, the hereditary enemy. But since Versailles I've come to think of the English and the Americans like that too.

"Not you, Kitty, never you. And yet . . . do you have the story of the glass mountain in America? It was like that. I couldn't climb over it. Only an innocent soul could, in the story at any rate.

"Things are getting easier here now; Landeck Steel is in full production again, though we're still terribly in debt. Recovery will be very slow, but there is a chance that we may recover.

"As for the rest—I don't know. I don't know what your feelings are about me; I'm not even sure what mine are about you. All I do know is that I've tried to forget you and haven't succeeded. Write to me if you can. Felix."

"I don't know," said David slowly. "It seems a kind of love letter to me."

"Do you think so?"

"Do you want it to be?"

"Oh yes. My feelings aren't nearly as complicated as Felix's."

"Dear Kitty. Then you're going to write to him. Give him my love, will you?"

"Write to him yourself," she said a little tartly, for she had never entirely forgiven him for not forcing his way into Landeck when he had been with the occupation army in Cologne.

"I have written. It's Felix's turn now. He'll write when he's ready." He looked at the crumpled, mud-stained letters on the table. They brought back the war so very vividly; these were the letters they had so often taken from the pockets of the German dead. He had no doubt that Kitty would read them over and over again, and save them in an empty chocolate box with a silk ribbon tied round them. Had they been his, he would have burned them.

"Don't forget," he said. "Give Felix my love."

Chapter 10

When Lucas Ryder's *Collected Poems* was published, many of his literary friends took the opportunity to write lengthy appreciations of his life's work in the *London Mercury* and the *Times Literary Supplement*, and almost all of them drew attention to the elegant prose and intricate perceptions of David's preface.

The slump in Lucas's reputation which Philip Goldenrod had predicted had not yet come to pass; in fact, what with the unveiling of a memorial plaque in Westminster Abbey and the publication of the *Collected Poems*, which very nearly outsold Mrs Ella Wheeler Wilcox's *Poems of Passion*, Lucas Ryder's popularity with the reading public was as high now as when the scandalous love poems *To N*. had first appeared.

Hermione Goldenrod, who kept a keen eye not only on sales, but straws blowing in the winds of literary reputations, suggested to her husband that David might be commissioned to do a biography of Lucas. Philip said, "Oh no, my dear. You know David. He'll want to be highbrow and literate, and people who read biographies want bad grammar, scandals, and duchesses."

"As for the scandals," said Hermione, "at least we can trust David to be discreet."

David, when approached, also had reservations. He pointed out that he had only known Lucas the last nine years of his life, of which four had been spent away in the army. Hermione said she didn't see why that should matter; lots of people did biographies of people they had never met at all—look at Plutarch and Carlyle. David said, "Yes, but by the time Plutarch and Carlyle were writing, there wasn't anyone else around who'd known Julius Caesar or Frederick the Great personally. There are lots of people around still who've known Lucas all their lives."

"I expect he'd like *you* to do it," said Hermione, and to this David could find no answer but to say he would try. "But it's to be a literary biography," he said, just as Philip

Goldenrod had feared. "I loathe those gossipy 'lunch with the Duchess of Blackpool' things."

"Oh, you must have a duchess or two," Philip Goldenrod said. "People expect it, you know."

There were duchesses and plumbers in Lucas's diaries, actors and prime ministers and even a burglar he had surprised trying to break into his house, with whom he had a long and interesting talk about the fine points of his craft. Lucas had been interested in everyone who had anything to tell him, and had written it all down in his diaries. His late Victorian childhood had been fed on Mangnall's *Historical and Miscellaneous Questions for the Use of Young People*, Pinnock's *Greece and Rome*, and *The Child's Guide to Knowledge*, and books like this (still on a low shelf in the library) had created in him, as they had in so many of his contemporaries, an endless appetite for facts and physical and mental exploration.

Whether it was a Victorian respect for the written word, or simply a squirrel mentality where friends and lovers were concerned, David did not know, but it did seem to him that Lucas could never have thrown out a single letter. David found bundles of them filling boxes and drawers. His own were there, from the first one, politely accepting an invitation to tea, to the last, written after Toby's wedding. Most of his had been written with the eye of the army censor peering over his shoulder, and were reasonably discreet, which could not be said for a good many of the others.

"I don't know what to do about them," David told Philip Goldenrod. "I've given back those that people asked me for, but there are still quite a few that might prove a considerable embarrassment for their writers."

"Give them to the British Museum," said Hermione, "and tell them they can open them one hundred years from now. By then everyone who could possibly be embarrassed will be dead."

"Yes, but it isn't just the reputation of the people who wrote the letters," said David. "There is Lucas's reputation to be considered as well."

"He had lots of warning, you know," said Hermione.

"He had two years to burn his letters if he'd been worried about his reputation. It seems obvious to me that he wasn't."

Philip Goldenrod had remained uneasily silent during this discussion. When Hermione was called away, David put him out of his misery by handing him a small packet of letters tied up with string. "I thought you might like to have those," David said. Philip Goldenrod looked more than ever like a snail who sees a gardener approaching with the salt cellar. "I only read the first paragraph of the first one," David lied kindly.

Some books are blessed from their very beginnings; they take immediate possession of the writer, and almost seem to beg to be written by him and no one else. Lucas's biography was a book like that for David. He gave himself to it completely, having indeed no choice in the matter, for the chapters spun themselves into his dreams and walks and meals. Sometimes he almost felt he was writing to dictation. And in all those quiet days in his study, with the Whistler drawing looking over his shoulder, David felt the house pervaded by Lucas's presence, as if at any moment he might hear the rustle of paper and look up to see Lucas sitting in the chair by the fire, turning the pages of a book.

Late one evening in November, Robinson climbed the stairs to the attic study to tell David that there was a strange gentleman at the door. David looked up from his manuscript and rubbed his hand across tired eyes. "How, strange? Straw in his hair, or simply unknown?"

"Foreign, like," Robinson thought.

"What time is it?"

"Half past eleven."

"That's rather late." David, whose mind was still on his writing, belatedly took in what Robinson had said. "Foreign! Good Lord, perhaps it's Felix. Really, Robinson, don't just stand there; tell him to come up."

The foreign gentleman was indeed Felix, looking very much like his old self, with his sleek dark hair and face like a handsome nutcracker. He said, "Hullo David," and

David said, "'Lo Flixy," and they both fell silent. They had not seen one another for eight years.

Felix's eyes went around the pleasant room with its many books and skylight, past David behind the desk littered with papers, to the drawing on the wall behind him. He said, "Is it a Whistler?"

"Yes, a very late one, done about the same time as *Daughter of Eve*. It's an awfully good likeness, that look of a Roman bust that some schoolboys have put a pince-nez on."

Felix laughed, but they were not easier with each other. It was as if they were looking across barbed wire and shell craters.

"This is a very nice house," said Felix a little desperately.

"Yes. It's mine. Sir Lucas left it to me."

Felix raised an eyebrow and said, exactly as he had at Oxford when he found David hunting with the Heythrop and far too intimate with a duke's son: "What *have* you been up to, David?" and at this the years of the war and the barbed wire between them seemed to vanish, David got up and came around from his desk, and Felix moved away from the door into the room. They embraced.

"God, Flixy, it's lovely to see you. Why didn't you let anyone know you were coming?"

"I thought I might get cold feet and turn around and take the next boat train back."

"I'm so very glad you didn't. Will you have a drink?"

"I could do with one. You can't imagine how frightened I was."

"Yes I can. I funked seeing you when I was in Germany after the war."

"I got your letter. Thanks." He did not add that he had burned it unread.

"Why have you finally come?"

"To see you and Toby, of course. But mostly to see Kitty if you'll pour enough whisky into me to give me courage. We've been writing to each other, you know. How's Toby?"

"Toby is a member of Parliament. He married my sister, and they had a son, but it wasn't a success, the marriage,

469

I mean, the son's an enormous success, so they live apart. It was a bit tense for a while, but he asked me to be godfather, so I suppose he's forgiven me for having a trollop for a sister."

In this assumption David was extremely unfair to Toby, who was far too just to blame him for the misdeeds of his sister. Nor did his asking David to be godfather mean that he had in any way relented in his judgement of David's own misdeeds. He was as much as ever at one with his sovereign's opinion that fellows like that shot themselves, or failing that, at least removed themselves to one of the less comfortable colonies to do kind deeds for the natives. They had no business living off illgotten money in a house Toby privately considered much nicer than his own chilly pile on Chesterfield Hill. Toby could condone none of it, but he also could not do without David.

Bereft of Julian, and desperately lonely, he was simply too much in need of the easy, undemanding companionship only a childhood friend can give. He satisfied the prefect in his mind who served as his conscience by pointing out to him that since Sir Lucas's death David had lived blamelessly alone, which made it appear that the whole thing had been Sir Lucas's fault in the first place. That Lucas Ryder had very likely had a predecessor in the person of Anthony Fielding, Toby conveniently chose to forget, for he needed his evenings with David, and often dined at Upper Cheyne Row, and, if the House was not sitting late, spent contented hours in David's study, turning the pages of a newspaper and getting gently sozzled, while David read or worked on his book. Sometimes they looked up from their reading and caught each other's eye, and each knew the other was thinking how pleasant it would be if Felix could be with them, and here Felix was, like an apparition from the past.

"Toby will be so pleased you're here," said David. "We'll ring him up in a moment. I'll have a dinner party for you and Kitty, if you like, or would you prefer to startle everyone in the middle of the night like the ghost of Christmas past?"

"It must have seemed strange. I've been here for ages, you know. First I walked up and down Tite Street for hours trying to get up the courage to ring Kitty's bell, then I thought maybe you'd be easier, but I had to walk up and down another hour or two before I managed it. Can I stay with you tonight, David? I'll find a hotel tomorrow, but I don't think I could drag myself out again."

"Yes, of course. Stay as long as you like. I should have asked you at once, but I haven't quite caught up with the fact that you're here at all."

"Do you live here all alone? I don't want to . . ."

"Except for servants," said David, answering the spoken as well as the unspoken question, "I am quite alone. I find it suits me. I never had the chance to find out before. My family, school, Oxford, the army—Lucas, of course—I'd simply never been alone before. My former tutor at Oriel says I have the monastic temperament."

"Do you?" said Felix surprised. "I can't say I ever noticed it."

"Yes, I think I do. So, as soon as I've finished Lucas's book I shall work for a fellowship, which is something I always wanted to do. Secluded from domestic strife, Jack Bookworm leads a college life. I shall become a well-known local character with breadcrumbs in my beard and birds nesting in my hat, and one day my dusty skeleton will be found among the minor Greek epigrammatarians in the Bodleian, and they'll dust me off and say, 'Why, it's Mr Harvey. He must have been dead since 1917. Funny how we never noticed.' "

"Is that how you feel?" asked Felix. "Dead since '17?"

"No. I did for a while, but not anymore. You?"

"I haven't had the time to think about it."

"Would you like me to come to Kitty's with you?"

Felix looked at his watch. "I think we'd better wait. It's awfully late."

"Oh, you needn't worry about that," said David. "Kitty's day starts when carriages turn into pumpkins and coachmen into mice. Hasn't she told you?"

"Told me what?"

"I can see she hasn't. Our Kitty has become famous. She dances with the Prince of Wales, has her photograph in

Vogue, and turns down proposals from the younger sons of dukes and earls every day of the week."

Felix looked as if he were trying to decipher a foreign language in which he understood only every tenth word. "Kitty? But how . . . I mean, what's she doing?"

"She is a singer in a nightclub. Or, as Mr Popkin prefers to call her, a shantooze."

"Mr Popkin?"

"Have another drink," David said kindly, and told a speechless Felix the story of Mr Popkin, his East End club, and Kitty's overnight celebrity. "I must say she looks remarkably well on it," he said. "She was obviously born to be a Bright Young Thing, but only Mr Popkin saw it. Now girls everywhere are starving themselves into advanced stages of tuberculosis to look like her, and if they could find some awful prison warder to ruin their voices with a feeding tube in Holloway, they'd pay her to do it. It's all a bit lunatic, of course, but she's enjoying it immensely. Indeed we all are."

Felix sat sipping his whisky in silence. David gave him time to think over what he had been told. He privately thought that Felix had continued his postwar sulks longer than either necessary or polite. If he had imagined all this time that Kitty would sit like patience on a monument waiting for him to make up his mind, it was a well-deserved lesson to him to find her doing so well on her own.

"She never mentioned any of this," Felix said finally.

"Perhaps she was afraid you wouldn't think it respectable."

"I don't."

"Oh, but that's where you're wrong. It's immensely respectable. When you meet the Popkins all your doubts will disappear. He is very rich and very round, and Mrs Popkin is, if possible, even rounder. They call each other Mother and Dad, though they haven't any children, and they guard Kitty's virtue as if she were their maiden daughter. So, what do you think? Do you want to go see her?"

With a diffidence very unlike him, Felix wondered whether someone who turned down the younger sons of dukes and earls every day of the week, and had danced with the Prince of Wales, would be interested in seeing a lame and stoney-broke German steel baron. He looked around Lucas Ryder's study, which seemed, with its shaded lamp and many books, a very cosy place. He would have liked to remain in it, sipping whisky till he got sleepy and dozed off in his chair by the fire. A visit to Popkin's became suddenly like a visit to the dentist, something to be put off as long as possible. Yet sooner or later it would have to be got over.

"Would you mind?" he said. "I don't want to drag you out if you're tired."

"I don't mind a bit," said David. "I'll go and ring up Toby."

"Do we dress?" asked Felix when David returned.

"It really doesn't matter." Suspecting that in the strange world of nightclubs Felix might feel braver armoured in his boiled shirt, David said, "If you brought your evening things we can change if you like."

He showed Felix to Lucas's bedroom and shouted for Robinson to bring up his suitcase.

"What a nice room," said Felix.

"It was Lucas's. You can have it tonight."

"Did he die in here?"

"No, he died in the country. But if that bothers you, you can have my bedroom and I'll sleep in here."

"You forget our prior. I'm used to haunts."

"Well, this room isn't haunted. I would rather like it if it were."

"Do you miss him?"

"Oh yes. Every day."

They met again presently on the landing. "A little wrinkled," said Felix, "but not bad."

"No one will notice at Popkin's," said David. "It's kept very dim. Coloured lights and cigarette smoke. Mr Popkin calls it hatmosphere." Then Toby arrived, full of excitement at seeing Felix again, and was shown in by Robinson.

The meeting between Felix and Toby passed easily, with none of the constraint that had coloured the first moments between Felix and David. Toby, genuinely happy to see his cousin again, had embraced him enthusiastically, and

Felix, warned by David about Toby's face, and in any case too preoccupied with the thought of seeing Kitty again, seemed scarcely to notice it.

When they left David told Robinson to call the nightclub and ask Mr Popkin to save them a table, he was bringing Colonel Strafford and another friend of Kitty's, but not to tell her because it was to be a surprise. The taxi driver, who had been told by Toby to wait, seemed not to be enchanted by the prospect of taking them all the way to the East End. "Where on earth is Commercial Street?" asked Felix, who was hardly aware of the parts of London not connected with the arts or wealth.

"Off the map," said David.

"Moiles and moiles," muttered the driver, and Felix, who was feeling rather shaky in spite of his boiled shirt, was glad of the reprieve.

They drove past docks and warehouses, until he began to hope the driver was lost, but finally they drew up in front of what looked like a temple, though the music which drifted out into the street was syncopated, not psalmodic. The doorman, who knew David and Toby, touched his cap and admitted them, and a waiter took them to a table in a corner away from the band.

"It's where Lord Altondale likes to sit," David said to Felix. "He can't abide the noise."

"Uncle Augustus comes here?" If Felix had been told that Nannie had turned trapeze artist he could scarcely have been more surprised.

"Whenever he is in town," said Toby. "I can't imagine what Mummy would have thought of it all, but Papa is tremendously proud of Kitty. He seems to think he invented her."

Very small, terribly crowded nightclubs with Negro jazz bands and tiny dance floors had not yet penetrated as far as Eschenbach, and Felix looked about himself with alert curiosity. He appeared to be particularly struck by the stained-glass window of Moses meeting the golden calf.

A waiter, wearing a fedora, asked them out of the corner of his mouth what they would drink. David, feeling that champagne might not be strong enough to sustain Felix through the next hour, ordered whisky. As friends of Kitty's they would be given Mr Popkin's private stock, not the rotgut from the bar, so Felix would come to no harm.

The band stopped playing; the dancers applauded and returned to their tables. The waiters rushed back and forth with drink, the pianist at his upright piano struck a melancholy chord, a spotlight made a wavering blob next to him, the saxophone gave a sob, and suddenly Kitty stood in the lit circle. She wore a dress of dark green, made of some smooth and glistening stuff, which under the spotlight made it seem as if she were wearing a sheath of water. Her eyes were outlined in black, the lids painted green, and a rosebud mouth was drawn over her own. David, who had not thought before about the effect Kitty in her war paint might have on Felix, slid his eyes sideways, then turned back to watch the stage. Felix appeared to be in a sleepwalker's trance from which David judged it might be dangerous to wake him.

The pianist struck his mournful chord again, the saxophone gave a sad little hiccough, then moaned, forlorn as a foghorn.

"Oh! Limehouse kid," Kitty's voice joined in, husky and mournful, "Oh! Oh! Oh! Limehouse kid, going the way that the rest of them did . . ."

It must be a new song, David thought; he had not heard it before. Looking around him he thought that the rest of the audience was hearing it for the first time too. They were as silent and intent as a held breath. A waiter stood transfixed with a glass on a tray, knowing what his life would be worth with Mr Popkin if he moved while Kitty was singing.

> *Poor broken blossom and nobody's child,*
> *Haunting and taunting, you're just kind of wild . . .*

A silly song, thought David, and yet there was something in Kitty's smoky voice which caught you up till you felt as mournful as the sound of the saxophone. Cigarette smoke curled in the rosy glow of a light slowly revolving, lingering briefly on a face, circling on.

The circling light moved across the room, reached the corner where Felix, Toby, and David sat, and moved on. Kitty's husky voice suddenly cracked, like a young boy's, and she stood, motionless, her hand at her throat. The pianist improvised some oh-oh-ohs, the saxophonist took over the tune, and it was a moment before people realized something was amiss. A murmur of talk could be heard under the music. Kitty found her voice, croaked, "Felix?" and again, as if she could not quite believe it, "Felix!" and jumped down from the stage while the band thumped away as imperturbably as if it were about to go down with the Titanic. Mr Popkin's round face appeared at the door to his office, but Kitty did not look his way. She ran between the packed tables, gasping for breath, threw herself into Felix's arms, and burst into noisy sobs.

David and Toby, very conscious that every eye was on their table, tried to look as if they were the kind of people to whom this kind of thing happens at least once a day, while Kitty wept kohl and green eye shadow all over Felix's immaculate shirtfront.

There was a sudden buzz of talk, a waiter arrived at their table, carrying an ice bucket and a bottle of Pol Roger, and was at once followed by Mr Popkin, spherical and smiling. Kitty lifted her head, said, "Oh, Pops, this is Baron von Landeck," caught sight of Felix's shirt, and with a wail of dismay put her hands to her face and rushed off to her dressing room to put herself to rights. Mr Popkin said, "Pleased to make your acquaintance, Baron," and Felix nodded absently. He was still staring at the place where Kitty had stood.

"Let's all have some bubbly," said Mr Popkin; "it'll keep us bright." Felix made no reply to this. "I'd better go and see that she's all right," he said, following the vanished green dress.

"Here," said Mr Popkin indignantly, "nobody goes into Kitty's dressing room. She doesn't like it." But Felix was already gone. Mr Popkin winked at David. "Tell you the truth, there isn't room in there for more than one." He drank down a glass of champagne, pulled out Felix's chair, and sat down. "What a commotion, eh? What's he want with her, then?"

"I think he's come to ask her to marry him," said David.

"First I've heard of it. You know this bloke? Know that he's all right, I mean?"

"How do you mean, all right?"

"Well, can he look after her? There's a lot of blokes call themselves Baron this and Count that, until you get them home and they're Baron Bankrupt and Count Stonybroke wanting a rich American widow to support them."

Toby, who did not much care for Mr Popkin, said coldly, "I think that part will be all right. Baron von Landeck owns the second-biggest munitions works in Germany. Not anywhere as big as Krupp, of course, but adequate to support our Kitty, I fancy."

"Hm," said Mr Popkin reflectively. "Wonder if that bit of shrapnel I had in my tum was made by him. Kitty known him long?"

"Yes," said David. "They got engaged the day before the war started."

"He doesn't make up his mind very fast, does he? Not like me and Mother."

David, who had frequently heard the story of Mr and Mrs Popkin's whirlwind courtship, laughed. Mr Popkin poured them all another glass of champagne. "Mother and I will miss her," he said sadly. "We're that fond of Kitty; we couldn't be fonder of her if she was our own. Well, least said soonest mended. Drink up; we'll have to celebrate. Wonder how they're getting on in there."

Kitty's face was clean and shone with cold cream in the unflattering light of her makeup mirror when Felix entered her dressing room. Her eyes were swollen with weeping and her nose was red. Felix drew the door shut behind him—Mr Popkin was right, it was a very tiny dressing room—and stood looking at her in silence. Then, formally, he went down on one knee and said, "I've been an awful fool, Kitty; I'm sorry. Will you marry me?"

Her tears began again, running slickly over the cold

cream. Her nose blew a huge bubble, and her voice came out squeaky and shaky as she said, exactly as she had eight years before on the beach at Fallon, "Oh, Felix, yes. Yes, yes, yes."

Though it was very late when he got home, David was far too wide-awake to want to go to bed. He went up to his study and sat down to reread what he had written earlier in the evening. Felix had stopped at Tite Street with Kitty, and David thought that he must send Robinson around first thing in the morning with Felix's bag, to spare him the humiliation of walking through Chelsea unshaven, wearing evening clothes. He had scarcely finished writing a note to Robinson to this effect when he heard a knock on the front door and went down to find Felix on the doorstep.

"You've broken off the engagement," said David.

"No, of course not. In fact we're to meet tomorrow morning—this morning, I mean—to buy the ring. Why do you look so surprised?"

"Well, frankly, I didn't expect to see you again tonight."

"Kitty was tired," said Felix, coming in and taking off his coat. "All her kisses ended as yawns."

"What an exciting lover you must be."

"I shall be, another time," said Felix tranquilly. "I'm tired too. It's been quite a day."

"Time for bed," said David.

"You'll come with us in the morning to choose the ring?"

"With pleasure. Goodnight, Flixy."

In spite of the fact that he had drunk a good deal, been out very late, and had probably not got much sleep when he had finally gone to bed, Felix was down to breakfast, bright-eyed and impatient, by nine o'clock. By ten he had on his coat and hat and was exhorting David to get a move on.

"It's no earthly use," David told him. "Kitty never gets up before teatime."

"Then we'll wake her," said Felix, who seemed to David to be growing rather masterful now that he was about to be a husband.

When Toby arrived he was allowed only a minute to gulp

down a cup of coffee, and they were in Tite Street by a quarter of eleven. Felix rang the bell in a resolute and Teutonic manner. The door was opened at once by Kitty, who had been waiting for them with her hat and coat on.

"I know that love is said to transform people," said David, "but this I would not have believed."

In the King's Road men in shabby uniforms were selling poppies. "Damn and blast," said David, "I'd forgotten it's the eleventh or I wouldn't have let Felix drag me out."

Toby gave him a sympathetic grin and Kitty said, "Why, what's the matter?"

"I hate all that assing about with poppies and two-minute silences. What good does it do anyone?"

They had turned the corner to the Embankment when the church clocks struck eleven, traffic stopped, and silence fell. Even the splash of a small, ornamental fountain in a garden across the road died back. Only the Thames flowed sturdily on, caring for none of it.

Kitty took Felix's hand. David said, "Damn!" From somewhere came bugle notes playing the "Last Post," a motor horn snorted, traffic moved again, and the fountain began to splash once more. Kitty sniffed and wiped her glove across her nose. David gave her his handkerchief.

"If you are really serious about marrying this creature," he said to Felix, "don't bother about an engagement ring; get a dozen large handkerchiefs instead. Kitty has been known to burst into tears at the playing of the Baluchistan national anthem."

"I can't help it," sniffed Kitty, mopping her nose. "The two-minute silence always makes me cry."

"Silly cow," said Toby affectionately, putting an arm around her shoulder.

David, suddenly in good humour again, said, "I can't think why, but all this patriotic nonsense has put me in mind of New Year's Eve. Let's go and buy the ring, and then we'll all go to Claridge's and drink champagne."